CITY OF SAVAGES

CITY OF SAVAGES

EE KELLY

SAGA PRESS

LONDON SYDNEY **NEW YORK** TORONTO NEW DELHI

First SAGA PRESS hardcover edition February 2015 | SAGA PRESS and colophon are trademarks of Simon & Schuster, Inc. | For information about special discounts for bulk purchases, please contact Simon & Schuster Special Sales at 1-866-506-1949 or business@simonandschuster.com. | The Simon & Schuster Speakers Bureau can bring authors to your live event. For more information or to book an event, contact the Simon & Schuster Speakers Bureau at 1-866-248-3049 or visit our website at www.simonspeakers.com. | The text for this book is set in ITC Veljovic Std. | Manufactured in the United States of America | 10 9 8 7 6 5 4 3 2 1 | Library of Congress Cataloging-in-Publication Data | Kelly, Lee. | City of savages / Lee Kelly. | pages   cm | ISBN 978-1-4814-1030-4 | ISBN 978-1-4814-1032-8 (eBook) | 1. Sisters—Fiction. 2. Manhattan (New York, N.Y.)—Fiction. 3. Regression (Civilization)—Fiction. I. Title. | PS3611.E443255C58 2015 | 813'.6—dc23 | 2014001540

FOR MY SISTERS, BRIDGET AND JILL.
WITHOUT THEM, THERE WOULD BE NO PHEE AND SKY.

PART ONE

*We're just lost migrants at the city's mercy,
survivors scavenging for a second chance.*

—From March 20 entry,
Property of Sarah Walker Miller

PART ONE

1   PHEE

Through our wall of windows, I watch dawn stand up and take on the city. It throws a thick, molten net over the skyscrapers, sets the river on fire, and makes me restless to be outside. It's our last day downtown, and I want to enjoy every second of it.

I untangle myself from the piles of blankets and clothes Sky and I share to keep warm this late in autumn, trying not to wake her. I take a peek around our apartment but can't find Mom. She must be up and already on the hunt for breakfast, and since there's no food left in our rooftop garden, she's got to be by the river. I press my nose against the floor-to-ceiling glass and pretend to fly for a minute, look down five stories to the small tuft of grass that hugs the water, but I don't see Mom anywhere.

After pulling on my boots and one of the coats we've scavenged, I rush out the door and practically sprint down the hallway to the dusty EXIT sign. But I take my time going down the internal stairs—a tunnel of darkness, but the only way out. Even though I know every chip on the railing and every groove on the stairs, I know I can't be too careful. Besides, there're far cooler ways to die in this world than tripping on a set of steps. When I reach the empty lobby, I crawl through the hole Mom bashed out of the glass door frame, maneuver around the Dumpster that hides it, and greet the morning.

The day is breaking open like an egg, the river runny with orange, red, and gold. I walk to the water's edge and look out at the statue Mom calls Lady Liberty, a green, rusted woman floating in a sea swamped with shrapnel and debris.

Even though I'm pumped to go back to Central Park for the winter, I'm really going to miss this place. I guess if I called anywhere home, it'd have to be this corner of the city—the glass towers bordering Battery Park, the Hudson River slapping the remains of the docks. But now it's October, smack in the middle of the month, and like on all my birthdays, it's time to join Rolladin in the Park for the POW census.

I hear a snap of a twig behind me and turn, in time to catch Mom taking down a couple of baby peacocks with two quick shots from her BB gun. The peahen and the rest of her chicks scream and scatter in a rage of feathers and tiny limbs.

"I couldn't see you from the window," I say.

"Good." Mom smiles. "Means I've still got my edge." She carefully finishes off the chicks with Sky's knife, removes the round pellets from the birds' flesh, and cleans them off for another day. She places the birds in her satchel.

"I don't know about that, old lady," I tease, 'cause it doesn't mean anything—Mom looks like she's only a few years older than Sky. Mom's tall with even features and long, tight limbs, as if underneath her skin there's nothing but steel and coiled rope.

"Speaking of getting old . . ." Mom throws her arm around my shoulders as we walk back towards the apartment complex. "Happy birthday, Phee."

"I was wondering if you remembered."

"Are you kidding? I could never forget this day, Phoenix-of-mine." She pulls me into her and pats her satchel, reminding me of the carcasses inside. "You ready for your birthday breakfast?"

"That's all I get? A couple of dead peachicks?"

"No, this day's going to be full of surprises." I can't tell if Mom sounds excited, or . . . nervous. Scared, even. "We need to hit the road, though. We don't want to miss check-in, and your gift means a stop." She takes a deep breath. "An important stop."

We round the Dumpster and Mom climbs back through the opening of shattered glass. "I've been debating with myself whether it's time to show you girls," she adds. "Whether we're ready."

I'm not really following whatever she's talking about, but one thing's for sure, I want the gift. So I say, "Come on, I was born ready," as I scramble through the opening after her.

And even though I'm clearly joking, Mom doesn't smile, and her eyes drift, like they do when she's thinking about her world of long ago. But this is how it is with her. You never know what's going to send her away, back into the past.

"That's very true," is all she gives me, and we walk in silence towards the stairwell.

When we get back to the apartment, my older sister's already laid all her favorite things across our bed. Sky sighs as she strokes all this totally impractical clothing, lace and feathers and sparkles and gems, biting her nails like what she packs has life-or-death importance. This is my sister—*everything* means more than it should for Sky. She cries over chopped-down trees, and she can't sleep the days we find a dead animal.

"Just pick some stuff and throw it in your backpack," I tell her, as I shove my own few things into my satchel—long underwear, boots, extra hoodie, and pants. "It'll all be here when we get back. Or at least it should be. You can wear those practical miniskirts next summer while we hunt for squirrels."

Sky smiles as she studies her clothes. "You know only one of us can get away with a year-round sweatpants uni-form."

I grab one of the hats she lifted a few years ago from what's left of Bloomingdale's, this big, stupid, floppy thing that makes her look like a sunflower, and throw it on. Then I use my high-pitched girly Sky-voice: "I'm thinking *sequins* for picking corn. No, no, the *suede*—"

She laughs and lunges for me. "God, don't touch the brim—look at your hands!"

"Come on, guys. Pick up the pace," Mom calls from the kitchenette. "We've got a long day ahead of us."

After a quick breakfast of peachicks roasted over the kindling fire Mom built in the fireplace, Sky gives me my birthday gift, a hand-woven necklace of grass. It's beautiful, and something I could never make: I don't have the eye or the patience. I thank her and put it on carefully. Then we gather up our coats and things and leave the apartment unlocked, just like Mom found it years ago.

We've spent summers in this apartment for basically my

whole life. But like most stuff, Sky and I know only half the story of why. Mom's mentioned in bits and pieces that she remembered the shiny skyscraper from "before." Something about visiting her Wall Street friends during "lunch hour," and being impressed with the "amenities." So we set up summer camp in the building's model unit after the Red Allies slackened their Park mandate. Mom said it was as good a place as any.

"Why are we heading east?" Sky says now.

"For Phee's gift." Mom checks the watch she's had since we were kids. "We need to get moving, it's already nine. You know we can't be late for check-in."

Rolladin has all these strict rules on timing—on everything, really. Sure, it bugs me as much as the next prisoner; but being on time's a small price to pay for front-row spots at the POW census festivities.

"Where's this present of mine again?" I ask.

"That's part of the surprise." Mom shakes her head, her eyes already watering from the cold. "It's better this way, trust me."

We brace ourselves against the chill and walk past townhomes with their windows blown out, through rows of mutilated storefronts. The corpses of the monsters Mom says once moved, she calls them cars, litter the streets and avenues.

"I'm freezing already," Sky says.

"That's 'cause you've got nothing on. Look at that coat." I fluff the wide collar of her flimsy leather jacket. "You know, one day those fancy-pants outfits are going to land you in Rolladin's den." I wiggle my eyebrows. "Our little Sky shacking up with the warden."

Sky fake gags as she pulls my parka hood over my face. "You're obnoxious."

"And you're asking for it."

"Guys!" Mom hates it when we joke about these things—about anything to do with Rolladin, really.

I laugh and nudge her. "Come on, we're kidding."

As the sun climbs up the sky, we reach the ratty mess of streets once known as Chinatown, hike a wide circle around where Broome had greeted Bowery, trek all the way to the East River to get into the Lower East Side. The tear in the earth we circle is blocks wide, and it adds about an hour to our trip.

Mom never lets us come up this way, even though there're no tunnels over here and the bombing stopped over a decade ago. But it's still far too dangerous, she always says, so whatever gift she has for me must be good. And I'm excited for it, really, but I'm also anxious to get to the Park, settle in at the Carlyle, and get prime spots for the 65th Street fighting. When I'm about to point out that this is taking all morning, Mom finally says, "This is it."

She stops in front of an ordinary row home. A pile of bricks, maybe four stories high. In fact, the only thing half-interesting about it is that it's still in one piece, what with being so close to the bomb crater.

Sky and I look at each other, confused.

"What's my gift doing in there?" I ask.

Mom's eyes are lost again. "This was my old home, with your father. This is where Sky was born."

Old home? I wasn't expecting this. Mom's never mentioned this place. Or much of anything, really, about her life Before. I don't know what to do with this information.

"So we lived here before the war?" Sky cranes her neck to

look up at the wall of brick and dusty glass. She snaps her head back to Mom. "Before the Red Allies attacked?"

But Mom's focus is on the front door, jiggling it open with a key I'd always thought was a necklace. "Only for a little while."

"Was I born here too?"

Mom shakes her head at me. "Just Sky."

The door sighs and clicks open. We walk into a musty stench so thick you can cut it, climb two sets of stairs, and stop in front of 3B. Mom stands in front of the bloodred door, waiting. Waiting for what, I don't know. Sky's trembling next to me like some cloud before a storm, so excited I think she's going to burst.

"It's getting late, Mom," I say, as patiently as I can.

"Right." Mom breathes deeply and clicks the golden key into the hole, and the apartment door opens.

It's weird. Mom's old place looks nothing like the glass box we live in near Wall Street, with its slate tiles, grays, and whites. This apartment's stuffed and soft. Pillows and blankets thrown over worn-cushioned couches, books tucked into corners and teeming from tall shelves. Yellow walls and dusty junk. Dust *everywhere*. And pictures. We can't see a tabletop, there're so many pictures.

"Is this *Dad*?" Sky clutches a large photo. A man has his arms wrapped around Mom. She's smiling, and younger around the eyes. "And is this *me*?" Sky shows me another one of a chubby baby.

My mom walks over to us carefully, slowly, like she might need to lie down any minute.

"That's you, Skyler," she finally says. "And yes, that's— Tom. That was, *is*, your father."

I can't take my eyes off him. "He's got my hair."

"A wild crop of blond, just like yours." Mom ruffles my wavy mane. "And Skyler's eyes."

"They are mine, right?"

"Definitely. Green eyes that were always probing, always questioning, just like you. Your curiosity and Phee's mouth. A brutal combination."

I look at Mom: she's trying her best to smile and joke, but this all feels wrong. Hollow or something. It just reminds me that I don't know this guy, that we've never even seen a picture of him. That the most we've ever gotten when we've asked what happened to him are vague answers or Mom's knee-jerk, bogus mantra, *Sometimes the past should stay in the past.*

I look back at the picture. *Tom Miller. Husband. Father.* I try to match these names with his face, but I can't shake the disappointing feeling—in my mind, he's played by someone different. Someone a little older and heavier, maybe, and with a beard.

I stare at him longer, hoping for something to register that this is the guy who made me, who willed me into the world. But he's just some stranger—there's no connection—and the sharp truth of it pricks my eyes.

"Why haven't you brought us here before?" Sky's bottom lip starts quivering before I can say anything first. "All the times we've asked you for something, *anything*, from before . . ."

"She wanted to keep it to herself," I answer.

"Phee—"

"Please, Mom, don't 'Phee' me."

I try not to get as worked up as Sky does, over all the

holes in the past that Mom refuses to fill, but still, my *own* lip's quivering. I walk towards the tiny kitchenette before either of them can tell.

"The Lower East Side was off-limits for years," Mom starts slowly. "After the bombing stopped, the Red Allies quarantined the area. Even if I wanted to show you, Rolladin—"

"Oh, please." Like Mom follows every order of Rolladin's. "You could've brought us here sooner. You know it, and we know it."

Mom shakes her head. "You're right."

She sits down on the ratty green couch for a minute and runs her fingers through her hair. "I know you two won't understand this, but I brought you here when I could. I wasn't ready to make these memories real. I'm still not ready. It hurts just to be in here, to see it frozen in time." She looks at us with glistening eyes. "God forbid, one day you two might understand what it's like to lose everything. To have to face it again, afterward—that might be the worst part." She stands and turns to the window. "Sometimes the past should stay in the past."

Mom stays there for a while, looking out to an empty street through dusty glass. I know what she's doing. She's centering herself, closing herself off before we can figure out another way inside her.

"We're running out of time." Mom turns towards the bedroom, her eyes on the matted carpet. "Let's not forget why we're here. Phee's birthday present, remember?"

"So that's it?" I call after her. "End of conversation?"

No answer.

Sky and I exchange a look. This is how Mom is. A closed book. It's useless to try to open her.

"This gift better be good, is all I'm saying," I finally whisper to Sky, and we follow Mom into her old bedroom.

Mom's sandwiched herself in between the nearby wall and a bed that nearly devours the room. She takes a blurry black-and-white photo off the wall to reveal a small steel door.

"What is that?" Sky asks.

"A safe. Your dad installed it when we moved here." Mom takes her time, twisting a knob on the safe's face round and round. Right, left, right, and the safe door clicks open.

"What's it for?"

"It does what it says. Keeps important things safe."

"Like what?" I try to peer around her, but she blocks me.

"Like . . . our passports, Sky's birth certificate—"

"A birth *certificate*?" I say. Some things from Before are just so dumb. "A certificate that says you were born? Isn't the fact that you're here proof enough?"

Mom gives a little laugh, continues fishing through a pile of things I can't see. God, I really, *really* hope my gift is not some lame piece of paper.

Finally she pulls something shiny and red from the safe, and my heart skips. It's—

A *gun*.

A real one, not a BB like my mom's. And the gun's painted red, just like the whorelords' few weapons in the Park. The ones sanctioned by the Red Allies.

"How'd you get that?" Sky whispers.

"It's not important." Mom opens the chamber, and I count four bullets, *real* bullets, fat silver fish that beg to be shot.

"Is it for me?" I ask.

Mom looks at Sky, and I can tell she's trying to get a sense

LEE KELLY

from my sister whether she thinks this is a terrible idea. I'm sure Sky thinks it is. But Mom knows I'm old enough now to protect myself, from holdouts during the summer, or from any trouble in the Park. You've got to be tough on this island, or else you don't have a leg to stand on. But Sky's never really understood this. She's never wanted to.

"So Phee gets the gun?" Sky just shakes her head. "You didn't think this would be a good gift, say, a year ago? When *I* turned sixteen?"

"Sky, come on," Mom says. "Don't make this difficult. This is Phee's day. I gave you what I thought made sense at the time."

"You're a lousy shot, Sky, everyone knows that," I try to help, thinking back to the first and last time she entered the census celebration's junior archery competition. But when I look up, Sky's face is all mashed up, like she's going to cry again. Damn it, I hate it when my words just slip out and cut her. "I mean, your knife is more your *style*. A more personal weapon. If you ever had the guts to use it, of course."

My sister shoots me a look more lethal than any knife.

"Phee," Sky says, "I really can't stand you sometimes."

She stomps off to the bedroom's bathroom, edging her way around her old crib. She slams the door behind her.

"Why do you say things like that to her?"

"I was trying to help."

"I'm serious, Phee," Mom pushes. "Try to walk in her shoes. If you two don't have each other, you don't have anything."

I look down at the worn carpet, and a warm wave of shame flushes my cheeks. I hate feeling like this, so I try to ignore it. "Come on, can't I hold the gun?"

Mom sighs. "This isn't a toy. I was debating even giving it to you." She fiddles with it, opens its chamber. So much power, potential, in her palms. "I thought Sky would be more careful with it," she says. "But I knew if you ever needed to use it, I mean really *use* it—"

"I'd be able to pull the trigger," I finish her sentence. I don't have to add that Sky would not. We both know. We all know.

"I can't protect you forever. This gift is a sign of trust. That you'll keep it hidden and only use it if you and Sky are in trouble. That you'll *respect* it. Do you understand that?"

I nod, but my heart and mind are racing. I want to be outside, firing this thing. *Pow.* One pull of a trigger and lightning comes out of my hand. *Pow.*

"Are you listening to me?" Mom's blue eyes bore into mine.

"Yes. I'm listening." And then I hug her, for the gun and for the trust, and take the gift out of her shaking hand. The shiny revolver fits into mine like a puzzle piece. Like it was made for me to hold it.

"Can I try it?"

Mom takes the weapon again, then digs back through the contents of the safe. She pulls out a small red box, torn around the edges, and shoves it into her pocket. "You get one shot. One blank. I don't want to make too much commotion before we travel uptown."

She pushes back the little lip of the gun. "That's the safety. Always keep it on." She fumbles with the chamber again, opening it. "And always keep the bullets separate from the gun."

She dumps the pile into my hand. "Keep them safe. It's

not like my BB. This is all the ammo I have. And once it's gone, it's gone. Do you understand?"

I nod, totally fixated on the weapon.

"Come on, let's make sure it still works."

I follow Mom to the window, a nervous energy creeping up my spine. She opens the glass pane that hasn't been touched in over a decade, and we step out onto the fire escape.

_____

The walls of this dark apartment are as thin as paper, and I hear them laughing outside as they climb onto the fire escape. Cackling and howling like two wolves. And I'm the black sheep who's locked herself in the bathroom. *The bathroom of the apartment I grew up in. Where I was a baby. God, I played in that bathtub.*

The tiny room is claustrophobic compared to the one in our apartment along the water—a small tub, a muddy-green-colored toilet that I don't dare lift the lid off of. I wish I could remember something, *anything*, about this place, from before. But like so much from the past, it's a stranger.

A sliver of a window casts a hazy glow onto the grimy floor, lets me see myself in the mirror. My face is still flushed from watching Mom give Phee that totally inappropriate gift, and I wish I could just turn the sink handles on. Let water run over my hands and face and cool me down. But of course, there's no water here, no water in any faucet. They're all teases, empty promises. So instead I study myself in the glass, look so hard that my features start to become foreign.

No wonder I'm the oddball of the family.

I'm small and frail-looking. *Tiny.* Phee's my younger sister and yet she has two inches on me, has towered over me for as long as I can remember. I've got limbs that tire easily, skin that doesn't like the sun. I poke at my white face and get up close to the glass. *Delicate,* my mother says when she's defending me to myself. *Girls of the old world would have killed to look like you.* I know she means to cheer me up, but it just makes me feel even more like an island on this small and terrible island—a relic of another time.

Girls of the old world.

I was born to be one of those girls.

I unlock the door and walk back into the bedroom, where shadows of Mom and Phee dance like puppets on the carpeted floor. Mom's behind my sister on the small landing outside, guiding her hands, showing her how to point and shoot. I taste something vile in my mouth, and I want to scream as loud as I can, let them know that I'm here.

But of course, I won't. *You're better than that,* Mom's voice echoes through my mind. *You're stronger than Phee, in a different way. Balance. Patience. Control.*

Sometimes I get so tired of being stronger than Phee in a different way.

I start to poke around the room, carefully open an old bureau caked in dust, and rummage through the narrow closet. There's very little in either, and I figure out pretty quickly that Mom must have been here already on her own, has picked the place empty like I've seen her pick the meat off her prey. Where were we, while she was making a secret visit to the Lower East Side?

Knowing our mother, we'll probably never find out.

I remember the safe and wander over to the far wall, where its door is still open. This little door in the wall feels magical, like if I touch it, *will* it, I can shrink and step inside, channel myself to places I've read about. Wonderland.

Narnia. Another time. It's childish, I know, but I try. I place my hand inside the silver vault and hold my breath, waiting for a transformation.

But nothing happens.

The safe is just a home to papers: Small blue books with official seals on them, envelopes torn and ragged, stuffed with faded pink papers and hard plastic cards. I shuffle through them, not sure what I'm looking for, growing angrier the longer I look. *What did I really expect to find in here? Three golden tickets to another life? The secrets of time travel?*

I'm about to shut the safe in disgust when my fingers brush against something soft and worn, most definitely *un*paperlike. I carefully dislodge what feels like a leathery box from the shadows of the safe.

A *book*. Without a title, without a name, just a book bound in the most unnatural color of leather I've ever seen. I open the soft, bright-blue cover carefully. Instead of what I expect to find inside—a title page, a few words large and bold in cold type, like my collection we've scavenged from libraries and apartments—there's lush writing by *hand*. Loops and bubbles and dips, ink racing across the page in a fever.

The title page reads *Property of Sarah Walker Miller.* Sarah Miller?

Mom.

A roar rips through my eardrums, jerks me out of my trance, and I jump, bang my head against the safe's tiny door. The boom echoes and echoes, until finally the aftermath of the gunshot is bullied over by Phee's confident cackling. She and Mom will be back any minute.

I know I should store the book away behind the fortress

of papers, as Mom wouldn't want me looting through here. But I flip to the next page, can't stop myself.

> *January 4—Every year it's the same. I swear that I'll finally give the stories that circle around in my mind a page on which to land. But now, with Sky's diapers and feedings and nonexistent naps, my dream feels even more indulgent. Ridiculous, even: Sarah Miller's trying to be a* writer!
> *More of a burden on my family than anything else.*
> *But I need something of my own, and the days keep blurring together. And I'm terrified I'll wake up one day and decades will have passed.*
> *So I need to start small, with you.*

Wait, so this book was *written* by Mom? The year's not marked, but obviously it was written when I was a baby.

I flip through it. Most pages are covered in that same ferocious ink. The markings look like they change: flowing handwriting, tight scrawls, shaky printing. But the pages are almost all full. So wonderfully full. *What do I have in my hands?*

I hear feet shuffle on the fire escape, and I know that I'm going to be caught any minute. I should throw the blue book back into the dark of the safe and forget it exists. If Mom wants to tell us about it, she will.

But I know she won't. There's so much she doesn't tell us. And I can't let the safe swallow this book whole. Whatever it is, it's about our mother. Things we don't know, things maybe she can't say out loud.

Before my mind knows what my hands are doing, I'm rooting through my backpack, digging for my own book collection. *Great Expectations. Charlie and the Chocolate Factory. Charlotte's Web.*

No, no, no. I can't let go of these, either.

But I hear the window to the fire escape being pulled back open, and I know I can't hesitate. I take a deep breath and whisper a small thank you to E. B. White and his spider for all their stories. I pull the cover off my hardback, drape it around Mom's book, and plunge it into my bag. Then I take the hardback and thrust it into the safe, camouflage it with the mound of loose papers.

Good-bye, Charlotte.

"Did you hear it?" Phee squeals as she scrambles around the bed towards me. "Did you hear the shot?"

My heart's pounding out of my chest, but not from the shot. *Have I ever kept something from Mom before?*

"Yeah, it was hard to miss. The whole apartment practically shook."

"I was aiming for a tin can across the street—if it had been a real bullet, I would have blown the lid right off it."

I give my sister a fake smile but don't answer. Phee's always making these types of wild, baseless proclamations. And I can't humor her right now; I'm still kind of mad at her and Mom. Plus, my focus is elsewhere. I study my mother, trying to figure out whether she can sense my nervousness, can tell that my bag's been ripped open and her secrets are tucked away inside.

"We should get going." Mom inches past me towards the safe. "It's time to hop if we don't want to miss check-in."

My breath catches. *Can she tell? Does she notice the switch?*

But Mom only looks into the miniature door once before she closes it and locks the safe.

And I breathe. For now, the truth stays buried.

As Mom locks the front door behind us, Phee extends the unloaded red gun out to me and shrugs. "You know, we can share it," she says. "Or rotate. Mom said I only got it 'cause I'm more trouble in the first place."

This is Phee's version of apologizing; she can tell I'm still mad.

"That's probably true. But no big deal, you keep it," I say, and I'm surprised I mean it. I clutch my backpack, knowing that I now have something far more valuable than a gun. "I'll just let you know if I need a good shot."

By the time we leave the town house and start walking uptown, it's square into the afternoon, but Mom still insists that we retrace our steps back to the East River and walk by the water to get to the Park. It's definitely out of the way, but she won't even entertain Phee's pleas to use Third Avenue. We never chance walking so close to the tunnels. Never. Even now, with a gun.

As we walk, I look across the river, to the sinking bones of the Brooklyn and Manhattan Bridges, and out to the gray boroughs that fence us in like barbed wire. I cover my eyes from the strong sun and search the horizon for our captors, the Red Allies.

I'm not sure I can remember the last time I saw a Red soldier on our island. I have slippery memories of men in uniforms with guns marching through our war-ravaged avenues, but these days, they pretty much leave us to fend for ourselves. The only reminders that we're prisoners of war are the fires and flares across the river from time to time, or messages from the Red Allies relayed by Rolladin and her Council. But today, as we travel to the Park for the annual census, I'm itching to see them. To see signs of life from those who have kept our own contained, imprisoned. Small.

There's no sign of the soldiers, though, and it makes me feel angry. And alone.

We reach the remains of the Queensboro Bridge quickly, but slow to a crawl as we navigate the sky-high piles of shrapnel, cracked cement, and debris that line the East River like tombstones.

"This is so stupid," Phee whispers to me, as Mom traipses ahead of us carefully. "When's the last time anyone actually saw a tunnel feeder?" She hops over a slab of cement. "We should be cutting up the center of the city. Why chance being late to the census?"

She's right, of course: If we miss check-in, Rolladin could throw us out of the Park and turn us back the way we came. A winter by ourselves along the water, with no guaranteed heat or food. But I doubt Rolladin would do that. Despite how much Mom hates her, Rolladin sort of has a fondness for our family.

"You know Mom, safety first." I study the sky. "We'll be all right. We're making good time."

A loud bang, like tin on tin, ruptures the silent city, and Phee and I both jump and look ahead of us.

"Mom!"

She's lying in a field of debris and chipped metal, holding her ankle, moaning. We rush to her side and fall down beside her, and she rolls over, breathes a few quick, punctured pants.

"What's wrong? What is it?" I inspect her. "What happened?"

"My ankle," Mom stutter-gasps. She tries to move her foot but winces and stops. "There must have been a ditch or something, hidden by the rubble. . . . I came down hard." She waves her hand behind her. A piece of metal sticks out of a small hole in the ground at a sharp angle, like one of the Park's seesaws.

"Do you think it's broken?" Phee shoots me a look over Mom's head. "Can you walk?"

"Yes. I can walk." Mom pushes herself into an all-fours position and begins to slowly lift herself off the ground— "Yes, I can . . . I can . . . *ARGHHHH* . . . God damn it"— but collapses underneath her own pressure. "It has to be sprained." Mom rolls onto her side again to get a better look at her ankle. It's starting to swell and rise like a tide. "You've got to be kidding me," she whispers, throwing her head back onto the earth.

Phee says, "Mom, we have to carry you."

"No, I'll be fine." Mom starts gearing up to try again. "Just let me get up."

"Mom," I say patiently. But firmly, as Mom would rather drag herself to hell and back than burden my sister or me. "We're walking you to the Park, okay? Let us do this."

Mom looks at me for a long time. Then she nods, reluctantly. "I'll move faster with a splint." She points into the rubble. "Phee, find a piece of wood, or metal, about this long." She holds her hands a foot apart. "Sky, give me one of your scarves. And quickly. We need to get moving." She runs her fingers through her hair, her trademark move when she's nervous, and I catch her panic. I'm starting to hyperventilate a little, digging through my bag.

"It's all right, honey," Mom says. But her voice is high and tight. "We'll make it. We always do."

We race against Mom's watch as the sky turns gray and cold, mocking us as we hobble alongside the East River. Mom winces every few steps, and Phee and I use every ounce of willpower we have not to keep stopping to attend to her.

We turn off First Avenue, onto 76th Street. We're all sweating, swearing, and I just try to focus on limping forward. I bite my lip every time I want to say that my shoulders are about to give in, that my neck is so strained I think it might snap.

"We're almost there." Mom pulls her hand around my neck to look at her watch. "We're going to make it."

By the time we reach the front doors of the old Carlyle Hotel, my skin is slippery, and my thin leather jacket's practically suffocating me. Phee's face is as red as a cardinal as she huffs and puffs on Mom's other side. Backpacks bouncing against our backs, we fling ourselves into the dusty Carlyle lobby. Phee bangs on the front desk bell just as one of Rolladin's warlords, Philip, carefully places a handwritten CLOSED sign on the desk's ledge.

"Too late," Philip mutters. He doesn't even look at us as he rearranges the raccoon shawl around his shoulders and tosses his thinning blond hair. "Census check-in's over."

"Philip." Mom tries to catch her breath. "It's a matter of minutes. My ankle . . . I tripped on the way up here. The girls have been carrying me. We did what we could—"

"You need to get that Rolex fixed." Philip purses his lips and rolls his eyes. "Pity there's no watchmaker left to recommend."

Phee and I exchange glances behind Mom's back. This

isn't good. But Mom's already after Philip, pulling our shoulders like reins to turn our three-man team around.

"Philip, wait." Mom calls after him as he saunters out of the lobby. "It was an accident. We can't be more than five minutes late, tops. Please—"

"You know the rules better than anyone. Take it up with Rolladin." He flings his words like weapons behind him.

"Please, Philip," Mom tries again as we hobble after him, her voice this time a desperate whisper. "We'd never say anything. Just look the other way, and the girls will get me upstairs. Rolladin will never have to know. For old times' sake—"

"Sarah," Philip turns abruptly, now with a red-handled knife in hand, so we know the conversation is over. "Check-in. Is. Over. Understood? Go to the Belvedere to plead your case."

Nearly in tears, Mom leans on us as we guide her out of the Carlyle, across 76th Street and over Fifth Avenue. Soon enough, the cement and brick give way to a thicket of trees, and then the crowded expanse of the Great Lawn of Central Park.

As we limp through the Great Lawn, tired fieldworkers eye us, nod their heads as we trudge around the cornstalks and cut through the small fields of potatoes and apple trees. Trevor, one of the young year-rounds, waves to us from the fields, his whole face breaking open like dawn when he spots us. He starts scrambling through the fieldworkers to greet us, but I shake my head and raise my exhausted hand to tell him, *Later.*

We reach the gates of Belvedere Castle after the sky's already been dusted with a rich blue powder. Per the rules, we shed our weapons and backpacks at the entrance, though of course, Phee keeps her new gun tucked and hidden in the folds of her sweats. As I drop my bag in the corner, my heart lurches—I can't take Mom's journal with me. *What if one of Rolladin's warlords finds it and decides to take it?* But there's so much else going on, there's no time to think of a solution. Two of Rolladin's lords are immediately beside us, ushering us into the belly of the castle.

"Stupid move, Sarah," one of the young, lithe lords whispers to my mother. The pair of lords grips our forearms and drags us all forward. "You know Rolladin doesn't like winters to keep her waiting."

I can't remember this young woman's name—*Cass or Kate or something?*—but I know her face immediately from past winters at the Park. She must have been pledged to Rolladin and accepted as a year-round warlord, one of Rolladin's "whorelords," as Phee likes to call them.

"Let me worry about that," Mom answers her, biting back a wince.

"Oh, I am," the lesser lord purrs. "I'm just looking forward to seeing you and your two lemmings thrown out this winter. It doesn't happen often."

My stomach drops as we continue down the hallway. Its walls are lined with small, contained firecups. The firelight dances merrily on the marble ceiling, a warm and festive chorus oblivious to our plight.

"Stay here," Cass/Kate tells us once we reach Rolladin's waiting room. Then she leaves the way we came in.

"Do you think she takes off that stupid squirrel shawl when she's kissing Rolladin's ass?" Phee whispers.

"Hush. Don't make things worse. Let me do the talking, all right?" Mom mutters. "I can't believe this."

Mom starts running her fingers through her hair again.

My own nerves are kicking into overdrive, and my teeth begin chattering even in the warmth of the firelit room. My sister's wide eyes reflect back my fears.

This might be it.

This might be our last winter.

"So, the prodigal Sarah and her lovely daughters have decided to join us once again." Rolladin's voice overpowers the room. She emerges out of a shadowed hallway, the one leading to her private chambers.

She looks taller than last year as she saunters towards us, then bores her wide weathered eyes right into Mom's. "Unfortunately, there's no room at the inn this year for you. You missed the census deadline. You know the rules. Every year, the middle of October. Before sunset. No one gets food and shelter otherwise."

"There was an accident," Mom says. "I busted my ankle— the girls had to carry me. We'll be here, working all winter to make up for my mistake."

Rolladin bends down to inspect Mom's foot. She hikes Mom's pant leg up, then pulls her ankle under the firelight as Mom hisses. "Sprained," Rolladin says. "Not broken."

Mom doesn't say a word, but I can tell she wants to scream.

"I don't know why you still insist on dragging your- selves back and forth each season," Rolladin mutters as she stands. "You should be in the Park year-round—enough with this *winter* business. This whole problem could've been avoided if you'd ever just look up to see the bigger picture."

"That's my choice to make," Mom says softly. She shifts her weight onto me to stand a little taller. "The Red Allies mandate check-in for winter, nothing else."

I can't help but think that this isn't the time to assert our part-time independence, but Mom's upper lip stays stiff. She doesn't flinch.

I watch Rolladin consider this as she slowly walks by us, surveying each of us like meat. "Of course you're right, Sarah," Rolladin says. "Rules *are* rules. So we're back to square one, unfortunately. Whoever misses the census deadline isn't on the books. We only feed and house who's accounted for." She picks up a massive leather-bound volume as evidence. "The many laws given to us by the Red Allies. Unfortunately, you can't pick and choose."

"Rolladin. There was an *accident*," Mom answers. "We were late by a few minutes. It'll never happen again."

Rolladin stands toe-to-toe with my mother, so close to us that I can see the deep wrinkles around her eyes, the skin beaten by the sun into burlap. She can't be more than a few years older than Mom, but time hasn't been as lenient towards her. "No one's perfect, Sarah, I get that." Rolladin smiles and begins stroking a lock of my mother's hair, like she's petting one of the Park's horses. And God, do I want to slap her hand away, spit in her face, and tell her to stop touching my mother. But Mom's voice echoes in my head again. *Balance. Patience. Control.*

"But you're putting me in a tough position," Rolladin continues. "As Park warden, I can't ignore the rules, despite a sprained ankle or a wrong turn or a failure in judgment. So as much as I hate the thought of it, I need to make an example of you three."

"The Red soldiers in the boroughs don't even know what's going on here anymore." Despite Mom's calm exterior, I hear desperation seep into her voice, and it kick-starts my panic again. "You can make an exception. They'll never find out. It was five minutes, Rolladin—the punishment doesn't fit the crime."

"Does it ever?" Rolladin turns away. "The lords and other fieldworkers saw you three sauntering in, disrespecting me. I can't just ignore this. But . . . I *can* make you a compromise." Then she extends her arms out to us, like she's actually offering something. "One of you will fight tonight."

"What? You mean on Sixty-Fifth Street?" Mom says. "But that's ridiculous. Those matches are for fighters. For pledges and warlords—"

"You get in the ring, take a few blows, survive a round to make sure the fight counts and isn't ruled a no-contest," Rolladin talks over her. "It might be . . . *humbling*, to say the least. But you'll show the rest of the prisoners that you respect the way of the Park. Eye for an eye," Rolladin says, "Nothing here is given, only earned."

"Rolladin, no. Think of something else," Mom says, taking a step towards our warden. "I'm in no shape to fight, and there's no way in hell I'm sending one of the girls into the Sixty-Fifth Street underpass—"

Rolladin's hand snaps across my mother's face. "Don't forget who you're talking to."

"Mom!"

Phee springs forward in fight mode, but I catch her before she can get her hands on Rolladin. "I'll do it, all right?" she says, hands flailing.

"Phee, no," I whisper.

"Absolutely not, Phoenix," Mom says.

Phee starts, "Someone has to—"

"NO. If you insist on this, Rolladin," Mom says slowly, "then put me in your ridiculous matches."

"Mom, there's no way you're street-fighting. Look at you." Phee eyes me for backup, but I'm speechless. Is Rolladin really doing this? Is it either my mother or my sister?

A cloying, masochistic voice inside me whispers, *Why isn't it you?*

"Rolladin." Phee breaks free of Mom and takes a step forward. "Put me down for the match."

"Reminds you of someone, doesn't she?" Rolladin winks at my mother as she leans over her desk and studies some papers. "I'll move some things around, push the contest for the Council position to the first round . . . then Phee can spar against my newest lord, Cass, for Cass's initiation fight." Rolladin looks up and flashes us a fat, hyena grin. "Everything's settled."

And now that she's given her decree, there's nothing left to say.

Mom manages to stay silent, but I feel her trembling next to me. I pull her in close and pull Phee even closer, try to be their pillar of support. Support's what I'm best at, after all. While my younger sister fights to save our places in the Park.

This isn't the way things should be. I know it—I hate it.

"Put your things in the Carlyle," Rolladin adds as she walks towards her chambers, back into the darkness from whence she came. "Your room's still open on the third floor. And for God's sake, Sarah. Make sure to use the washbasin. You three smell like shit."

3   PHEE

It's been nearly an hour since we left Rolladin's castle and settled into our tiny Carlyle room, but I'm still all worked up. I'm on the bed, gripping my new gun, wishing that I too could spit bullets and roar through the city.

"I just can't believe it," Mom says, as Sky comes back into our room with a washbasin and some walking sticks for Mom. "I can't believe you're actually doing this."

"We've been through this already," I say. "There wasn't a choice. If we miss the census deadline, we're on the books as CCs."

"Rolladin shouldn't be able to mark us as civilian casualties because we don't get here on time," Sky mutters as she helps Mom get adjusted to her new crutches. The long wooden sticks hit Mom right at her waist, fit almost perfectly, and she nods in thanks.

"The census is supposed to be a prison count of who's left, not a deadline," Sky adds as she flops down on the bed next to me. "Rolladin just twists the rules to do whatever she wants. That's not the way things should work."

"Who cares how things *should* work?" I say. "What matters is how they do. You know Rolladin. We don't play by her rules, and she shuts us out for good."

"Maybe it'd be a blessing," Sky answers. "The Park's not

the only way to survive the winter—think about the holdouts, Phee."

Seriously? I mean, I know Sky's pissed, but that's just crazy talk. "So . . . you're cool donating your books as kindling to keep us warm on Wall Street."

Sky flinches.

"And buddying up to tunnel feeders for food every once in a while, to beg for an arm or a leg—"

"Phoenix," Mom scolds. "Don't even joke about that."

"Well then, we've got to do what Rolladin says," I say. It's not rocket science. Survival means the Park, and the Park means Rolladin's rules. "One of us has to street-fight."

My mother leans her crutches against the bed and sits on my other side. She dips a cloth into the washbasin.

"But that someone should have been me." Mom wipes the dirt from my cheeks. I look into her eyes and see tears itching to fall. "My job is to protect you, not the other way around."

"Look at you. You can't even walk." I shake my head. "We're not kids anymore, Mom."

But despite my argument, she pulls me in and cradles me like a baby. I can feel her whole body shaking as it holds mine.

"Then it should have been me." Sky gets up and starts unpacking her things in the corner. I pull away from Mom to look at her, but she keeps her eyes on her stuff. "I'm the oldest."

I'm surprised Sky still thinks this way. "But you're the littlest." Does she really think I'd expect her to protect me? Plus, the image of Sky sparring in 65th Street in her leather jacket and leggings is so crazy it's laughable. "It's okay."

"It's not okay." Sky pounds her hand on the wooden bureau, and I jump. My sister's never really pissed off or out of control. But she doesn't meet my eyes, just carefully places her things in the drawers. "None of this is okay."

I let Mom finish wiping down my face with washbasin water as she lectures me on street-fighting . . . *throw a jab, maybe two, get through the first round. After that first bell rings, you let Cass hit you, then you FALL DOWN* . . . then I carry the bucket into the bathroom to finish the rest of my body myself. Firelight spills out of a small cup lodged into a high corner of the room, and my shadow grows and dances as I bathe. The whole room's warm, not just one corner, and it's a nice change from our place near Wall Street.

Sure, there're a lot of things that sometimes bug me about the Park—the whorelords, the rules. The way the rules only seem to work against us, especially tonight. But there're some awesome things too. Like, the Park keeps us fed, safe, and alive. And it gives us all a purpose—survival together through the winter, one crop at a time. At least until the war beyond the skyscrapers is over.

I take a deep breath and pretend that's what I'm fighting for—for my family and all the prisoners—not Rolladin and her fat book of Red Allies rules.

But as I put my clothes back on after washing, my resolve kind of cracks and falls apart. And a fear about tonight starts to rumble in my belly. I think of the matches, how excited I was this morning to watch the whorelords kick the crap out of one another, and how now I'm part of the show.

And then, even though I try so hard not to, I think of the brawls from winters past. Young pledges knocking each other around to within an inch of death, all for the sake of joining Rolladin's ranks. Junior whorelords pulling each other apart to impress our warden. Then I think of the bruises and fat lips of the losers, and the ones who can't walk all winter.

What if Cass slashes up my face or something?

What if I break an arm? Or a leg?

What if I die?

I shake my head like I can physically shake off the fear. I just have to get through one full round in order to avoid a call of no-contest. Then get to the second round, take a blow, and stay down.

I exhale like I can breathe out all the worry. *Take one minute, one step, at a time.*

When I come out of the bathroom, Mom's gone to get some cloth to make handgrips for her crutches, and my sister's hunched in the corner of the room under another firecup. First time we stop today, and she's already lost in a book. I'm relieved to see it, though. I want the distraction more than I care to admit.

"Haven't you read that, like, twenty times already?" I say, pointing to her beat-up copy of *Charlotte's Web*. I've never understood reading a book twice. Or once, if I'm honest.

"I'm just trying to keep my mind busy," Sky says, without lifting her eyes. The hollow way she says it pinches me with something I can't explain. Sometimes I swear Sky likes her book characters more than me.

"Well, then go be productive and wipe yourself down already, dirty bird." I flop next to her, rip the book from her hands, push to get her real attention.

"Stop, it's fragile!" she cries.

"Lunatic. It's a *book*."

But she scoops up the hardback like I've crushed Charlotte underneath it or something.

"Look, I didn't mean to snap, okay?" Sky's face goes through a wardrobe change, and now she's wearing only sympathy. "I'm sorry. I can't imagine what you must be going through right now."

But I don't want pity. I want to do something with all this fear and aggression I've got bubbling up inside me. "You're being totally psycho." I lean in and rip the book away from her again, just 'cause I know she doesn't want me to have it.

"Phoenix—"

And when I get the old hardback into my hands, I finally figure out why she's making a big deal over it.

It's not *Charlotte's Web*.

I flip through the pages, front to back to front again. I've never seen so much handwriting in one place, not since Mom forced us to learn as kids, anyway. Never more than a scribble from Mom that she's gone to hunt near our Wall Street apartment, or that she's up in the roof garden. Come to think of it, the writing reminds me of Mom's, loopy and tight at the same time.

As if reading my mind, Sky whispers, "It's a book by Mom."

"What do you mean, 'by Mom'? Like she wrote it? When?"

I flip to the front page, expecting some sort of cover page like all of Sky's other novels, but instead it just confirms what Sky's said—*Property of Sarah Walker Miller*.

Sky shushes me and looks back towards the door. "When I was a baby. Before you were born."

Her lip starts quivering, and I have to hold back an eye roll 'cause I think she's going to cry. But instead she says, "I took it from Mom's old apartment. She doesn't know. This is just our thing, okay? I don't think she'd want us to have it. It was hidden away in that safe."

Sky's waiting for some sort of reaction, I know, but I can't speak. I'm shocked. Stealing from Mom isn't something I ever thought Sky would do, was even capable of, really.

She gives up waiting for an answer, takes the book back from my outstretched hands, and flips a couple of pages.

"It's from before the war." She drops her whisper to a hum. "Look."

> *January 4—Every year it's the same. I swear that I'll finally give the stories that circle around in my mind a page on which to land. But now, with Sky's diapers and feedings and nonexistent naps, my dream feels even more indulgent. Ridiculous, even: Sarah Miller's trying to be a writer!*
>
> *More of a burden on my family than anything else.*

So many thoughts and questions fly through my head. I can't sort them out, and the messiness brings on a rush of feelings. If Mom's book was locked in that safe, it was obviously never meant to see the light of day. Should we really know what's in it?

I want Sky to understand this, that I feel weird and unsettled by what she's shown me. But as usual, I can't find the right words, and Sky's waiting for me to say something.

"Not much has changed," I finally come up with. "You're still a shitty sleeper."

Sky just shakes her head, turns the page, and buries back into Mom's book.

> *February 15—So it's official. Tom decided to leave Robert Mulaney's studio to work for his dad and Mary at the firm. I feel like I've gutted a bit of his soul—*

We both jump when we hear the creak of the door to our bedroom. Sky quickly closes the handwritten book, so all that's visible from her lap is a faded picture of a pig and a spiderweb.

"Still trying to get Phee hooked on *Charlotte's Web*?" Mom gives Sky a forced smile. She looks a million years old, tired and hunched over those walking sticks, and a wave of guilt hits me over the idea of feeding her lies, especially tonight. But Sky's right. Mom would definitely take the book if she found it on us. And the only sure thought I have about the thing is that I'm not ready to say good-bye to it.

But before I can jump in, Sky shrugs and answers, "It's a classic."

I stare at her, shocked at how easily the lie rolls off her tongue.

"It used to be one of my favorites too, when I was a kid," Mom says, and a lost look conquers her face. "Come on, let's finish getting washed up. There's no reason to make this any worse."

After Mom hides my contraband gun under our mattress, we take some more of the rationed cloths and smaller sticks left at the end of the hall and make traveling torches from the firecups in the hallway. Then we leave the Carlyle to join the rest of the stragglers on their way to the Park.

The sky's settled into twilight outside, lighting up the bordering trees, making the whole scene wildly creepy. My fear has already kicked into overdrive by now, but it's not a cut-and-dried feeling. I want to run, shout, and fly all at the same time. There's so much terror and excitement flooding my veins, I kind of think I might explode.

"Protect your face, protect your stomach," Mom says. She hobbles forward on her makeshift crutches, towards the mass of people gathering to hear Rolladin speak in Sheep Meadow, hundreds of torches waving in the air. "You've got to last through the first round."

"Right."

"Next round, you fall down as soon as Cass touches you. You got it?" Mom keeps lecturing, with these crazy-wide eyes. "Fall down and stay down."

"Yes." I can barely hear my answer over the sound of my obnoxious heart. "Stay down."

"You don't have to do this, Phee." Sky grabs my hand and looks into the hungry crowd. "We can run away. Or I could take your place."

It's an empty offer if I've ever heard one. Like I'm going to sign Sky's death sentence. And where would we run?

But it still makes me feel better. Like this really is a choice. And it empowers me, gives me just an inch of confidence to keep on walking. And I say, "No. I've got this. I'll be okay."

Sky lets go of my hand, puts hers on my back, and we push our way into the maze of people. The crowd is bodies deep, a fog of dried sweat and earth from today's tilling. We wade through the masses—Mom's best friend, Lauren, calls out to us from the mess of people—but Mom just nods absently and keeps moving with us towards the front.

I feel sort of terrible thinking this, but I really need to lose Mom and Sky. They're making me nervous, even more nervous than I already am. As if they're more weight on my shoulders. More people I'd disappoint if I get hurt. Or worse.

We're about nine or ten rows from the front when I hear a familiar voice.

"Phee! Phee!" I barely hear over the crowd.

God damn it. And I *really* can't deal with Trevor right now. He bounds over to us and somehow manages to insert himself in between me and Mom.

"Sarah, are you okay? What's with the crutches?"

"Trev, I'm fine, honey. Just an accident."

"And what's going on with the street-fights? I saw the schedule of matches. Phee's on it." He looks at me. "How are you on it?"

"Trev, we'll catch up after the fights. Give Phee some space, all right?" Mom says, but she sounds totally spooked.

"Is Phee going to be okay?" Trevor calls after us as the crowd pulls him back, and we keep rolling forward. "Will she be okay?" His voice gets softer, like we're floating away from him, farther and farther out to sea.

"I'll be okay, Trev," I somehow manage to call out. "It's going to be okay."

Whorelords come crawling out of the folds of the crowd, nod at Mom and Sky, take me from them. And now that I've gotten what I wanted—we're separated—I'm actually not sure I can stand on my own. But as my knees buckle, the whorelords pay no attention and just keep ushering me past Rolladin's podium.

"Phee—no!" Mom yells. I twist my neck and manage to catch her and Sky swimming against the tide of the crowd to keep up with me. "Clara," Mom calls out to the old flaxen-haired guard on my right. "Please don't do this."

"What's done is done, Sarah," the guard mumbles.

I pass Rolladin's stage just as she gets ready to mount it to address the Park, her Council surrounding her with a halo of torches. Somehow I manage to catch Sky's eyes one more time before I'm dragged into the forest to be prepped for my match. "It's going to be all right," I call to her with a voice I don't recognize. "We're going to be okay."

4   SKY

I watch, helpless, as Phee is pulled towards the trees that border the Park Lake. As she disappears into darkness, I unleash a hatred within my skin that threatens to eat me alive.

Phee's words echo through my brain. *The littlest.*

The black sheep.

The one on the sidelines.

I'm the oldest. It shouldn't be Phee.

It should be me.

I try to shake away the demons and focus my efforts on Mom, on being that shining pillar of support for her, and grab her hand.

"Welcome," Rolladin's voice booms through the Park, "to the few winter fieldworkers who've just joined us. To my year-rounds, my Council. My lesser lords. Fellow survivors—all glorious three hundred eighty-two of you, according to this year's census—we live another year. And for that, we have much cause to celebrate."

The crowd hurrahs, and a wave of torches rises and falls.

"The war wages on beyond the skyscrapers, and yet because of our determination, our honor, our *refusal* to give in, we live," she continues. "Our city has fallen, our shores have been surrounded. The Red Allies have cut us off from the rest of the world. And yet we live. They give us nothing but our bare hands to survive. And yet—WE LIVE!" Rolladin throws her hands up to the stars, and another rally from the crowd echoes like thunder through the Park.

"I've been with my Council of Lords to the Brooklyn borders and back this summer," Rolladin continues. "I've begged the Red Allies to spare us once again, to leave us here in captivity as the war goes on. And because of all of you, we can continue to survive here. We can afford to be ignored. We have made an oasis in the middle of a war zone. And we will *continue* to thrive."

She steps down onto the matted grass and the crowd rallies again, parts like wheat in a windstorm.

"Tonight I am not your warden, but your fellow prisoner. Your fellow sister who emerged from the tunnels when the skies were black and the streets were singed, and we clawed our way back to life all those autumns ago," she says. "Tonight I give you a gift, a celebration worthy of your courage. And we will rejoice and dance and fight for all that we have to be thankful for."

I can barely see over the rows of people in front of me, but it looks like Rolladin is signaling to a cluster of lesser lords behind her. The warlords break away and move towards the forest. The 65th Street fighting is about to begin. This is it. This is real.

"So without further delay, let us commence the census festivities. To the Sixty-Fifth Street underpass for the first of our competitions!"

The crowd cheers and a chorus of drums kicks up, percussion thumping against the night sky. We move as a herd across Sheep Meadow, in and out of the trees, spill onto the cement roads that cut through the Park like frozen rivers.

Mom skip-hops next to me on her crutches, wincing a bit with every step.

"Rolladin said the first round's for the Council position, then the second round will be Phee and Cass." I swear my heart is pounding louder than the drums. "We've got to be right under the bridge, so Phee can see us."

Mom nods. "We need to pick up the pace."

Mom's friend Lauren catches up to me and my mother, and the three of us navigate our way together through the crowd, move quickly to get to the front of the pack before it floods both sides of the 65th Street underpass.

"Do you see her?" Lauren asks us.

"No, we lost her," Mom says. "They must be prepping her in the forest."

The music's grown so ferociously loud I can't hear myself think. There are guitars in the crowd now, and singing, no words but moans and chants. Haunting, oddly beautiful sounds, like the odes of nightmares.

We spill under the 65th Street Transverse. We nearly collide with one of Rolladin's lesser lords, holding her arm forward to signal *stop*, her other arm waving a torch high above. Some of the Park kids giggle as they race around the guard and scale the rocks up to the abandoned street above, then lie down and hang their heads into the underpass, attempting to watch the matches upside down. My sister and I used to do this. My sister, who's about to spar tonight.

I exhale and try to focus only on my mission—protecting our spot in the front, in the first rows right at the edge of the archway's shadows. Lauren and I start throwing elbows, and I put my hand out like a protective gate in front of my mother as prisoners file around us. Others come under the 65th Street Transverse from the other side, so now the underpass is caged by bodies. Guards with torches puncture the crowd like fence posts, the firelight casting odd, frightening shadows on the archway above.

"Keep the underpass clear! Keep it clear!" Clara, the guard who took Phee, hollers as she walks in a long, wide oval, her stride marking the ring. "Save the aisle for Rolladin!"

The drums and chanting quiet as Rolladin pushes her way through the crowd and into the underpass.

Mom grabs my hand and looks at me. "Tell me Phee's going to be okay."

"She's going to be okay," I say, for both of us.

"The Sixty-Fifth Street fights are not only a Park tradition." Rolladin's voice booms through the tunnel as the drums fall into a steady beat: *BUM bum BUM bum BUM bum BUM.* "They are a testament to the prisoners taken from us. A celebration of the lives that were sacrificed for the amusement of the Red Allies, those who were beaten senseless in this very street for sport. We honor them with these matches. Let us never forget our desperate beginnings. And let us always remember that strength and sacrifice keep us alive."

The crowd gives a huge collective *"HURRAH!"*

"For the first match, I give you my two lesser lords Philip and Lory. They're both fighting for the chance to join my Council, since we lost my dear friend and confidante Samantha this past summer." A few of the lords murmur in sadness. "But as we've learned from this treacherous city, from death comes life and opportunity." Rolladin raises her arms to the archway. "Three matches! To be followed by the archery contests, and of course, the races. Then last but not least . . . the feast of your year!"

Another "*HURRAH!*"

"Without further delay, we begin!"

A soft cloak of mink brushes my arm as Lory pushes her way past us into the open underpass. Philip plows through the crowd on the other side, and the two begin circling the torch-lit underpass, a dangerous dance of light and shadows.

"Philip's as good as dead," I tell Mom and Lauren as I study Lory's chiseled arms, her legs as wide as tree trunks. Lory wears a scratched helmet long past retirement age and carries no weapons but her bare hands.

Not that I feel sorry for Philip. After he turned us away from check-in today, I'm rooting against him with my whole being. The very fabric of my soul prays for his destruction.

"He's getting old," Lauren says. "It was a stupid play for power. Rolladin will take his cloak if he loses."

The chatter has reached a fever pitch, as bets and side bets are being swapped and argued over—who will win, how many rounds, how many licks. I try to calm myself in the chaos, try not to think about the fact that my sister is next. That she might have the worst odds of any street-fighter who's ever sparred in the Park.

I put my arm around my mother, holding her close, letting her lean on me. I crane my neck behind me, trying to look past the thicket of bodies, to see if I can spot Phee approaching.

I can't find her, but for a second, I spot something else moving across the lawn beyond the crowd. It cuts in and out of the shadows, darts over the pathways of cement and into the trees, bounding away from the madness of 65th Street. I'm about to shrug it off as a startled deer, but it's slower and bigger. It almost . . . it almost looks like a person.

But before I can think through it, before I can say anything to Mom, the mania of the underpass overpowers me. The drums, the catcalls, the cheering—they build like a raging storm. Then Lory's animal war cry thunders through the underpass:

"You're mine!"

Philip steps onto the curved brick wall of the pedestrian walkway and leaps forward towards Lory, like he's flying.

But his fist meets air as Lory ducks and sends an elbow right into his stomach. Philip doubles over, and Lory kicks him square in the chin, sending him staggering back into the brick wall. He hits it with a *slap*.

But he gets up quickly and dances away from Lory.

She throws a jab, he ducks, she throws a hook, he jumps . . .

"TIME!" Clara, the referee, comes bursting out of the folds of the crowd on the other side. She separates Philip and Lory, pushing them to opposite ends of the underpass.

The crowd is wild at this point, and I feel hands and hot breath on my neck, tugs on my clothes, as the prisoners behind Mom and me lean in to get a better look.

"Round two!" Clara yells a minute later.

Philip repositions his helmet, then steps back into the ring. He starts to stutter-step, like some pathetic warm-up lap, but Lory's already barreling towards him.

"Philip's a goner!" Mrs. Warbler declares behind me, in between hacks. "She has him. She has him!"

Lory punches Philip in the face, once, twice, sends him flailing backward.

"Use a rock!" someone yells from the crowd, tempting Lory to raise the stakes.

I wince with expectation as Lory searches the shadows of the bridge and picks up a flat, smooth rock the size of a fist. Philip tries to slither away, but Lory grabs the collar of his raccoon shawl and pulls him under her.

"Stop!" Philip cries. "Stop!"

But no one pays attention. This is 65th Street fighting, after all. There are no rules. And there's no "stop" until someone's down and out cold.

Lory whips off Philip's helmet, then smashes the rock over his head. A river of blood springs from his temple, flowing over his eyes, his hair, his . . . I can't look anymore.

"Finish him, Lory!" the crowd rallies.

I keep my eyes closed, take my mother's hand once more, and squeeze as hard as I can.

Then I hear the referee: "One, two, three, four, five . . ." The crowd joins in. "Six . . . seven . . . eight!"

Then, silence.

"Bravo," Rolladin's voice echoes through the tunnel. "Bravo."

My eyes snap open. Rolladin's hovering over Philip's heap of a body in the corner of the 65th Street underpass. She bends down to survey him, some mess of emotions crawling across her face. Then she's nothing but a blank slate again.

"Lory will join my Council of Lords for her bravery. Philip's service was commendable." Rolladin waves a team of lesser lords forward to take Philip's body away. "But over. If he survives the night," she tells her team, "he'll start as a fieldworker tomorrow."

The crowd booms with cheers and laughter as three young warlords carry Philip out of the underpass. Rolladin takes the victor predator pelt from the referee, throws it over her shoulder, and crosses the open ring to congratulate Lory. She grabs Lory's face and crushes her own into it, a fierce, possessive kiss.

"Do you understand what you're watching, why I give you these matches, year after year?" Rolladin addresses the crowd. "To show you *evolution*. Survival of the fittest. Only those of us who are strong, like our champion here"—she thrusts Lory's arm into the air—"will survive. There is no room for weakness in this city."

And it's only when Rolladin drapes her newest Council member with the prized pelt of a zoo tiger that I realize Mom is crying.

"I'm going to rip your hair out. Gouge out your eyes. Make your teeth into a necklace," Cass calls ahead to me as a pair of whorelords pulls me across Sheep Meadow and towards 65th Street.

One of my whorelord goons tightens her grip around my forearm. Then she turns around and tells Cass, "Save the fighting for the ring."

We stumble through the dark field, then over the walkways of cracked cement and towards the underpass, the 65th Street Transverse crested over it like a half-moon. Fieldworkers and whorelords with torches spill out of both sides, and kids are hanging over the bridge for cheap-seat views of the fights. The whole scene's chaos, basically: shouts and cheers and flashes of fire against the night sky, side gambling and bickering. Every year I've been in the thick of it, just part of the bloodthirsty audience, calling for some whorelord to get what's coming to her. I never thought about how it looked from the outside. I never realized it feels like some sort of crazy sacrifice.

Someone comes sprinting towards us out of the madness. "They're ready for her," says Clara, the old referee.

"Who won?" Cass asks behind me.

"Lory."

"Figures. Philip was a relic." Cass laughs. "I was sick of that old queen anyway."

But Clara doesn't laugh along with her. "Show some respect. He got his face rearranged." The referee takes me from my escorts and nods at Cass. "Maybe you should focus on your own match."

Cass adjusts the little squirrel shawl around her shoulders, the only stupid thing separating her from me. "You think I'm worried about this lemming? Please." Cass smiles at me. "She's as good as dead."

The drums have kicked up again, and now I know we're minutes from starting. My heart starts sputtering, climbing, clawing its way to my throat. *God, I think I'm going to be sick.* Referee Clara leads me away from Cass and my two bodyguards, then pulls me down a small hill and into the crowd of people.

The underpass is humming, a fat, soupy stew of grabby hands and catcalls—*Wait, is that Phee? Sarah Miller's youngest?*— as Clara pulls me through the crowd. My head starts spinning, my heart keeps pounding, and I swear I'm going to drown in all of this. Like it's all going to wash over me and pull me under.

I say, "I don't think I can do this," before I even realizing I'm saying it.

Clara pulls me into her side as we plow forward. "You can, and you will," she says into my ear. "Do whatever it takes to make it through the first round." And even though she's giving me advice, her eyes are hard. "The only place there aren't rules is the ring."

But before I can pump Clara for more, she thrusts me into the center of the underpass.

The crowd falls to silence as I stand there, alone, in the middle of hundreds of prisoners.

I look around, the faces of friends and fieldworkers blurring together in the light and shadows of the underpass. I try to take a deep breath, just try to find Sky and Mom, but the crowd's gasps and shocked whispers rattle me like thunder.

I start backing up, into the hands of the crowd behind me, then look over to the other side, where they're packed in like matches.

Even if I wanted to escape, there's nowhere to run.

"And now, I have something quite *unusual* for your viewing pleasure." Rolladin steps into the center of the ring and calls over the crowd. "One of your own has pledged a street-fight to me, as a pleading for mercy."

The crowd grows louder, a hive buzzing with questions.

"Her family has disrespected the rules of the Park," Rolladin adds, "and extends this offering in desperation. As you can see, I have accepted. But let this be a lesson to all of you. *Nothing* is given for free in the middle of a war."

Rolladin looks at me. Her face is weird, though, all mashed up, almost like she's worried, or upset. Then she gives me a little nod, so small and serious that I almost don't catch it. But I can't stand to look at her. *Screw you, Rolladin.*

I reach for the grass necklace Sky gave me for my birthday this morning, pretend it's her hand. I *need* to see my family, and the need is quickening my breath, shaking my hands. I search the crowd frantically, run through each face as quickly as I can.

Where are they?

Clara comes back with some loaner helmet with a hole on the right side and a fat pockmark in the middle.

"Keep this on, whatever you do," she says as she fastens it under my chin.

But I don't answer, I *can't* answer—it's all going so fast, none of it feels real. I'm watching from a cage in someone else's nightmare.

Rolladin's still blabbering on about Cass, and the match, and about me being an example, but I can't process her words. They're just flies, buzzing past me.

"Eye for an eye—"

All I can think is, *Where are they?*

"The way of the Park—"

And the shadows dancing across the arched ceiling of the underpass, Rolladin's voice, the gasps and the whispers—it all comes to a quick boil, and before I realize what I'm doing, my vocal cords are straining under the pressure of, "WAIT!"

And then it's only me talking. Fear is flattening me, crushing me on all sides, but somehow I'm talking.

"I'm not doing this for Warden Rolladin," I say. I'm surprised I sound powerful, my tone as flat and steady as a drum. "I'm doing this for my family. For my mom and Sky." I look around at the worn, tired faces of the Park on both sides of the underpass. "For the fieldworkers."

"How dare you speak—," Rolladin begins, but she's interrupted.

"Phee!"

Sky angles past one of the whorelords who's guarding the crowd on the other side and moves a few steps into the ring. Mom's trying to pull her back, but Sky shrugs her off. I close my eyes and open them, and when I do, there's no longer any crowd. It's just the two of us. Back by the water on Wall Street, laughing and sparring, ready to begin our own fake fight. And in that crazy way Sky can read my mind, she reminds me of what I've forgot.

"Remember your weapons," Sky yells.

The crowd murmurs, confused.

But I'm not confused.

I take a deep breath, close my eyes again, and do what she says. I think of the weapons we made as kids, the ones hammered out of my sister's stories and dreams. Swords from wizards and magic dust from fairies that Sky swore lived in Battery Park. We'd pull the weapons out and be ready to battle anything. Even the ghosts that made Mom scream in the middle of the night. Even the skeletons we'd find in bed when we'd scavenge downtown apartments.

Cass can't touch me.

"Silence!" Rolladin roars. "Enough delay. It's time to begin!"

My sister runs back to the sidelines. Then it's just me and Cass, on opposite sides of the underpass. She starts pacing sideways, surveying me like some zoo animal, so I start mimicking her and stalk the other way. The crowd's alive again, and a swell of cheers and catcalls erupt out of the Park and shake the underpass.

"PHOE-NIX. PHOE-NIX."

Even through my fog of fear, I hear the cheers. I grit my teeth, crack my knuckles, and swallow the tight ball in my throat down, down, down.

Cass crosses the ring. She comes at me in a burst, sprinting, jumping, fist framed against the torch-lit underpass. . . .

I duck and roll away.

Cass gets to her feet, dusts herself off, turns around and smiles. "You can't duck forever."

She growls and runs at me again, both fists up and ready to strike. She grabs my shoulders before I can wriggle away from her. My hands go up on instinct, reaching for her face, her eyes, her dumb squirrel cloak. . . .

BOOM. My rib cage rattles. Then Cass whips her hand up and brings it crashing down against my cheek. The blow burns, feels like candle wax against my skin, and I yelp and turn to run away from her. But Cass has got me, pushes me, and now I'm flailing backward. I fall against the pavement, the wind knocked out of me in one tight whoosh, as gasps echo through the underpass.

Get up, God damn it, Phee, get up—survive the first round.

I take a breath out of my battered lungs and crawl my way to stand.

"You're a masochistic little bitch, aren't you?" Cass leaps for me, grabs my hair, and pulls me towards the brick wall.

"Stop," I'm yelling. "STOP!"

Somehow I manage to elbow Cass in the ribs and fold into her side, and I send us both careening onto the pavement.

Cheers roar through the underpass:

"Phoenix, hang in there!"

"She's nothing but a Rolladin lackey!"

"Stay in it for me. For my daughter! May she rest in peace!"

Then Referee Clara is untangling us, shouting, "TIME!"

Cass comes at me again, but Clara pulls her into the opposite corner.

"Don't make me *try*, bitch!" Cass is shouting, fighting, as she's dragged away for the one-minute break between rounds.

The crowd is just a loud wave of voices, like an ocean under 65th Street, but somehow I pick out the one voice I need to hear. Mom. "Phee, next hit, stay down!"

LEE KELLY

I scramble to my feet, desperate to see her and Sky again. But they're no longer on the front lines. The crowd must've swallowed them whole.

"Round two!"

Cass bursts out of the fieldworkers and comes running at me. She wastes no time. Blow to my right side. Then she undercuts my chin, and I swear, I feel the jab in each tooth. The next hit comes fast as lightning, across my cheek, and the pain sears me like a flame.

I double over.

Cass kicks me in the stomach, and now I'm hurling, just bile and spit and blood as I crawl to the side of the underpass, to the rows and rows of legs and feet marking the borders of the ring.

"Enough!" I can't see my sister, but I can hear her. Sky's voice rings out, panicked and desperate above all the others. "Phoenix, stay DOWN!"

Referee Clara begins the count. "One . . . two . . ."

Then time does a funny thing as I'm on the ground, bleeding.

It stops, hands me a slice of forever, and I *feel* all the fieldworkers around me. All the prisoners, especially the young ones, like Sky and me, even Trevor, the ones who have only known rules.

And even though I know I'm supposed to just . . . *stop*, and stay down, I said I came to fight for them.

". . . five . . . six . . ."

Before I can even think, *Yes, okay, this is what I'm doing*, I spot a thin red-handled blade poking out of a whorelord's boot. I lunge towards the leg and dislodge the weapon, then with every shred of fight I have left in me, I whirl around and thrust it forward, the referee's words whispering in my ear: *The only place there aren't rules is the ring.*

The small knife lodges into Cass's forearm, but I pull it out fast as a reflex. Her eyes fly open, and she shrieks and falls to the ground, folds around her arm. I scramble to my feet, blood and heat and pain attacking me from all sides, just as Clara jumps between Cass and me.

"TIME!" Clara says, pushing us to opposite corners.

I look at Cass's arm, a cut the size of a finger lacing blood around her forearm. *I did that.* I exhale. Wipe my lip, wipe my brow, readjust my helmet. *I did that.*

"Time?" Cass is sputtering. "*Time?* That bitch is a cheat! You can't bring weapons into the ring! Rolladin," she appeals to our warden, who's standing in her cushy spot on the sidelines.

Rolladin's face is hard, cool . . . she doesn't answer.

So was that fair? Does it matter?

I can't think, I can't process any of this, 'cause time's now skipping forward like some kid hopped up on honey, but somehow I manage, "I didn't bring it in."

Cass gives this tight, twisted little laugh. "You're giving me technicalities?" she shouts. "You are so fucking dead."

Again the crowd is all whispers, grunts, and groans. Out of the thick madness, I swear I can hear Sky and Mom call to me. "Phee, enough!"

But time keeps skipping forward, and Clara shouts, "Round three!"

And then Cass is coming for me like a lion from an open cage. I try to keep the small, bloodstained knife between us, thrusting it in all directions like some moving wall she can't scale.

But she catches my arm and brings it crashing over her knee, and sends her other hand into my stomach. And I can't hold on anymore. It's like someone's taken my heart and thrown it against the cement. I fall to my knees, and the knife goes flying.

I lunge for it, but Cass pulls me back into her, and then we're locked together, rolling around in the underpass, nothing but the cheers throughout the Park to buoy us. She's feet, inches, away from the knife. I know it's over when she gets her hands on it. But I can't hold her, I—I can't stop her. . . . Her fingers wrap around it. . . .

"ENOUGH!"

Cass looks at me hungrily. Then at Rolladin, confused.

I want to roll away from Cass and run, run as fast as my legs will carry me, through the crowd now as quiet as Wall Street in winter. But I can't move.

"I said enough." Rolladin's voice is louder, closer now, like she's right up next to me, in my ear, and then I feel Cass release my hand. And now Rolladin somehow *is* beside me. One rough tug by her, and I'm on my feet. Rolladin's gripping my forearm, holding me steady, with Cass pulled close on her other side.

"The match is a push," Rolladin booms through the underpass. But her voice sounds funny, shaky, like it's balancing on the edge of a skyscraper. "Cass has secured her place as newest lord on my lesser council. And for her courage, Phee and her family will remain with us in the Park. Extra rations to the three of them tonight."

The crowd's not quiet any longer, as hundreds of voices let out a roar, and a bloody smile creeps across my lips. *A push.*

And even though the world's spinning, I stand a little taller.

"Final match!" Rolladin calls over the crowd. But before she gets back to the best spot in the underpass, she pulls me in tight to her, so close that I can see where the blue of her irises fade into green.

"Go to your mother." Her eyes are haunted, two tortured ghosts in the firelight. "Now."

6   SKY

The fire pit laps at our faces and hands, warms our full bowls of peacock stew, and for a moment, the world is a mirage, the crest of a dream. My sister is safe. With a patched eye, a fat lip, and some bruised ribs. But safe. *Alive.*

We eat shoulder to shoulder, huddled over our soup bowls. I've even slipped my arm through hers, just to convince myself that she's really there. It's an awkward way to sit, I know, but when Phee tried to shrug me off and dig into her dinner with both hands, I couldn't let her go for some reason.

"All right, weirdo." She'd shrugged but had flashed me a wide, uneven smile. We both knew how close she had come, *we* had come, to losing everything. "Arm in arm it is."

Sheep Meadow is now peppered with small fire pits, each one encircled by hungry, tired prisoners perched on stones and logs, since the races have ended and the official census feast has begun. Most of the pits are crammed with people, but after Phee's brave performance, Rolladin gave us our own fire pit near the solace of the trees, at the edges of the crowd. Ironically, even though she'd demanded that one of us spar in the first place, afterward Rolladin kept asking Phee if she was *okay*. She even checked out Phee's injuries herself during the archery competitions, instead of letting one of the medics do it, almost . . . almost like she cared. Mom gave her steely eyes the whole time, of course, but that part I expected.

"I still can't believe that match," Mom says now, after she comes back from the ration line and settles in close on Phee's other side, like we're fencing her in. We had our big reunion on 65th Street, right after Phee's fight, but Mom and I don't trust our luck. Like Phee might disappear any moment on us. "Your sister and I were beside ourselves."

"What, you really thought that Cass-hole was going to take me down?" Phee says to her bowl. But as she plays with her fat lip, I can see fear lingering behind her eyes. And for some reason, I'm still afraid too, as if I've just woken up from a long stretch of feverish nightmares. *We came so close.*

Mom pulls both of us into her. "Never, ever, *ever* pull something that crazy again, you hear me?" she whispers.

I can't help but laugh when I feel Phee shrug next to me and say, "We'll see."

The festival becomes warm and loud, as the music kicks up again and some of the warlords begin dancing in the center of the fields, raising and clanking their mugs of Rolladin's moonshine as they twist and writhe across the Park.

Every year it's the same. We watch the street-fights and scream for bloodshed. Then some of the fieldworkers compete in the archery contests and field races for extra rations or a day free of duties. Then we're fed, well for once, and relax under the stars while music plays until midnight. Or until Rolladin's warlords get sloppy and fights break out, whatever comes first.

It's one of the few easy days in the Park, and I want to

enjoy it, just let myself celebrate—but it's kind of hard to do. My nerves are still fried, and I can't seem to sort my feelings out. Fear, adrenaline, envy, anger. And in the dark corners as always, like dust swept under a rug, a sadness I never fully understand.

"Oh God," Phee mutters next to me. "Here he comes again."

I follow her eyes and watch Trev bound across the Park with a huge grin on his face and a steaming bowl in his hand. I shake my head and start laughing, try to herd my disconcerting thoughts back into their cages.

"Be nice," Mom warns my sister.

I feel bad for Phee a lot of times, I really do. Gangly Trevor, self-proclaimed Miller family adoptee, has such a monster crush on my sister that most times, it's painful to watch them together. But other times, it's total entertainment. Right now Trevor's practically sprinting over to our fire, bobbing and weaving through the crowds, arms outstretched like he's praising the heavens. His peacock stew is spilling over half the Park.

"Phee, the birthday victor! You were amazing!" He breathes excitedly as he approaches us. He looks around for a seat, and I gladly oblige.

"Sky, don't get up—," Phee grits through her teeth.

"Oh, I don't mind." I know she's been to hell and back tonight, but we're still sisters, after all. She's going to kill me for this, but it's worth it.

Trevor sits down hastily, right up close to her, his silky black hair flopping over his eyes. "You. Were. Fantastically Incredible," he sputters. "I didn't know you had it in you! I mean, of course I knew you did, but to see it, in the flesh."

He looks up at Mom and me, making sure we're hanging on every word of his eloquent synopsis. "Cass pummels you. Cass knocks you around. Cass beats you senseless. Then you whip out a weapon from some whorelord's shoe, and whoop! You slice her!" He laughs this choppy, tight little laugh as he wields an invisible knife over the fire.

My mother, saint she is, gives Trevor a huge smile like always. Then she begins stroking Phee's hair. "She's pretty amazing, isn't she?"

I feel something small and jagged in my throat, but I nod along with them.

"I've known it forever. Since she was a kid—"

"Trev, you're younger than I am." Phee rolls her eyes, and mouths to me, *Help.*

"I even bet rations on you with Old Lady Warbler," Trevor barrels on. "Two full days of meals. This is the first course of many tonight." He beams as he shoves his stew under Phee's nose. He then looks into the fire in sudden realization. "Man, I hope I don't kill the woman."

"Mrs. Warbler's been through worse." Mom laughs and keeps playing with Phee's hair. "And she's still as strong as an ox. I think it's safe to collect on that bet."

I slowly drift away from the fire as Mom helps Trevor recount Phee's street-fight scene by scene. It's not that I *want* to be jealous. That I want to act like a shadow while my sister shines. But I don't know how to turn these feelings off sometimes. My smile starts to feel hollow, my heart races, and I wonder if people can see right through me, can see how different I am inside. That I'm not hammered out of steel, like Phee is. That I'm not made for this city—while my sister is practically its prodigy.

I wander over to the trees as the music's tempo picks up and the cheers through the Park become deafening. I stop short of the forest line, just in case any raiders or feeders are lurking out there, waiting to pick at scraps—or lingerers—from the festival. But I'm sure I'm safe. A holdout hasn't tried to poach the Park since we were kids.

As always when I'm feeling tense and unsettled, I let my mind wander, let my thoughts chain together and drag me to a better place. I think of the past and how much I don't know about Mom and this city. I picture Mom writing her secrets in that small, tattered blue book, which now belongs to me, and soon, tonight even, I'll read and share those secrets. Maybe if I know what's come before, I can take comfort in where I am, and why I'm here, instead of wishing with every fiber of my being to be anywhere else.

I hear a sharp crack of a branch coming from deep in the forest, and panic jolts me. I'm being reckless, have stumbled too close to the woods. But before I can turn to rejoin my family, a swift flash of green darts from tree to tree. It moves again, this emerald lightning bolt, and my heart starts jumping around like a fish in bare hands. Is it an animal? A person? *What kind of person?*

I try to remember Mom's warnings about the tunnel feeders. *Don't panic. Back up slowly. Then run like hell.* And about the raiders. *Empty your pockets. Put down your weapons. Then curl into a ball of submission.*

But what if you don't know what kind of holdout you're dealing with?

I start shuffling backward, when the green form stops

in between the trees, just for a second. It's a man, a *young* man, his face covered with mud, leaves in his hair like camouflage, the pupils of his eyes so white against his dirty face, they glow like a pair of moons. He meets my gaze.

I give a short, startled gasp. I know the faces of all the male prisoners in the Park—the fieldworkers, the lords. There aren't many of them. And I'm positive I've never seen this one. My mind starts swimming, a realization crashing over me—*was this the stranger outside the crowds, during the street-fights?*

But before I can think through it, he's gone.

I take a step closer to where this disappearing woodsman was, sprint back and forth a bit between the trees to try to find him. But the woods are unassuming, the trees stoic. *We saw nothing*, they seem to whisper. *You're conjuring ghosts.*

Am I really starting to see things? My imagination has gotten the better of me before. But not like this . . . and not twice.

I take a deep breath and quickly scout once more around the wide, knotty oak where I saw him.

Nothing. No footprints, no markings, no proof.

I don't say anything about what I think I saw to Mom, Phee, or Trevor once I get back to the fire, or during the walk home after the festival. I try to stop dwelling on it, try to convince myself that it was the firelight bouncing off the underpass, and the moonlight hitting the trees, creating shadows. And by the time we ride the wave of the crowd through the Carlyle lobby and up the grand marble stairs, I've managed to quiet my mind.

As soon as we're back in the room, Mom's first in the bathroom to redo her ankle splint, so Phee and I fall down on our fluffy bed with its soft, sinking middle. Phee flops her arm over my stomach, and I laugh and push her away. We smell of blood, air, and earth, but it's comforting instead of gross. We're warm and alive. And together. I breathe deeply, think only of what I have to be thankful for, just try to focus on this moment.

Mom pokes her head into the bedroom and sees us lying on our mattress. "Up," she says.

"I'm never moving again," Phee murmurs into her pillow. "I just saved our butts for the winter. That's like a lifetime of free passes."

I laugh and nudge her gently. "Come on. You know she won't stop hassling us until we do what she says."

Phee groans and finally gets up to let Mom help her change her wound dressings. And now that Mom's occupied, I burrow under the bed to dislodge her journal from my backpack. It's still covered with the tattered *Charlotte's Web* book jacket, so I prop myself up against the dirty silk headboard, making sure it's impossible to see the handwritten pages from any other angle. It's dangerous, I know, to jump right into reading this in plain view, but I've been impatient to get back to it since dinner. I've wanted—no, *needed*—more about my mother my whole life, and now her journal from the old world rests in my palms, ready to share.

> *February 15—So it's official. Tom decided to leave Robert Mulaney's studio, to work for his dad and Mary at the firm. I feel like I've gutted a bit of his soul—I know how much he loves working with*

Robert. I loved the two of them working together too—at least some of our old NYU crowd was getting to pursue their dreams. But we need the money, and even though we've debated the pros and cons since Sky was born six months ago, we both knew, all along, that this was the only long-term solution.

Tom starts as an admin on Monday. He says he's fine with it, but I know he's lying. We dance around each other these days.

I really, really hope he and Mary don't kill each other.

February 28—I've been feeling crappy recently, tired and stretched thin. It's just me at home, and there's been no break from Sky. There's been no break at all.

I feel a pang of guilt but keep reading.

Plus, Tom's been getting back to the apartment and making a big stink each night, like he's the only one put out by our new arrangement. Mary apparently takes every chance she gets to remind him that he's crawled back to his family. How he's low man on the Miller totem pole. How he failed as an artist. Blah, blah, blah.

I try to be empathetic, but I'm so tired by the time he gets home that I'm resentful that he thinks he has the right to complain. He gets to talk to adults! Put on fresh underwear! Order out for lunch! While I've essentially kissed good-bye any hope of actually starting my novel. The days keep flying by in a whirl of feedings and diapers.

And between you and me, most times I think he's lying, that he's just dressing up his own insecurities. I've never really seen that side of Mary. Tough-as-nails negotiator, yes. Spitfire CEO-in-training, sure. But vindictive? Belittling? Impossible?

Tom's a drama queen.

March 3—I hate the subways. Really. We've been sitting here for the past hour, and the conductor hasn't even bothered to let us know when we'll be moving. MTA, aka Majorly Thoughtless Assholes.

Mary's been holding Sky and is somehow keeping her quiet. Whispering these cute little stories about all of Mary's favorite animals, the shy giraffe and the noble polar bear and whatever else keeps Sky giggling and gurgling in the corner.

She's so good with her. It makes me feel sad, and guilty, that Mary will never have any of her own. And the sadness is uncomfortable, sits like another passenger squeezed between us. On New Year's Eve, after we put Sky to sleep and were way too drunk on Tom's Manhattans and Jim had passed out on our couch, Mary admitted that she'd had a fourth miscarriage. Since then, she's stopped talking about her and Jim trying, and I've stopped asking.

Anyway, we're on our way to the zoo now, where Mary's going to give us her special "zoo

*volunteer" behind-the-scenes tour—she even bought
Sky a stuffed monkey. We're giving Tom a Daddy
Day Off to work on some big installation with
Robert up at the studio. I know how much he
misses it.*

*March 3, later—Still haven't moved, and it's been at
least two hours.*

"Hey!" Phee says as she emerges from the soft firelight of the bathroom. I instinctively shut the book. She looks far better than she did a few moments ago. Her bandages are changed, and her face is clean. She looks nervously at Mom and then shoots me the stink eye. "I thought . . . I thought we were reading *Charlotte* together."

"We are," I tell her calmly, my eyes wide to telepath, *Please don't blow it. Please don't go all Phee on me about this.* "You can catch up later."

"But," she fishes, "it's not the same as reading it together. Wait for me next time."

And I can tell she's really hurt that I'd even think of moving forward without her. I shake my head. Sometimes Phee still surprises me, even though I know her better than I know myself. "I will. I'm sorry."

"Your sister usually has to twist your arm to get you to open a book," Mom says to Phee, then laughs as she waves me into the bathroom to get ready. "Guess you're making progress, Skyler."

As Phee and I swap places, I whisper, "Stop at the subway."

———

Once Mom is asleep, Phee and I sit together in the large marble tub in the bathroom, where the firelight is brightest. We waited until we could hear Mom's trademark wheeze of a snore, and then I pinched Phee's arm, as we'd agreed, and we snuck into the bathroom together. I don't know about Phee, but I'm planning on staying up until I finish the whole journal. I want Mom's words, her old life, to wash over me like one big wave.

"This tub is uncomfortable," Phee whispers.

"Well, the light over there is terrible," I say. "Did you get to the part where Mom and Mary are taking me to the zoo, and they're stuck on the subway?"

"And Dad's out making art or something with his friend?"

I nod and open the book again. The firelight dances across the crinkled pages, and we jump back into Mom's world of long ago.

> *March 3, later—Still haven't moved, and it's been at least two hours. My claustrophobia started to kick in about thirty minutes ago, so Mary, Sky, and I moved to an empty bench in the corner. "Just breathe," Mary keeps telling me. "Someone will open the doors soon."*
>
> *Sky's been asleep against Mary's chest, rising and falling with her breath, like she's on a life raft. Where's my life raft?*
>
> *There aren't many people in our car, maybe ten—a few Spandex-clad cyclists. A homeless guy wrapped in trash. A willowy teen with a cover-girl face, who could plunge even the securest of women back into the mires of high school insecurity.*

But it feels like there's not enough room for all of us. Like we're all expanding, stretching, hoarding air into our mouths and bags and purses.

"No one's stealing your air," Mary said. "Just breathe."

Mary rarely humors me, and I kind of count on her not to.

March 3, later—We heard muffled, empty assurances from the train conductor, garbled through the speakers.

Silence.

And then darkness.

Sky started to cry and pass out intermittently, so Mary and I took turns dozing off against each other. While Mary was sleeping, I found her lighter (I knew she hadn't quit). I managed to locate my nursing cover at the bottom of my bag, and draped it around myself to feed Sky for a little.

Ideas have been thrown around of prying the doors open, or breaking the windows if no one opens the emergency exit soon. The man dressed in trash bags suggested pooling our brainpower and using mind control, while the teenager, Bronwyn, played with her hair and told us just to call MTA.

But no one's doing *anything*. We're just talking in circles, providing ourselves with a quiet soundtrack.

March 3, later—I swore we were going to die.

"We're not going to die." Mary rolled her eyes. "Please."

But she grabbed my hand anyway, and my
heart slowed down just a bit.

It's funny how different she and Tom are. Tom's
such an artist, frazzled, impetuous. His sister's
always been the steady one. And even though
I wished so desperately that Tom was with us,
holding my hand, Mary's the one who knew what
to do and say to calm me down.

"Mom's never mentioned this Mary chick, has she?" Phee sits up and asks.

"Never."

"And she's Tom's—I mean Dad's—sister. So she's Mom's sister-in-law."

"Right . . . but this journal was written before the war started," I think out loud. I fan the pages quickly. "There's no mention of soldiers, Dad's family firm was up and running, Mom was taking me to the zoo. Mary probably died during the attacks, and so Mom doesn't talk about her."

I think about all the people, like Mary, who didn't survive the attacks. All of Mom's ghosts, and how many there must be. Ghosts who haunt her thoughts, who leave her screaming in the night. And for the first time, I sort of understand Mom's mantra, maybe even sympathize. *Sometimes the past should stay in the past.*

"Don't you still think that's weird?" Phee asks. "For Mom to never mention Mary, even if she died?"

"You know Mom. She doesn't talk about *anything*. It took her over a decade to bring us to our old apartment."

"True. Okay, wait, hold on a second," Phee grunts. "My butt is killing me. This tub's as hard as cement."

She shifts her legs up and over me and almost kicks me in the eye. After some finagling, we end up with our knees hanging over the side of the empty bathtub, our heads propped up by towels on the tiled border, like we're sunning ourselves under the torchlight.

"All right, I'm ready," Phee says, and I crack open the spine to continue.

> *March 6—It's been days. I haven't been able to stop to write down what's happened until now.*
>
> *Suffice it to say, no one came to save us. So we had to save ourselves.*
>
> *Mary somehow shaped Sky's stroller into a weapon, and the three men dressed in cycling gear helped her stab the glass and gut the windows of the train. Each one of us carefully crawled out of the belly of the beast, and then we worked on rescuing the other cars. If I didn't have Sky, I might even have laughed, been excited by the bizarre Saturday adventure.*

"You ruin everything," Phee teases.

"Would you be quiet? I'm trying to get into this."

> *But my nerves were so fried all I could think of was getting home.*
>
> *Once everyone was out, we reconfigured the stroller and rolled Sky down the tunnel with the rest of our ragtag crew. It was so black that the dark had texture. The dull blue light from people's phones did little to light the way, and*

hardly anyone had a lighter. Now that New York
is smoke free, smokers are rare commodities,
I suppose. It was just Mary and the lithe teen,
Bronwyn, along with every member of a group of
sixty-year-old women from Kansas, visiting for a
girls' luxury weekend away.

The women with lighters leading the charge,
we all walked carefully on the tracks to the next
subway stop, a group of about fifty of us. Mary
announced at some point that we were between
33rd Street and Grand Central. It was clear from
both her lighter and her stroller-weapon move that
she was somehow leading our pitiful brigade. She
said the power must be out, that it might be the
whole city. And that once we got to Grand Central,
we'd know what was going on.

We hear a moan from the bedroom. And then a startled gasp.

"She's up," Phee whispers. "Ditch it."

I close the book and shove it in between Phee and me as Mom frantically opens the door.

"What are you two doing?"

Shadows carve out Mom's eyes and cheeks, and she looks ancient under the torchlight. I can tell she's half-asleep. For a second I consider coming clean and telling her that we have her book, that we stole her past, and let her wake up tomorrow and write it off as a dream.

"Just talking," I say.

"Tomorrow's our first day in the fields," Mom mumbles, visibly more relaxed now that she's found us safe and sound.

"You both need to rest. We've got a big day ahead of us. Come on, out of the tub."

We begin to climb out as she limps back to the room.

"When do we finish?" Phee whispers.

"Tomorrow." I think of this morning, how it feels as if we've lived lifetimes since then, and I realize I'm excited for a new day. Even if it means we have to wait. "Hey, Phee?"

"Yeah?"

I put my arm on her shoulder and help guide her into the dark. "Happy birthday."

We stumble back into the room and I return the journal to the folds of my backpack, then push the bag to the center of the floor under our bed.

I climb in next to Phee and drift in and out of sleep. I dream of dark tunnels. Heroes fighting by firelight. And lonely, beautiful woodsmen.

7   PHEE

I sit down on a rock in the shade of the trees that border the Great Lawn and massage my bruised ribs. For, like, the tenth time this hour. There're hundreds of workers in the fields, collecting corn from the stalks and plucking apples from the trees. Rows of bent backs and beaded brows. I'm obviously the only one who's taken a million breaks since dawn.

But no one's giving me any grief.

Something's changed since the street-fights last night. I've seen it in the looks of other fieldworkers. In the smug smiles of the whorelords during the feast last night, and at this morning's rundown of duties. There are nods of respect, talks of my "resourcefulness," whispers of my "potential."

Sarah, Rolladin has to have her eye on your youngest now, I'd heard Lauren say to Mom this morning.

You'll be wearing a warlord shawl by this time next year. Mark my words, Old Lady Warbler had cackled to me at the festival, as I'd moved past her crowded pit to our own penthouse of fires.

Trevor even overheard Council member Lory talking with Cass last night after they were good and wasted, telling Cass she needed to lay off me from now on. That with how impressed Rolladin must be with my performance on 65th Street, someone will pledge me, and I'll be one of them soon enough.

One of *them*.

I've been raised my whole life to hate the whorelords. And I do. At least I think I do. They're technically prisoners of war along with the rest of us, stuck on this dead island just like we are. But they're the "chosen" ones—when our city was surrendered to the Red Allies, the story goes, our numb-nuts captors put them in charge. Well, I guess they put *Rolladin* in charge, and she fleshed out her ranks with bruisers and eye candy. Bruisers that get to beat us up and boss us around in exchange for food and safety.

A bit of a bullshit exchange, obviously.

I start picking at my lip as I sit, and the scab that's formed overnight breaks apart. I think more about the matches, about the way the crowd cheered for me, and the way people looked at me differently afterward, like I wasn't someone to be messed with. And I wonder, would being a warlord really be the end of the world? Extra rations for my mom and Sky, rooms at Belvedere Castle. And I could pretty much guarantee that no one would ever hurt my family.

I watch Mom and Sky in the fields, as they rip the light-green husks from the yellow cobs. I don't know why I'm even entertaining this. Mom would kill me. It's not just that the warlord gig is dangerous—combing the Upper East and West Sides for feeders and raiders, being on the front lines of Rolladin's crazy moods and whims. It'd also be the biggest insult Mom could think of. She hates Rolladin so much, it's like a drug, and sometimes I think she's so hopped up on it, she can't see straight. If I ever "worked" for Rolladin, Mom might very well disown me.

I think of Mom's beef with Rolladin. Then I think of Rolladin breaking up my match, of stopping Cass before she reached for that knife—even though Rolladin

who forced our family into the whole mess in

Why? It doesn't make any sense. It works me

when I realize how little we know about my mo_

this city, and why things are the way they are. But unlike

Sky, I refuse to let it drive me crazy.

So I take a breath. Then I glance at my mom and sister, at the way the light hits the grass so it looks like they're working in a field full of silver. And I say thanks for what I *do* know: that I'm lucky.

I eventually get up and work for a few more hours, before a couple of whorelords start shouting over the fields, "Break time!" We all drop our tools and converge on the ration lines like an army of ants. Today's midday ration won't be anything as glamorous as last night's stew, but who cares? I'm starving. Mom takes a break to talk with Lauren near the farming edges, but I can't wait. I push Sky towards the front.

"Cornmeal or potato hash?" I quiz Sky as we take our place in line behind about thirty fieldworkers.

"Hash, definitely," she says as she bends backward to stretch.

"No way," Trevor says as he just magically appears on my other side. "I heard we just started pulling the potatoes. They can't be ready to make a hash."

"Um, where'd you just come from?" I ask.

"The zoo," he says, missing my point. "I saw you near the front and didn't want to miss my window."

Sky and I both wrinkle our noses as Trev's stink settles around us. A few fieldworkers in front of us start murmuring in disgust. Then a couple of boys, maybe a little younger than Trev, start snickering behind us. Soon we're bordered by two feet of empty grass in all directions.

I take a closer look at Trevor. He has small pieces of carcass on his shirt, red stripes of dried blood across his arms. His smell is so intense it nearly gives me a headache.

"What the hell were you doing this morning?" I say.

"Trevor was on animal guts," one of the boys behind us answers.

I turn around to a pair of dirty faces, all ratty clothes and tweeny smirks. The boys are definitely younger than Trevor, maybe twelve or thirteen. Not that it matters. Trev doesn't stand up for himself, no matter who's pushing him down.

The one talking gets all flustered, pink face and everything, now that he's got my attention. But he recovers pretty quick. "Stupid Red bastard," he nods at Trev. "Rolladin makes all the rejects do her dirty work." Then he laughs and looks at me hungrily, like he's waiting for props.

But something has snapped inside me, and my heart starts clamoring into fight mode, almost like I'm right outside that 65th Street underpass again. Sure, most days I want to strangle Trevor. But that doesn't mean I want anyone else messing with him.

"That's a bogus theory," I tell the kid. "Else your whole family would be working the slaughterhouses all winter."

Sky shoots me a smile as the boy's friend starts heckling him behind us: *She got you. You should see your face!*

But Trev doesn't say anything. He never does—in fact, these types of rumbles are the only times the kid's quiet. He just keeps tailing me and Sky like some fidgety shadow as the line snakes us up to the front.

　　　　　　　　　　　　　　　　　　　　　　　　　　　　　　　　　LEE KELLY

We get our bowls of what turns out to be some kind of apple and wheat concoction in silence. Then we all settle on a small patch of grass bordering the fields. The midday break is for half an hour. It's the first and only one before the end of the workday and our nighttime ration.

"This actually isn't too bad," Sky says in between bites. Her hands are shaking a little bit, and I can tell she's already exhausted. I'm exhausted too. We got about four hours of sleep last night, and most of it was just tossing and turning.

"Agreed. The apples are just ripe enough," Trev says with his mouth full.

"I forgot you worked apples last season," Sky says. "Hey, why'd they move you off tree picking this year, anyway? I thought you were the Park's quickest picker."

She sneaks me a wink. Trev's always telling us these tall tales that make him out to be Boy Wonder of the Park. My sister humors him more than I do.

"I'm getting older." He shrugs. "And they want the men and stronger women handling the meat."

"Men?" I snort. "Aren't you being a little generous there?"

Trevor blushes beet red, and for a minute I feel terrible. It was just such an easy shot.

"We're just surprised," Sky says, covering for me. "You're only thirteen, right?"

"Fourteen! Almost fifteen. And if not me, who? It's not like there's a ton of . . . of *guys* to pick from. I stepped up to help and do my part."

Well, he's right on that point. We're four-to-one females to males on this island, based on Rolladin's last census. Even less if you take out all the kids and "guys" like Trev. But now I'm wondering why *I* wasn't sent to the zoo this morning along with the rest of the strongest workers, instead of tilling the fields. Maybe it's my bruised ribs. Or some weird reward for last night.

As if reading my mind, Trev whispers to Sky, "So how long till you think someone officially pledges Phee?"

Sky looks at him curiously, and I make eyes at Trev to shut it. I didn't tell Sky any of the rumors I heard about me being plucked to be a warlord. I don't know if they're true, and besides, I know how she'll feel about them.

"What are you talking about? Phee, what's he talking about?"

"Nothing," I say loudly, at the same time Trevor blabs, "Pledge her to become a warlord."

Sky's face freezes up.

"Trev, you're as bad as Old Lady Warbler with the gossip." I look at my sister. "It's dumb. Just some rumors, Sky. Rolladin's not going to make me a whorelord 'cause of one measly fight."

"Duh, of course not. One of the lords would have to pledge you, but that's easy." Trev keeps making it worse. "And you'd probably still need to spar next year for your initiation and everything—"

"Assuming all of that happens," Sky talks over him, her voice all shaky, "Phee, would you really think about doing it?"

I mash around my porridge, trying to find the easiest way to dig out of this. "Why bother with what-ifs? No one's pledged me."

"Phee, come on. Answer me. If someone did—if *Rolladin* picked you herself—what would you say? You wouldn't really think about it, would you?" Sky's staring at me so hard it's like she's trying to see through me.

"I'd say no, of course. No way." I hate holding back from Sky; it makes my insides churn. But I tell her what I think

LEE KELLY

she wants to hear. "Are you kidding me? Mom would kill me."

"So because of Mom, you wouldn't." Her eyes become a little watery as she looks at me. Sky rarely full-on cries, but anytime she's worried or confused, or angry, her eyes swell up like storm clouds. They're like that now, all glossy and unfocused.

"Exactly," I hesitate. I can't tell whether that's the right answer anymore.

"Not because the warlords are animals. Not because they beat people senseless for stealing an extra ration." Sky's shaking her bowl so hard now that little bits of apple porridge bail out onto the grass. "Or because even though they're prisoners too, they treat us like we're slaves. But because *Mom* would be *mad*."

I look back and forth between a flushed Sky and a confused Trevor. He looks how I feel. He doesn't say a word, though. He knows better.

"One match, one night of cheers from the crowd, and you just—*forget*—that they're monsters?"

"No," I say quickly. "I just meant it's pointless to even think about it. 'Cause it's not like I'd really have a choice."

"But if Mom didn't care, you'd be ready to throw on that lesser lord pelt and start doing Rolladin's bidding. Just turn on a dime. Everyone you've loved and known and worked with, you'd be fine treating them like trash. And for what? Didn't you see how they threw away Philip after he lost?"

Of course I'd seen Philip the match loser this morning. He reached too high and got cut down, so now he's limping around the Great Lawn like any old fieldworker. Rolladin threw him away, and no worker can stand him. He's a one-man island now.

"Sky, you're totally putting words in my mouth. I didn't say I wanted to be one—"

"You didn't have to." Sky shakes her head. "It's what you didn't say."

I don't know how to come back at that one.

My face is on fire and my mind is racing, but I can't find any words. I can't retrace how we got here. Why's she so pissed off? All I know is now I'm angry too, but I can't pinpoint the reason. Maybe it's because she's angry with me.

Or maybe it's because Sky *always* makes sure I hear her feelings, but most times I can't figure out how to voice my own.

I break from her eyes and look down at my lunch.

"Trev, I'm going to kick your ass," I finally mutter into my bowl.

"What the heck are you mad at me for?"

"Just shut up already about the street-fighting, all right?"

We finish our lunches in silence before the lesser lords start poking everyone to get back to work. Trevor heads back to the zoo houses, and I follow Sky into the cornstalks. Sky settles on Mom's left and I stand on Lauren's right. I think we need a break from each other. It's like this with us, sometimes.

Most days I feel like we're the last members of some awesome tribe. Just me, Sky, and Mom against the holdouts, the whorelords. The whole world, if they'd ever stop screwing around and end this stupid war. But sometimes Sky and I just don't speak the same language. My sister's always dreaming about the world beyond the skyscrapers, but the truth is, we live *inside* their fence. And while we do, this is the way things are. Questioning things, wishing things were different, seems like a total waste of time.

I roll up my sleeves to start picking, still lost in thought. I know the whorelords can be assholes. Of course I know that. But sometimes bad things, used in the right way, can bring about good things—like my fight on 65th Street. It let us stay in the Park and score double rations, and earned me some respect. Being a warlord might be like that all the time, for all three of us. What's that saying?

The ends can justify the means.

But I know Sky wouldn't get this. And after sixteen years, I know it's pointless to try to make her, even if I could find the perfect words.

I take a deep breath to calm down, and grab a collection bucket.

Day bleeds into evening in the cornfields. We work in silence, picking the corn off the stalks one by one. Tearing the silky husks. Cleaning the cobs. I have to admit, I like working with my hands out here. It's peaceful, letting the hours slide by as your fingers work in silence. The quiet massages my mind, the evening wind cools my temper. And by sunset, I'm not mad anymore. I'm just wiped. It's a good wiped, though, a soreness that says, *You've been useful.*

The sky finally turns dusty and pink, promises food around the corner. But it's not until the light is nearly gone altogether that someone finally speaks.

"Sarah," Lauren whispers to Mom. "Look at the lords. What's going on?"

I follow Lauren's gaze over the stalks, to the borders of

the fields. The lesser lords are in some kind of panic, one by one racing towards the forest. And behind them is the Council of Lords—the six of them all have their fancy predator cloaks on and are fully loaded with red-tagged weapons—swords, knives, and the few guns that Rolladin keeps safe in Belvedere Castle.

"I have no idea," Mom whispers. "But it doesn't look good."

Most of the fieldworkers have already dropped their tools and begun moving through the stalks towards the warlords. We join them, plunk the last of our corn into our collection buckets, and make our way to the front for a better view.

"Get the rest of the lesser lords," Lory tells Cass and a few of the other junior whorelords. "Stay back!" Lory shouts at all of us. "Whoever leaves the stalks will be shot. No exceptions."

Lory heads into the forest with the five other members of Rolladin's Council, as Cass leads a few junior lords on a mad dash to the castle.

Of course, now the cornfields are buzzing.

"What do you think it is?"

"Could it be a holdout?"

There're so many questions floating around that the cornfields start to feel crowded.

"When was the last time they found a holdout sneaking around the Park?" Sky whispers.

"Years ago," Mom whispers back.

I look past Lauren and Mom to Sky, and we exchange glances. This feels major. Suddenly me becoming a warlord is the least of our concerns.

I leave Lauren's side and go to Sky, and she gives me an anxious smile. Whatever tension existed between us from this afternoon is gone. She puts her hand on my shoulder and keeps it there, like she's anchoring both of us. Trevor runs up beside me on my other side and pushes down the cornstalks for a better view.

There're gasps and shudders as Cass comes running from the northern fields with the thirty other armed lesser lords in tow. And behind the small army is Rolladin.

This isn't typical. Rolladin's never in the fields. It's beneath her. Seeing her now starts to truly freak me out.

Plus, she's carrying one of the island's few assault rifles.

"No one leaves the fields," she roars towards us. "Or I will have your head as a doorstop."

She plunges into the forest. We hear yells, muffled orders, a shot ring through the air.

"This is crazy," Sky whispers to me. "They never use the guns."

No one moves their feet past the farming border, but necks are craning, fields of eyes are scanning through the dark.

The Council slowly emerges from the forest in a wide ring, weapons extended like a mouthful of fangs. In the middle of the circle stand a crew of strangers with their hands raised. Dirty, ragged, caked in leaves and mud. There're four of them. All males, which is kind of weird, considering how women-heavy the Park is.

I do a quick scan.

The oldest looks about fifty. There's one around Mom's age, then a tall, thin guy who looks maybe twenty-five or something, and then a teenager. The two youngest ones kind of look alike, actually; both have wild black hair that sticks up at all angles.

Funny, these guys don't look like crazy tunnel feeders, or even raiders, the rough bandits Mom always warns us about. They just look tired. I hear Sky's breath quicken next to me as the men come into better view.

"It's okay," I tell her. "Rolladin's got them. We're safe. It's over."

She looks at me fearfully but just shakes her head.

"Fieldworkers!" Rolladin calls to the lot of us cowering in the fields. "These selfish pigs have come to rob the Park, steal your food . . . poach the fruits of your toils. What should I do with them?"

Nobody says a word.

Rolladin storms towards the cornfields and barks, "What do we call these *cowards*? These spineless prisoners who refuse to surrender and earn their way?"

And then there's a spark among the crops, a small chant that rumbles into a war cry. "Traitors."

"Traitors."

"TRAITORS!"

Rolladin smiles wide as we chant, then extends her rifle over us and shakes it, as if to say, *There, there. That's what I was looking for. Now quiet down.*

She turns back to the holdouts.

"Please!" the oldest of the bunch cries, but Rolladin rails him in his stomach with her gun.

"Quiet. You fools are fucking with the wrong woman. I've got no time for freeloaders." She spits on the ground in front of them. "Or psychos. Whoever you are, *whatever* you are, we follow POW rules to the letter here." She paces like a hungry tiger. "Lory, lock these holdouts in the zoo."

"Wait, wait, please! I think there's been a mistake." The

old guy looks to his buddies for backup. "We don't know what you mean. We're not holdouts, or . . . or psychos."

His voice sounds funny, kind of like he's singing, his vowels rounded out big and bold. *An accent?* I mouth to Sky. She nods.

"Please," the oldest continues. "We've traveled so far. Let us rest for one night. Let us rest and then we'll sail away and leave you and your city forever. We swear. We only came to New York because we heard there was hope here."

Wait, *came* to New York? From where? From Brooklyn? Are these guys Red Allies troops in disguise?

I'm not the only one who's confused. The crowd buzzes again.

"Came to New York?"

"Is that what he said?"

"Did I hear him right?"

"SILENCE!" Rolladin roars. But I see something in her face I've never seen before.

Fear.

It all happens in a whirlwind, a storm of commotion. Rolladin and the Council members with guns take the hold-outs, or enemy spies, or whoever they may be, to the zoo to imprison them, while Lory leads an armed team of lesser lords through the fields. They bark at us, push us into the stalks, rip our tools from our hands. We leave the fields in disarray, and then we're led back to the Carlyle for a full night lockdown.

I don't remember this ever happening before. My heart's in my throat the entire time, as if it's threatening to leave me and find its own way out of this.

Still, through the mayhem, I can think only one thought, over and over. And I can't believe it. The woodsman.

My figment from the forest.

He's real.

Warlords fence us in as we all stumble through the Park and bottleneck at the bridge to 76th Street. I get separated from Phee and Mom as we're led back to the Carlyle tenements, and then minutes later, from Lauren. I take a deep breath, try not to erupt into panic. Trevor and I hold on to each other as the crowd carries us home.

"No one leaves their rooms, you all hear me?" Lory shouts over the mob. "Rolladin's orders. Each to their own quarters. Rations will be delivered to your door tonight.

Don't report to the fields tomorrow for duties unless you're told."

The crowd is a sea of gasps and mutters, of questions.

"What about the Brits?" Mrs. Warbler bellows above the noise. "What's to become of them?"

Lory raises her bow and arrow into the air over the crowd, feigns aiming for Mrs. Warbler's head. The only problem is there're about ten people—including Trevor and me—in front of her target.

"Shut it, you old bag, or eat wood," she answers. "You heard Rolladin. They're traitors. We're locking them up, she'll try them, they'll likely hang in the morning. Now move!"

We enter the dark, dank lobby of the Carlyle. Trevor tries to follow me upstairs, but a warlord grabs him and pulls him down the hall to the singles quarters.

"Wait, Trev—"

"Skyler!" he calls behind him.

"Each to their own rooms!" The warlords push me up the stairs with the rest of the crowd. "We haven't got all night."

When I reach our room, Mom and Phee are thankfully already there and safe, and I relax a little. They're in the process of relighting a few of the firecups with some of our allotted wood.

"Sky, thank God," Mom whispers. She drops the wood and limps towards me, throws her arms around my neck.

"Mom," Phee says behind her. "What's all this about?"

I take Mom's hands in mine. "Has this ever happened before?"

"A lockdown?" Mom asks us. We all walk to the window,

and the three of us peer out of the dusty glass. A couple of warlords are now stationed outside the Carlyle with weapons, flanking the entrance like twin gargoyles. I have no doubt several others are pacing the halls, making sure no one dares to leave their rooms.

"The last time something like this happened, you both were really young," Mom answers. "A band of tunnel feeders had come to the surface to scavenge. It was during the occupation, when a few Red Allies platoons were still stationed in the Met and the natural history museum." Mom's wearing her faraway look again. "We were locked up for days. The Park was swept for holdouts, and five tunnel feeders were found, tried, and killed. The Red generals let Rolladin's team execute the order. They hung them on crosses along the southern border. Like lampposts," she whispers. "From Fifth Avenue to Columbus Circle."

Mom's eyes have grown teary. Rarely does she share so much, and I want to give her a minute to collect herself.

But Phee, like always, rushes in. "The guys in the woods tonight. Could they be feeders too?"

"You two can't remember what tunnel feeders are like." Mom doesn't look at us, just keeps her eyes focused on the window. "I've tried to make sure of that. But you'd know a feeder if you saw one." She takes one of each of Phee's and my hands and kisses them. "They're not right. Inhuman. They're shells of people who lost themselves in the tunnels, to the dark."

Mom's words oddly bring me back to the journal, to when the tunnels were "subways." I picture her all those years ago, wandering with Mary and me through the darkness. I desperately want to know what separates the woman of then from the woman in front of us. What separates her carefree city from the bones of Manhattan that cage us in now. But I know Mom won't tell us, even if we ask again, and again.

And the only comfort I take is that we have some of her story on paper, whether she likes it or not.

"Then are these guys raiders from outside the Park?" Phee asks.

"Raiders are lone wolves; they don't travel in packs like those men. They hide in the rubble of the city, poaching food and supplies here and there. I can't imagine any raiders survived these last few years of rough winters." Mom shakes her head. "There's always been . . . rumors . . . of other hold-outs on the island. But by now, the Park and the last of the feeders must be all who's left."

Mom runs her fingers through her hair, while our questions just get more and more tangled.

"So where did they come from, Mom?" I coax. "Brooklyn?"

"Yeah, are they Red Allies spying on us?" Phee breathes deeply. "Rolladin wouldn't have the guts to kill them. Would she?"

"Those men had English accents." Mom lets go of her hair and thrusts her hands to the windowsill. "I refuse to believe the Brits sided with the Red Allies. The United Kingdom was always our ally. *Is* our ally," she stresses, then sighs. "Then again, who knows what the hell is going on out there. Rolladin doesn't share news of the war. Not news of substance, anyway."

I'm trying to follow, trying to put the pieces together. But they don't make a full picture.

"Mom, if they're not holdouts, and they're not Red soldiers," Phee asks what I'm thinking, "then who the hell are they?"

"And more importantly," I add, my stomach now sinking, "how are they here?"

A deep rip of a knock on our door makes the three of us jump, and I let out a small reflexive yelp.

"It's okay," Mom says. "It's just the lords."

"Three rations. Miller family is served," a raspy voice booms from the other side of the door. "Get it while it's luke-warm."

We bring the small trays of rations into the room, spread some towels out like blankets under the candlelight, and set up our picnic. Phee and I both try to push the conversation forward, find out more, but it's clear that Mom doesn't know any more about the Englishmen than we do. We end up eating in silence under the dim lights. Through the thin walls of the Carlyle, we can hear arguments in other rooms, the clanging of metalware, muffled whispers.

"You guys want to play cards?" Mom asks, once we've cleared our trays away and stored them in the shadows of the bathroom.

"It's kind of dark," Phee says. "Can't we light some of these other firecups?"

"We should save the wood in case we're here for another night. I doubt the lords will think to hand out more supplies."

A few days ago, had someone told me that I'd be forced to stay indoors, playing games, reading, safe and warm, I would have been thrilled. But tonight the hotel feels claustrophobic, overcrowded with all the questions that have elbowed their way into our room.

Why do I need that book to know my mom? Why are we cooped up in here? Why are things the way they are?

And why do I care about that boy in the woods?

Thinking of the boy brings on a flush that spreads across my face like fingers.

"I don't really want to play cards," I say.

"Should we read then?" Mom says. "Sky, what are you reading now? *Charlotte's Web* again, right?" She puts on her best smile, trying to entertain us, make us forget for a moment that we're prisoners. "Why don't you read some to us?"

Phee's eyes open wide, and I look away or else I think I'll lose it. *We can't read you* Charlotte. *It's in the safe in your abandoned apartment. What about your journal instead?*

"I'm kind of tired, Mom," I mumble into my lap. "Maybe we can just go to bed, and start over tomorrow."

"All right," she says quietly. "I understand. I guess it's been another long day."

Later I lie in bed awake. Moonlight dances across the water-stained ceiling, creates the illusion that we're sleeping under a slow, lazy tide. It reminds me of the river at home, back on Wall Street, of the way the water stretches so long and wide that you can almost hear the waves beat *Freedom* if you listen closely.

I readjust my pillow and turn to face Phee. She's wheezing softly, already sound asleep, not a care in the world. Her mouth is turned up in a little smile, as if even her dreams are working out for her. It makes me think of what she said earlier today. About joining the warlords, becoming one of them. Not that she'd said that exactly, but she didn't have to.

And it haunted me all day.

I watch her sleep. Strong, bold, brazen Phee, protector

of the family. A future leader of the Park. A seed of worry takes root in my stomach.

If she becomes a warlord, what happens then? Do I become a year-round fieldworker? Do I just keep following her around like a shadow? Continue to shrink and shrink as she burns brighter, until one day I'm gone completely?

And what's really bothering me: Am I more upset that Phee would make the crazy decision to become a lord, or that I'll never have the chance to?

I flop on my back to watch the rippling ceiling. I think of the street-fights, of the rules of the Park, of the way I float through here unnoticed. My mother's favorite attributes of mine rattle inside my head. *Balance. Patience. Control.*

Am I really patient? Do they really see me as in control? Or am I just defined by what my younger sister isn't?

The worry blooms, works its way from my abdomen and curls up my spine, until I can't sit still anymore. I need air. And space. I need to be outside myself, to burst out the door, to dive into someone else's world and hide there.

But of course, I won't do it alone.

I shake Phee's arm gently and she wakes with a start, but I'm quick to put my hand over her mouth. I poke my chin over her towards our mother. If we don't want to wake her, this all needs to be in the sister sign language I taught Phee—a mix of basic ASL I learned from a textbook, plus a few of our own trademark gestures.

Phee rubs her eyes and then looks over her shoulder. Mom's sound asleep, snoring in the darkness. Phee's eyes light up as she figures out why I'm waking her. She puts her hands out, palms facing up, and then turns her left wrist back and forth, like she's flipping invisible pages. I nod. *Exactly. The journal.*

She points to the bathroom.

I shake my head no, point to Mom and then to my eyes. *Not the bathroom—she'll wake up if we light the firecups.*

She throws her hands in the air. *What do you want, then?*

I can't believe I'm doing this. I solemnly point towards the door. *I want to sneak out, down the hall.*

Her index finger shoots up to her temple and twirls around. *What are you, loony?* Then she swipes her thumb across her neck. *Suicide.*

I just shrug and ignore my shaking hands. I carefully dislodge my legs from the pile of frayed blankets and sheets. I'm not sure if I'm bluffing, until Phee's hand wraps around my wrist.

She shakes her head slowly. *No.*

And for a moment, the first moment in perhaps our entire lives, I'm ready for something dangerous. And she isn't. It empowers me, chops at my weed of self-loathing, excites me to the point of recklessness. I take a deep breath, point to her, and then bring my hands to the side of my head in prayer position. *Go back to bed then.*

I give her a small wave, crawl the rest of the way out of the covers, and grab the journal from under our bed.

Phee's by my side before I can even crack open the door.

So I'm not sure when Sky decided to turn all daredevil on me, but I'm not going to pretend I like it. Breaking out of our room during lockdown feels stupid, half-baked. What if we get caught? What happens then? Of course I want to read that journal as much as she does, but there're other ways.

I don't tell her any of this, though. I'm not going to stay behind—it just doesn't make any sense. That's not the way we work. In fact, if anything, she's usually the one trailing me.

We creep into the hall, and I reach for one of the firecups attached to the walls, but Sky grabs my hand and shakes her head. She keeps up with the secret sister sign language, points to both of us and then down the hall. Then she starts signing way too quick, and I can't catch anything else. *Enough of this.* I throw up my hands. Then I raise my index finger. *Hold up a second.*

I duck back into the room for one of our torches. At least one of us is going to be prepared. I pause for a second and think about my gun, which I haven't really carried since Mom gave it to me. Talk about being prepared.

No, stupid idea, Phee. It's not necessary.

But a part of me, one I'm not so proud of, begs and pleads to grab it. *You're the one who's supposed to be badass,* my little instigator taunts me. *Not Sky.*

I honestly can't spare a minute for this *Who am I really?*

crisis. Since I don't have the time to debate, I just listen, and dig the gun out from under our mattress. I stick it in the right pocket of my sweats and put the bullets in the left.

There. Things feel right again. I head out the door.

"No, leave the torch. We'll feel our way up the internal stairs," Sky whispers when I get back. "We need to stay in the shadows. Follow me."

I ignore this idea and keep the unlighted torch, and follow her down the hall of the Carlyle.

It must be almost midnight. I'm so jumpy I'm starting to see and hear things, whorelords climbing out of the shadows, whispers in the walls. Then I'm sure I hear two guards talking quietly at the opposite end of the hallway. I grab Sky's hand and we flatten ourselves against the wallpaper, like we can push ourselves through it. We watch the pair of whorelords cross our hall and head towards the lower-numbered rooms. After they disappear, we scramble to the stairway door, open it, and duck behind it. I open it again to light my torch with a nearby firecup, then rejoin Sky on the other side.

"This way, we can see where we're going," I say.

"Yeah, and they can see us." Sky shakes her head. "I told you to leave it and just follow me. We could have made a fire on the roof."

"With what? You'll thank me later."

She just shakes her head again and begins climbing on all fours up the few flights of stairs. "Stay down," she cuts at me. "There're lords roaming every floor. They see that flame, we're finished."

"Well, we trip on the stairs and we're finished."

"Phee," she huffs. "No one insisted you come along."

Really. Would Sky have actually gone without me? So I just say, "Get real."

We continue to climb in silence, then finally reach the rooftop door. It's bolted and locked with about four monster chains, but the chains are loose, so we manage to push the door open enough to wiggle through. Sky goes first, and then I pass her the torch and slide through behind her, into the open air of the roof deck.

We run across the empty lounge, from couch to beat-up couch, towards a long rectangular shape in the far corner of the space. It's bordered with rusted stools on one side, and we crawl into its belly. Half-empty bottles and broken glass are everywhere. I read the labels: JIM BEAM. JACK DANIELS. JOSE CUERVO. A bunch of other guys.

Sky nudges the glass away with her foot, and we settle down against the shelves. I hold the torch as she whips the journal out from the elastic of her shimmery stretch pants. Sky's pajamas put all my outfits to shame.

"We finish this tonight," Sky says as she cracks open the journal. I lean the grip of the torch against my knee and the journal comes alive, firelight breathing into the old words. And for the first time since she woke me up, we're on the same page.

"Without a doubt."

We pick up with Mom and her sister-in-law, Mary, walking through the tunnels.

> But before we reached Grand Central, we felt
> a rip, a jolt so powerful it seemed like the world's
> carpet was being pulled out from under us. I
> leaned against the raised subway platform and

pulled Sky close to me. She started wailing, like she was being tortured in the dark.

"We need to get out of here," a woman dressed far too nicely for the subway on a Saturday implored, once the earth had stopped trembling. "Now."

I could feel a new undercurrent to our group, a collective, breathless panic. We all started scrambling, throwing elbows and grunts as we moved towards freedom. The teenager from our train, Bronwyn, started sobbing behind me, moaning that she wasn't ready to die.

Mary dropped her voice an octave, even as the murmurs and the cries began to bubble and rise around us. "Whatever happens," she said to me, "we stick together, okay?"

Her voice was shaking, and it scared the shit out of me.

"Mary—"

"Just promise me," she said.

I told her of course.

The crowd began clambering its way up the stairs to the terminal. The lighters were extinguished by the rush, and then we were blind, a thicket of hands pawing our way through the dark. We jumped one by one over the turnstiles into the station. But there was no sunlight to greet us. Instead we combed through a thick, dusty fog. We heard brittle rounds of machine guns, the barking of foreign tongues. Wails.

We were lost, lab rats in a maze of fog, and I wanted to scream, just sit down and scream, I was

*so panicked. But instead I clutched Sky and prayed.
For her, for her dad. Where was Tom? Was he safe?
Were he and Robert at the studio, or were they
somewhere underground?*

*I felt a hand on my waist, and Mary was at my
side. "Everyone back to the subways," she told us.
"Now!"*

*Mary herded us back down the stairs, to the
hungry, empty belly of the city. We descended
the stairs carefully, and by that point, Sky was
shrieking. Hungry, tired, sitting in her own filth.
I promised her I would get her home. But maybe I
was full of shit. Maybe the world was falling apart.*

"Wait a minute." Sky yanks the book from me and then
leans over it so close, it's like she's trying to hear it whisper. "Wails . . . foreign tongues. Machine guns." She looks at
me, her eyes wide and spooky under the torchlight. "Do you
realize what this is?"

"What? What are you talking about?"

She starts flipping Mom's journal pages so fast, the ink
starts to blur together. "This isn't . . . some slice-of-life journal about Mom before the attacks." Sky's words are practically tripping over one another, they're so excited to come
out. "This *is* the story of the attacks. It's happening right
here, in these pages. Maybe all the secrets, all the missing
links . . . about Mom . . . and *Dad* . . . even me and you, they
could be in here. Phee, this could explain everything."

I peer over the journal and think about all we don't know.
All the times Sky would ask about Mom's life Before, or even
After, and Mom's face would just cloud over.

I don't want to tell Sky that it feels like spying, like we've broken Mom open and are just dumping all her secrets out.

'Cause right now, I'm having trouble breathing.

Right now, the idea of figuring out what happened to Mom, to our family, is so huge and heavy, it almost knocks me over.

"Everything we don't know about our family could be in there?"

"More than just our family, Phee." Sky shakes her head. "Everything we don't know about this *city*. About Manhattan."

March 8—We lived through another day. We camped out in the dark just shy of where the 7 train pulled into Times Square. In the process, we freed the passengers of two other subways.

No one knew what was going on at the surface. No cell phones, no computers, no television. Those who had gadgets with power left bounced and roamed for service like stumbling drunks.

"We need to send a team of scouts to the surface." Mary finally broke the silence.

We'd been debating for hours about what was happening up there, arguing, hundreds of voices reaching a fever pitch until Lauren, the well-dressed woman, finally pointed out that regardless of what was going on, we were in hiding and should be quiet.

"Mary, are you insane? We don't know who— or what—is up there," Bronwyn said from the corner. The alpha teen's mask of confidence from the subway car had faded, right along with

her makeup. And now I saw only a pale, lonely girl drowning in a sea of strangers—somebody's daughter lost in the dark. "The police'll find us, they have to," Bronwyn said, and shivered. "Someone will save us."

"Don't be a fool," Mary said. "We can't just sit here forever. We need to save ourselves."

Of course Mary looked to me for support, and even though I was exhausted, I mustered my conviction and said, "Absolutely. Yes, we need to do something." Then I clutched Sky tighter, dropped my voice, and whispered to Bronwyn, "This will be okay."

The crowd started murmuring in agreement, and soon we were making plans, selecting scouts to send into Times Square station. The cyclists from our subway car volunteered, and we gave them careful instructions, used our collective knowledge, and drew a map in someone's notebook of the various hallways and passages of the subway stop. We started a collection and sent them along with money, a lighter, and hope.

"Be quick about it," Mary warned them as they jumped the subway turnstiles. "We're all down here, waiting for you."

It was then that I finally saw that fire behind Mary's eyes, the power that Tom often told me was there, ready to burn him to the ground. But I was grateful for it. I was starting to think that without Mary, I would go insane down here. Might run until the blackness enveloped me, claimed me as its own.

The cyclists never returned.

March 20—It's been weeks. Or maybe it's been
a lifetime. I can't be sure. I've divided my mind
into two—the anxious, fully conscious part of me
has been put to sleep. There's only my animal left,
which roams this dark labyrinth. I breathe, eat,
and care for Sky. I don't think. I can't think.

We're just lost migrants at the city's mercy,
survivors scavenging for a second chance. We
camp out at different subway stops, swapping tales
from our past lives like trading cards. Lauren has
shared stories about her overachieving fifth grader.
Bronwyn's told me about her "perfect" boyfriend,
some arrogant freshman at NYU . . . then more
quietly, as she played with Sky, about her little
sisters back home.

A few of our doomed pack have volunteered
to scout and loot on the surface. Many of them
haven't returned. Some have with food, clothing.
Flashlights and candles. And of course, images.

"New York is under fire," they said. "We're at
war. The streets are filled with corpses. There are
soldiers on every corner. There's nothing left."

I don't believe it. I can't believe it. I stay in
my dark cocoon, taking rations for Sky and me,
keeping an eye on Bronwyn, clinging to Mary. I
feel so sick these days.

April 1—Our numbers are dwindling. The brave
ones are dying faster, one by one volunteering or
being chosen for a near-certain suicide mission.
Those who are left are young or old, scared or sick.

*We get by on looted goods from abandoned corner
stores and restaurants. We ration. We want to
give up. But Mary keeps us focused and moving.
There's really no one else to lead this pitiful crew.*

*Most days we spend wandering or cowering in
corners, speculating. We've compiled a collective
mental montage of the surface, from the few who
have made it back with supplies. Our theories
start out each morning as a slow simmer, building
throughout the day into a boil, until by evening
we're whistling louder than a teakettle.*

"It was China."

*"I met survivors from the N line on the surface.
It's definitely the Middle East."*

"I heard Brooklyn's bombed out."

"No, it's Queens. And it started with Japan."

*"You idiots, it's a land invasion. No one dropped
a nuke."*

But no one knows for sure.

*April 15—The pain has gotten unbearable. I feel
like my insides are trying to crawl out of me, and
recently it hurts to even walk. Where is Tom?*

*Some days I picture him hunting through
the dark, looking for me. I hear creaks, noises
underground, and I think he and Robert are
around the corner, coming for us.*

We hear a frustrated rattle of chains from the other side
of the bar. An angry door trying to break from its hinges. I
jump and nearly burn the journal. Sky's eyes are wild under

the firelight. She quickly tucks the journal back into her stretch pants, then motions for me to blow out the flame.

Our light disappears just as we hear a series of keys click into the door's padlocks. The chains fall one by one, clang to the floor, and then a team of voices stampedes the roof.

"This is ridiculous. We should be at the zoo, or the castle."

I close my eyes. I'll never forget that voice. The one that taunted me before my 65th Street fight. The one that promised I wouldn't walk away from it. Cass.

"Fieldworkers are like sheep. They know to stay in their pens," Cass adds. "We don't need to be at this shitty hotel missing all the action."

Her voice grows louder, and I hear a few footsteps moving towards us. Beside me, Sky starts breathing heavy, so I reach out to hold her hand. Our palms, slick with fear, slip together.

"Sheep, huh?" Another voice, a deeper one, male, answers Cass. "Then why'd you call me up from the lobby?"

"Darren, Lory called you up. Not me."

"Enough bickering," a third voice chimes in. *How many of them are there?* "Cass, for being low lord on the totem pole, you've got an awful lot to say. As Council member, I make the calls here. And I saw a flame in the stairwell."

A flame in the stairwell. A flame. My flame. My stomach does a backflip and lands on the glass-covered floor.

"Darren's squad was guarding the lobby. Yours was on two, Clara's was on three, and I was patrolling four. So if not for the sheep, then who the hell was on the stairwell?" The third speaker, which by now I'd bet a ration is Lory, pauses for dramatic effect. Then I hear a groan and a gasp—like there's some sort of power play happening on the other side of the bar.

"Now shut the fuck up and do what you're told," Lory says. "This is the last place we have to look."

Sky lets go of my hand and moves up my wrist with her fingers, then ever so slightly digs her nails into my skin. A bona fide *Told you so*. Damn it, I hate it when she's right. I should never have lit that torch.

I'm wondering how pissed she'd be if she knew I had the gun.

I take a small breath and look around at the bottles and glass that barricade us in. If we don't move, we're surely caught. If we move in the middle of all this glass, we'll make noise, and we're caught. I close my eyes and briefly consider shooting our way out of this. How many bullets are there? Four? Probably not enough. Assuming I have the guts to pull the trigger.

The footsteps are splitting up and shuffling around us in all directions. The whorelords must be checking under couches and in corners, looking for the rogue sheep.

"Lory, there's no one up here," Cass whines. "Come on, can't we go back to the castle? You promised I could see the trial."

And for one short, amazing moment, I think we might be safe. Sky takes my hand again, and we squeeze. *Yes, yes, yes, go back to that whore's den of a castle.*

"They must've snuck back to their rooms," Lory says with a sigh. "I guess the other lords can handle babysitting for the night. Just check the bar and then let's get the hell out of here."

The bar.

Sky and I look at each other, mirrors of panic. Footsteps start pacing towards us from the opposite side of the roof.

Half-baked ideas start bumbling around in my brain.

The whorelords. Lockdown. The castle. Rolladin. Street-fighting.
Think, think, think.

The ideas finally roll up their sleeves and start working together to build the beginnings of a plan.

I put one hand on my chest, like I can actually keep my heart on lockdown, and with the other, lean on Sky's shoulder for support. Then I dislodge the small gun and bullets from my pocket and shove them into the seat of my long underwear. Sky watches me in horror.

You brought your gun? she mouths. *Moron.*

She's right, of course. Again. There's no precedent for getting caught on the roof during lockdown, let alone with a weapon.

But I don't admit this, and instead just whisper, "Do what I do."

I scan the bottles. Out of the lot of booze, Jim Beam looks like a solid, rational guy—a real straight shooter in a jam like this. His cap is crusted over from years of disuse, but he finally cracks open and I pour the caramel-colored liquid onto my hands, rub it behind my ears, take a long, deep swig of the gag-worthy stuff and pass it over to Sky before I stand.

Here. Goes. Nothing.

"We're over here," I fake slur across the roof terrace. I try to remember all the nights of watching the sloppier whorelords stumble around the Park, and channel them. "Cele-bra-ting."

I look down at Sky, plead with her. *Drink it, bathe in it, and get up. Please.*

She debates whether to hide the journal on her, but then thinks better of it, weasels it into a cabinet, and camouflages it with a few bottles. Then she takes a long pull from the Jim and, choking on it, pats some on her face before she stands.

"What the hell are you two doing up here?" Lory demands. "Getting wasted? On our stash?"

She stomps over to us and grabs the half-empty bottle from Sky. The other three whorelords converge on us.

"Ugh, you lemmings reek."

Lory and Clara begin searching Sky as Darren drags me out to the center of the roof-deck lounge. He holds my arms behind my back with one hand and does a quick check of my sweatpants pockets with the other, scouting for booze or weapons or God knows what else. I buckle my knees a bit. I squeeze my thighs together and pray he can't see or feel the gun poking out from my sweats. *Moron*, I repeat silently. *Moron.*

But he backs away, satisfied I've got nothing. The cold lead of the gun slides between my legs uncomfortably, but it's nothing compared with the shit I'd be facing for holding a weapon.

"Well, if it isn't the famous Miller kids, cel-e-brating," Cass spits into my ear as Lory brings Sky around the bar. "What, now you think you can do anything you want, just 'cause Rolladin didn't let me finish you on Sixty-Fifth Street?"

The smell of Cass's breath is layered—meat and booze and a heavy, smoky smell—and I cringe and angle my face away from her. The fur of her lame little squirrel cloak scratches me in the eye.

"Don't think I'll ever forget you cut me. Bitch."

"Cass," Lory snaps, pushing Sky forward as she does so, like my sister's just a puppet on a string. Sky looks at me, her eyes wide and hollow, and I can tell she's scared shitless. I am too. I close my eyes and breathe. *Come on, just trust in the plan.*

"What?" Cass answers Lory. "I'm just having a little fun with her."

Cass grabs my hair and pulls my head backward, and I have to bite my lip to keep from yelping. My ribs are still sore from the fight, and Cass is standing so close, she's crushing into me.

Darren reaches across the back of my body, and for a second, I'm sure that he's going to touch me again and find the gun, and this will be all over. I close my eyes—

But his hand just grabs Cass's wrist.

"Cass," he says quietly. "Let's not do anything we'll regret."

Cass releases her death grip on my hair. She straightens herself out and clears her throat. "Fine. We're taking them to the zoo prisons, right? Then let's go. We don't have that much time before the trial."

"Not the zoo," Lory answers. "The castle."

"The *castle*? These two lemmings were found drinking the lords' booze. After curfew. On *lockdown*. And we need *Rolladin* to weigh in on whether we lock them in the zoo?" Cass's eyes inch up and down my features. "I don't get it," she adds, her hot mess of breath crawling across my face. "What's so special about you? Why does she even care?"

"What did I tell you about that mouth, Cass? Don't forget your place." Lory pushes my sister towards the door and the puddles of chains. "Now shut your fat face and get moving."

As we feel our way down the stairs, I keep my thighs locked, hugging the gun.

"Can we at least tell our mom we're being taken?" Sky calls out over the stampede of footsteps. "If she wakes up and we're not there . . . Please."

The whorelords get a good laugh out of that but don't even bother answering.

Sky's right. Mom's going to be totally spooked if we're not there when she wakes up. I pray that she stays asleep through all of this. That somehow we get back by morning. But if things go according to my plan, it's pretty doubtful.

"Clara," Lory barks back to my street-fight referee, now flanked between Lory and Sky, and me and my captors. "Stay behind and let the squads know we're taking these fools to the castle. They're on their posts until told otherwise."

"Yes, ma'am." Clara drops behind as the rest of us burst into the slick-floored lobby, and then out into the midnight air.

We shuffle over the sidewalk and then dive into the shadows of the Park, through the woods and over the 76th Street bridge towards Belvedere Castle. Cass is pressing her fingers so hard into my forearm that by tomorrow I'll have a whole new set of bruises from her. But I don't flinch. In fact, I don't even look her way.

I get it. She's taking jabs while she can. I know she's livid, and I guess, in a weird way, she has a right to be. If Sky and I were anyone, *anyone*, else in the Park, we'd be thrown in the prisons at the zoo for months for disobeying direct orders, maybe even years. Our rations cut, our families threatened. Instead, as I'd bet on, we're on our way to Rolladin.

Like I realized on the roof, there's something special about us. I don't know what or why. I just know it's true.

We get the easiest jobs at harvest. We get the same room every year at the Carlyle, regardless of when we show. Last night Rolladin absolutely should've thrown us out of the

LEE KELLY

Park, but we got a pass instead, a chance to fight on 65th Street to prove our worth. And as much as I hate to admit it, I should have been handed my ass in that fight. But Rolladin stopped us right when things were going south for me. I saw it in her eyes when she broke us up, but really, I've known it for a long time. There are rules that don't apply to us. Now it's time to test how far that goes.

I take a deep breath as Darren and Cass pull me out of the dark of the Park and into the dim light of the castle hall.

I'm just going to need to kiss some serious ass in order to test it.

I'm so furious I'm seeing colors, the candlelit hallway of the Belvedere no more than the tunnel of an angry kaleidoscope. All I wanted was a tiny shot of adventure, an escape into another world. But like always, Phee took over, and instead of a night of reading Mom's journal on the roof, I'm being restrained by one of the most feared warlords of the Park, on my way to appeal to Rolladin.

What was Phee *thinking*, grabbing that torch, bringing the gun? And if we lose that journal, I will never, ever forgive her.

Lory thrusts me forward as she pushes open a wide, thick wooden door, and we're once again in the study of Rolladin's chambers, as we were a night ago, begging for mercy.

"The one thing I'll give you, you've got nerve," Cass snarls into my sister's ear.

For once, my stomach doesn't lurch forward, and my mind doesn't clamor into protective mode. I just look away, upset, frustrated. Maybe even a little glad Cass is giving Phee trouble. Phee doesn't listen to *me*; maybe the lords can knock some sense into her.

"Cass, take this one," Lory says, passing me over to Cass. "I'll get Rolladin."

Cass holds my hands behind my back as Lory opens the door to Rolladin's inner chamber, and then retreats into darkness. We're left in the study. I look over at Phee and try to figure out if the small handgun is noticeable in the folds of her sweatpants. Thankfully, she never wears anything formfitting, and the thick cotton reveals nothing.

I look up and meet her gaze, and I can tell she's trying to carefully wiggle one of her hands free from Darren's grasp to sign something to me. Her eyes are wide and determined, and she has that crazy look in her eye she sometimes gets when she's about to hatch a less than fully formed plan. I don't know what she's thinking, but I quickly and slightly shake my head. *No. You've done enough.*

Rolladin bullies open the door to her study, Lory in tow, before Phee can respond.

"Did I hear this right?" Rolladin demands, thrusting her wide features into mine.

"Breaking out during lockdown?" She moves like a cat on the hunt, is on Phee before I can blink. "Drinking on the roof? Tell me, do you think I just give orders as *suggestions*? That I'm open to interpretation? Do. Not. Leave. Your. Rooms. What is so fucking hard to understand?"

She looks like she's about to strike Phee, and every ounce of ill will I wished my sister over the past few minutes washes away. I battle against Cass's grip to break free, but Rolladin's already diverted her anger, is pounding her old wooden desk in frustration. Crumpled papers and folders jump in surprise, then fall to the tabletop in surrender.

"What the hell am I supposed to do with this information?" Rolladin runs her hands through her fire-colored hair. "You've left me no choice, you imbeciles. Lory, take them away."

Lory waves Cass and Darren to start moving back the way we came.

This is it. Mom, forgive us.

"Rolladin, please," Phee fake slurs. "We didn't mean any disrespect. In fact, the opposite. We were celebrating your recent capture of those holdouts. No one steals from the Park. No one."

Phee does a little stutter step forward for emphasis, but Darren pulls her back. I watch as Rolladin gently takes hold of Lory's wrist to wait a moment. Phee takes this as a sign to continue. My God, I hope she knows what she's doing.

"I want to stay here," Phee blurts out. "The whole year. I want to be safe. I'm tired of leaving every summer. Tonight I realized that—and I went with Sky to the roof to convince her, too. Without Mom hearing us."

She looks over at me, nodding encouragingly, and for the life of me, I can't tell if she means what she's saying. This is a lie for Rolladin, right?

Of course it is.

But then I think about our conversation today about Phee becoming a lord, about our countless debates about the Park. And if I'm honest with myself, as much as I've always wanted to ignore it, we've never seen eye to eye on this place. Somehow this ruthless city is home to my sister. Where for me, it will never, *ever* be more than a cage.

I get an unsettling, anxious feeling in my abdomen. So how much truth is in this speech of Phee's? Is it for Rolladin's benefit, or mine?

"We had a few drinks. And I'm so, so sorry for taking what isn't mine, what belongs to the lords. Please show us the lords' mercy," Phee continues, pulling out the ultimate line of deference in the Park. The one people use when they have nothing else to offer, and I can't believe Phee is able to make the words cross her lips. If Mom could hear her, she'd explode. She's taught us never, ever to give in and say this.

"I'll pull extra shifts," Phee continues. "I'll clean the prisons. We'll do whatever you want. But after tonight, I know who I am and what I want. And I think Sky does too. Right, Sky?"

Rolladin turns her attention to me, stalks forward. But her features are softer than they were before. There's something new—hope?—in her eyes.

"Yes," I stammer, not sure of what to say or do, only sure that *yes* feels like the best answer. "That's right."

Rolladin's mouth sets in a hard line, and her eyes don't leave mine.

"Wait outside," she finally says to her lords.

"Rolladin," Lory says softly behind her. "If the other sheep knew what happened—"

"What are you, fucking deaf?" she barks. "I said leave us."

The lords slowly slither out of the room like snakes in the grass. Rolladin slams the inside lock shut with a snap.

Then it's just the three of us.

"So," Rolladin says to the ground, and if I didn't know better, I'd say she seems . . . nervous. As nervous as I am. "Take a seat."

Phee and I find our way to two cracked leather chairs on the near side of her desk, and Rolladin bends down and examines the contents of her cabinet on the other side. She emerges with three glasses and a half-empty bottle labeled JOHNNIE WALKER BLUE. She pushes away her mounds of dusty files . . . *Third Geneva Convention* . . . *Red Allies Code of War* . . . before slapping three glasses on her desk.

"Lory said you two liked whiskey," she grunts as she opens the bottle and pours us each a hefty amount. I'm pretty sure Phee has no idea what she's talking about either, but we both take a glass without protest.

Rolladin sits and leans back in her throne, probes us with her stare, then finally takes her whiskey and tips it towards us in the air. "Bottoms up."

I take the liquid to my lips. This one's still beyond brutal-tasting, but it goes down a little easier than the Jim Beam. It's smoother, and I somehow manage not to gag. I regroup and take another sip. With each one, I get a little less anxious. A little less afraid. A little less conscious of sitting with the leader of the Park, discussing our future over a glass of whiskey. I take a deep breath and a long, long pull from the glass.

"Well," Rolladin says. "You were saying."

Phee clears her throat but doesn't look at me. "We love our mom," she says carefully. "But now that we're older, I think we should be able to make decisions for ourselves. And when those holdouts emerged out of the woods, it all clicked for me."

"It clicked for you," Rolladin repeats slowly. "And what, may I ask, *clicked*?"

"It's—it's like you were saying at the street-fights. About the whole survival-of-the-fittest thing. And after my match, I got it. I mean *really* got it, you know?" Phee's voice is starting to betray her a little, quiver just a bit. She takes another gulp of the Johnnie, and I do too for good measure.

"We're in the middle of a war," Phee says with new vigor. "And I don't want to be cowering in the background. I want to be on the front lines, with you, keeping this city in order. Making sure we're as strong as we can be when we're finally released to fight and end this war for good."

She sells it, *hard*, so hard I'm believing her, and I have to look away.

I focus on Rolladin instead. She's toying with her glass, batting it around on her desk, like a cat with a caught mouse. "And what makes you think that I'd want you as a lord?"

Phee stutters, "Uh, nothing. I don't think that." She runs her hands in circles under the desk, pulls at her sweatpants, gives that hidden gun some breathing room. "I don't expect anything at all. I just wanted to say that I hope to be pledged. And if you'll have us, we're yours."

Yours. I no longer care if Phee is being serious, or if this is all some elaborate tactic to escape the zoo. It's too much either way, and my stomach curdles in disgust. I can't look at either of them anymore. I grab my glass and pour it down my throat, finish every last drop, wish I could transport myself back to our room at the Carlyle. Or better yet, to the other side of the world, to another dimension, where there is no Rolladin and *eye for an eye* and *survival of the fittest.*

"Interesting," Rolladin finally answers. "Well, I'll have to think about that offer."

She finishes her drink as well, and then promptly pours herself another one.

"And what about you?" Rolladin suddenly turns to me. There's a smile threatening to reveal itself, but she smothers it before it can escape. "You've always reminded me of your mother. It's always seemed to me that our Park way of life doesn't suit you."

She leans forward, I swear, like she's about to jump over the table and devour me. "So I'm quite sure that you're just playing along on this one."

My stomach drops. And I'm shocked. Rolladin has paid

that much attention? Knows me well enough to even guess at the truth? I feel a flush in my cheeks, and I don't know whether it's from the alcohol or the sickening feeling that I might be flattered.

And I know I have two options.

I can tell her how much I hate the Park, and this city, and her and all the sorry excuses for human beings who do her bidding.

Or I can tell her the bigger truth. The one that, regardless of how jealous I am, how insignificant I feel, is more a part of me than any limb or organ, whether I like it or not. It rumbles inside me and bursts through my lips, armed with new ammunition from the whiskey.

"I would never leave Phee," I say, but don't look at my sister, as my answer is so fundamental I'm scared by it. "What she wants, I'll live with."

Rolladin looks at me for a long time, and a thin film glazes over her, steals the color out of her eyes. And for just a sliver of a second, she reminds me of my mom.

"Well, that," she says, "I can believe."

Phee's fingers find mine under the desk, and she gives me a little squeeze.

I feel like a traitor, a terrible, sorry excuse for a daughter. If Rolladin takes us in, how are we going to answer to Mom tomorrow? Are we even going to see her? As the whiskey settles, I start to realize that here, right now, we're forever altering the course of our lives. Not to mention Mom's.

Will she stay here with us?

Will Rolladin force her to stay in the fields? Or will it be Mom's choice instead, and she'll disown us?

I close my eyes and think of this uncertain future,

LEE KELLY

picture Phee a lesser lord, and me—what? Some sort of council to Phee? A castle whore? I shake my head.

Stop it. Stop thinking. Just stop.

"You'll stay here tonight." Rolladin stands quickly, the shove of her chair interrupting my thoughts. "Tomorrow we'll discuss and make arrangements. I'll tell your mother. She'll have to come to terms."

Then she pounds on the door, and the moment is lost. We're just two young prisoners of war again, being handled.

Lory opens the door, and I see the other two warlords have just been waiting behind it patiently.

"Take them to the guest chambers. Lock them in," she tells Darren. Then she looks at us and nods like a fat cat, satisfied. "Until tomorrow."

Darren hurries Phee and me up a few flights of circular stairs and down a hall lined with windows, then throws us into a small, simple room. He slams the door and snaps on the chain lock on the other side, and we're left with each other.

"Phee." I sit down on the narrow bed, shaking, and put my head in my hands. The whiskey causes the room to bend and flex its muscles, bully me for sport. "What have you done?"

"What do you mean, what have I done? Isn't it obvious? I just saved our asses."

Phee moves into the corner's shadows, pulls open her two layers of pants to dislodge the gun and the bullets, then sits beside me. She carefully places the small weapon down next to her, like it's an esteemed guest instead of an interloper.

"Were we in the same room down there? You just signed

us up for a lifetime with *Rolladin*. Are you insane? I mean, really, have you lost your mind?"

Phee cranes her neck back, like she's sizing me up. "You're drunk."

"That's hardly the point." I leave her and walk to our window, look down to the torch-lined entrance of the castle. Lory is leaving with a fully armed troop, down the cement path and into the night.

And I realize it's possible we might never leave this castle as fieldworkers again.

"What were you thinking, bringing that gun?" I say to the window. "And that show for Rolladin down there—"

"Oh please, they don't even know I have the gun."

"Not the real issue here. Seriously, why couldn't you have just listened to me? Why'd you have to light that fire on the stairwell? Now Mom's journal's locked on the roof!"

"Well, don't blame me for that. You had to know that was a risk. No worries, I know we'll get it back—"

"Phee." I sit back down on the bed. I want to shout or cry, but I'm so frustrated I can't bring myself to do either. It's always like this with my sister. She deflects, she rationalizes everything away, and then we end up talking in circles. And I can't do it right now, I just can't. I take a deep breath. "Just be honest with me, for once. No twisted words. No dance. You're happy with the way things turned out tonight."

"Come on. I thought we dropped this whole me-wanting-to-be-a-warlord business in the fields today," she says slowly. "We were in a jam. A jam, in case you forgot, that was sort of your fault in the first place. And I got us out of it. That's all."

"You got us out of it," I parrot. *Calm. Calm down. Measure and weigh your words.*

But for some reason, I can't seem to get calm, and my words fly out of me before I can pin them down. "Phee, there were a lot of ways we could've gone on this, had you—I don't know—let me do the talking maybe? For once? We could've pleaded for a shorter sentence. Or agreed to leave the Park with Mom. But your go-to is pledging to Rolladin, practically *begging* her to keep us? What do you think's going to happen tomorrow, huh? How are we going to explain this nightmare to Mom? Because I'm pretty sure Rolladin's not open to 'Sorry, just testing the waters. Thanks but no thanks.' We're finished, Phee. This, this castle." I raise my hands as if to summon the room. "It's home now."

Phee shakes her head. "Okay, these options you're talking about? Involve legit jail time, or starving and freezing our butts off on Wall Street. We're alive, we're warm, and we're not behind bars. We'll just explain the situation to Mom and make her understand."

"*If* we're ever alone with her again—"

"*Second*, if I do say so myself," Phee talks over me, "we had about two seconds to come up with a plan. And for all your big talk now, I didn't see you stepping up on the roof. So you can say thanks anytime. We just dodged a heck of a lot worse."

"In your eyes." I roll over on the bed, thrust my hands under the flat pillow, and curl my knees into my chest. The room starts quivering again, threatening to spar. I close my eyes. "You're just not getting it," I add. "This isn't a game."

Phee lies down beside me and makes a big show of pulling the thin lonely blanket, threatening a tug of war. I let her have it.

"I know it's not a game," she snaps. "You always think you

know better than me. But maybe I know what I'm doing. Maybe I get the Park, all right? And I know how these whore-lords think, more than you ever could."

"Why, because you're such a 'badass' warrior now?" I throw back at her. "One fight, Phee. You were in *one* fight."

"Oh, just forget it. You're such an asshole sometimes."

She grunts and thrusts the blanket over her, and the old bed moans and squeaks in protest. And I know I might have gone over the line, but I'm not apologizing. I'm tired of her, of the whole thing. The self-proclaimed stronger, braver sister. And me, just the sad little storm cloud that follows her around, threatening to rain on her parade. Of course I meant what I said to Rolladin, that I'll never leave Phee's side. But Phee could at least acknowledge it. She could at least pretend we're in this together. We're going to need each other tomorrow more than ever.

I'm beginning to shiver a little, now that my anger has scared the whiskey away. But I don't reach for the blanket. I don't say anything for a long time.

"We'll figure this out tomorrow," I finally whisper to Phee.

And that's the most I can give.

11

I wake with a start. Sky's shaking me frantically, cover-ing my mouth for the second time tonight, I guess in case I wake up all disoriented and scream. I remind myself to tell her that the fake gag doesn't help. I push her hand from my mouth and shake the sleep from me. She's breathless, excited, eyes-wild, and I almost get swept up in it till I remember we're sort of in a fight.

"What is it?" I say as coolly as I can. "What's got your panties in a bunch?"

"Come look," she whispers, totally ignoring my dig, as I know Sky hates the word "panties." She runs to the window, and I sigh, throw off the blanket I've managed to hijack, and move beside her.

"The men from the forest," she says. "They're bringing them in for the trial. Cass was talking about it on the roof, but I didn't put two and two together."

Sure enough, below us some Council members are ushering the four guys from the woods into the castle. The prisoners' hands are tied, and the whorelords have them strung up and connected by chains, like a sad bunch of flies in a spiderweb. The oldest one is in front. Then there's the one around Mom's age, then the thin twentysomething guy, who's carefully trying to wiggle out of his binds, then the teenager. As the group slinks out of sight and into the castle entrance, I really see the teen's face for the first time, without all the dirt and leaves and everything. He's pretty cute, actually.

"Who are they?" Sky whispers.

"So now you want my opinion? I thought you were the one with all the answers." I rub the sleep from my eyes. I don't really feel like fighting with her anymore, but what she said about the 65th Street fights pissed me off.

"Phee," Sky says to the ground, "I was out of line before, okay? I know you've been through a lot. And I know you were just trying to help on the roof. I'm sorry."

"Fine, I'm sorry too." I mutter. For good measure, I add, "You don't always have lame ideas."

She looks at me funny, and I try to remember whether I'd said that last part out loud or not. "So, who'd Mom think the guys were again?" I change the subject. "Not feeders, right?"

"And not raiders," Sky whispers. "And definitely not enemy soldiers, unless, like Mom said, the English are aligned with the Red Allies against us. . . ." She trails off. "What do you think's going to happen to these men? And why's this trial taking place in the middle of the night, anyway? The field-workers and lesser lords are at the Carlyle." She reaches for the doorknob and carefully twists it. The door releases and opens a couple of inches before a chain reminds it of its limits. "No one but the Council would even be here to see it."

Here's the thing: Even though Sky's brain could run laps around mine, it has a blind spot. I won't bring it up again—what's the point? Sky railed me for it last time, but honestly, I get how Rolladin thinks. And it's this kind of stuff that Sky doesn't understand, or even pay attention to. She can read a book in a couple of hours, recite page-long poems by heart, explain physics. But she just doesn't get the way of the Park, or the way things work in this city.

"She's having a trial so she can take her list of rules and put a big fat check mark next to them," I tell her. "All POWs get a trial, even holdouts, so she's having a trial. No one says it's got to be fair."

Sky's eyes grow wider. "Then we might never find out who these men really are," she says. "They might be dead by morning."

"Exactly. A quick, dirty trial and a fast cleanup that Rolladin can tell the whole Carlyle about tomorrow. A sketch of justice, no more, no less. And poof. It's like they never were."

"No. That's crazy. This is all insane." She looks at the door, determined, like she's gearing up to run through it. "Phee, I need to know who they are." She's got that same lunatic look in her eyes like she did when she woke me up the first time. "No more secrets."

"Well, what the heck can we do about it?"

She pauses for a few seconds. "We're going to need your gun."

We quickly wipe ourselves down over the washbasin in the room's corner, since we both stink like a bottle, and Rolladin might smell us coming. Then without a sound, Sky and I take my gun and manage to stick its skinny red nose into the crack of the door, and after what feels like an eternity of jiggering, we release the chain. We snap the chain back on the door to make it look like we're still inside, just in case any whorelords will be stalking the halls. But I doubt there'll be anyone checking. The Carlyle's on lockdown, after all—and Lory told Clara to make sure the whorelords hold their posts.

We hurry down the hall in silence. This time there's no sign language or bickering. There's no finger pointing or words. Sky was right, this isn't a game. After my pledge to Rolladin, us sneaking around her castle, spying on her, and betraying her from the inside out will end in our own sham of a trial. Then on a cross, hanging on 58th Street.

But neither one of us says it. Why remind each other? Why scare ourselves shitless?

All I have to say is, these guys' secrets better be worth it.

We're positive that the trial will be in the Great Hall. We see the room once a year, when a few "lucky" fieldworkers are picked to have Christmas dinner in the warmth of Belvedere Castle, and listen to Rolladin's retelling of the prisoners' emancipation from the zoo prisons to the Carlyle. She explains how she got the Red Allies to trust her, how her becoming warden gave us all a bit of our lives back. And even though the dinner's always awesome, it's totally weird that we always get seats at the table. Sky pesters Mom every year about why, but I've always written it off. Like I said, we're not just any prisoners.

The Great Hall is one flight up from the main floor and spans the whole length of the castle. We round down the marble stairs from our floor, and then tiptoe down the dim hallway of what should be the third level. We're looking for the mezzanine, where Rolladin gives her speech from. It's our best chance to hear the trial and stay hidden, before we sneak back to our rooms.

"Do you hear that?" Sky grabs my hand and whispers to me. "This way."

Sky's right. I'm starting to hear echoes of hushed conversations, and I breathe easier that we're headed the right way. Before we reach where the light from the Great Hall puddles on the marble floor, Sky stops me and points to the ground. We crawl on our hands and knees over the hard flooring and enter the mezzanine without a sound.

I look at Sky, point to my eyes, and then raise up my hands in confusion. *How are we going to see?*

She rolls her eyes and pulls on her ear. *Just listen.*

I hear boots, shuffles, then a door closes with a snap and a boom.

"What the hell is this, Lory?" Rolladin's voice. "Why are they here?"

I figure she's talking about the men from the woods, but then Lory answers, "They stayed to see the trial."

"I was clear as fucking crystal. I didn't want any lesser lords here, just the Council."

"I-I'm sorry," Lory stutters. "I thought it was harmless. . . ."

"Harmless?" Rolladin gives a sharp laugh. "Please, explain. Explain how your feeble pin of a brain can construe this whole thing as *harmless*."

"Apologies, I— Then I'll just take the lords back to the Carlyle—"

"It's too late for that," Rolladin snaps. After a long silence, "Bring them all in."

The door swings open and smacks the wall, and then we hear more boots and clanging metal, like the sounds of some distant chain-gang parade.

"Welcome to our humble abode," Rolladin's voice booms through the Great Hall. "I apologize for the chains, but I can't be too cautious when strange men emerge from my woods."

A few chairs scrape against the floor below—Rolladin and her whorelords must be getting settled.

"Gentlemen, Park rules on holdouts found poaching the Park are very clear," Rolladin continues. "But I can be merciful, as my lords know, when the situation warrants it. So I'll make you a deal. You tell me what I want to hear, and I'll spare your lives."

"Please, miss, we don't understand. How could we possibly know what you want to hear?" I think the old guy, the front man for the strangers, answers.

Rolladin says, "Because I'm going to tell you."

A few of the whorelords laugh.

"Listen and repeat after me," Rolladin continues. "You and these other sorry excuses for men are raiders from downtown. You underestimated your supplies for the winter and came up to the Park in desperation."

"What's a raider?" the old guy interrupts.

"A traitorous thief." A big sigh from Rolladin. "We haven't got all night. Say the words. Make this easy. 'I and the rest of my crew—'"

"Miss," the old guy jumps in. "What do your people call you? Rolladin? You're not—you're not giving us a chance to speak. We're not from downtown. We sailed from London to see if others are alive in the States—"

"Stop," Rolladin snaps. "Now, I'm going to give you one more chance. I understand that the best of us get disoriented, stuck on this little island. Forgotten about as this world war wages on for years."

There's this weird long pause, and I look at Sky. She seems as confused as I am. Mom said raiders never travel in such big packs. And by this point, it's pretty clear these guys aren't

LEE KELLY

enemy soldiers in disguise. Wouldn't they be giving Rolladin orders or something, instead of the other way around?

"But you, lads, are New Yorkers," Rolladin says, before I can sort my thoughts out. "So whatever your warped little minds are telling you, it's not true. They're voices. Hallucinations. I'm sure you came over from England a long, long time ago, and you're mixed up. I take pity, I really do. I've seen so many people fall to madness in these troubled times." She takes such a big breath, I can hear her inhale from here. "But I'm not going to entertain your lies any longer. Do you understand what I'm telling you? Do you comprehend what I'm saying? So I ask you one more time to tell me what I want to hear before I render a judgment of insanity and sentence you to solitary. 'I and the rest of these traitorous fools came to poach from the Park. I ask you to show us the lords' mercy—'"

"Rolladin," the English leader interrupts once more, and Sky and I look at each other. These guys are finished. No one interrupts Rolladin, let alone twice. "We're not crazy. We sailed across the Atlantic and docked at the Brooklyn Yard but a week ago. We're here for you, for others like you. The war is—"

"The Brooklyn Yard," someone else mumbles. "Psychos."

And I know, without having to guess, that the interrupter is Cass. Her raspy voice.

Her fat mouth.

And even though I hate her, I shake my head in pity. *Cass, you are a total idiot.*

"Excuse me, gentlemen, one of my young worthless bitches apparently thinks she has something to add here," Rolladin snaps.

"Sorry, it's . . . it's just, that's crazy," Cass stammers. "The Brooklyn Yard's the Red Allies' docking port. It's crawling with platoons . . . these guys would've been in body bags before they reached the shore." She laughs high and long and terrified. "Psychos."

But before Rolladin can really tear Cass a new one for speaking up, the Englishman jumps in.

"Platoons? Red Allies? Are you mad? The war destroyed everything . . . everyone. There are no *Red Allies* anymore. There is no *England* anymore. There is no *America*, for God's sake! Now please. Can't you comprehend what *I'm* saying?"

12   SKY

His words come at me like an army of arrows.

No Red Allies.

No America.

The war destroyed everything.

Is Rolladin right, are these men from the woods just sick, deranged poachers—desperate lunatics?

Or are they the bearers of an almost impossible truth?

Are we alone?

Are there no soldiers camped outside the island, holding all of Manhattan prisoner?

If no one's out there, then what's keeping us in?

I want to doubt the Englishmen. I want all my instincts to rush to their feet like angry jurors and cry out, *No! That's crazy. These are empty, desperate lies.*

But deep, deep in my heart, in my bones, I somehow know. I knew it when I saw my young woodsman in the forest after the street-fights. These men are here for a reason.

And the thick, slick snake of their truth slithers up my throat and stays there. There are no Red Allies out there anymore.

It's only Rolladin and her Council, keeping us penned in like animals. Keeping us small, our lives frozen in time.

I think I'm going to be sick.

I look at Phee. Her face is contorted in confusion, her

eyes glistening, and I want to hug her. I want to take her hand and run across the fields and back to Mom. I've never wanted to see her so badly.

But Rolladin's answering the Englishmen before I can even think about how.

"Yes," she responds icily. "I think I comprehend. My lesser lords, Darren, Cass—take these men back to the zoo. My verdict? Not guilty by reason of insanity. A life sentence of solitary confinement in the primate tower. Transfer them tomorrow."

"Insane? *Insane?!*" The Englishmen all start roaring through the marble room. "You can't do this! You can't keep spewing these lies!"

"Such a tragedy." Rolladin clucks in disapproval. "This war took so much from so many—people's loved ones, and futures . . . and sanity." Then I hear the steel door of the room below burst open once more and slam against the walls. "Council members, hang back a moment."

"Rolladin, no!" the men bellow. "Please!"

But Rolladin doesn't answer.

There's a shuffle of boots on the floor, and the heavy door is pulled shut below us, leaving Rolladin alone with her Council.

"Rolladin, I had no idea who those men were," Lory starts slowly. "I never would've brought the lesser lords if I'd known—"

A smack of a hand, a whack of metal, the sound of flesh dragged against the floor. Then a long, guttural cry.

"What did I tell you when I gave you that Council member cloak?" Rolladin snaps. "Now you share the truth. And you *protect* this city—the Park, the fieldworkers, the lesser lords—from that truth. Or don't you remember your oath?"

"I remember," Lory whimpers. "Please. Please show me

LEE KELLY

the lords' mercy." Even though I know it's her voice, I still can't picture this beast of a woman breaking.

"The lords' mercy," Rolladin repeats slowly. Then, softer: "Those men are *insane*, do you all understand? It explains all their ramblings about England and traveling overseas . . . about the war being over." She takes a deep breath. "We'll tell the rest of the Park the official verdict tomorrow—that we moved the men to the primate tower. That they'll be in solitary confinement indefinitely."

Silence.

"But the Council needs to tie this up for good," Rolladin snaps. "I don't want any loose ends. So give that fat mouth, Cass, the order. Get her hands dirty. Shut her up."

I don't understand Rolladin's orders, but the Council must. Because there aren't any questions.

In fact, there's not another sound, let alone a word, below for a long, long time.

"Well, what are you waiting for?" Rolladin adds. "Tick-tock."

The steel doors open and shut below us, and then the Council members are gone.

But I can't look at Phee. Not yet. If I look at her now, I'm going to crumble, and Rolladin is still in the Great Hall, pacing below us, muttering in frustration. I keep my eyes closed, slide one of my hands around my sister's wrist, and raise the other to my lips. *Quiet. Stay quiet until she leaves.*

Finally the steel door flies open and smacks the wall below us, and Rolladin's heavy footsteps carry her down the hall, down the stairs, back to her chambers.

Phee slowly pokes her head above the mezzanine to check that we're alone, but she starts whimpering before I can get a word out. "What the fuck?"

It's been a long time since I've seen her cry.

"Are those guys really telling the truth?" she whispers. "Is there actually no one freaking out there? But doesn't Rolladin go to the borders every season? Haven't we seen the fires over in Brooklyn?"

"But . . . but that could have been the Council, for appearances," I say slowly, putting the pieces together. "These British men could be lying, Phee. Or insane, like Rolladin's insisting. But their accents, and how sure they seem. Besides, what holdout—insane or not—would just show up at the Park in the middle of a field day?"

"But if those guys are legit, if—if they're telling the truth—" Phee's face is twisted and frustrated, her brow knitted, like she's trying to wrangle a wild animal. "What the hell is all of this for?"

I shake my head and tell her the only truth I have. "I don't know."

I can't begin to make sense of this, or get a handle on my thoughts. I'm breathless at the possibility of a world beyond this terrible city, regardless of what state it's in. I have so many questions for these men about the war, about England. God, the ocean.

But I'm also furious. Is this all Rolladin's twisted game? Does no one know the truth about the war but Rolladin and her Council members? They can't.

"Sky," Phee whispers, interrupting my thoughts. "What do we do with this?"

I look at my sister. For the first time in a long time, she looks helpless. Terrified, even. And I realize, for as much as what we've heard excites me to the point where I might burst, Phee definitely doesn't feel the same way.

LEE KELLY

"We need to leave," I say softly, grabbing her hand. "You know we can't stay here now, Phee."

She wipes the betraying tears from her eyes. "I just don't understand. Where would we go?"

And for the first time in my life, I let myself entertain the question. "We could go south." I start to let the hopeful smile that's been begging to cross my lips see the light of day. "For the winter, like birds. Or we could go west—or to England, with these men, and start a new life overseas. They said they came by boat. We could cross the Atlantic, like Columbus in reverse."

But Phee doesn't catch my excitement. "We can't just walk out of here. We just begged Rolladin for a chance to be whorelords-in-training. We leave, and she'll know we were playing her. She'll hunt us down through the city. We won't make it to the water."

Phee's right, of course. The madwoman at the helm of the Park would never let us go. This dangerous, maniacal hoarder of lives, who we're double—make that triple—crossing. And after the Englishmen showed Rolladin the tears in her web of lies, she'll be even more paranoid, more controlling. Will lockdown continue? Will there be random searches in the fields? More innocents thrown in solitary, to prove a point?

"We leave tonight," I whisper.

"What? You mean get Mom and pack up our stuff at the Carlyle? And just run? What if—what if those men weren't telling the truth? I mean, honestly, how do we *really* know for sure?"

"We question them ourselves," I say, nurturing my plan as it slowly takes form in my mind, like wind that laps a spark into a fire. "We find out everything we can. They told

Rolladin they got into the city undetected, so they should be able to tell us how to get out of it."

"Sky, they're in prison—you did hear that, right? They're being sent to the primate tower. We're never gonna see them again."

"Rolladin told the warlords to transfer the men tomorrow," I say slowly. "So we go tonight to the cells, and talk to them. Maybe we can even figure out the way to their boat."

I picture Phee, Mom, and me sailing into the horizon, breaking past the fence of skyscrapers and out into the great unknown. For a second I let myself see the young woodsman beside us—the image further warms me—but I don't tell Phee about that part.

"But that's crazy. What if there're whorelords at the prison?" Phee asks. "What then?"

"Then we'll forget it and find a way out on our own. Sneak back into the Carlyle, get Mom, get the journal. Get out before sunrise." I stare at the ceiling, like I can break it open and conjure the sky, show Phee that the stars are still governing. Right now, I feel like anything's possible. "There's still time. This is our only chance."

But even as I'm saying it, deep down, I know. This plan is ludicrous. Reckless. Brash. All I need is for someone to tell me otherwise. All I need is a voice of reason. One that cuts through all the secrets and the lies and the double-crossing and tells me I'm pushing too far, risking too much. Usually, I am this voice of reason.

But after tonight, I'm not sure I know myself, or this world I've taken as fact. Everything seems up for debate.

After a moment of thinking it over, Phee shakily says, "Okay."

I paste on a grin to hide the storm of terror and anxiety that rumbles within. "Then let's get moving."

I guess who needs a voice of reason when you have a partner in crime?

I scramble to my hands and knees, heart clamoring, palms slick, and slip with Phee along the dark marble hallway of the Belvedere. We slowly feel our way back to the stairs, slither undetected into the entrance hallway—and then burst out into the night, the cold air of October smacking us as we run for the cover of the trees.

The stars are out, and the moon is full, bulbous and glossy like an onion. It paints the forest in deep greens and blues, drapes branches in cloaks of steely gray. A couple of times I stop and swear I hear something in the trees— *warlords? Raiders? Feeders?*

But I shake off my fear and grip Phee's hand, and we rumble forward.

Phee and I don't say another word until we reach the old polar bear pit on the north side of the zoo. Down a cobblestone path about a hundred feet are the reptile house and aviary used as the prisons. Past that, the primate tower— solitary confinement.

The pit's guarded by a faded sign that reads POLAR BEAR BEWARE! and really isn't a pit at all, but a sunken room bordered by walls on three sides and a window which looks out to an empty pool. I've never actually been in here, but I know the warlords sometimes use it for questioning.

Once we've settled between two of the pit benches, Phee finally breaks the silence. "Did you see? Some of the Park's horses are tied up at the reptile house."

"The lesser lords must have ridden them over here—they

must still be in the prisons," I answer her. "The lords have to be leaving soon—Rolladin said they aren't moving the men to the primate tower until tomorrow."

Phee shifts onto her left side and dislodges the small handgun from the pocket of her sweatpants. "I guess I should load the gun, right? If we're breaking into prison."

She looks at me for encouragement. I've never even held a gun before, let alone know how to use one. Plus, I'm still pretty angry that Mom gave it to her and not me. "We're not going to need that."

"Well, in case. I think I'll set it up." She pulls the bullets out of her pocket but doesn't do anything. Just looks at the pistol for a long time. "What if it goes off in my pants?"

"I don't think it works that way."

She annoyingly starts to slot the silver cylinders into the empty chamber and rolls it closed. "Mom said this safety thing should keep it from going off," Phee says. "At least we'll have it if we need it."

"Trust me." I could strangle her. Even though this is clearly my plan, she's somehow managed to grab the reins. "We're not going to need it. The guys are behind bars."

Phee shrugs. "Yeah, but what if we need to get information out of them?"

"What, you'll *shoot* one of them to get them talking? Phee, that gun has already been more trouble than it's worth. Keep it in your pants, okay?"

Phee shakes her head. "You never think I know what I'm doing."

But before I can argue with her anymore, we hear voices waft over the abandoned zoo, then soft clomping of horses' hooves on pavement.

"Quiet, all right?" I whisper. "They're leaving."

I can catch only snippets of the warlords' conversations. . . .

"You think Cass and Darren can handle this?"

"They'll have to. An order's an order."

Then there's a chorus of neighs from the horses as they break into a gallop, and the crew of warlords is off, pounding against the cobblestone walkway, past our pit and back towards the castle.

"Okay," I whisper. "Let's go."

We climb out of the pit, run across the cobblestone walkway, and duck into the shadows of the animal houses on the other side.

We pass boarded-up shacks labeled SNACK BAR and RESTAURANT, creep behind the aviary, and stop once we reach the back entrance of the reptile house. The thin flap of the back door isn't locked, but all the cages will be chained with padlocks.

I take a deep breath before opening the door. I'm anxious, so anxious I can't seem to catch my breath. What are we going to say to these men? What if they refuse to speak with us, or start screaming, and the warlords hear them and come back for us? Or what if there are other prisoners in here, and they give us away?

Phee puts her hand on my shoulder, grips it firmly, and gives it a little squeeze.

"I'm scared too," she whispers. "But like you said, this is our only chance to find out the truth. One step at a time, right? Just open the door."

I nod, pat her hand with mine, and then pull open the flimsy back entry.

As soon as we crawl into the belly of the reptile house, we hear moans. Whimpers. Pleading. It only takes a moment for my eyes to adjust, but what I see freezes me in my tracks.

Cass is in the middle of the floor, red crossbow in hand, firing on the men behind steel bars at the end of the hall. One by one.

"What are you doing?" I yell.

Cass rests her crossbow beside her. "What the hell? How the—"

"Cass." I take a step forward, instinctively look around. It's just her and us. And the men in the far cage. No one else. "Stop. You don't need to do this."

"Oh really?" She laughs at me, spits her words across the reptile house. But she's rubbing her eyes. "I'm pretty sure I do. That's what being a warlord is all about. Following orders. Doing things you don't understand. Or didn't you know what you signed up for?"

I don't answer her, and that forced smile falls off her face.

"I knew it. I told the rest of them, and no one listened. You played her, didn't you?" Cass says.

I shake my head. "No, we—"

"You kissed Rolladin's ass just to be spared an arrow up your own."

"Who's there?" one of the men calls from the cell. He sticks his fingers out between the bars. "Help! She's already killed our mate. Please!"

Cass takes a hammer out of her pants pocket and whacks the bars. The guy cries out in pain, but Cass ignores him and stalks towards us like a cat on the hunt. "Maybe I can see what Rolladin can't see. And I'll do what she doesn't have the heart to do. I don't care what any of them say, I've had enough. It's just you and me now. No Rolladin or Lory to save your sorry ass."

"Wait," I plead with her. "Cass, wait!"

But she keeps moving. As she positions the arrow, loads the bow, and gets ready to point it between my temples, Sky starts yelling. "Phee, come on!" and pulls my arm to go back the way we came.

But I let my instincts take over.

There's no time to run, no time to hide.

Cass's bow is fully loaded, and as she raises it towards my face, aims it right between my eyes, I dig out my gun, push off the safety, wrap both hands around the weapon, and pray.

The shot goes off before Cass can fire the bow.

Cass's abdomen bursts open like a blooming rose, and her weapon clangs to the floor. She hits the ground, moaning, clutching her stomach.

And I can't think, I can't feel. I've been emptied, unhinged, rewired.

The front door swings open. Another warlord, Darren, quickly surveys the room. For a moment he's shocked, paralyzed with surprise, but then he starts moving, running towards us, barking at Phee and me. But I can't hear him— all I hear is the nagging ringing of Phee's gunshot.

Darren dislodges his own gun from the folds of his cloak and points it at us, his mouth an angry hollow, a silent scream, but Phee fires first, and the bullet dives across the room. The warlord falls, faceless, to the floor.

It takes a moment, but my heart starts working again, pumping, feeling. Sound, senses, they all return. But my mind is fixated; it says one word, over and over, tormented by a mantra I can't quiet.

Murderers.

Murderers.

Murderers.

My hands are shaking so badly that I nearly drop the gun.

I just killed someone.

Me. I ended someone's life. I stole it.

"You. You are so f-f-fucking dead," Cass stutters from the ground. She's bleeding, curled like a baby on the floor. "When Rolladin gets to you, she'll rip . . . rip you in half."

As if my arm has a mind of its own, it raises the gun again, points it right at her. Cass looks up at me, her eyes liquid with fear. But she says nothing.

Do it, the voice of my little instigator is louder than it's been in a long time. *Do it, do it.*

I shove the trembling gun into my pocket.

I'm no monster.

But you are a killer. A killer.

I grab the keys from Cass's belt and take her bow.

"Get the other whorelord's gun," I tell Sky. A raw survival instinct has grabbed hold of my throat. After this, it doesn't matter how special we might be to Rolladin. After this, there won't be any more forgiveness.

I finally take a good look at the men in the cage. There're three of them still alive. The fourth is wrapped around an arrow and is lying on the straw-covered floor.

"Get us out of here," the oldest pleads with me. Up close,

the men look beaten, raw eyes, scraped cheeks, clothes tattered and torn.

"We leave the Park. Tonight. You're taking us with you." I'm still shaking, the keys jangling in my hand, betraying the voice I'm selling as steady.

"Anything you want. Just open the door," the old guy urges.

Sky stands beside me, with the dead whorelord's gun in hand. "Let them out," she tells me. She's got a look on her face I can't read. It's not fear. It's—it's emptier than that.

I take a deep breath and turn back to the men. "You try anything, anything at all, and we'll shoot you. We need to get our mom at the Carlyle. Then you take us as far as we need to go." I stop, think—what else do we need? "And you tell us what the hell's going on. You hear me?"

"We'll get you out of the Park, sure. But you need to finish her off," another guy, the thin one in his twenties, says from the corner of the cage. "She'll track us."

I look at Cass, in agony on the ground. I hate her. I hate her so much, I'm tempted again to shoot her.

But there's a line somewhere, a hazy, shaky line that dances in front of me. My little instigator's begging me to cross it, sure, but deep down somehow I know. If I do, I'll never be the same. "We've got the weapons, we make the call."

The thin guy shakes his head. "Mistake."

I ignore him, hand the keys to Sky, and back away from the cage. I put my two-bullet gun in my pocket and cock Cass's bow like I'm ready to use it. I can tell Sky thinks these guys are our heroes, but I'm not sold. After the night we've had, I don't know whether I'll be able to trust anyone again, besides Sky and Mom.

Sky fumbles with a key in the lock, tries another, then another.

The door to the steel-bar cage finally staggers open, and the three men pour out into the reptile house. The thin one—the same guy who told me to finish Cass—watches me carefully, and I get the sense he's sizing me up, debating whether he can take me. I grip the bow, wishing I had a full deck of arrows, limitless guns.

"Let's go," the old guy says.

I nod at my sister. "You follow Sky, and I'll trail you. No funny business." I wave the bow for good measure. "We'll run up the east side of the Park, to the Carlyle. We'll regroup up there."

The thin one shakes his head again. "We should leave the Park as soon as possible."

"Are you seriously trying to take the reins here?" We don't have time for this tough guy's bullshit. "You were going to die. We freed you. We're holding guns. You do what we say."

The thin guy takes a few threatening steps forward, and I get a good look at him. Dark hair, dark eyes, skin that's been rubbed raw by wind and weather. Probably a few years older than Sky, maybe more.

"Sam, these girls just saved our lives," the old guy says softly. Then he asks me, "What's your name?"

"Phee. This is my sister, Sky."

"I'm Lerner." The old guy points to the thin, snarky one. "My mate, Sam." He nods towards the youngest. "And his brother, Ryder. Now, Phee and Sky—let's get the hell out of here."

We lock Cass in the men's prison cage, leave the reptile house a bath of blood, and cut across the zoo grounds to the east side of the Park. Me, then the three men, then Phee in tow. We hug Fifth Avenue as we run, follow the narrow cement path along the Park border sunken from street level, attempt to move as fast as possible.

I try to stay focused on our flight, but images from the reptile house keep tormenting me: Cass bathed in blood, Darren's face opening like curtains. I can't shake the images. They replay over and over, in real time and then slow, as if to say, *In case you missed anything, here it is again. Watch carefully.*

We killed someone. Someone a few years older than me.

We're all on high alert. Phee keeps ordering the Brits to slow, to give me some breathing room.

But I'm not afraid of these men. I knew, the moment I saw the young Englishman in the woods—Ryder—that things were about to change. That he was here for a reason. Now we have minutes to capitalize on that reason, to get out of the Park before Rolladin finds out what's happened at the prisons and tracks us down. And there won't be any third chances.

If she finds us, we're done for.

"Stop here," Phee calls from behind when we approach the stairs of 76th Street, the ones that lead out to Fifth

Avenue and down to the Carlyle. "You still have his gun?" she asks between breaths.

I look down at the long red-nosed pistol, the weapon of the dead warlord. We don't say Darren's name. We've taken his life, captured his soul, and yet we can't say his name. "Yeah, I've got it."

"All the year-rounds and the winters are kept in the Carlyle," Phee tells the men. "About a block east."

"*Winters?*" the oldest man, Lerner, repeats.

"The ones like us. The prisoners who're on their own in summer months," Phee says impatiently.

"Wait, so you *choose* to be here?" Sam jumps in. "Lerner, these girls aren't prisoners. They're guests."

"*Guests?* You don't know the first thing about us," Phee snaps at him. "You've got no clue about this city. What it takes to survive—"

"Sam, right?" I interrupt Phee in the most patient voice I can muster, trying to ignore that precious minutes are falling around us like rain. "I know you've got no reason to trust us. But we're prisoners too. We've been held on this island our whole lives, lied to, deceived. Please believe us, we're on the same side here."

No one answers me—my words just hang in the air, ripe for picking. Finally Phee plucks them and kills the silence. "Our mom's on the third floor, all right? We've gotta get her before we can leave."

"Okay, okay." Lerner runs his fingers through his silver blanket of hair. "We help them get their mom, and then we're off. Everyone got it?"

Sam mutters to himself in the dark but doesn't argue further.

"This Carlyle. Is it guarded?" Ryder says. It's the first time I'm hearing his voice, and I don't know what I expected, but it wasn't this. He has that beautiful, melodic accent like the other men, but his voice is gravelly, like water running over stones.

"There're whorelords in there, sure," Phee says.

"Whorelords?" Ryder probes.

"Guards, like the ones who threw you in prison," Phee says. "But there should only be a squad or two roaming each floor."

Despite the fact that I haven't stopped trembling since we burst into the reptile house, I know I need to be the one who guides the men into the Carlyle. As far as I'm concerned, there are two stops, the roof and our hotel room. Perhaps it's crazy, perhaps it's pitiful, but regardless, there's no chance I'm leaving Mom's journal behind. "Sam, will you stay with my sister out here?" I ask.

"Wait? Are you serious?" Phee pulls me aside and whispers. "Sky, that guy's the worst. Plus, I think it makes more sense for *me* to get Mom."

"I don't trust him," I whisper back truthfully. "Please, you've got the gun we know works, right? And you know how to use it."

She thinks this over, then finally gives a little nod, satisfied. She hands the bow over to me. "Take it. In case."

I give her a quick hug, and then motion for Ryder and Lerner to follow me.

"Go in from the west," Phee tells me. "We'll figure out a distraction and pull the door guards away. Meet in fifteen minutes at Seventy-Seventh and Madison, all right?" Phee's eyes are wide as she grips my hand.

I want to hug her again. Part of me wants to throw my arm around her and head upstairs to sleep, then wake up tomorrow just a normal prisoner, plodding along in the fields, ignorant, my hopes small, my dreams smaller. But I know that's never going to be possible again.

Besides, a bigger, stronger part of me now wants so much more.

"Seventy-Seventh and Madison," I repeat. "Fifteen minutes."

Ryder, Lerner, and I run up the Park stairs and cross the deserted highway.

"It's been at least nine minutes already," Sam whispers. "Maybe even ten."

The two of us are holed up behind some ancient Dumpster in the back of a Madison Avenue storefront. I'd never agree out loud with this psycho, but it's got to have been at least ten minutes. I'm worried. I should've gone with Sky. What if Rolladin already got wind of our shootout in the reptile house, and there're tons of whorelords crawling around in there? What if my sister's now being dragged back to the castle?

I readjust myself against the brick back wall of the store and try to think about anything but what's going on at the Carlyle, but it's impossible. I close my eyes for a second to relax—

But my mind's eye offers blood and dead whorelords.

"I thought you said your mum was on the third floor?" Lerner says. We're on the fifth-floor landing of the internal stairwell, the three of us crouched together in the dark. It's taken a lot longer than I ever would've imagined without a fire torch.

But we had to get the journal. I can't say good-bye to it, not without a fight. And once I get Mom and she knows what's happened, I'll never be able to come back for it—the past will be lost forever.

"She is," I whisper. "I left something up here that I need to grab first. I'll be quick. I can slip through the door."

"This has taken too long already," Lerner says, but he doesn't argue further.

I make my way to the roof-deck door. I think twice and pass Ryder the bow, as a consolation prize for waiting, or a sign of trust, I'm not sure. Our fingers touch in the darkness. His hands are field hands too, rough like sandpaper. "I'll be right back."

I round the half-flight and push open the door to weasel through the crack, as Phee and I did before, but the warlords must have locked it tight. Oh God. I wasn't expecting this.

I pull out Cass's thick set of keys and start fumbling with them—there are at least ten, maybe even twenty.

A surge of panic passes through me.

"Time's a-wastin', desperado," Sam says from across the alley. "At the fifteen-minute mark, I'm taking that revolver, grabbing my brother and Lerner, and hightailing it off this island."

I raise the gun to remind Sam who's got the ammo here. "You're not leaving without us."

Even though I fake calm pretty well, I'm starting to freak out. I need to get out of here, to breathe, and think. My sister and Mom are at the Carlyle, maybe in danger, maybe caught, and I'm just supposed to stay here, in this tiny alley, with this jerkoff, and be *patient?*

I think about flying the coop and just taking off for the Carlyle myself, but I know it's impossible. Even if I wanted to run, we can hear the Carlyle door guards searching Madison Avenue, trying to find the holdout who howled like a psycho in front of the hotel and then dashed into the night. I'll give him this, Sam's cover let me sneak up Fifth and across 77th. And I don't know how Sam pulled it off, but he lost the guards and somehow found me hidden behind this store.

"Why'd you come here, anyway?"

Sam sizes me up again. "Manhattan was the only POW camp we knew of still standing."

"Who's *we?*"

"Our army. England."

I gulp. "You fought in the war?" I study him, long and lean in the alleyway's shadows.

"Both sides had pretty much destroyed each other before I saw any action off base." I watch Sam watching my gun. "But I was a Royal Marine."

I have no idea what that means, only that it doesn't sound good for me. I swear, I'll shoot this guy if he tries anything, *Royal Marine* or not—if he pushes me. I've shot two people.

I've killed one.

I shake my head. I don't want to think about Darren right now.

"How many bullets are actually left in that thing?" Sam nods his head towards my small pistol and shuffles a little closer. Then the bastard actually smirks. "Mind if I take a look?"

I position the gun in between my knees, so that it's ready to go. "That's close enough."

Now it has to be at least twelve minutes. Thirteen even.

Sky, Sky, Sky. I focus, try with all my might to tap into her mind and bug her. *I'm worried. Please hurry your ass up.*

I return to the stairwell breathless, Mom's book tucked into the back of my leggings—our old torch in one hand, and the dead warlord's gun in the other—to find a frantic, wild pair of Brits.

"A torch," Lerner says. "You made a pit stop for a *torch*?"

"Lerner," Ryder pleads with him. "Come on, that's not helping, man."

"We'll need it," I say cautiously. There's no reason anyone needs to know what I have, what we've found in this journal, besides Phee and me.

"Well, that torch might have just cost us *our lives*."

I listen, slowly catching the men's panic. There are footsteps shuffling, and a stairway door swings open somewhere below us.

"We still have time. We need to get to the third floor," I say as calmly as I can.

"That's what I've been saying this whole time!"

I don't answer Lerner—even though he's only speaking up for the dissidents inside me, the angry Greek chorus that's been howling during the agonizing minutes I spent finding the right keys to release the door's chains. *How could you waste so much time? For a book of secrets? You would choose to know the past rather than to save your own mother?*

I force myself to tune them out, focus only on moving

quickly, quietly in the dark. All that matters now is getting Mom and getting out.

We creep down the stairs as the warlords inch their way up. They talk about inane things—who's going to be stuck watching the fieldworkers tomorrow, who owes who a pint of vodka from old bets. It's chatter, nothing about the murders at the zoo, so I know that the news hasn't reached the castle. If it had, the full guard of warlords would be patrolling for us. My guess is there's a squad or two, just rotating floors.

We reach the third-floor steps ahead of the warlords and slink out the door. I think we're unseen, until I hear one of the lords whisper, "Wait, did you see that door open?"

The quicker shuffling of boots.

Then a long bellow, "Stop!" behind us. The warlords' crawl becomes a stampede. We don't look back, just race down the hall.

"I said STOP!" a warlord calls.

I stutter-step, eye the approaching lords, then glance down the long hall to our room. It's clear we're not going to make it to Mom's. Lerner grabs the bow from Ryder's hands.

"Sky, give Ryder your gun. Now!" He backs up slowly, nods his head at me. "Run and get your mother. Don't look back."

My heart is pounding, my vision is blurred, but my body jumps at his command, thrusts the old revolver into Ryder's hand, and starts sprinting towards our room down the hall.

I hear shouts, barking orders. "Attack, do you hear me? Take them down!"

I burst into our room, shake Mom out of sleep, start throwing clothes and the remains of our half-eaten dinner into my book bag. She's lying there, looking fragile, the sleep still on her, and I want to embrace her, just curl into her arms and forget the world.

"Grab a torch, get your crutches," I say as I add the journal and the knife wedged underneath the mattress to my pack. "We need to leave. We need to leave now!"

Mom attempts to argue, but sleep's tentacles still hold her captive. I throw her arm around my shoulders and try to propel her forward.

"Sky, wait—stop! What is this? What's going on?"

"Mom, not now. Later, trust me. Where's your coat? Where's your shoes?"

We hear a gunshot, and then another, and Mom's eyes fly open in fear. She thrusts her coat over her pajamas, stuffs her feet into her shoes, and lurches towards her crutches resting in the corner. "Where's Phee?"

"She's okay. She's outside."

There's a heavy, panicked knock on the door.

"Lerner's hit!" Ryder calls from the other side. "We need to get out of here!"

I help Mom to the door, then crack it open. "Watch her ankle, it's sprained."

Ryder nods and huddles Mom and me into his chest. Lerner's behind us. He's been shot by an arrow—his leg is red and raw—but he's still managing to load our bow and get in one or two shots at the warlord team trailing us with knives and makeshift weapons. We move like a snake together, down the hall, down the stairs—

We round the marble staircase to the lobby, breathless, devils on our heels.

"Out the door!" Lerner calls ahead to Ryder.

Ryder pulls us out of the lobby, into the night. We're

greeted by two door guards coming from the east. They stop, shocked at finding us, raise their knives—

But Ryder takes the gun and shoots one of the guards in the chest.

"Drop your weapon," Ryder barks to the other. It's a younger lord—a man, maybe a decade older than me. He's carrying nothing but a small spear.

The man slowly places his spear on the ground as we push past him, out into the night air. We race to Madison Avenue, with a team of warlords on our heels.

"PHEE!" I hear Sky bellow, a shaky war cry across a dead highway, and Sam and I scramble to our feet and run out to the sidewalk.

Sky, Mom in pajamas, Ryder, and Lerner are being chased by a mob of whorelords up Madison. It looks like a parade out of somebody's nightmare.

I wave my hand, start running towards them without thinking, on instinct. My gun out and dancing in the air, ready to rumble—

But Sam grabs my hoodie before I can get very far.

"Forget it, there's too many of them," he says. "We need to run."

"Run? Where?"

Sam looks uptown. "The tube. We can lose them in the dark."

He's speaking gibberish. "What are you talking about? What *tube*?"

"Whatever, the subways. Underground."

The tunnels.

No.

No. No. No.

But he doesn't wait for a reply, just inserts himself front and center of this cat-and-mouse chase, and there's not a second to waste, to think. Soon me, Sky, Mom, Ryder, and Lerner, we're all following him, up Madison.

"Lerner, Ryder, the tube, on the left!" Sam shouts, and I swear Mom almost screeches to a halt.

"Girls, we can't." She starts trembling.

I put my hand on her and look behind to the army of guards. They're literally on Ryder's and Lerner's heels.

"Mom, it's our only option."

We approach a set of stairs, with a green rusty gate that reads 77TH STREET ENTRANCE and has a big green circle around the number 6. The stairwell cuts back and forth below us until it disappears into darkness. Sam's already stumbled into the pit. But he doesn't know what's down there.

"Come on!" he calls up to me.

I stop at the railing for a second. The whorelords are still firing arrows behind Ryder and Lerner, who both push us into the tunnel.

"It's the only way," Ryder tells us. "GO!"

Mom gives a low, long wail, like an animal that knows it's seen its last day, but I can't listen to her. I turn my back on the whorelord army and tuck her walking sticks under my arm. Then I grab her hand, and Sky grabs the other. We stumble down and into the dark.

PART TWO

Save yourself. Whatever it takes. Save yourself.

—From September entry,
Property of Sarah Walker Miller

PART TWO

The warlords march over the steel grates above us, shouting, cursing, firing hopeless arrows into our abyss, literal shots in the dark. But they won't come down here, not unless Rolladin puts a rifle to their heads.

No one comes down here.

I squeeze Mom's hand tighter as we burrow into the deep, the torch that Phee now holds our only guiding light in this twisted labyrinth. We run past an abandoned box of a room labeled INFORMATION, then hop over a series of steel gates.

"Sky, where's that other torch?" Lerner asks. He takes Mom's hand to help her over the steel bar. "We need all the light we can get down here. And those guards will be down soon enough."

"The guards won't come down here," Mom says, quivering, as she makes her way over the gate, wincing as she lands on her ankle. We hobble with her after Lerner, Ryder, and Sam, down another set of stairs. "Listen, we've already attracted too much attention ourselves. We should stay quiet and get back to the street at the next stop."

We climb down onto the tracks. Sam stops to patch up Lerner's leg, ripping shreds from his own shirt to wrap it like a mummified limb.

"What do you mean, no one will follow us down here?" Lerner asks Mom as Sam works. "You mean we lost the guards?"

"Yes, but now we've got a bigger problem." Mom settles herself onto her crutches. Her hands are shaking so badly, she's making the walking sticks tremble. "We shouldn't be down in these tunnels—they're not safe. We need to get back to the surface—"

"Lemme get this straight." Sam looks up at her. "We've got a mob of ruthless guards prowling New York for us. We've got a clear-cut path downtown, underground. You're positive no one's going to follow us down here. And you want us to go back to the *streets*?"

Mom grips her crutches tighter and straightens her spine. "I'm sorry, I didn't catch your name."

"Sam."

I haven't really looked at Sam—my eyes have been on my woodsman, Ryder—but he's younger than I originally thought, probably in his twenties. He's wartime thin, with big, deep-set eyes, and his own shock of black hair.

"My brother, Ryder." Sam points to my woodsman, then nods up to his older friend. "And you know Lerner, since he just saved your hide."

"Well, all due respect, Sam," Mom keeps her icy tone, "but you don't know anything about Manhattan. This city is haunted. There are monsters down here. Not humans, monsters—"

"*Monsters,*" Sam repeats. He gives a frustrated laugh. "Funny, I don't remember seeing any of these monsters when we walked through the tube from Brooklyn."

"Well, you must've gotten lucky."

Sam shakes his head. "Boys, any of you get the feeling this whole city's gone mad?"

He stands and starts tugging my backpack open for the

extra torch. I try to pull away from him, but he pins me against his chest. I give a little yelp.

"What do you think you're doing?" Mom hobbles forward as Phee starts clamoring, "Hey, asshole, lay off her!"

"Sam, please," Ryder pleads. "Easy."

"Everyone, just . . . *stop*." Sam tightens his grip around my shoulders. Then he whispers calmly in my ear, "Give me your torch, then you and your family can crawl back to the surface alone." He looks at Ryder. "These chicks aren't worth it, trust me. They're just extra baggage."

"Extra baggage," Ryder repeats. He takes a slow step towards his brother. "You act like there are other places we have to run. But you said it yourself, Sam—Manhattan was the endgame. So where the hell are we going?" I hear Ryder swallow in the dark quiet of the subways. "I'm tired of doing things your way, all the time. These women saved our lives, so we save theirs. Baggage or not, we figure the rest out together."

My cheeks begin to feel warm in the frigid tunnels.

"You've always been too quick to trust." Sam shakes his head. "Too quick to play savior, Rye. Even still."

That "still" holds the weight of worlds, and I want to know more. As I watch my woodsman, I realize I want to know everything about him, who he is, where he's from, and where he wants to go.

"We do owe them, Sam," Lerner says softly. "Ryder's right about that."

Finally, slowly, Sam eases his grip on me.

Under the dim light of the torch, Mom studies Sam, then Ryder and Lerner. I can tell she has a million questions for these men, not least of which is why they feel indebted to us.

But something more powerful has precedence, has taken hold of her face.

A raw, primal fear.

"We don't need your help," Mom says. "We'll give you a torch. Then you can run off into the night and take your chances. I don't know what you and Phee have done at the Park, Skyler," she says to me. "But it's fixable, it always is. We're not going to tempt death, walking down here. Rousing the tunnel cannibals." Her eyes become glazed and gauzy under the torchlight. "We can beg for Rolladin's mercy. We've done it before."

"Did she say cannibals?" Ryder whispers.

But my gaze is fixed on Mom. I finally realize, after the rush and adrenaline have taken their toll and left me exhausted, that Mom has no idea what we've found out. What these men's arrival even means.

And someone needs to tell her.

I unzip my backpack, careful to keep the other contents in, and dislodge the torch Phee and I used on the roof. Phee hands me our other one so I can light mine. I look at my sister. Who's going to tell Mom? Who's going to tell her that whatever demons haunt these tunnels are nothing compared to the one that rules the city?

"Mom." Phee finally takes the bait. "We've found out some things you don't know, okay? Before we go back to Rolladin, you need to hear this."

Mom looks a little shaken but doesn't back down. Not that I'd ever think she would so easily. "Fine," she tells us. "You can tell me on the walk back."

"Mom." I put my hand on her shoulder, as if I can literally transfer my sincerity, along with everything I've come to learn over the past few hours. "We can't go back. Not anymore. We can never go back to the Park again."

After she finally relents, Phee and I tell Mom everything—well, almost everything—as we continue our cautious trek downtown. We tell her about getting caught on the roof . . . stargazing. We explain about the castle and the trial. How Rolladin and her Council have lied to us, stolen our freedom. Then we tell her about Cass, and about freeing the men.

We leave out the parts about the journal, and pledging allegiance to Rolladin. And about killing the other warlord. It's not as if Phee and I have rehearsed this, but somehow we both know what boundaries not to cross, where the pressure points are in our story. There are things Mom just shouldn't know.

She embraces us, thanks God for us, stifles tears. It's a long time before she collects herself. I know she must be a mess of emotions, as I was when we found out about Rolladin's lies. And I'm sure that on some level she's livid with us for sneaking out after hours and getting caught. But when she does speak, there's no scolding, or pleas to return to the surface.

Instead, she fires off questions to the men, hushed, desperate whispers. I know this feeling all too well—this raging urge to know—I've felt it ever since I laid eyes on Mom's journal. Still, it's kind of surreal to see my *mother* the one so hungry for information.

"I don't understand," she asks Lerner in front of us. "China attacked us in '16. Manhattan was officially occupied. . . ." She turns in on herself, thinking. "By the end of '17? '18, even?"

"That's right," Lerner answers. "But by that point China had aligned itself with Russia and Korea, among others. Britain got involved right after they bombed your bridges and Ellis Island. If I recall, the EU splintered soon after that."

Mom pauses, as if she's reloading her question pistol, then fires off another round.

"Did you know?" she whispers. "Did the UK know they were keeping us on this island? That there were survivors?"

"Sam knows all of this best." Lerner tries to defer.

"I'm letting them tag along," Sam throws behind him. "That doesn't mean I've got to catch them up on the last decade." He's a good five feet in front of Mom and Lerner, scouting the tunnels with the torch he managed to steal from me.

Lerner and Mom just look at each other. "He'll come around. He always does," Lerner whispers as he and Mom traipse forward together, and Phee and I fall into lockstep with Ryder behind them. "Put it this way, the whole world knew what happened here. It sparked another world war, drove most of the globe to align with one side or the other, escalated combat from land invasions and air raids to weapons of mass destruction." Lerner pauses. "An escalation that ended us all." He looks around the tunnels. "How much do *you* know?"

Mom pauses. "Hardly anything."

"I remember it began that March of '16," Lerner says, "after a year of worldwide droughts, with trade concerns driving China to the brink. They attacked New York, DC, L.A., and San Francisco the same morning. Their plan was to take hostages, gain hold of four major American cities—"

"So how'd you learn to fight like that?" Ryder's gravelly

voice interrupts my eavesdropping, and I realize he's talking to Phee.

"What do you mean, like how'd I figure out how to use a gun?" Phee says. "I guess I taught myself."

Ryder laughs—a deep, melodic, hearty laugh. A good laugh. "No, though that was impressive. I mean how'd you learn to box?"

"Box?"

"Or fight in the street, whatever you New Yorkers are calling it now," he says. "You had some serious moves."

I try to ignore their conversation and tune back in to Mom and Lerner's, but I can't seem to do it. A thick, familiar wedge lodges itself in the base of my throat. So Ryder saw Phee in action. Of course he did: He must have been the shadowed stranger, darting away from the street-fights and back to the woods. And suddenly he no longer feels like my woodsman, but just another Phee admirer, another person floored by my sister's bravery. I feel him slipping away.

"Wait—you were there?" Phee asks. "In the Park, last night at the street-fights?" The self-satisfied grin on her face nearly becomes a third torch.

"Yeah, we were in the woods when we heard all the commotion. We snuck down to that underpass and caught some of the performance." Ryder gulps, then steals a glance at me. "What a show."

"Yeah, the street-fights happen every year at the Park census celebration," Phee says. "And they're awesome to watch for sure. But being in that ring was a whole different story." Then she promptly clarifies: "Not that I was scared—I stepped up, obviously. So wait, you were in the Park that whole night? How'd no one see you?"

"Oh, someone saw me." Ryder laughs. "Your sister over there is quite perceptive."

My cheeks become hot and flushed, but I'm pretty sure the torchlight reveals nothing.

So he *had* seen me, just as I had seen him.

I want to say something, to use the kernel of his comment to pop open a full conversation, but all I come up with is, "I thought it was you."

"Wait, Sky, you saw these guys? And didn't tell me?"

"I saw Ryder for a *second*, Phee. When I went to look, I didn't find anything. I figured . . . I figured it was just my imagination," I answer. "And you'd been through so much with the street-fights, I didn't want to bother you."

"Yeah, I guess you have a lot of false alarms." Phee shrugs, and then flashes Ryder a smile. "Once Sky *swore* there was a dragon downtown. In the stock exchange building."

"Phee, I was like eight," I say, feeling my face growing hot again. "Plus, I had just read *The Hobbit*. It kind of made sense."

"You read *The Hobbit*? At eight?" Ryder sounds impressed, and my face flushes with something new.

"I've read it a bunch of times since then, but yeah, I guess I did."

"All she does is read," Phee mutters.

I remind myself to tell her she's being a brat later.

"Where do you get your books?" Ryder presses. "I'd think that crazy lady, Rolladin, keeps everything under lock and key."

"There's a small library at the Carlyle, but most of the good books have been taken," I say. "We've found others during the summer, when we're on our own. From the libraries when Mom takes us uptown, or from scavenged apartments. Do . . . *you* read a lot?"

"Whenever I get the chance," he tells me.

Mom, Sam, and Lerner stop moving in front of us, and we catch up to them and grow quiet. Two giant forms have emerged out of the darkness. They're like the abandoned taxis on the street, but monsters, like the one in Mary Shelley's *Frankenstein*, car after car stitched together by thin cables and wires. The monster cars take up the entire width of the track.

"What are they?" I whisper.

"Subway cars." Mom skips over to me on her crutches. "People used to ride in them. This is what the tunnels were for before the war."

Her answer brings me back to her words of long ago, to the story of her journal. But now the story's leaping off those old crinkled pages. I look around, breathless. *This* is where Mom was when the Red Allies attacked. This is where she lived with Mary and me, for months. The shadows creep closer, the subway cars loom larger, and I feel my throat tightening like a lid on a jar.

"They've never seen a subway?" Lerner whispers.

"Long ago, they did," she tells him. "I've made sure they never have since."

She turns on her crutches to address our motley crew. "Listen, if we're going to keep moving, we need to trust one another. I swear there are disturbed people down here," Mom says. "We need to get out at the next stop."

"Wouldn't that be the first place your psycho leader would look for us—the stops along this 6 line?" Sam sighs. "You say there are . . . 'monsters' down here. But when's the last time anyone was actually in these tunnels to see for themselves?"

"Sam's got a point, Sarah," Lerner chimes in. "The lies this Rolladin woman was touting, it's like she has your entire city under a spell. Maybe the reason the subways are off-limits is because they're the only real way of leaving the island, since all the bridges are gone."

The men's words hang in the air for a moment, and I watch Mom fold into herself as she often does, debate with her own demons. "I've seen the monsters down here myself," she finally answers.

This is new information.

"It was a long time ago, yes. But the tunnel feeders are real." Mom pauses. "We need to find another escape route down-town."

Lerner shakes his head, his silver hair sparkling under the torchlight. "I think Sam's right on this one, Sarah. Better the devils we don't know in this case, than the devil we've met."

Phee and I exchange a look. I know my sister's think-ing about the Park's devil too, just like I am: Rolladin's lies, her assassination orders given to her warlords in Belvedere Castle. Not to mention our betrayal, our shootout in the zoo, and us flying through the Carlyle, battling teams of guards on our heels.

"Mom, we need to go with the guys on this one," Phee says what I'm thinking. "It's the only way."

Mom looks to me hopefully for backup, but I just shake my head.

"Well, I guess I'm outnumbered," she snaps. But then she takes a deep breath and grabs each of our hands. "All right. You two stay close."

We hoist ourselves onto the platform from the tracks,

one by one, passing the torches forward until our entire squad has risen. By torchlight, I can just make out the black plaque of writing on the far, white-brick wall: 68TH STREET— HUNTER COLLEGE.

As we walk past the college stop, I swear I hear a low, long wail. A soft scuffling, like pattering feet.

"Quiet," Mom whispers. She grabs my hand and motions for Phee to come closer. "You hear that?"

"I don't hear anything—," Lerner starts, but Sam shushes him.

"Listen."

It grows, moves closer to us, the tiny wail building into a full-on whimper.

"Ryder, you've got that bow?" Sam asks.

"Yeah."

"Hold it like I taught you," Sam says, as he supports Lerner on his injured side. "Get ready to take aim."

Ryder moves forward on the platform, towards the approaching noise. It has to be a feeder. Is there one? *Many?*

Phee takes her gun out of her pocket and moves to join Ryder.

"No way," Mom grabs her. "You stay here."

"Who are you?" Sam calls into the darkness. "Show yourself, or we'll shoot."

But the only thing that answers is a moan, and then a breathless panting.

"Last chance," Sam calls. "You hear me? I'm counting to three. One . . . two . . ."

And then, finally, from the darkness comes a tiny, hesitant answer:

"Are the Millers with you?"

It's Trevor.

I don't know how, but it's Trevor.

I never thought I'd be so happy to see him.

We pull him from the tracks onto the platform. He's shivering, eyes wild, spooked like he's been chased by ghosts.

"What the hell are you doing here?" Mom shakes him. "Why would you *ever* come down here alone?"

Then she gives him a tight, suffocating hug.

"I'm—I'm sorry," Trevor whimpers. Under the torchlight, I see he has a few nicks and bruises, probably from falling as he stumbled through the tunnels. What the heck did he do, follow us down here? Just hope he ran into us? I knew Trevor had a few screws loose, but I didn't think he was suicidal.

I hate to admit it, but I give him some credit.

"I woke up to all this commotion at the Carlyle, shooting and everything, and I cracked open the door. You guys were running into the street with these guys I didn't know. I got scared. . . . I thought you might be in danger."

"So what, you were going to rescue us?"

"Phee," Mom shushes me. "Let him finish."

"No—I—I didn't think I'd be able to do anything. I just thought—"

He's getting all worked up, so Mom starts stroking the top of his silky head. "Calm down, Trev, okay? I'm not mad. I just would never want you to get hurt. You're too important to me. Take a breath, tell us what happened."

He takes a deep breath. "I just thought—there goes my family. My sort-of family. I don't know what I was thinking. Lauren's going to flip when she checks my room tomorrow." He shakes his head. "I just panicked and snuck out after the whorelords. I've been trying to track you, but I couldn't keep up and I got lost and scared and—"

"Send the kid home," Sam says.

"Excuse me?" Mom answers.

"I said send the runt back to that spooky old hotel you're all penned up in. We can't handle any more kids in tow."

"This boy is practically family," Mom turns to Lerner and argues. "My best friend's his guardian, and he's got no one else." She takes another step towards him and drops her voice. "Please, I've left him before and it nearly ate me alive. I swore I'd never do it again. If he goes back now—"

"Lerner, don't even think about it," Sam jumps in. "Helping her and her kids was one thing—"

"You keep calling us *kids*," I say. "But we're not much younger than you—"

"—but turning into a traveling day care is another. This one goes home. Or game over. We leave them behind."

I meet Trevor's stare, and he mouths me a silent, *Sorry*. I shake my head. I still don't know how he managed to find us. He's already come so far, it's just so unfair to turn him back around. Not to mention he'll probably get caught sneaking back into the Carlyle, and he'll be punished for sure. Whippings, definitely jail time.

Plus, as much as I can't stand the kid when he's around, the possibility of never seeing him again really bothers me. No more late-night street-fight reenactments in our Carlyle room as Mom and Lauren shush us. No more gossip sessions during midday meals.

The thought brings me back to the last time Sky and I were in the fields with Trev, actually. How he was selling himself as this tough guy of the slaughterhouses. Maybe Trev's bragging wasn't totally pointless. 'Cause for as one-way as Sam is, he's obviously not stupid—he knows how to survive. I've just gotta convince him that Trev will help, not hurt, our cause.

It's a long shot, clearly.

"We could use him," I say cautiously to Sam. "You lost a buddy, in the zoo, right? And if we're traveling by boat, we'll need a good team. Far as I see it, we need as many able bodies as we can get."

"He'll just be another mouth to feed," Sam snaps.

"Yeah, but he can help with food, too. He's resourceful," I lie through my teeth. Trev's a lot of things, but resourceful ain't one of them. "He knows how to skin an animal, and he's one of the best young hunters in the Park. Even though he looks small, he's strong. And we're going to need a strong crew."

Sam studies Trevor but keeps his face unreadable. It's the first time he's not wearing some scowl or smirk, though, so I know we're making progress.

"Come on, Sam," Ryder says slowly. "He's a kid. And he's all alone."

Sam's face changes for a split second—looks more like Ryder's, softer or something. But by the time he grabs the bow, it passes. "There's being a Good Samaritan," he mumbles to Ryder, "and then there's just being dumb."

But he doesn't fight us anymore. He just breathes this big put-on sigh and starts walking into the tunnels.

Ryder shoots me a smile, then follows his brother. But the smile sets something off inside me, a warm buzz that runs from my shoulders to my fingertips.

"One thing's for sure, Phoenix-of-mine," Mom throws her arm around my waist. "At least one of us is resourceful."

We get back to trekking downtown. The plan is to take what Mom calls the 6 line all the way to city hall, wherever that is exactly, and then wait for the right time, make our way to the surface, and regroup at our summer place on Wall Street. Sam was pushing to head straight into Brooklyn through the tunnels to board his boat. But since Mom thinks staying underground that long is way too dangerous, and since she and Lerner will need some care anyway, we settle on making a stop on the surface.

I don't say this out loud, but I'm relieved. The idea of just getting on a boat and leaving everything, and everyone, we know panics me. I know this might sound lame, but I'm not ready to leave this city . . . or I don't want to. I know Sky's all set on finding this perfect paradise, but as far as I'm concerned, we've already got one.

But I don't argue now. It's not worth it. At this point, we need to take one step at a time, and save the fight for when we get downtown. *If* we get downtown.

The college stop becomes 58th Street, then 51st, then 42nd. Our two torches are down to stubs, and by now, I'm basically sleepwalking. Sky and I have been up all day and night by this point—it has to be almost dawn—and I'm dying to sit down. Just rest for a little bit . . . even an hour'd make a difference. But out of the crowd, I'm not going to be the one who admits I'm tired first. Forget it.

Trevor's been yapping in our ears since we found him. Asking us how we escaped, and why, and who are these guys who talk so weird, and where are we going to go if Rolladin's after us, and, and, and. I'm so tired I think I might actually clock him, but Sky and Ryder both humor him.

"So. England, you said, right?"

"Right," Ryder answers him. "We sailed across the sea for the New World and all that. Pity the natives were just as unfriendly this time around."

My sister gives him a little knowing laugh, but I don't get what's funny. And for some reason, it bothers me that Sky does.

"What's England like?" Trevor presses. "And why'd you want to leave?"

Ryder laughs. "It's sort of complicated."

"I can do complicated," Trevor says.

Ryder looks at Sky, then me, like we might know some way to save him. I shrug, wishing I had an answer for him. Trev's relentless, and I know from personal experience that every dodged question just leads to two more.

"Our . . . family situation changed, after the attacks on England," Ryder says slowly. "So Sam found his way home. . . ."

"From where?"

"From where he was camping out in Dover, with what was left of the British Armed Forces. Sam's the one who thought it was best if we moved on, started over. Too many ghosts in the graveyard called London." Ryder clears his throat. "Anyway, Sam hooked up with Lerner and his mate on the long road home. After fixing my Dad's boat and stock-piling supplies, the four of us set sail this past summer for the City of Dreams." Ryder flashes us a grin under the torchlight.

I study Ryder's face in the shadows of the tunnels. He's not "pretty cute," as I thought when I first took a good look at him out of the castle window. He's—gag me for using a phrase from one of Sky's girly novels—*devastatingly hand-some*. Jaw strong enough to cut wood, nice even features. Plus, he's about three inches taller than me. I like him. I mean, I like his look. I'm suddenly very conscious of my own presence, and I stand a little straighter.

"But why'd you pick New York?" Trevor keeps up with his twenty questions. "I mean, you must have known about the POW camp and everything, or at least your brother must've. Why sail into Red Allies territory?"

Oh God, here we go again. No one tells you that having a secret comes with so much responsibility to spread it around. And so we tear the blind from Trev's eyes, tell him what a fat, fat liar Rolladin's been, how there's no one guard-ing Manhattan anymore. He takes it pretty hard, which I sort of feel bad about. But on the plus side, the shock of it finally shuts him up.

We pass 33rd Street, then 28th, then 23rd, all the stops marked in white type against a thin black board, a taunt-ing little white 6 in a green circle. Will they never end? I don't know the whole 6 line, but I'm sure that after 1st Street, there's still the mess of Soho and Chinatown, and then the Financial District. I'm almost tempted to blurt out, *Isn't anyone else exhausted?!* when Lerner stumbles into Sam in front of us.

"Whoa, whoa, easy, man." Sam holds Lerner up by his shoulders. "How's the leg?" Sam kneels down to get a good look at Lerner's wounded calf with the last of one of the torches.

"Not too good," Lerner admits. As I get closer, I see that all the scraps of clothes wrapped around his calf are soaked through, and his forehead is caked in sweat.

Mom leans on me before bending over her crutches to examine the damage.

"I need to get off it for a minute," Lerner says.

"Mom, you've gotta rest too," I say. Even though she's been trying to pretend she's okay, I know she's hurting. She's been wincing since 33rd Street.

But Mom doesn't answer, just looks at Ryder. "Can you and Sam carry him?"

"Lady, come *on*," Sam spits. "You've gotta give up these horror stories, all right? Ryder and I aren't carrying him through the subways. That's ridiculous."

"It's far from ridiculous. Lerner, I'm so sorry you're hurt." Mom looks at him. "And on our account, no less. But we need to keep moving—"

"See what happens when you give somebody an inch?" Sam tells Ryder. He waves the stumpy torch into the black pit ahead of us. "There's another train car down the tracks. We'll camp in there for an hour, elevate Lerner's leg, and all take a rest. Then, and only then, do we go—no debates. Come on, man."

He puts his arm around Lerner's shoulders, takes the bulk of his buddy's weight onto his own, and guides him forward.

LEE KELLY

"You don't believe me about the tunnel feeders either, do you?" Mom asks Ryder.

Ryder looks at Sky, then me, then Trevor. "I don't know," he finally says.

"Right. How could you?" Mom says. Her eyes are pinched by the past again.

"I know my brother's tough to deal with," Ryder says slowly. "Trust me, I do more than anyone. But Sam knows what he's talking about. Lerner can't walk on that leg any longer, you saw it. Plus, you should take care of yourself, too." He gives my mom a cautious smile. "I promise, I'll get us moving soon."

We form a human ladder, each of us scrambling up and through the broken windows of the abandoned subway car. The car is empty, the space heavy with the stench of old air. We use the torches to get situated. Lerner lies down in the middle, with his leg propped against some useless silver pole in the center of the room, while Sam takes off Lerner's old bandages and rips some more of his own shirt to make new ones. Sky and I set Mom up on a stretch of orange seats that border the subway car, and elevate her leg with Sky's backpack. Then we spread out on our own beds of plastic chairs. We finally blow out the last of our light to save it for the rest of our trek. A rusty, heavy stench of blood and sweat overpowers the car, but nothing could keep me from sleep at this point.

It's weird—I rarely dream. When I do, it's just a mixed-up replay of things that happened the day before. But tonight it's different. It's not a story, not the telling of some elaborate fairy tale, like Sky says sometimes happens to her. It's weird, trippy pictures. Fear, mixed with hungry rumblings. Squeals that seem to jump out from corners and lodge themselves in my ear.

Then I realize I'm not dreaming.

A wild roar erupts from the center of the car.

"My leg!" Lerner howls.

"What the—"

Before I can even think, I'm thrust against the back of the subway car. There're footsteps all around me, gurgles, cackles, and then I'm off my feet, being pulled in two directions.

"Sky! Mom!"

"Phoenix, Skyler, where are you?" Mom cries from the dark. "Where are you?"

Dank breath on my face. Rough hands in my hair.

"Mom!" I scream. "Mom, please!"

"Get this fucking thing off me!" Lerner's screaming, but I can't see him. I can't see anyone.

But I feel roaming hands writhe around me like an army of snakes.

"Mom!" I thrash my arms and legs, trying to break free of whoever, whatever, has ahold of me, but I can't. "Let me— ahhh!" I scream, pain stabbing me in the side.

A snapped match punctures the dark of the train.

I'm surrounded.

By three feeders.

Three real, live feeders.

Feeders that are about to feed on me.

I look up in terror, my eyes scrambling to find Mom, Sky, Trevor—

But I only see four more feeders climbing through the windows. An army of pale faces, snaked and matted hair. Sweat-soaked rags.

The match goes out.

Sky, then Mom, screams my name. *Do they see me? Can they help me?*

"Somebody help!" I call out desperately, so desperately I don't recognize the sound of my voice. But it's not me. It can't be me. I'm somewhere else, actually dreaming.

One of the feeders whispers in my ear, a soft purr, "Shhhhh. This won't hurt."

"Someone PLEASE!"

"Ryder, take the ones on Phoenix!"

Another spark. The light blinds my captors for a second. In that second, Ryder slices a pair of arrows through the two monsters on my left.

Without thinking, I grab my gun from my pocket, shove off the safety, and fire it right into the temple of the third feeder attached to my other side. Warm blood soaks my sleeve and splatters the car.

"RUUUN!" Sam bellows.

"Girls, Trevor, the windows—jump!"

As we move, one, two, five feeders pour into the subway car from the platform side of the car. We fling ourselves through the opposite windows and fall onto a set of tracks below.

"Mom." I can't see anything. "Sky!" I reach out, arms thrashing, like I'm possessed.

"It's okay." Ryder's gravelly voice is in my ear, his arms around me, and for a second, I feel safe. "It's all right, I've got you."

"Where's my mom?"

"Phoenix, I'm here. Sky—Trevor?!"

"I've got Trevor, we're here," Sky answers.

"Where's Lerner?" The darkness takes on the voice of Sam. "Lerner!"

No answer.

"Ryder, quick, the matches," Sam whispers.

Another spark.

There's all of us—all of us except Lerner.

We look back to the subway car, now full of hungry cannibals. And they're crawling through the bashed-open windows on our side, worming through the cracks. Coming for us.

"We can't leave without him!" Sam says.

"They have him, Sam." Ryder's shaking his head as Sam's match burns out. "I'm sorry."

Sam takes a second to recover. "Sarah, give me those crutches. Get in the middle. Everyone support her. We'll move faster." He lights a torch and passes it to Mom with shaky hands. "Link up," he says. "Let's go."

We fling ourselves away from the subway car, a messy chain of hands, stumbling, breaking, attaching and reattaching in the dark.

We run and run until my side is burning.

Until my feet are numb from the pounding against the tracks.

And just when I think we're done for, when I think we're going to die here, in this pit of crazies, in this hellhole of darkness—

A puddle of dawn appears like a mirage on the platform.

We scramble towards the light, propelling Mom forward. We climb onto the platform and over the subway gates, trip up the steps slick with fresh drizzle. The open air greets us, a fierce breeze pummels us with rain, but I don't think I've ever been so grateful to see daylight. We hear groans and rumblings somewhere beneath us—the bright white of morning should stop the feeders, blind them for a moment— and we cross a wide, abandoned Avenue of the Americas, hopscotch around taxis frozen in time to reach the other side.

"Where are we?" Sam calls behind him as he shields his head from the piercing rain.

Mom cranes her neck around. "Fourteenth and Sixth Avenue. We must have crossed tracks to the L line. Phee, are you all right?"

Mom stops to inspect my sister, pulls up her sweatshirt, and takes a look at her new wound. There's a superficial cut that runs about three inches down her left side. Even though it doesn't look too deep, she'll have to be bandaged.

"We need to get you patched up," Mom says, reading my mind. "You okay?"

Phee just whispers, "I think so."

Mom kisses the top of her head. "Come on, we have to get out of sight."

Mom hobbles with us down half a block, then scrambles

up a set of cracked cement stairs. She shakes a set of glass double doors, begging them to open, but they don't budge.

"A gym? You want to hole up in a gym?" Sam pushes. "There're a thousand flats to choose from. Pick one, any one—"

"There'll be medical kits in here, splints, bandages. And there's a lot of us." Mom scans the building, then peers down the narrow alley that hugs its far side. "This means more room, a better vantage point. Plus, apartments are hit or miss. Trust me, I know."

Mom puts one hand on the rusted railing, and her other on my shoulder. She limps back down the stairs, grabs her crutches from Sam and lurches over to a pile of debris littering the abandoned back lot. She carefully leans down, picks up an old rusted pipe, and points it at Sam. "You've got to break a window."

"Are you crazy?" Sam says. "Those monsters could already be out of the tunnels and hear us. No, we move on."

Phee shakes her head and starts walking towards Sam. I know that look in her eye.

"Phee, wait—"

"No, Sky, I'm sick of this," she says. "Last time we did it your way, *Sam*, it cost your buddy his life and I nearly got a bite taken out of my stomach. So I say we go with my mom on this one."

Phee's pulled her gun out and points it right at Sam, of course taking it too far. The weapon might have one bullet left in it, but my sister was never one for details.

I barely can follow what happens next, it's so fast. In a flash, Sam has Phee's arms pinned behind her back with one hand and holds her gun in his other.

Mom and I both lurch forward. "Phee!"

"Sam," Ryder says. "Come on, man. Easy!"

Sam grips my sister against his chest, hard, and my heart kicks up once again. I can't believe it has any fight left in it.

"Lerner wasn't my fault," Sam says to Phee. "I did what I should have. I got him bandaged. I made him rest. . . . I . . . I followed protocol." He takes a long, deep breath. "A man's injured, that's what you do."

Phee shakes her head, and her long, tangled hair splashes Sam in the face. "Whatever to protocol," she says. "You need to start listening to my mom, or we're all going to die."

Sam releases her, pushes her forward, and Phee clutches her side. Sam pauses, clearly thinking twice, before he carefully hands her gun back to her.

"Why not move on?" he repeats.

"Because Phee and I need a med kit." Mom walks back through the rain-slick alley, where a row of closed windows just beg to be broken. "And from the looks of it, this place hasn't been touched in fifteen years. It's the perfect place to wait out the weather."

Sam punctures a window with three quick jabs of the steel rod, and we hoist one another up and take turns crawling through the opening and inside to a dark, musty lobby. Then Sam and Ryder pick up a large bureau and move it in front of the broken window, a makeshift door to a makeshift home. Dripping wet, we cross the checkerboard-tile expanse of the lobby, past a wide desk with empty chairs, and then under a red-letter sign that reads YMCA. We climb two flights of stairs and emerge on the third floor.

"The yoga studios should have candles." Mom slowly combs the wide layout, checking the signage of each glass door that borders the open floor, as Phee and I flank her on both sides.

The main space looks like a graveyard of headless, strange dinosaur skeletons, arranged in row after row. Some tall and hunched, like pictures I've seen of T. rexes in books; some small and tight, as if they once ran fast and close to the ground. "What are all these things?"

"Workout equipment. StairMasters, ellipticals, bikes." Mom points to a glass door. "Bingo."

We lead her into the small room, with a wood-paneled floor and lush red velvet curtains painted in dust. Sam lights a long row of white candles in the center of the room, while Trevor starts digging through the open cupboards on the far wall. He pulls out some black foam mats and tattered blankets. "I think I could sleep for a year," he says, before splaying out on the ground.

"Don't get too comfortable," Sam mutters, as he curls into a ball on the floor next to Trevor. "Those Park twats are on the hunt for us. We move at nightfall."

"Says the guy in the fetal position." Phee moves to plunk down as well, but Mom and I grab hold of her arms.

"Not yet," Mom tells her. "We need to get you bandaged up."

"You ladies need any help with anything?" Ryder's voice echoes against the wood. And I feel an unexpected, jealous surge—does he want to help because of Phee?

"Actually, Ryder," Mom says, "we should take advantage of this rain. I'm sure there're buckets and old water jugs in the storage closets we passed. Can you guys take care of it? Sky, come with me."

Ryder nods. "Sam and I are on it."

Sam starts muttering obscenities in the corner, but he gets up.

"Aren't you forgetting someone?" Trevor moves from corpse state to standing in about two seconds. "I've gotta do my part too."

I watch Ryder stifle a smile. "Of course, man. We were counting on it."

My sister's practically falling asleep as we clean her wound with the treated gauze Mom dug out of an old first aid kit. But after our collective nightmare, I don't know how Phee could even think about sleeping. Every time I close my eyes, I see split-open faces, an army of warlords on our heels, or worse, hungry tunnel feeders.

I watch Mom rummage through the kit attached to the wall. She pulls out a cardboard box with a sorry-looking man clutching his head on the front of it.

"Mom," I say.

"Mmm." She opens the box and unravels a long flesh-colored dressing.

"In the subways," I say softly, "you said you saw the feeders in the tunnels before, personally. I don't understand."

She doesn't look at me as she pulls apart the bandage, but I take it as good a sign as any to continue.

"I always thought the feeders were lost people, traitors who stayed underground after the city's official surrender—holdouts who never came up to the surface again."

"That's right." But she doesn't give me anything more.

"So . . ." I struggle with how to phrase my next question. "So, what were you doing down in the tunnels after Manhattan surrendered?"

She keeps her mouth in a tight, thin line as she wraps the gauze around Phee's middle, then gives me the same to wrap around her other side.

"Not too tight," Phee grunts, eyes closed.

I let my hands wind round and round, helping Mom, playing nurse, but I don't take my eyes off my mother. She must feel it, my desperation for her to just let me in, to tell me what she keeps hidden. Secrets are spilling out of this city, emerging from the shadows, rising from the ground—and I'm tempting hers, begging hers to join them.

"I was lying to the Englishmen." She doesn't look at me.

"Mom—"

"Not lying, really. Just bluffing. I knew the stories. I knew some people who had tried to escape the Park years ago, who'd gone into the tunnels and came back with the fear of God in them. I knew the feeders were real. And I didn't want to risk our safety for a shortcut." She pats Phee's side gently and then pulls down her sweatshirt to cover the dressing. "There."

Mom's smiling, but it's hollow. And I don't know how I know, but I do. She's lying, or *bluffing*, to me. She's keeping something, something dark and terrible, from me.

"Mom, please—"

"Stay with your sister a minute, okay?" she says as she walks to the windows.

And that's it. My own window to the past is closed before I find a way to prop it open. "Sometimes you have to lie to survive, Sky," Mom adds behind her. "I hope you'll understand why I did what I did. One day."

And then she joins Sam, Ryder, and Trevor as they arrange buckets on the fire escape to capture the rain.

I toss and turn for hours, even though I know I need to rest. Even though my muscles are aching, quaking, *pleading* with my mind to just stop working for a moment so they can truly relax. But I can't. My conversation with Mom has me so anxious to figure out the missing pieces of her story that I'm tempted to pull out her journal and start reading it right here in the yoga room.

A collective wheeze whispers through the room. The candles have been blown out, and the only light that remains is a small sliver that sneaks through the velvet curtains. Phee's snoring softly next to me, and I wonder if I should wake her up again, or if that's too cruel, especially considering all that we've been through. Any normal person would be sleeping. So I grab my backpack, tiptoe over the field of bodies, and slip out the glass door.

Filled water buckets now line the entryway to the yoga room. I pull a small canteen out of my backpack and tip over one of the buckets to fill it. I take long, luxurious gulps as I navigate through the dinosaur field, or "workout" room, then settle against a far window and pull out the journal.

I look at the *Charlotte's Web* cover for a long time. I feel guilty moving forward without Phee, even though I can't wait to jump in.

I settle on reading until there's something I know we should share together. I crack open the pages, and the morning light pours across Mom's words.

*I hear creaks, noises underground, and
I think he and Robert are around the corner,
coming for us. Sometimes I even trick myself into
thinking Tom's cologne is wafting through the
subways.*

Other days I know Tom must be dead.

*But I won't let myself feel it. Otherwise I know it
would be the final straw, and I'll crumble. And Sky
needs me.*

*April 25—The pains returned again, but this time
with a vengeance. Dry heaves and aches and
pains and a headache that knocked me sideways.
And I knew it, I knew it so deeply and tragically
that I started wailing.*

"I'm pregnant," I told Mary.

Pregnant. *Phee.*

Phee and I always knew she was born during the war, but
not . . . in the tunnels. Not when bombs were being dropped
above and people were living in the dark, cold shadows of
the city, on rats and borrowed time. I close my eyes and
picture Mom, without Dad, with Mary, with one baby and
another on the way. And even though I know the ending
to this story—that Mom survived, is sleeping and snoring
in the next room—I'm still terrified of what happened in
between.

I know I should stop reading, should tuck the journal
back into my bag and wait for my sister. Phee should read
this. This is her story too.

But the past has me under its spell, keeps my eyes

LEE KELLY

transfixed and my hands wrapped protectively around the journal. And I don't resist.

I *can't* resist.

> *I didn't want to tell her, but in the dark Mary and I have come to share everything, and it's scary how much I need her.*
>
> *I couldn't breathe after I said it. Me, with two. Her, with none. Mary. Strong, wonderful, beautiful Mary. For a moment, I wondered if her husband ever knew her like I'd come to know her. If Jim ever saw what I have seen.*
>
> *"What do we do?" I whispered. "I need him, Mary. I need to find Tom."*
>
> *She didn't say anything for a long time, just stroked my hair, hugged me and Sky towards her, and rubbed my belly tenderly.*
>
> *Finally she answered me, her voice as faint as rain on the surface, "We'll figure out a way."*

> *May 5—I'm lying down after a night of celebration, if you want to call it that. The tunnels for the first time feel festive, hopeful, though the day started out in a panic.*
>
> *Early in the morning, somewhere between First Avenue and the crossover to Brooklyn on the L line, we woke to the pitter-patter of their footsteps on the tracks. Three people, maybe four. Was it other survivors? We listened.*
>
> *Then we heard the harsh, strident sounds of foreign tongues. The smacking of boots.*

Soldiers.

Mrs. Warbler, one of the cursed vacationers from Kansas, just started rocking and mumbling, "This is our end."

"We're never going to make it," Bronwyn sobbed into her hands.

I wrapped my arm around her shoulders and pulled her in, as Sky swatted Bronwyn's matted blond hair from my lap. Bronwyn's somehow become my charge in this dark underworld, where the lines between stranger and family, right and wrong, have been erased. She doesn't have anyone else.

But Mary has no time for the girl. She snapped at Bronwyn to keep quiet. There were still a lot of us, she said. And we knew these tunnels. "We might not all make it out of this alive," Mary added, "but we sacrifice for the greater good."

We quickly dispersed and perched ourselves like long rows of gargoyles on the platform above the tracks. The front row of our crew was armed with knives, flashlights, Sky's stroller, and a few other Bugaboos and UPPAbaby Vistas from other moms who've joined our doomed crew. Mary wouldn't let me anywhere near the front line.

As the soldiers approached, our crowd blinded them with the last of our light, then converged on them like a swarm of hungry roaches. Jumping them, beating them senseless. One, two shots went off. We lost another survivor and then another from the shots.

But the soldiers were dead, and there was cause for celebration.

We now have uniforms, and guns.

A young orphan, Lory, and her little toddler shadow, Cass, immediately started playing with the guns—the hand-me-down toys of this lost next generation. But Mary yanked the weapons away from them. Then she dislodged the bullets, put them into her pocket, and addressed the crowd.

"Like everything," Mary said, "we ration."

I don't understand how she's doing it, how she's managing to lead us and stay so calm, so strong. But I'm proud of her.

June 5—New York has settled into summer, and the heat has invited itself into the tunnels, pushed its way down here to make us all that much more uncomfortable. Sweat is a constant, above my lip, on my forehead and back, paints me with my own clothing, until by night I'm mummified.

But I barely have to lift a finger. Mary always makes sure Sky and I are fed first, holds my hand through the pain, sleeps by my side in case Sky and I start crying in the night. We've become a ragtag family, a patchwork quilt of the scraps of who we were before. And though I'm grateful for Mary, beyond belief, it's not enough. My need to see Tom, to know he's okay, has begun to plague me like a fever.

"Where is he? Where could he and Robert be?"

"We've been over this a hundred times, Sarah."

Mary shook her head under the soft candlelight,

*and odd shadows were thrown against the dank
tunnel walls. "You said they were working at the
studio. But Chelsea's a wreck—the Piers have been
blown to pieces."*

*I didn't let myself process that. "Tom and Robert
could've been on the subways, like us—trapped on
the 1 or 2 lines."*

*"You know we've been over there, and nothing.
If they're alive, they've moved on by now. We
can't chase ghosts, Sarah. Look at this group, the
number of people. Every one of them has someone
missing. There're far, far too many ghosts to chase."
She dropped her voice to a low whisper, so that
those sleeping nearby couldn't hear us. "Right now,
you and I, we're in a good position. We're in charge.
But it's so fragile, can't you see that? We need to
think of the group. I don't want to give anyone
reason to question my priorities."*

*She used "me" and "we" interchangeably, and for
some reason, it unexpectedly warmed me.*

*"Just promise me, when we can, we'll look for
them again," I whispered.*

"Of course."

*July 4—Independence Day. But the sounds above
weren't fireworks. They were air raids. Land raids.
Bombs.*

*We've been trapped under here for four months.
I can't believe there are still so many of us left,
over a hundred wandering the tunnels as a unit.
Scavenging the surface, hunting rats, sharing*

water, and swapping food and supplies. Mary has kept us alive.

There've been dissensions, of course. Small fights and brawls. Two or three people, usually the younger ones, who think they have a better answer, who curse Mary and disappear into the tunnels to fend for themselves. Or the ones who work her from the inside, the fragile ones like Bronwyn, who fear everything, who question everyone, who still wait for someone to save us.

But in general, we've become a well-oiled machine that hums along steadily in the dark. I try to be a cog, do my part, not ask questions. Though sometimes the old me bubbles to the surface, and I cry and I scream and I'm so angry I can't see.

"Lie down," Mary often says. "You need to think about that baby."

I can't believe I'm bringing another person into this world.

August 4 (or 5)—I've started to lose count of the days. The heat arrested all of us, and we lay around on the tracks just trying to breathe, a thick swamp of survivors.

Mary and I were next to each other, with Sky between us, sharing a jug of water.

Mary had her hand on my belly and was stroking it, carefully, cautiously. And I knew I shouldn't have asked, but I did.

"Are you ever going to try again?" I whispered. "I mean if, when, we ever get out of here."

"No."

Mary was quiet for a long time. Then she told me that after her third miscarriage, Jim told her that she must be doing something wrong. "That on some level," she said softly, "I must not want it badly enough."

Her breathing was heavy, loaded.

"Mary."

"Jim was drunk. But I knew he meant it," she said. "He never loved me. Not in the way I needed, anyway. I know that now."

I rarely saw her soft underbelly anymore, and it scared me. She'd become our fearless leader, our resourceful commander in the dark.

She grabbed my hand. "Being down here with you, it's awakened something inside me. Like my whole life I was supposed to be someone else."

I thought about what she said. It wasn't news. I knew, for a long time, how unhappy Mary was.

"Do you ever think things happen for a reason?" she whispered again. "That we're given second chances?"

Her words were full and promising, almost visible against the dark. They floated towards me like those soft dandelions on my parents' farm in Iowa. The ones we'd blow on to make wishes.

I couldn't see Mary's face, but somehow I could sense her tears, could tell that she was inches from me, with Sky and my stomach pressed between us.

Then I felt the softest of pressure against my lips, and I sighed. It felt wrong and yet so wonderfully

right. The tunnels faded away, as did the thick
moat of bodies lying around me. And the only
thing that ran through my mind was, I knew this
was coming. And I wanted it. I couldn't do this
without her.

> *Tom, please, if you're out there . . . If it's*
> *possible—forgive me.*

I can't believe what I've just read. My face, my hands, my
whole *body* is on fire, yet I force myself back over the flames
and reread the last passage:

. . . against my lips . . . I sighed . . . I wanted it.

Mom cheated on Dad. With his *sister*, no less—Mom
cheated on Dad.

I knew this book would contain secrets, things that
might change how I see my mom, her world, her place in it—
but not this. A twisted knot of anger lodges itself right in my
throat, and no matter how I try to sugarcoat what I've dis-
covered, I can't swallow it. How could Mom have done this?

And how can I *ever* see her the same way again?

I want to talk to her. I want her to explain this away and
show me how this was possible. No, how it was *right*. These
pages couldn't have captured everything. There has to be an
explanation.

But I know I can't go to her, not now, not when I'm in the
trenches of her past. Not when I'm peering in judgment
over its casualties.

Besides, at this point, I'm covered in lies and deceit
myself.

I take a deep breath and do the only thing I can do.

I keep reading.

September—There's no use pretending I know what day it is. It feels like September, in my belly, in my bones. That's what we're all whispering. That we survived the heat wave of August and lost only a handful. That we've got a few cool autumn months ahead. That we're fortunate.

And in a small, bizarre, unfettered way, I do feel fortunate. Mary and I have become something. Something undefinable. Something we shouldn't be, of course I know that. Am I falling in love with her? Is this love? Is this need? I'm not sure. When you inch through life as we're inching, you're desperate for something deep and grand. You cling to feelings like this, nurture and feed them, let them pull you up and out of yourself.

Sometimes at night we lie in the dark and hold each other. Sometimes . . . it's more, and it feels as if the dark has stolen our borders and we've merged into each other.

When the sheen of immediacy dulls, when I think about Tom, about what I'm doing, the guilt drives me to madness. But a small, self-preserving voice inside me keeps whispering that I need this: Save yourself. Whatever it takes. Save yourself.

"Can't sleep?"

"Oh my God!" I jump, bang my elbow against the window-sill, and glance up to find Ryder perched over me.

"Sorry, didn't mean to scare you."

"No, it's my fault. I'm jumpy. Too wrapped up in this, I guess." I quickly close the journal and wave *Charlotte's Web* in front of him, then immediately wish I hadn't. I curse myself for picking the spider over *Great Expectations* back in Mom's old apartment. "What are you doing up?" I say, trying to divert his attention. I shove the journal back into my knapsack, trying to bury Mom's words—*I sighed . . . I wanted it*—and chase her out of my head.

"I couldn't sleep either." Ryder takes a seat opposite me in front of the window. "I was sick a lot, on the boat ride over here. Guess I've gotten used to being up around the clock."

He smiles at me, but it's a sad smile, one that hides things I bet I'd like to know more about. But maybe I shouldn't pry. "I know how that goes," is all I say.

"What, getting sick on a boat?" he teases.

I laugh. "No, battling insomnia." I look out the window for a moment, at the street below us frozen in time. "I hope I get the chance to be seasick, though," I say, allowing the possibility of a world outside this city to warm me once more. "I hope we get out of here."

He gives me a flash of that hollow smile again.

"I'm sorry," I add. "About Lerner."

"Thanks. I didn't know him very well, though," Ryder says. "He was my brother's mate. Sam met him and Frank— the one who didn't survive the zoo prisons—on his trek back from Dover."

"Well . . . I'm sorry just the same."

Ryder doesn't say anything for a long time.

"Your mom was right." He finally breaks our silence. "Sam and I couldn't believe it. There're . . . *monsters* on this island. The world has turned men into monsters."

"Mom's warned us about tunnel feeders since we were little," I say slowly, "but I'd never seen one before today.

That I remember, anyway." I close my eyes and they appear again. The ravaged, hungry cannibals, loose packs of wolves roaming the dark, hunting us, hurting Phee. I try to shake off the images.

"What do you call the monster of the Park?" he says softly.

"Who? You mean Rolladin?"

Ryder nods, then leans in. The stark white sky catches his hazel eyes and turns them into gold. "What kind of monster can brainwash an entire island into thinking the war's still going on?"

"Manhattan's not brainwashed," I say, snappier than I would've liked. I take a deep breath. Why am I getting so defensive about Manhattan? I sound like Phee or something. "I mean, you just don't understand how it works here. Rolladin's been our only window to the outside world for a long time. She's run the Park since the island became an occupation zone and the Red Allies started withdrawing. People just don't . . . *question* her. And even though she's warden, the prisoners still think of her as one of their own. They'd never think she'd betray them."

"But what happened to the whole American way?" he sputters. "Democracy? Checks and balances?"

I give a choked laugh, surprised that he knows anything about US history. He can't be much older than I am.

"Well, we devolved into a monarchy," I answer, testing the waters. "A true kingdom in the Park."

He smiles again, this time wide and uncompromised, and I see that it's a little off center—lopsided. Contagious. "I guess every country goes through its 'Queen' period."

"Some longer than others."

"Touché. But I don't identify with Britain pre-Parliament,"

Ryder says. "Or post-Parliament, for that matter. The country really went to pot when Parliament disbanded. I prefer fictional governments, mostly."

"Oh really?"

"Really. *Atlas Shrugged*, *1984*—"

"*Animal Farm*," I add, getting a little more excited.

"Oh, *Animal Farm*'s a classic."

I can't contain my enthusiasm when I ask, "So you really do read a lot?"

"Every book I can get my hands on."

"Even textbooks?"

"I'm a textbook *junkie*," he says.

And I just might have found my soul mate.

"Not just history," I say, still not believing that this beautiful boy in front of me prefers to spend his time reading old textbooks from a forgotten world. "I'm talking biology, chemistry, physics—"

He stares at me straight-faced. "Prentice Hall is a god."

And I can't help but burst out laughing. "What do you do, scavenge libraries?"

"Universities, mostly. But I went to school for years before Britain bit the bullet. Almost graduated year eight and everything."

"Year eight." I match the grin he's now wearing, and will my mind to keep working overtime, to pull out all the shreds of the past I've managed to stitch together from books and papers. I have this desperate need to show him what I know, even as the world forgets it. "Not quite high school, but you were clearly going places. Your parents must be so proud."

I'm the slightest bit horrified when his eyes start watering.

Sam and Ryder obviously came over here alone. Why did I just mention parents?

"Ryder, I'm sorry—God, I didn't mean to say anything wrong."

"Not your fault." He turns away from me, towards the dusty pane. And my skin feels like it's on fire, as if this is what I get for flying too close to the sun.

"It's just—" He lets his words hang between us for a while. "My mum was the big reading advocate. She'd still walk me to school every morning, even with England's shelter-in-place. Still kept rallying for textbooks, even after the city declared a state of emergency. Petitioning until there was nothing, and no one, left to petition." He gives me one of those lopsided smiles again, but it doesn't strong-arm his sadness. "I miss her, is all."

"I'm so sorry, Ryder."

I want to ask him so many questions. I want him to share whatever happened to his mom, to his family, to *him* . . . with me. I want him to trust me.

I want him to like me.

Before second-guessing myself, I whisper, "We've lost a parent too. My dad. I mean it was a long time ago, obviously. And I don't remember him, so I know it's not the same."

I look at Ryder for a second, trying to judge his reaction, but he keeps his face neutral.

"So it's not like I miss him, but—I miss him *for* my mom, if that makes any sense. I wish she had someone, so she didn't have to raise us without him. It's—it's a hole in her I wish I could fill."

I know I'm reaching, blubbering on about secondhand pain, when Ryder's is real, immediate. He must think I'm

LEE KELLY

clueless. Insensitive—a self-centered little girl on a sheltered island.

"That's exactly what it feels like," he whispers. "A hole."

"You don't have to talk about it, if you don't want to—"

"It's okay," he whispers to the window. "Mum was beautiful. Smart as a whip, strong, rebellious. She took the state of emergency as a guideline. And when the bombing finally died down, after everything was in pieces and survivors started leaving to see what was left of the mainland, we'd go on these *tours* . . . walks through London's bones to make sure I didn't forget the past."

Ryder's story pinches me with something: longing . . . maybe even jealousy. I picture him with his mother, walking through the skeleton of a foreign city, her whispering well-kept secrets, giving him the gift of a dying world. Secrets Phee and I needed to figure out for ourselves. Secrets we needed to steal a journal to uncover. On cue, Mom's mantra springs from a well-worn river in my mind: *Sometimes the past should stay in the past.*

"Was it just the two of you?"

Ryder nods. "My dad was deployed early on, not long after Britain joined the war effort," he says. "When he died, Sam just . . . *changed*. He closed up. It became all about joining the marines, going to war, moving on. He was out the door way before he actually went to Dover for training."

"So you just had your mom."

"And she just had me." Ryder rubs his eyes. "You ever look backward and wonder how you missed something?" He laughs a different laugh—this one's bitter and sharp. "I can't believe I didn't see what was going on, having a mom scream at police, and holler and run through minefields. A morn who took me on walking tours of a bombed-out city. I just thought it was us . . . being explorers. A game. Our own private world."

A wave of tingles hits me, right at the top of my spine. I think I know where this is going.

"Sam put all the pieces together for me, after, when he finally came home. Things must have deteriorated without her medicine, he told me—Sam hadn't even known about her diagnosis, until he checked the cabinets. He told me it wasn't our fault. That it wasn't even her at the end, just sadness and mania." Ryder turns to me. "But it still drives *me* mad, that I didn't see it. Our last conversation plays on replay in my mind, over and over. Mum saying she couldn't handle it. That she couldn't see her baby wither away."

I want to say—*do*—so many things. I have an uncontrollable urge to grab Ryder, hold him, but I force my hands to stay where they are. All I can do is ask, "When?"

"She was depressed for a couple years after the last of the London air raids. She took . . . her life last summer. Carved a hole right out of me." He runs his fingers along the windowsill. "Sam pretends his isn't there. Sam just keeps . . . fighting, like he can avenge her and Dad. Like he can somehow . . . escape all of it, if we just keep moving forward."

"I'm so sorry, Ryder," I say again. "I can't imagine what that must have been like."

"I can't either," he says. "Not really. It's almost like . . . like I shut that Ryder down. I didn't understand." His voice is controlled, even, like he's reciting from a script, speaking for someone else. "I couldn't accept it, so I didn't. I just locked it away."

What he's said makes me think again of my own mom—

how she keeps her pain in an airless jar, preserved but inaccessible. "But you and Sam must talk about her?"

"We don't talk like that." Ryder shrugs. "There's stuff we just can't say to each other."

I nod, even though I wouldn't survive if I didn't talk about something like that with Phee.

"It actually feels really good saying this stuff out loud," he says, "just to hear it. To remind myself it's real." Ryder looks at me, as if only now realizing that I'm not just a reflection, a character in a therapeutic dream. "The more I see, the more I think that I just can't make sense of any of it. The world's a mess, right? Death, destruction, lies." Then he gives another bitter laugh. "And now cannibals."

I nod again, knowing I should tell him we should get some rest, and end the conversation. But he's touched on something I just can't nod my head and agree with, especially the more I learn about what really happened here, to Mom and everyone else in this city. And despite the fact that I know I might isolate Ryder, upset him to the point of no return, I say, "You don't really believe that, do you?"

"What?"

"That the world is just some random, messed-up place?" I break his gaze, a flush starting to crawl over my cheeks. "People make choices, and those choices add up to the world we see. Nothing's random . . . nothing's *senseless*." I can feel my eyes start to pinch as they do when I get emotional, and so I turn my face away from his, embarrassed. "And right or wrong, what we do—our choices—matter."

Of course, I know my world's been small. A couple of square miles, tops. Less than five hundred people. A few momentary glimpses into other worlds—some real, some fabricated—worlds of good and evil, heroes and monsters. But I know, deep in my heart I *know*, that things can't just be written off as the product of chance, no rhyme or reason to any of it. "And I think you believe that, too," I finally add, no more than a whisper.

Ryder doesn't say anything for a long time.

I think I've ruined it, whatever "it" is, the beginnings of a friendship, or maybe more, all with my big, fat, self-righteous mouth. How do I know what he believes in, really? Because I have a hunch? Because, through this warm cocoon of a conversation, I feel like I actually know him?

He doesn't want to hear my theories, least of all when he's so fragile.

But then, slowly, an off-center grin breaks across his face.

"I knew I was going to like you," he says, "Skyler Miller."

Skylah Millah.

My ears feel like they're on fire, and my face must be crimson by now.

Ryder changes the subject. We get back to books—thrillers this time.

Horror stories.

Even some romances he begrudgingly admits he's read.

We talk until the rain comes down so hard, the highways become rivers. I don't remember falling asleep against the window. The last thing I remember is debating *The Great Gatsby* versus *Gone with the Wind*.

The rain keeps us cooped up inside all day—but it doesn't bother me, since I'm so tired and beat up, all I want to do is sleep for a week. Plus, these black mats and blankets in the yoga room are somehow more comfy than our sinking bed at the Carlyle. Not that I've been thinking much about the Park since we got out of the tunnels.

I've been trying not to, anyway.

The thing is, I know Rolladin's a liar. And I know we can't go back to the Park, not anytime soon anyway. But that doesn't mean I want to hop on a boat and sail into the wild blue yonder. Ryder and Sam came over here looking for answers, they said so themselves. So what's to say the rest of the world isn't worse off than Manhattan? What's to say we can't all make a better go of it here? Eventually make peace with Rolladin, after this killing-her-guard thing blows over?

I look around at our sleeping crew. I know I'm the only one who feels this way. Well, besides Trev, of course. But having his support in this crowd is about as worthless as a dollar on Wall Street.

We all get up by midafternoon. Mom lights the long row of candles in the yoga room, and we crowd around the fire-light, debating, trying to figure out our next move. Sam says we're heading south to Bermuda, since the rest of America's in shambles. But Mom's pushing to try the "Midwest," and Sky and Ryder are giggling like fools, throwing out options like Narnia and Middle Earth, wherever the heck those are. After a while, I can't stand that they're giggling together, so I plop my yoga mat right in between them. Sky shoots me this look that says, *Seriously?* But I just ignore her. Ryder's warm, smells like leaves and daytime, and his face is so close that I kind of shut down for a little.

Pretty soon everyone's stomachs join the debate, and in no time, the whole yoga room's one big growl. At least we all agree we've got to eat before we move on, since Sky's scraps from the Carlyle are long gone and we'll need some strength to keep moving. We settle on sending scouts to the streets for food tomorrow morning, whether it's raining or not. Trevor and I will take the Brits, since I'm a good shot and I sold Trevor as this big-time hunting ace in the tunnels. And Sky and Mom will stay behind to man the fort, since my sister wouldn't know what to do with a wild animal, and Mom's ankle is still pretty busted.

We get up before the sun the next morning. Ryder quietly shakes me and Trevor awake, as Sam slips out of the yoga room. I empty my backpack for storage, throw it over my shoulders, and tiptoe out with the guys. But I make sure I don't wake Mom and Sky—I just can't handle another round of *Be careful*s.

The four of us grab jackets from the YMCA closet, and then we climb out of our makeshift door. We hit the alley just as the gray sky's pulling dawn out of its pocket.

"Anywhere but east," Sam says as he peers out to Sixth Avenue. "No way we're tempting those subway cannibals again. And I'm sure that Rolladin bitch is trailing the 6 line— she knows our boat's at the Brooklyn Yard." He places his bow on the ground and loads it with arrows faster than I can blink.

"Let's ask the natives for recommendations." Ryder nudges me in the ribs. "Phee, Trev, what are the West Side's best options for fine dining?"

My face gets all hot when Ryder looks at me. 'Cause I dreamed about him last night, and like I said, I rarely dream. All through the night, too—his strong jaw, his jet-black hair. His hazel eyes that almost look yellow in the daylight. Now I feel like I'm wearing a sign, HEY, I LIKE YOU! and I can't figure out how to take it off.

"What's wrong with you?" Trev asks.

I shake my head. "Nothing."

I close my eyes to focus, try to picture the hand-drawn city maps Mom, Sky, and I would use when we'd search for our own game during the summer on Wall Street. One's no doubt tucked into the bottom of Sky's backpack, and I curse myself for not thinking to bring it. "Our best option's probably some form of game along the river parks. Squirrels, pigeons. Plus occasional deer, peafowl, monkeys, that've wandered down from Central Park."

I open my eyes. Sam and Ryder are looking at me like I've lost it.

"Come again?" Ryder asks carefully, just as Sam repeats, "Monkeys?"

"Warden Rolladin overbred all the zoo animals for food," Trevor says. "Now she lets them run wild to fend for themselves."

I nod. "Sometimes we've found peacocks as far south as Wall Street."

Ryder gives me a big, lopsided smile. "A true concrete jungle."

"And besides the game," I add, now gunning for another smile from him, "there should be some plants and grass, too."

Sam fiddles with the bow. "Where are these parks you're talking about?"

"I'm pretty sure there's some stretches of grass along the Hudson up here," I say. "We'll have a better chance of finding food there than in the streets."

"All right." Sam throws the crossbow over his shoulder, then waves us back towards the small parking lot. "Let's try the Hudson."

We cross town, hug tight to the storefronts, all shattered windows and angry black spray paint. At first Ryder and Sam are obsessed with checking out each store, like maybe someone's been magically stocking the shelves the past decade. One of them stops to look in an old bodega, while the other pops into a bookstore. And Trev gets caught up in the scavenger hunt too, crazy-excited since he's never been south of 58th Street. He keeps coming back with all these odds and ends, begging for some of my backpack real estate.

"Guys, come on, this is a waste of time."

They finally abandon the lost cause, and then we start making progress, the numbered avenues falling away along with the storefronts. Finally it's just a stretch of road that dumps us into a thick, six-lane street called the West Side Highway. We cut around car after abandoned car until we reach the small stretch of pavement near the Hudson River, and the thin slice of grass sandwiched in between.

"You call this a park?" Sam hisses.

"I didn't promise rolling fields," I snap, feeling defensive and sort of dumb in front of Ryder. "We can't go back north, and you said we can't go east, and all the parks till Wall Street—the ones that weren't blown up, anyway—are made of pavement. So, yeah, this is what we've got."

"Easy, everybody." Ryder points past me, to where the walkway loops around a cluster of buildings. "Maybe the stretches of grass widen out as the trail runs downtown."

"They better." Sam starts trotting south towards the buildings. "Stay here," he calls back to us. "I'll check it out."

Ryder leans against a skinny tree as Trev collapses Indian-style on the coarse grass below us.

"Sam's kind of a boss," Trev says.

I plunk down next to him. "Trev, that's Ryder's brother. Don't be an ass," I say, even though I'm thinking the same thing.

Ryder just laughs. "It's okay. Trevor's right. Older brothers can be like that."

"I guess." Trev's studying the grass, so I can't really see his face, but he doesn't sound like himself. His voice is as small and hard as a pebble. "I mean, I wouldn't know."

Ryder looks at me before settling on Trevor's other side. "No siblings, then?"

"No siblings, no parents," Trevor says with a sigh. "No friends, really, but Lauren, and the Millers, when they come back for the winter."

My stomach churns a little bit as I watch Trevor pull out the grass in ratty clumps. I try not to think about Trev during the summers. It just makes me feel guilty, picturing him without me around to get his back, without Mom and

Sky listening to him babble. Even with Lauren looking out for him, he has to get pretty damn lonely. But what were we supposed to do? Orphans stay in the Park. Plus, we couldn't afford another mouth to feed. Especially a loud one.

So I say, "Stop feeling sorry for yourself. You've got friends. You're fine."

It comes out a lot harsher than I wanted it to.

"Either way," Ryder covers for me, "us orphans'll have to stick together."

Trev doesn't answer, but as he keeps ripping the grass new bald spots, a little smile escapes his lips. And I get this crazy impulse to hug Ryder, or kiss him or something, for saying that.

But then Sam jogs towards us, and the moment's gone.

"All right, the trail does open up ahead." Sam takes big gulps of air as he collects himself. "There's even some trees, some bushes and stuff, a ways down."

The jerkoff acts like this is some big discovery. "So, basically, you'd call it a *park*?"

But Sam doesn't say *Sorry*, or *Yeah, Phee, you were right*, or anything else that would make me forget about wanting to punch him. He just gives me a blood-boiling smirk as Ryder, Trev, and I scramble to stand.

The four of us begin traipsing south. We march down the pavement path, eyes on the hunt, hands on our weapons, as the sun throws its arms around the city.

"Are we near your summer place on Wall Street?" Ryder asks as we pass a squat, colorless building marked NEW YORK SANITATION.

"We're not too far. But we never come up this way." I shrug. "Mom likes us to stay close to home base."

"So while Trevor's in the Park all summer, you three really brave the city on your own?" Ryder scans the sad, empty trail that cuts downtown ahead of us. "Seems like it'd be almost impossible outside the Park."

I think about all our summers on Wall Street—Mom and I hunting in the Financial District, Sky and I learning the herbs in Mom's garden. "It wasn't too bad," I say. "We just had to find our own food sources, like we're doing now. After a while, there wasn't anything useful in apartments and stores and stuff. We scavenged as kids, but it became a lost cause eventually."

Ryder looks shocked. "So, for the past few years you've just lived on squirrels and peacocks?"

"Rye, they're still here, aren't they?" Sam says as he readjusts his bow. And I could be imagining things, but I swear it sounds like he's impressed. "Not everyone needs three-course meals and a library to survive."

Ryder shakes his head. "I'm just saying, zoo cuisine's not a balanced diet for two growing girls."

I laugh. "We ate more than squirrels and peacocks. Our summer apartment had a roof garden. We've got crops that come up every year, and we add each time we get our hands on seeds at the Park."

"Couldn't have been an easy way to live, though. Just the three of you," Ryder says.

"Nope."

"Then why do it?"

Trev laughs behind us. "I've asked myself the same question, like, a million times."

I have too. Even though I love our place along the water, I've sometimes wished for the Park so bad it hurt. Like when it snowed in April, or rained so hard in June that our little farm was nearly flooded.

"The Red Allies only forced everyone to the Park for the winters, 'cause of the land and animals and timber and everything," I tell them. "Mom said she wanted the summers to be ours. That we deserved a taste of freedom. So even though it's tougher on our own sometimes, Mom feels like it's worth it."

Ryder studies me with wide, probing eyes. Then he asks softly, "Do *you*?"

His question jars me, 'cause I've never thought about it—that was just the way it was. But now I try to consider both sides—what we'd be doing at the Park right now if we weren't hunting game along the Hudson. Maybe waking up, warm in our tiny Carlyle room, getting ready to pick crops in the shock-cold air. Then I think about Wall Street—our summer kingdom of three. All those lazy days of lying in the sun with Sky in our roof garden . . . all those long nights of freaky noises outside our walls. A kingdom every bit as awesome as it was terrifying.

I want to explain all this to Ryder: that the answer is messy, that I haven't let myself sort it all out, 'cause no good would come of the sorting. Plus, I don't want him writing me off as some Manhattan savage, especially compared to my brainiac sister.

But like always, I can't find the right words. And I've got to settle for, "I don't know."

I'm waiting for Sam to grunt or make a crack at such a lame answer, but he doesn't.

In fact, no one speaks for a long, long time.

"I get that," Ryder finally says as he flashes me this big,

awesome smile. And his voice is full and knowing, like I've said something important. It warms me even more than his smile and pretty face. "There aren't many straightforward answers anymore. Are there?"

Sam grabs Ryder's arm to slow him on his other side. Then he whispers, "Quiet." He points to a bunch of scraggly trees a stone's throw down the path, then steps onto the grass and crouches behind some bushes. "Get down, guys."

Ryder, Trev, and I all crawl behind Sam and follow his gaze. A family of squirrels runs up, down, and around the near-bare branches of the trees, frantic little figure eights one after another. I focus and count. Six squirrels. Jackpot. With these and some mushrooms, and if we're lucky, some herbs, it's a stew to feed all of us.

"A gun might be better," Sam whispers. "You've got extra ammo for yours, right?" he says to me.

I clutch the small handgun in my pocket. The little pistol with one measly bullet. And even though by now I should probably just trust this guy and come clean about my lack of replacements—at this point, we're all in this together—it still feels safer to lie.

"I left the other rounds with Sky," I tell Sam. "Sorry. Guess it needs to be the bow."

Sam mutters to himself and then looks at Trevor. "What about you, the big-time hunting prodigy? Where's your weapon?"

Trev gulps. "I don't have one."

"Naturally." Sam rubs his forehead and sighs. "So basically, this was just a kiddie field trip."

My heart starts rumbling into fight mode again—I've helped Mom hunt and held my own in the Park for as long as I can remember, and this jerkoff's been dismissing me since I saved his ass in the zoo.

"Call me a kid one more time and we're going to have problems. Seriously, what are you, like, twenty or something? And what have you actually *done*, besides gotten us in trouble in the tunnels and taken up a mat at the YMCA?"

Sam stares me down.

"She's got a point," Ryder answers. When Sam glares at him, Ryder just shrugs and says, "What? Step up and show us that fancy marine training you're always bragging about, or knock the insults."

Trev nudges me in the ribs as we stay silent behind them. But Trev's mouth is twitching, and his eyes are all big and animated, like we've somehow stumbled on a secret street-fight no one else knows about. I totally feel that way too. But there's something else going on under my skin, that same urge I had before—to grab Ryder, and hug him or something. I somehow manage to keep my hands on the ground.

"Fine," Sam mutters. "Watch and learn." He repositions himself on his stomach, with his forearm propping up the bow and his eye resting in the scope. He scoots forward, army-style, so his head's peeking out of the bushes.

He waits a long time—watching the squirrels, fluff and fur parading round and round the trees. I almost lose interest, until he whispers, "Now."

His arrow slices through the air, stapling two squirrels against the trunk with one shot, one's tail and another's face pinned to the bark.

The rest of the family scatters in a frenzy, jumping to the nearby branches as Sam gets ready to fire off another arrow. He's quick this time and catches one of the squirrels in midair. Two shots, three squirrels.

I can't pretend I'm not impressed.

The four of us scurry over to our victims, and Sam takes Sky's knife and finishes off the squirrels. He shoves the carcasses into my satchel.

"Good morning," I say to Sam breathlessly, before I remember I hate him.

And for the first time since I've met him, Sam looks up and gives me a real honest-to-God smile. "I'd say a pretty damn good morning."

Phee, Ryder, Trevor, and Sam burst back into the YMCA like they're soldiers returning home from a glorious battle, with good cheer, a satchel full of squirrels, and Phee's pockets bursting with mushrooms. Mom and I abandon our card game in the workout room and walk to our makeshift door as soon as we hear them.

Mom brings the mushrooms into the stark white light near the window to double-check Phee's work, even though Phee and I are both near experts at distinguishing edible mushrooms from poisonous ones. Phee just rolls her eyes.

"Half the time I feel like she can't believe anything good can happen," she whispers to me. It's not an unfair statement.

Speaking of Mom and her lack of faith in a better future, I really want to pull Phee aside, to let her know what I've found out from the journal. But before I can, Ryder says, "Phee, we need to get these squirrelies in a pot, before the natives get too restless."

Then he grabs Phee's backpack of carcasses and throws it over his shoulder, as my sister cackles and follows him. Ryder throws me a wink before he climbs the stairs, but it doesn't stop my stomach from sinking.

To be honest, I've been driving myself insane most of the morning, thinking about the two of them together. Imagining that Ryder was so awed by my tough-as-nails sister that by the time they returned, our conversation yesterday would feel like no more than a dream. But seeing them all chummy still stings more than I could ever have prepared myself for.

"You guys need any help cleaning them?" I swallow my pride and mumble after them.

"Nah, Ryder and I've got this," Phee says quickly over the stairwell.

"But we'll need candles, and bowls," Ryder calls down. "Trev, help the woman!"

Sam trails his brother—"Rye, hold up, let me skin them first"—but Mom gently grabs Sam's wrist over the banister.

"Sam, seriously, thank you." It's sweet, but almost uncomfortable, watching my mother thank someone genuinely: She doesn't do it often. Then again, she doesn't need to. "You deserve a rest. Leave this part to me—there's a kitchen on the fourth floor. I'll make a true stew over a fire."

Then Mom shoots me a look, reminding me that I'm supposed to feel grateful, instead of consumed by jealousy.

"Thanks, Sam," I muster.

"No big deal." But I can see the faintest hint of a rare smile on his lips. Sam throws his arms over his head, revealing two inches of lean torso, and yawns his way to the yoga room. "Wake me up when it's ready, I guess."

Mom slowly follows my sister and Ryder upstairs, while Trev grabs my hand to collect some candles.

"So did you have fun? With Phee, Sam, and Ryder?"

"Yeah, it was a good trip," Trev says. "Sam's okay, kind of a jerk, but I think he just doesn't know how to *not* be a jerk, if that makes sense. And Ryder's beyond cool. He's an orphan too and everything. And he's really . . . *accepting*.

Just . . . nice." Trev shakes his head as he piles candles into his arms. "I was kind of hoping he wasn't so nice."

I laugh. "Why?" I take a wicker basket off one of the shelves and load Trevor's candles into it.

"Because then it'd be easier to hate him."

His words pinch me as we return to the main workout room. And I ask the question, even though I'm pretty sure I know his answer: "And why do you want to hate him?"

Trev's face twists into a grimace. "'Cause Phee's crazy about him." Sometimes Trevor's more mature than I would ever give him credit for.

Trev shakes his head. "At least he's nice. At least he'll be good to her." He looks at me. "We should get upstairs, right? They're waiting on us."

But I can't move my feet. Even though my mind knows that Trevor's analysis hasn't changed anything, my heart feels like something monumental has shifted. "I'll be right there." I hand him the basket, and he shrugs and bounds up the stairs.

So Phee likes Ryder too. Of course she does.

If I'm honest, I've known this for days. I knew it in the tunnels, and saw it in that look Phee flashed me last night in the yoga room, when she literally inserted herself between Ryder and me. Then this afternoon on the stairs as she took them two at a time—this *possessiveness*, this claim to him— *Ryder belongs to Phee*, just like everything else in this city.

And even though part of me is itching to barge into the kitchen, pull a Phee and just plunk myself in between them . . . I turn away from the stairwell. Then I tiptoe back into the dark of the yoga room and dig Mom's journal out of my bag.

I feel like a kid again. Jealous, overshadowed, sneaking off into corners to escape into other worlds, where younger sisters aren't always the heroes or the belles of the ball.

The most frustrating part is, I thought it was different with Ryder. I thought for some reason we had connected yesterday, and for the first time maybe ever, I could give someone something that my sister could not.

I wade through the equipment room and situate myself near my favorite window in the corner, *Charlotte* smiling up at me from my lap. I know I shouldn't be reading this, making this trip through Mom's past alone—it's just not fair. Once is one thing. To keep sneaking off by myself, without Phee, quite another.

But I also feel like she deserves it.

Right before I crack the spine open, there's a musical whisper—

"There you are," Ryder says as he hovers over me. "I was looking for you."

"Hi," I say, unable to contain my surprise. "What are you doing here?"

"You're quite taken with *Charlotte*, aren't you?" He smirks and sits across from me, each of us mirror images of our yesterday selves.

"She gives sage advice, what can I say." I flash Ryder a smile before I remember I'm kind of confused by him. "But really, what are you doing here? What about Phee?"

He looks at me strangely. "What *about* Phee?"

"I thought you were busy cleaning your spoils together or something," I mutter, unable to prevent bitterness from seeping into my voice.

"Your sister can handle it." Ryder grins. "Plus, Trevor

showed up as I was leaving. And he was all too willing to lend a hand."

Now I can't help but match his smile. "Phee's never going to forgive you for that."

"Well, I thought Trevor might appreciate it at least." He laughs. "He's a good kid, isn't he? Sounds like he's had it rougher than most."

Ryder's words warm me, gravitate me towards him like a sun. I've always hated that Trevor floated through the Park for half the year alone, with no one but Lauren to anchor him. Having a guy like Ryder around who cares, who gets him, would be just as good for Trevor as it would be for us. "You're right," I say. "He has."

Ryder pauses before breaking into another grin, and starts mining through the pocket of his jacket. "I got you a gift today, on the road."

"What—like an extra squirrel or something?"

"No, I'm not a caveman." He laughs. "I picked it up from the rubble. Your sister nearly killed us for all our detours, but when I found a quarter-full Barnes and Noble, I couldn't resist. I thought everything would've been burned by now."

"We must be a lot more civilized on this side of the Atlantic," I tease him.

"Yes, you and that Rolladin troop are the pillars of etiquette."

"Oh, come on, don't lump us together like that."

He pulls what he's hiding in his jacket forward with a great flourish and presents it to me with a bowed head. "A classic for your collection."

I look at the front cover. A tired-eyed soldier stares back at me, the title *Waverley* written in looping handwriting.

"It's about England," Ryder says. "A young English soldier. Some say it's the first real historical novel."

"Thank you," I whisper.

"I think the blending of the two is the most exciting. History with poetry, fact with fiction. Sometimes I find the story aspect truer than the truth, if that makes any sense."

Ryder's brow is stitched, almost like he's nervous about how I'm going to react. I don't know how to tell him how much this book means to me. That he thought of *me* when he was away. How his words just now echoed a part of me I don't share with anyone. How I kind of want to kiss him. All I say is, "I feel the same way."

"Anyway, the first fifty pages or something are a bore—but get past it. I promise you, it's worth it."

My hands wrap around the book so tightly my knuckles turn white. "I love it."

"Well," he says mischievously, "maybe now you can finally retire that spider."

I watch him carefully, filled with a sudden compulsion to tell him what I really have in my hands. He's been honest and open with me. But can I trust him? Or worse, will he think I'm terrible for stealing something so personal from someone I love, not to mention lying about it?

"Ryder," I say slowly, taking the risk. "This isn't *Charlotte's Web*."

I open the handwritten pages and turn the book around to show him the mad, frantic scrawls of ink across the page.

"What is it?" he whispers.

"It's—it's a journal. It belonged to my mom, before the war." I look up at him for a moment but quickly break under the pressure of his gaze. "We were in her old apartment a few days ago, and I saw it and took it. Mom keeps all these memories hidden away inside. Jeez, the *journal* was even hidden inside a safe. It'd kill her if she knew we have it."

"Then why'd you do it?"

My lips start trembling, and I know I'm about to cry. "I just wanted to know her, in a way she'll never let us, since she's locked so much of herself away. When I read it, I feel like we're talking to her. And she's saying all the things she wants to say but can't."

A stray tear runs down the side of my face, and I wipe it away quickly. I definitely don't want Ryder thinking I'm this soft, fragile girl, especially after he spent the morning hunting with my sister the Spartan. "But I'm probably saying that to make myself feel better."

"Doesn't make it any less true," Ryder whispers.

I laugh a little, and in a brutal act of betrayal, my eyes spill more tears. Ryder reaches out and holds my hand.

Before I can say anything else, Mom's voice is calling down to us, echoing through the linoleum-tiled hallways and bouncing over the carpeted floor. "Sky, Ryder—I need people to set the table!"

Ryder and I look at each other for a long time before he stands and helps me up. We don't say a word as we navigate through the cemetery of workout equipment. It's only once we climb the stairs, and the thick scent of stew envelops us, that Ryder whispers, "You seek the truth, and meaning, Skyler. Never think that's a bad thing."

Then he squeezes my hand before he drops it, and he walks into the kitchen. I immediately want more from him.

But I take a deep breath, shrug off one hunger in favor of another, and follow him to set our table.

I finally get some alone time with Phee the next day, since Sam and Ryder are hunting for supplies and food for our journey, and Trevor's roped Mom into watching him play tennis against a wall on Level B—Tennis & Pool. Mom felt bad about leaving us alone upstairs, but I told her that Phee and I could use the time together. That it's been awhile since we caught up.

I wasn't lying, technically.

"I didn't even know you had that thing," Phee says incredulously, once I tell her that I read Mom's journal yesterday. "What'd you do, go back to the Carlyle roof?"

"I had to," I say. "We couldn't lose this."

She nods, as if she's agreeing with me, but her eyes stay wide. "That was really dangerous."

"Well, there was no other choice." I wave the book at her. "These secrets? The past? It would've been lost forever. We never would've known."

"No, I get it," she whispers. She carefully picks the book up from my lap. "So you've been reading it, alone?"

"Just once." It's not untrue, though I know it easily could've been. "It was when we first got here, and I couldn't sleep." I watch her scan the book, flip the marked pages carefully, as if there might be a hidden symbol, or a clue, that I could've missed. "I'm sorry I did that."

"It's okay." But Phee looks at me with eyes that want to say more. I'm desperate to say more too. For most of our lives, Phee and I have been each other's worlds—we've barely been apart for longer than a hunt since I've been old enough to remember. And yet, sitting here, just the two of us, feels awkward—as if now there's a library of unsaid things between us. As if now that our world's been broken open and strangers have stepped inside, we somehow don't recognize each other, or know what to say.

I want to address the weirdness. Despite how mad, or envious, I am at Phee's attempts to claim Ryder, I'm sick over the idea of not knowing how to bridge this gap. But before I can figure out how, Phee bulldozes in with, "So catch me up."

I relax a little. And I force myself to get excited again about the journal.

"You're never going to believe this." I check behind me and across the workout room for any signs of Mom and Trevor, but we're alone. "But Mom was pregnant with you in the *tunnels*. And this Mary woman? She wasn't just Dad's sister. She was caring for her. She was Mom's—" I pause here. My enthusiasm falls away, and I'm suddenly very conscious that I'm talking about our own mother, not a book character.

"Mom's what?" Phee prods.

"Mom's—lover."

"WHAT?"

"Shh. She could be coming up any minute."

"Wait—you mean like they were a couple? Mom cheated on Dad?"

"Yeah. It's completely insane, right?" I wait for Phee's outrage, her shock, her anger, the same wild roller coaster of emotions I had felt before Ryder had gratefully whisked me away.

"She was alone," Phee finally whispers. "All alone in the tunnels, with a baby, and another on the way. She must've thought Dad was dead. She must've thought it was the only way to survive. Oh man—can you imagine?"

Now I'm the one who's shocked. "Wait, so you think this is *fine?*"

"Not fine but—understandable."

"Understandable to cheat on Dad?"

"Sky, honestly, we don't even know the guy."

This is just like Phee, to erase all the boundaries between right and wrong, to rationalize whatever's thrown at her. But right now, her annoying pragmatism, her *refusal* to judge, bothers me so much that I almost want to scream.

"But it was Dad's *sister*. You heard that, right?"

"I know, but—"

"What if it was me? What if I was married"—I immediately think again about Ryder, which causes my face to break out in hives of embarrassment—"and you couldn't find me? You think I'd be okay with you shacking up with my husband?" My voice keeps rising, even though I'm trying to whisper. "Because I'm not. I mean I wouldn't be. I hope you know that."

"But Sky, this isn't about you and me," she says, so forcefully she surprises both of us.

We stare at each other, daring the other to speak first.

"Is it?" Phee finally adds.

And this is my chance to say something, to tell her that, *Yes, there is something about you and me that isn't right. That feels like it's dying.*

"No, obviously." I try to regroup and get back to the book. "Anyway, Mom's pregnancy with you wasn't going so easy in the tunnels," I mumble to the journal, my voice still shaking from our tension, trembling, preparing to pounce. "That's where I left off."

We position ourselves against the window without another word.

*September—One of our surface scouts, Lauren,
came back with news. Huge news. Potentially life-
changing news.*

*"We found missionaries on the surface, while
we were in Whole Foods," the once well-dressed
woman from the subways started sputtering.
Lauren wore a dead soldier's uniform, and it
hung loosely on her frame. "They came from the
West Side, and they're caring for people in the
subways. The missionaries told us there's going to
be some kind of . . . of convention down here, for
survivors. From the 1 line, the 2, the F train, the
R line . . ."*

*The 1 and 2 trains. The lines Tom and Robert
would've used to get to the studio.*

*"There're still other groups of scavengers hiding
in the subways, and in the city—"*

"Lauren, cut to the chase," Mary barked.

*"Tomorrow, at noon," she answered breathlessly,
"every group's going to send a representative to
the tracks at the West Fourth subway stop, on the
uptown E train track. With a list of names of their
survivors, and who they're looking for. Don't you
see? My son—your daughters and husbands and
sisters and brothers—might be out there!"*

*The crowd fell into disarray, shouts and
laughter and tears. Lauren whispered stories about
her son to the Kansas women, Bronwyn prayed to
God for her boyfriend from NYU.*

*But I only had eyes for Mary, to see what she
was thinking.*

Hope. Tom. Our lives. Tom and Robert could be out there. My God, they could be out there.

I grabbed Mary's hand and tried to get her to look at me, to share what she was thinking, but she shrugged me off and talked over the crowd.

"We don't know who these people are. They could be lying."

Lauren shook her head. "This is real. We need to meet them. I promised—"

The crowd turned in to itself again, whispering, arguing, until Mary finally shouted, "Enough. All right. I'll go. As our leader, it should be me."

And even though the possibility of finding Tom had my nerves electrified, my stomach plummeted. "Wait, Mary, no. Send someone else, it's too dangerous."

"You can't go alone, Mary," Mrs. Warbler agreed.

"Fine. I'll take someone with me. Sarah, rip a page from your book. Pass it around. We all write our names and our missing loved ones next to them tonight."

September—I'm a mess. Vomiting, dry heaving, shakes. I can no longer stand without feeling dizzy. Lauren is kindly taking care of Sky as I lie here, sick and sobbing, on makeshift bed rest in the corner. Mary and Dave must be at West 4th Street by now, determining our fate. Figuring out who's left. God, I hope she's safe. I hope Tom's safe.

I'm terrified.

My feelings are warring inside me, guilt and

anger and longing. If Tom's alive, have I ruined everything?

September—The next day Mary stumbled back to us covered in blood. Alone.

I wanted to rush to her, but I was cemented to the ground.

"What happened?"

"Who hurt you?"

"Where's Dave?"

Mary just shook her head and collapsed as the crowd swarmed around her.

"They killed him. They almost killed me," she whispered.

Lauren gasped and clutched Sky to her. "That can't be. They promised, they seemed like us. Trustworthy—oh God, Mary, I'm so sorry."

Mary motioned for water, and one of the young orphans, Lory, opened a jug and brought it to her.

"The E-train summit started out calmly enough, reading and comparing names, asking one another how we've been surviving. But the lists revealed nothing. There weren't any matches."

She rolled onto her side to rest and moaned from the pain. "I did find out a little. The enemy is headquartered in Central Park. It's dispatching its ground forces from there. The Lower East Side, the Piers, most of Chelsea and the Villages, are gone." She exhaled. "As Dave and I were heading back home, they jumped us. They stole our weapons, they finished Dave off. You see what's left of me."

The crowd helped clean Mary's wounds. No one spoke as we retreated into our dark corners and relinquished the hope that we had secured without credit.

Late into the night, Mary finally came to me. I wanted to comfort her. I wanted to tell her that I'd take care of her now, that at least she was safe.

But I couldn't. First I needed to know.

"You said the E-train summit compared lists, before they hurt you," I pressed her, my voice cracking from disuse. "Did you ask about Tom and Robert? Did anyone know them?"

It was a long time before she said anything. "They weren't on any list, Sarah."

I shrugged off her answer. "Then they made it to the studio," I said matter-of-factly. "We could send someone up, to the surface—"

"Sarah," she interrupted as she rubbed her fight wounds with alcohol. "I'm sorry, baby, but I need you to give up chasing Tom's ghost. Robert's art studio is in Chelsea. In shambles. Wrecked. Sarah, they didn't survive."

"But—" I let the word hang there, like bait on a hook, prayed that I'd catch something, anything. A glimmer of hope. A concession.

"Sarah. It's time to let them go," Mary told me softly. But firmly. "It's time to face reality. It's time to let them go."

It was a long time before either of us moved. Finally I turned away from her.

I got on my hands and knees and crawled.

Nothing, no one, could soothe me as I cried. Sky
must have wiggled away from Lauren and
scrambled beside me, mimicking me, wailing, until
I pulled her in and hugged her fiercely, our tears
running together.

Mom. Tough, stoic . . . *fragile* . . . Mom. I'm crying as I listen to her, young and broken in the belly of a dying city. All my judgment and my anger about her and Mary fall away. And just like all those years ago, I want to run to Mom and bury my head in her shoulder.

"It's okay," Phee says. Her hand snaps forward, reaching for me like a reflex, but then it retreats back to her side. "This was a long time ago, Sky. Mom's okay."

I wipe my nose on my sleeve. "Right."

October—I'm not human anymore.

I'm just bodily functions and urges. Eat, throw
up, bleed, cry. Mary is beyond worried. And the
whispers—all I hear is the whispers.

"Hemorrhaging."

"Hyperemesis."

"She won't make it, not without a doctor."

I try not to listen as I slip in and out of
consciousness.

October—"We're getting you to the surface," Mary
said, and I realized I was being carried on a wide
life raft of some sort, a makeshift stretcher.

"Where's Sky?" I mumbled. I didn't know how
long I'd been out.

"She's with Lauren and Bronwyn. She's safe, baby. We're leaving the tunnels."

"Mary, no—" I struggled to get the words out. "Not on my account. They'll kill us up there."

She grabbed my hand. "I put it to a vote. People are tired of hiding. We can't do this forever." She leaned in and stroked my hair as the crowd carried me forward. "I can't live without you, and you and the baby will die down here. We're surrendering."

"Everyone?" I managed.

"No, not everyone. Only those who are smart. Those who can fend for themselves. Survival of the fittest."

I couldn't help but smile. It might have been my first one in weeks. "I'm hardly the fittest."

"Well," she said, kissing me as I was propelled forward. "The fittest and those they love."

They carried me on the stretcher, like an offering, and we emerged out of the tunnels and into the light, blinded, stumbling around like drugged animals towards the fields. I got down and leaned against Mary, and slowly, we walked forward. Bronwyn brought Sky to me, and I clutched her like a doll.

Light, oh how I missed you.

Grass.

Air.

Food.

Rich smells saturated the air—meat, boiling vegetables. Blood and sweat.

The smells wafted over the Park, through the

rows of tents and huts that were built by our
invaders.

"Put your hands in the air," Mary ordered the
crowd.

We raised our arms, walked slowly, showed
our attackers that we were coming in peace. But
that didn't stop the foreign tongues thrashing at
the sky, the cocked rifles. The team of soldiers that
surrounded us, yelling, barking, thrusting their
weapons into our faces.

"Please," Mary said. "We come to surrender.
Woman. With Child. Please."

She took out her Central Park Zoo volunteer
keys and dangled them. "Surrender. You lock us up,
take care of us."

We were ushered into the heart of the Park, to
be given to the mercy of those who could make
these kinds of decisions. A short man shadowed
by a large general's cap approached us with a thin
young interpreter right on his heels.

The general ran through a litany of foreign
syllables, harsh alien words that snapped and bit
at our ears.

Then the interpreter spoke. "The general has
heard your plea. He accepts on his terms."

Mary gave a choked, nervous laugh. "His terms?"

The general grabbed the keys from Mary,
grunting and smiling at them. He nodded to the
team of soldiers behind him.

"His terms are women and children," the
interpreter said.

"Wait, I said we have a woman with child—"

The interpreter interrupted Mary, barked to the platoon behind him in his native tongue, and then we were separated and herded, the women and children pushed to one side, the men to the other.

The general moved up close to Mary, so that he was inches from her face. "What is your name, woman?"

Of course he spoke English himself.

"Mary," she sputtered. "Mary Rolladin."

"Oh my God." My breath catches as I read over those words, repeat them just as Mary did. *Mary. Mary Rolladin.*

Mary is Rolladin.

"What?" Phee says, frantically grabbing the journal to catch up with me. I watch her eyes move swiftly back and forth, devouring each word. "Wait, that can't be. Mary *Rolladin?*"

"Oh my God," I say again. My mind shuffles, bends, and bridges my memories of the Park leader like cards in a deck. Rolladin barking orders.

Rolladin bullying guards and fieldworkers—

Rolladin protecting Phee in the street-fights.

Rolladin offering us drinks in her chambers.

I think of what she said to me, that night we told her we wanted to join her. *You've always reminded me of your mother.*

Rolladin knows my mother, because she's our aunt.

Because she was with our mother.

"I knew it. I knew there had to be more," Phee says. "I knew she cared about us—"

"We just didn't know why," I finish for her.

And she's right, of course. This news doesn't surprise me. Instead it completes the picture and clicks everything into place.

I tug the book back between us, so that it lies across our knees. "This isn't just Mom's story." My head is reeling, overloaded, sputtering from trying to process too much information.

"This is Rolladin's story," Phee's voice catches as she finishes. She looks at me. "Like you said back at the Carlyle—this is our city's story."

The men were gathered into the center of the Great Lawn as we were pushed towards the sidelines. Soldiers moved quickly, lining us up, lining the men up, counting, running numbers for an equation for which none of us knew the variables.

"WOA-WA-DIN," the general repeated back to Mary, smiling. "Women and children, Rolladin. Nothing for free."

And then, with a whistle, he called all his gunmen to raise their rifles. They fired on the men in the field.

One at a time.

October—Our captors, the Red Allies, are picking New Yorkers off the streets one by one and slowly flushing them out of the subways. They're storing us in the Central Park zoo houses like it's some kind of makeshift internment camp.

Our original 6 train crew, we're some of

the lucky ones. We're kept in the aviary, a big, greenhouse-looking structure that smells of zoo and manure. We see the stars through the glass roof every night, and every morning, we wake to the sky blooming pink and orange. We're reminded that there're still things left to wonder about in the world, and we're still human enough to wonder.

But not everything's so rosy.

There are rumors passed like notes from cell to cell, that some of our women are trading themselves for beds. Soon it's all Bronwyn can whisper about through morning and evening rations: how anything is better than prison. How the loneliness is slowly killing her. How she could make somebody love her.

I do what I can do from my cell, which is just shy of nothing—I tell her she'll break, I tell her she'll hate herself, I beg her to think of her little sisters. But she's volatile, desperate—just a kid with nothing left in a cruel and apathetic city.

And then one morning I wake up, and she's no longer there.

And the failure I feel cuts so deep, I can't bandage it.

There are other rumors too. That soldiers send groups of new captives running across Sheep Meadow, and that only the fastest survive. That at night, troops walk through the reptile house and pick the strongest-looking men, only to have the entire platoon kick the shit out of them on the other side of 65th Street.

We hear their pleading and groveling each night
outside the aviary's walls: Have pity. Spare us.
Show us the Lord's mercy.

We don't speak of them in the morning. Just like
we've never spoken of the men in the fields, the
ones gunned down so we could live. Mary and I
cry ourselves to sleep each night as we listen to
the begging, thanking God for at least each other.
We hold Sky between us, like she belongs to both
of us.

October—In the corner of the aviary, Sky's sister
was born under a full moon. It somehow felt
appropriate. I still can't believe this baby was
born at all. She came out wriggling and screaming,
thrashing at the world.

"I think we have a fighter here," Mary whispered
in my ear.

"What should we name her?" I asked Mary and
Sky. Sky just giggled. She has a couple of words
now, Mommy and May-May. But these days, she
mostly laughs. It's as if she knows we've somehow
crossed a threshold and have gotten our second
chance.

"Phoenix," Mary finally answered me the
following night. She pulled me and the girls into her
lap as we relaxed in the corner.

"Phoenix?" I asked her.

"This little girl pulled us out of the dark," Mary
said. "Let us all rise from the ashes."

And immediately, I knew she was right.

We hear Trevor and Mom coming up the stairs. I quickly take the journal from Phee and fold it closed again, trusting *Charlotte* once more to keep our secrets. As I do so, Phee springs from the ground, but I manage to catch her wrist.

"What are you doing?"

"I need to ask her." Phee's face is taut. "I need Mom to tell us all this herself. This is too big. We should have known this."

"Phee, you can't."

"Why not?" Phee growls. "Why add secrets to secrets? I'm tired of this. I need to come clean. I need *her* to come clean. Everything's getting messed up. Everything's changing."

I tug her forcefully, until she finally stops wriggling and relents. "We will figure this out," I say. I study her glossy eyes, her brow stitched in confusion, and I soften my grip. "Just you and me. But until then, keep it to yourself. Okay? Promise me."

She finally nods, and I let go of her sleeve.

"Can one of you guys help Trev with the water buckets? I want to prepare for today's meals," Mom asks cheerfully as we approach, but Phee sprints past her, down the stairs.

Mom looks at me. "Everything okay?"

I close my eyes. *Focus. Show her nothing.* "Yeah it's fine. I can help," I tell her. "We'll bring the buckets up in a second."

I let the light streaming in from the smeared windows cover me like a sheet. I'm on my back, watching the steady rise and fall of my stomach. Forgotten toys are scattered around me, and shrunken chairs pepper the room. The door says this room's called DAY CARE. That's exactly how it feels, like care for today—a safe and secret hideout—and I don't want to go back upstairs till I calm down.

It's not just keeping secrets that's killing me—although that's gnawing at me too. It's all the changes, coming at me one after another, like an army I'm trying to ward off with one sword.

I used to take this city as a given. Manhattan is where I belong. Of course I thought the war would end one day and we'd be able to leave, but I never really thought about *actually* going. Now we're planning to escape the only home I've ever known, the only one I'd ever want, for the lame idea of finding something better.

But it's not just Manhattan. My family's becoming unrecognizable. I've found things out about Mom that I never thought were possible. That Rolladin's my *aunt*, for freaksakes, might have been the reason I was ever born. Christ, she even named me.

And of course, the kicker: Sky. The person I trust the most is now on the other side of some wall that never existed before. And the crappy part is, I don't how to scale it. I don't even know who built the thing.

I'm trying to deal, to take it all in stride, to breathe it in, then let it go, like I always do. But I'm really starting to suffocate.

I hear quick footsteps on the stairs outside the playroom, so I know Ryder and Sam must be back, and with food, most likely. But even that doesn't cheer me up.

I flop on my side and stare at the smooth square of green slate hanging on the wall. I focus on it until my eyes start to droop and my breath becomes soft and controlled. And then, what I knew was coming—what I hate anyone seeing— starts happening. Tears fall, one by one, on the thick carpet. My ribs start to shake, but I don't make any noise. I just lie there.

Then, when I feel like my eyes have run out of tears and I can't feel sorry for myself anymore, I pick myself off the ground.

Maybe all this will sort itself out. Maybe everything will go back to normal, if we just give it more time. And maybe there's a chance Ryder and Sam can stay with us, right here in this city.

I realize I need to believe it.

"Where've you been?" Trevor's in my face as soon as I get back to the third floor. "I was looking for you."

"I took a walk." I rub my eyes for good measure, making sure I didn't leave any evidence of weakness. I look around and realize that we're the only ones on the workout level. "Where's everyone else?"

Trev's face becomes serious. "Someone's here. From the outside—from a hotel or something."

"What do you mean, from a hotel?" I ask as I follow Trev up a flight to our kitchen.

"Some guy who knows your mom," he whispers. *A guy who knows my mom? From a hotel?* Who does she know who's not at the Park right now, or in this gym? Mom said all the city's raiders must be dead.

But we reach the kitchen before I can sort it all out. And perched around the small table are Sky, Mom, Ryder, Sam . . . and like Trev said, some guy I've never seen.

"What's going on?" I ask the crowd, which is now dead silent. Like a reflex, I look at Sky, hoping to get a read on her. Her eyes are big, telling, like I've missed something important.

"Phee, sweetheart." Mom waves me over. She grabs my hand when I approach, and I see that she's been crying. Then she gives this tight little sigh, like everything she's got tied up and twisted inside her is loosening.

"This is a friend," she says. She does that gasp-hiccup thing again. "Robert Mulaney. He's been close with your father since we were kids. He found Ryder and Sam while they were hunting along the Hudson."

Robert Mulaney. The name sounds weirdly familiar, but I don't know why.

I finally look this Robert in the eye. Even sitting down you can tell he's tall, and thin. He has that tight-as-steel look Mom has, like he's seen far too much, so he recast himself in iron. And he's handsome, for an old guy—blue eyes, pale skin. Paler than anyone I've ever seen at the Park.

"A friend of Dad's?" I say instinctively, my native New

Yorker sense kicking in. "How do you know he's telling the truth?" I wasn't raised my whole life here to just take someone at their word. We know better.

"Phee," Sky says, but she lets my name hang there. When I look at her, I can tell she's trying to telepath something to me. But I'm not getting it, and I guess it'd be way too weird for her to start signing.

"You raised them well." This Robert guy smiles. "This isn't the kind of world anymore where you can believe something without proof. Phoenix, right?"

I nod, still not sure what's going on.

"Phee, Robert's a friend of *mine*, too," Mom says. "From before the war. He used to work with your father as an artist. We were all close, all friends, in the city. Before."

Robert, I rack my brain. *Robert*.

Then it comes to me, Mom's words—not her words from the present, but the ones from the past. *Robert and Tom*, she had said, over and over again in the journal. Robert and Tom. Robert and Dad.

Could it be? Robert, the guy with Dad, who Mom and Rolladin were looking for in the tunnels all those months? Mom hoping and praying they'd be just around the corner? This Robert survived, somehow. But if he survived . . .

"After we searched him and got talking, we found out these two were long-lost mates." Sam nods at Mom and Robert, interrupting my train of thought. He's polishing our bow in the corner, and I notice that small bits of squirrel meat are still wrapped around the couple of arrows lying on the table.

Then I notice the plastic-wrapped hunk of meat beside him—a huge rack of deer or some other big game—definitely not squirrels, unless Sam managed to kill about a hundred of them this morning. I suddenly need to sit down, and pull up a chair next to Ryder.

Ryder points to the meat sheepishly. "Your mom's friend is quite generous."

Robert laughs and squeezes Mom's hand. "The least I could do, as we have plenty of it to go around. I spent more than a year with Tom, searching for your mother and Skyler in the tunnels. And sadly, we gave up hope. Never in a million years would I have guessed that you had survived. And brought more life into this world, no less." He looks up at me with big genuine eyes and gently rubs my arm. "You're a miracle, Phoenix. A testament to the fact that life persists, despite all things."

But I don't care about testaments. I want to know how this guy found us, why he's here, and what it means. "How'd you get all that food?" I ask him. "Did you ransack the Park?"

Robert never breaks his smile, but he looks to Mom. She nods, encouraging him to go on. "Phoenix, I've never registered at the Park."

I don't understand. So this guy's a holdout? "But everyone was ordered to the Park during occupation, right, Mom? They swept the streets."

"There were plenty of people who weren't found, Phoenix. Especially people who didn't want to be." Robert leans in, his blue eyes wild and animated. It kind of reminds me of how Sky gets when she's about to tell me a story, about something so fantastical, it can't be real.

"As I was telling your companions here," Robert says, "Elder Tom . . . rather, your father and I, spent months combing the subways and the streets, desperate to hear of something, anything, that would give us hope you girls were alive. It was a dark, dark time for your father."

Robert rests his hand on Mom's shoulder for support. "Most of the people we had been scavenging with were captured, broken, or dying. The two of us were on the brink of death ourselves. Just . . . lost. That's when angels found us, Phoenix," Robert says.

I blink. "Angels."

"Yes. Missionaries who were combing the subways, committed to bringing the fallen back to life. They found us and brought us to the Standard Hotel, on the West Side near the water, where a man named Wren was making a home for so many who had lost their own. I've been there fifteen years." Robert looks around the table. "We have more than enough food and provisions for everyone. We've been blessed: Our community is home to botanists, and scientists, and pharmacists . . . it's almost as if the Standard was destined, was made to be the world's second chance." Robert's smile widens so much, I'm half-afraid his face can't contain it. "We've stayed hidden all these years, Phoenix. From the Red Allies, and the war, then from the warlords in the Park. We're an oasis on this devastated island."

"Robert," Mom says, and rubs her eyes with her hands, hiding her face, then gives one of those gasp-hiccup things again. And I want to hug her, just pull her in, but Robert's already got his arms around her. "I still can't believe it's you."

"Like I said, Sarah. Miracles can still happen on this island."

I look down at my hands.

A friend from Mom's past is alive.

Alive and well, in an oasis in Manhattan.

And he found us, right on the brink of leaving. Right on the brink of turning our backs on this city.

Despite my best attempts to remain doubtful, I feel the tiniest spark of hope inside me.

I run Robert's words through my mind again. *A home for so many who had lost their own. We've been blessed . . . destined . . . the world's second chance.*

I feel the hope start to grow stronger, until my insides are warm, until I feel my muscles relax, just a little.

Miracles can still happen, Robert said.

Maybe he's right. 'Cause minutes ago I was hyper-ventilating—about the idea of sailing into the unknown, about leaving home and everyone in it behind. Then Mom's past jumps right out of her journal and knocks on our door with an answer.

Maybe Robert'll take us to this Standard, all of us, and we can start over in Manhattan. Maybe we'll never have to leave. Maybe all this—the cannibals that sent us running to the YMCA, Ryder and Sam hunting, meeting Robert—maybe all this is *destined*, or whatever, too.

I want to believe all this, so badly that I'm embarrassed. But after all the lies, the double-crossing, the changes, I need to know the whole story. There are too many secrets buried in the wreckage of this city—even with Mom's journal, there's so much we don't know.

"Robert, you said you went to the Standard with our dad," I say, not meeting Mom's or Sky's eyes. "So is he there? Is . . . our dad at the Standard too?"

Mom's breath catches again, and Robert turns to comfort her.

"I'm afraid your father's no longer with us. He was sick and passed away several years ago," Robert says slowly, carefully. "But he had a good life."

A little sob escapes from Mom, and she buries her face in her hands. Sky and I both jump to comfort her, but when she looks up, she's sort of smiling through the tears. "I'm okay," she tells us. And I think she's telling the truth. There's no sadness or pain or anger in her face. There's just relief.

"Tom was happy, Sarah," Robert says. "He was happy at the Standard. And I know he would've wanted this, more than anything in this world." He stares at me with those blue, blue eyes. "He would have wanted his family to share the Standard."

Mom starts cooking Robert's generous gift of meat over the fire for a midday feast, while Robert stays with her, huddled close over the cauldron. It's clear Mom wants some time alone with him, so the rest of us eventually slink out of the kitchen.

Maybe I'm being paranoid, but something doesn't feel right. It's been bothering me since Phee asked about the Park, and whether Robert's ever been there. Of course I saw the hope, the relief, the joy in Mom's eyes as she sat there, listening to Robert convince us he was a walking miracle. And then the peace settle over her, like a door was finally closing, when he told us that Dad had passed away, that he'd had good years at the Standard. And I want Mom to relish these feelings, of course I do. But I need some loopholes closed before I can believe that all our problems will be solved at this oasis of a West Side hotel.

"Your mom seems different, with this guy around," Sam says to Phee as we traipse down the stairs and into Level B—Tennis & Pool. Sam takes Phee's torch and lights a few of the candles left over from Trev's tennis match. "Lighter, or something."

"Doesn't she?" Phee shakes her head. "I still don't know how the heck you managed to find that Robert guy."

Sam smiles. He's given her two or three today already, and I'm wondering if they declared some sort of tough-guy truce when I wasn't looking, or if Robert really is some kind of miracle worker. "Still wowing you, am I?"

Phee rolls her eyes, but I can tell she's enjoying the teasing.

"You're so full of it, man." Ryder laughs. "Robert found *us*."

Sam just smirks. "Semantics."

In a rare display of brotherly love, Ryder laughs and pushes Sam against the tennis cage. Sam spins him around and puts him in a fake headlock, then Trevor starts imitating Ryder: "Easy, everybody! *Easy!*"

Everyone's jovial. Everyone's clearly basking in this new development, the best news we've had since Ryder and Sam landed on this miserable slice of an island.

Everyone, except me.

"You get what this means, right?" Phee whispers to me as the guys continue horsing around against the cage. "We can actually stay in Manhattan, together. We could make a home here. With as much food as we wanted, and medicine and all that other crap Robert was talking about. Can you believe this, Sky?" She looks at me expectantly in the candle-light, like she needs something from me. And I know what it is. She needs me to acknowledge this, for me to believe it before she can accept that it's real. "Isn't it amazing?"

"Come here for a second." I pull Phee onto the bench near the stairs. It's been so long since it was just the two of us, figuring things out—maybe if we can make sense of Robert's news together, all of this really is possible.

"Just walk through this with me. Dad's Rolladin's brother, right?"

Phee nods. "Yeah, obviously."

"And Rolladin's in charge of the Park. So what I don't

understand is . . ." I drop my voice an octave lower. "Robert said that he never surrendered to the Park, that they didn't *want* to be found. But why wouldn't Dad and his friend want to be found by Dad's own sister?"

Phee takes a minute, then shrugs. "Don't over-Sky-ify. The timing could be off—like maybe the Standard missionaries saved Robert and Dad way before Rolladin took over. They probably had no idea Rolladin was in charge. How would they, actually, if they were living at the hotel?"

I nod, wanting to accept what Phee's saying. But things still don't feel right to me. All these puzzle pieces, past and present, still lie in front of me at odd angles. "Sure, but they must have found out at some point—Rolladin was working for the Red Allies. The whole island must have known who she was eventually. And Dad *knew* that Mom and I were with Rolladin in the subways when the city was attacked— Robert basically said so himself."

"So?"

"So if Dad knew we were in the Park, and he only passed away a few years ago, like Robert said, why didn't he come to the Park? Why wouldn't he come if there was a chance we were still alive?"

"And . . . how do we know he didn't? We know what a fat liar Rolladin is." Phee sighs, her tone as sharp and flat as glass. "How do we know she didn't send him away, or lie to him? Just like she lied to the rest of us?"

"I guess," I say.

"You *guess*? Sky, Mom knows all this. She just doesn't know that *we* know from the journal. Don't you think she's thought all this through? Don't you think we should trust Robert if she does?"

"Yeah, but . . ." Phee has a point, of course. But I'm desperate for her to understand that this just feels *off*, that all my instincts tell me this doesn't add up. It feels like we're forcing the puzzle together. Like we want to believe that there's a picture so badly, we'll tear the edges of the pieces to make them fit.

"Sky, honestly, *enough*," Phee says, no more than a rough whisper. "I know you hate it here, all right? And I know you think you've got all the answers. But don't ruin this for Mom, or for me."

I feel stung. "I'm not ruining anything. I'm just trying to figure out—"

"You're so stuck in that journal, in your books, in your . . . *hatred* for this city that you just question things until everything's wrong."

"Phee, come on—"

"Seriously, Sky, when are you going to just let things lie? We're poring over that journal like it contains the keys to everything. But it's just this old book, okay? Maybe Mom's right, you ever think of that? Maybe the past *should* stay in the past. She's not in that journal—she's in the next room, right here, right now. Talking with this Robert guy, who's *real*. Who might give us a second chance in Manhattan."

"Phee," I try again, as patiently as possible. "You can't always rationalize everything away. You can't just turn a blind eye to the past. It's stupid—"

"I'm not stupid," she cuts at me.

"I didn't say that," I try to correct her, but she tramples over me.

"I'm just not fixated on being miserable here, like you are," Phee says. "You have a problem with *everything*. You hate the apartment. You hate the Park. The whorelords, the city. You spend all your time in these novels imagining a better world. Well, what about the one we're really in, huh? What about believing good things can happen here?"

"I do. That's not true—"

"It *is* true, and you know it. You live in a dreamworld 'cause you think it's better than the one that's right under your nose. You just won't give this place a chance, 'cause it's never given you one."

"Phee, you're totally not being fair!"

I can barely catch my breath. We've never talked about this, ever—my deepest, darkest fears. My insecurities. And honestly, I never knew Phee sensed them, or if she did, that she'd ever, ever say them out loud.

I have that same feeling again, that we're drifting away from each other. That as we're trying to bridge a gap between us, we're just floating farther and farther apart.

But before I can answer her, she's already walking away. "Where are you going?" I blurt out.

"To play with the guys," she throws behind her. "I'm tired of analyzing things to death, okay? I've gotta get outside your head."

She storms over to the tennis cage and thrusts herself through its gate and onto the tennis court, where Ryder and Trev are playing Sam. Then the game stops. Phee camps out at the net, hands flailing, brow creased with frustration. No doubt telling them what happened, her side of the story, spinning all of this out of control. That I insist on being miserable. That I'm just a sad little storm cloud, raining on her parade.

I feel tears start to prick my eyes, and I curse myself for crying again.

I watch Ryder watching me as Phee talks animatedly to him, Sam, and Trevor. I can't see his features well, but he isn't moving. He's staying right where he is. He knows we've gotten into a fight, and he's staying put. Right next to Phee. Strong, bold, brazen Phee. Versus her black sheep of a sister.

I dash off the bench, throw myself around the dark stairwell, up to the third floor, and burst into the yoga room. It feels like the walls of this cursed gym, the littered highways outside, the tall, ominous skyscrapers, they're all closing in. Reminding me that I'm chained to this cursed island, to this dead city stuck in a small corner of the world.

I wrap my hands around my knees and curl into a ball to try to calm myself down. But I can't seem to catch my breath, and Phee's words keep encircling me, poking me, turning me inside out.

You just won't give this place a chance, 'cause it's never given you one.

The worst part is, I know she's right.

For my entire life, I've dreamed of leaving this city, of exploring a world beyond the cold towers that fence us in. Towers that dwarf me, warlords that bully me, fieldwork that reminds me every day that I'm not strong enough.

Am I just so desperate to escape this prison that I'll twist everything around until I wring all the goodness out of it? If a miracle presented itself from underneath the city's remains—a chance for us to start over here—would I even want to listen?

I think about Mom's journal, about our entire lives, really, hearing the clipped, pained snippets of Mom's life from before. A life that was full of color and meaning, so beautiful that it pains her to even think about it, so fragile that she insists on keeping it locked away. Now we've been told that Mom might have a happy ending with her lifelong friend—that a second chance is possible for all of us, here. And I can't accept it.

Maybe Phee's right. Maybe there's nothing amiss. Except for me.

"Hey," Ryder says, poking his head into the yoga room. I quickly wipe away the rest of my tears and stand.

"I looked for you in the kitchen," he adds. "And at our spot at the window." His face is creased with concern. "Phee told us you guys got into a fight."

I take another deep breath. "Is that all she said?"

Ryder looks away from me sheepishly. "That, and that you don't want to be happy here." He's about to grab my hand, and then pulls away, as if he's thinking better of it. It makes me wonder if he's starting to see what the rest of this city sees. "Maybe you give this guy a chance, Sky. Give this whole thing a chance."

A small, dark part of me wonders if he's saying this for my benefit, or for Phee's. But I just nod and watch his hazel eyes trace the carpet.

"Just think, we wouldn't have to brave the boat this winter, or worry about supplies. We wouldn't have to search for an answer," he continues. "We could start over *here*, have enough to eat, have a place to call home. You don't know what we've seen, across the ocean, Sky. There's nothing left."

Ryder looks up at me with those pleading eyes, and I feel myself growing hot under his gaze, wanting him to reach for me and pull me into him, despite who he's here for. "This really could be a second chance," he adds. "Robert said we'd be safe at the Standard. They've got security and everything—we'd never have to worry about Rolladin and her goons again. There's plenty of room, and whenever we want to try someplace new, our boat is right in Brooklyn."

"I want to believe Robert," I say after a while. "I do."

Ryder smiles, clearly relieved. So I don't elaborate. I don't want to cause that off-center smile to fall from his face. I don't want to be the sad little storm cloud anymore.

"That's brilliant, Sky," he says. "You've got to come upstairs and listen to what Robert's saying about the Standard. It's what my brother and I have been hoping to find—what I think we've all been searching for. Apparently they even have school, Sky. Like, *real* school. And the adults work, not the kids. It's nothing like the Park. It'd really be a new life, for all of us."

I can't contain myself any longer. I grab his hand. "I really hope so, Ryder."

We round the flight of stairs up to the kitchen together, to a table set for seven. Mom and Robert are still talking near the smoking cauldron. And Phee and Trevor are hovering over Sam at the table, debating all the ways you can prepare venison so you never get sick of it.

"There you are." Mom pulls me over to the table. "We didn't want to start without you."

She sits me down and puts a huge pile of meat in front of me. The steak is so tender that it falls apart, and it's a bigger helping than I think I've ever had at one sitting. Ryder takes a seat next to me, and Phee, without a word, settles down on his other side. She doesn't look at me, though. Not once.

"This is unreal, Sarah," Sam says as he gobbles down his portion.

"Incredible," Ryder agrees.

"Truly, Robert." Sarah sits down next to him. "How can we ever thank you?"

Robert beams at her. "There's no need to thank me. And there's plenty more where this came from. You're all welcome at the Standard as long as you like. There's no need to be hiding in terror from the Park. I promise you, Sarah, the nightmare's over."

But Mom's not looking at Robert. She's studying me with her wide, clear eyes, the clearest they've been in a long time. And in that moment I know for sure: Phee's right. Mom wants this. Phee wants this. Everyone wants this.

So I nod, and smile, and pray with every fiber of my being that it's true: *The nightmare's over.*

PART THREE

Sometimes the past should stay in the past.

—From October entry,
Property of Sarah Walker Miller

We walk over to the Standard the next day. Like we did on our hunt a couple of days ago, we take 13th Street all the way across the city to the West Side. Then we climb what Mom and Robert call the High Line—an elevated track that runs north to south above the abandoned highway. The Standard Hotel sits on top of it, two shiny skyscraper tablets hugged around the platform. When I see it, I try to picture it as home.

Mom and Robert catch up more on the walk over. They're walking arm in arm—even though Mom's ankle is basically healed—comparing notes and time lines, trying to build the two sides of their story from the ground up. They're trading whispers, naturally, but I've read enough of Mom's journal to kind of follow what they're saying. Mom's talking about the E-train summit in the tunnels way back when, and Robert's explaining how he and Dad met these missionary "angels" who saved their lives.

I still need to pinch myself that this is all going down, and we're really getting to stay in Manhattan. But I force myself to believe it's actually happening. The Standard is real, and my family's getting our second chance in this city.

Call me crazy, but I think we deserve it.

Speaking of family, Sky and I still aren't talking. On the walk over, I managed to sandwich myself in between Ryder and Sam, so my sister and I didn't have to walk next to each other. There's no room on the sidewalk for four, so Sky's stuck with Trevor in the back. It's not just that I'm still mad at her, or that we've had a fight. That's happened before, obviously, way too many times to count. But this one just feels . . . different, like we've both crossed some line and don't know how to uncross it.

I was planning to say sorry after we blew up on Level B at the YMCA, even though I thought it was Sky's fault in the first place. But when I went upstairs to find her, I saw her holding Ryder's hand. She's got to know I like him, it's obvious. And having her move in just feels like she's trying to get back at me.

Sometimes I secretly wonder if Ryder wouldn't be better with my sister, which annoys me. Like right now, Ryder's gushing on and on to me and Sam about the "opportunity for learning" at the Standard, and how he hasn't been in a real classroom since the eighth grade.

Sam rolls his eyes at me. "Rye, you're boring us."

I have to bite back a laugh. I was thinking the same thing, not that I'd ever tell Ryder.

"Crap, really?"

"No, it's cool," I'm quick to say. "I like hearing about United Britain."

Sam gives this flat little laugh, then nudges me in the ribs. "It's the United Kingdom, or Great Britain. Pick one, but not both."

I start blushing. There goes my attempt at playing the smart card.

"It's challenging, remembering so many names we don't use," Ryder saves me. "That's why I'm excited for school, and history, English . . . all of it. It's important to remember, you know?" He gives me one of his huge lopsided grins.

And I start nodding. 'Cause I'd pretty much agree with anything Ryder's perfect face is saying . . . even if what makes him excited puts me to sleep.

We follow Robert down the platform of cracked pavement and hungry weeds and enter the Standard's lobby.

"I present to you," Robert says real dramatically as he opens the glass doors and walks past a couple of guards, "the Standard."

The place is, hands-down, awesome-looking. The lobby's a huge room with ceilings as high as the sky, slate floors, and floating white wall-divider things made out of plastic or glass. And instead of the old torches that are pinned to the wall at the Carlyle, here they somehow managed to secure cups of fire below the light fixtures, and each one throws off so much light that it pools on the floor. In the far corner sits a smiling woman at a huge stone desk, a check-in girl behind a slice of a mountain.

"Not quite the Carlyle," Mom whispers as we take in every inch of the lobby.

"Exquisite, am I right?" Robert says to her. "We were lucky. This hotel was nearly untouched by the West Side bombing. Mas—Wren kept all the prewar details." He looks up and around him, as if he's impressed by his home all over again. "You might remember how much I love architecture, Sarah."

Mom smiles at him. "Practical art."

"That's right. Practical art." Robert rests his hand on her shoulder. "Why don't I give you all a tour, then maybe we can settle you into your rooms for the night . . . or however long you want to stay. Community dinner is at sundown, and I'm sure you don't want to miss that."

"Community dinner," Ryder whispers. "I'm hungry already. Sounds promising."

"Hopefully more venison," I say. Then I add just to bug Sam, "But anything beats squirrels."

Sam just shakes his head and smirks. "You know those squirrels were clutch."

"We'll take the internal stairs," Robert interrupts our bickering. He leads us down a slate hallway off the lobby to a stairwell.

As we climb, he tells us all this stuff about "the roots of his community." How the head honcho of this place, Wren or whatever, used to be some big "preacher," and how his missionaries saved "countless souls in the tunnels." I'm catching about half of it, but it seems like Ryder's eating all this history stuff up, so I smile and nod like, *Oh, isn't this fascinating?*

We pass a couple of people in the halls every once in a while on our tour, but otherwise it's fairly empty.

"Is there really a whole . . . *community* here?" I finally ask, testing out the word, once we wind our way around another hallway, past rows of white doors. It's weird—unlike the rest of the hotel (which feels brand spanking new), the room doors look roughed up. Like there were once symbols or numbers on them that were removed and painted over. Maybe they're fixing them.

Robert laughs. "I believe there's at least a hundred of us. Maybe more. I know, you can't tell, right? Most of our members spend a good deal of time in their rooms. Solitude and reflection are extremely important for the Standard. But I'm

LEE KELLY

getting ahead of myself," he says. "I want to show you the big reveal."

He takes us up one more flight of stairs, and then pauses expectantly in front of the door. "I've told you about our past," Robert whispers excitedly. "Now, on to our future."

He pulls the door open to showcase a huge farm behind glass. It stretches the whole length of the hotel floor.

Sunlight filters in through the ceiling and fills the entire room with blinding light, and green is everywhere. Grass planted somehow in the ground, trees two stories high, bushes. There's even a shallow moat on one side, teeming with fish. Monkeys and squirrels scramble from tree to tree. And there's a family of *deer* grazing in the stretches of grass.

It's a mini Park—a mini Park inside a hotel.

"How did you manage to do this?" Mom asks what all of us are thinking. "This might be the biggest greenhouse I've ever seen."

"Innovation, mostly." Robert pulls open the sliding glass door and helps Mom inside. "What was once a restaurant is now a controlled ecosystem, though of course it serves the same purpose. To feed the Standard."

"It's beautiful," Sky says.

"Breathtaking, really," Ryder adds.

"Thank you," Robert says. "It took years. Missionaries raiding abandoned homes, lifting seeds from Central Park and surroundings. Gathering animals, instead of hunting them, as I was doing yesterday when I had the pleasure of meeting your company." He nods to Ryder and Sam. "In two words really, patience and sacrifice."

"Can we back up a second?" Sam asks. "How the hell did you manage deer?"

"My friend, our innovation will astound you." Robert smiles. "We've been truly blessed by the genius and scope of expertise of our community members. We've created tranquilizers, weapons, and aqueducts, among a great many other things. Honestly, the only thing we haven't managed to do is turn the lights on, but we're not the first community to survive without electricity." Then his smile breaks wide open. "Like I said, it's as if the Standard was destined."

I take a look around the wide green expanse and inhale the scent of the trees. I close my eyes and listen to the echo of the water within the glass. It's not the Park, but it's a slice of it.

Mom comes up behind me and grabs my hand. "I've always wanted something like this for you girls," she whispers. "I gave up on it long ago. But now, seeing this place, I think maybe we've found something special."

I tighten my hands around her shoulders, squeeze, and pull her in. It's been a long time since I've seen her truly happy.

"Ladies, I hate to interrupt," Robert says gently behind us. "But it's almost time for supper. I'd love to get you settled in your rooms so you can fully enjoy tonight."

"Of course." Mom squeezes me back before she turns to go.

Robert waves us out of the glass paradise and back towards the stairwell. "Let me show you home."

I take my time cleaning up in my own private washroom, the first space that's ever been "mine" in my life. Robert assured us that there are plenty of open rooms in the hotel, so each of our group was given their own suite, a floor-to-ceiling box of glass with views of the entire city.

It feels beyond luxurious, having so much space: a bed of my own, a bath, and a mirror. But strange as well. Part of me feels like I'm missing a limb, not hearing Mom right outside, or Phee banging on the door to hurry up already. Today, though, I'm glad for the space. Today I really need a break from my sister.

After she practically took my head off at the YMCA, she spent the entire walk over here buddying up to Ryder, acting like she cared about what he had to say. About books and lessons, and learning about places beyond this tiny island. Which is ludicrous, as half the time I try to engage with Phee about a book, she ends up falling asleep on me. I tried to tune out her conversation with Ryder and Sam, but I couldn't—which prompted poor Trev to ask if I was okay about four times on our walk over.

I have to give Phee one thing, though I'll never admit it to her. She was right about giving this place a chance. The Standard feels magical, somehow, a true oasis—especially that glass atrium teeming with life, *food*, on one of the top floors. Even more magical is the idea that our father lived here, in this very hotel, and that the road he blazed, the sacrifices he made, might have come full circle to give us a home here too. I can tell, it's ignited things long dormant in my mother—happiness, and *hope*. Mom never lets herself see the bright side of things. But today it was like her shell was cracked open, like her hard exterior might actually be fracturing.

Robert has a whole fancy evening planned for tonight: A member of the community is going to escort each one of us to supper, so we can start to meet people and get acclimated. It feels very royal, like something out of Cinderella or King Arthur's court, and I'm surprised at how excited I am. Compared with eating outside in the bitter cold as Rolladin barks orders at us, this dinner sounds like a page out of a Brontë novel.

After I finish getting ready, there's still no sign of my escort, so I start to poke around my room. The bed linens are clean and white, and there's a small chair and bureau in the corner. I go through all the bureau drawers, but they're empty, save for a fine layer of dust. The only personal items I see besides my own are in the bedside table: two books stacked on top of each other. I move aside a small, tattered copy of the Holy Bible and pull out the hardback underneath it. On the front cover is a man with his arms crossed, dressed in a black robe, with a small white square of fabric stitched into the robe's collar.

I scan the cover, and the title page . . . *The Standard Works: God's New Test for America.* I've never heard of it.

It's been so long since I've read anything but Mom's journal that I find myself bashful about jumping in. So I flip to the introduction, testing the waters:

> *Today's generation has been wooed by the*
> *temptations of our all-consuming Information Age.*
> *Brothers and Sisters, we are failing God's test . . .*

I jump at the knock on my door, then carefully close the hardback and slip it inside the end table.

"Good evening, Sister Skyler." A young man about my age stands on the other side of my door. He doesn't make eye contact, just keeps his head bowed and his hands locked in front of him, taking this whole royalty thing a little far. "I'm here to escort you to supper."

"Thank you." I peer around the hall—it's empty. There's no sign of my mom, Ryder, or Phee, who all have their own rooms along my corridor. "Aren't we waiting for the rest of our group?"

"No, Sister. Master Wren and Elder Robert asked that I bring you right away." He extends his arm, anticipating that I grab it. I hesitate, for a second.

"But they're coming, right?"

"I'm sure, Sister."

The "Sister" and "Elder" thing definitely feels odd, maybe even old-fashioned, but then so do personal escorts. Then I think about all the weird rules we were subjected to in the Park—the arbitrary check-in hour, the lockdowns, the street-fights. And the nuances of every world I've read about, real and unreal. I guess every community has its quirks.

I smile, shrug off the uneasiness I'm determined to keep

at bay, and take my escort's arm. I study him as we walk—he's kind-looking, if a little bit bland, with pale skin that looks like it hasn't seen the sun in a decade.

"What's your name?" I ask, uncomfortable with the silence.

"Brother Quentin," he says with a nod. His eyes dart around the hallway suspiciously, even though it's obvious that we're alone.' "I'm not sure if you and I will be sealed or not. But I hope so." He gives me a tentative smile, and I return it, completely confused as to what he's talking about.

"Me too," I say, to be polite.

He walks me down the blue-carpeted hall, down the sleek metal stairs, and into a tiny dining room, no larger than my own suite. In fact, on second look, it *is* a converted suite, but the bed and bureau have been taken away and replaced with a small circular table. Six people are already seated, and two open place settings remain for Quentin and me. I do a quick scan. Everyone's a stranger.

"Quentin," I whisper. "Where's my family?"

He offers a tight-lipped smile. "Master Wren and Elder Robert will be stopping by to greet us soon. You mustn't worry."

I nod and try to take him at his word. I think back to what Robert said about meeting the Standard community—maybe he thinks splitting us up will maximize the opportunity.

I look again at the odd assortment of people around the table. Quentin to my left, an older man and woman to my right, a young couple, and two small children across from me. But no one's looking up. No one's even acknowledged my presence. So much for getting to know the other Standard residents.

Finally, when the silence becomes so intense that I'm almost prompted to laugh I'm so uncomfortable, there's a swift knock at the door, and Robert enters the room with another man in tow.

"Robert," I rush, glad to see a familiar face.

He gives me a smile, but it's contained, hesitant, and he takes a step back as he says, "Skyler, this is the man I was telling you about, the man responsible for everything you see here. This is the true Master of the Standard, Wren."

A wave of hard-to-characterize energy washes over me. Because I know this Wren person too. Not personally, but I've just seen his picture. He's an older version of the author of the *"New York Times* bestseller" resting in my end table— the man behind *The Standard Works*. Same intense eyes, same long face. All that's changed is a softness around his jaw, a few wrinkles, and streaks of silver hair where there used to be brown.

Wren gets down on one knee and kisses my hand, and gives me a wide smile. "Elder Tom's daughter, in the flesh. I never thought I'd see it. I never thought I'd have such a chance. I can't tell you how delighted I was when Elder Robert told me he had found your family."

"It's . . . it's lovely to meet you," I say, trying to be patient, just like my mother always says. "You mention my family, Wren. May I see them? Are they joining us here?"

Wren exchanges a look with Robert. "Your family is getting acquainted with our little community, just like you."

"But," I say. I tread as carefully as possible, trying not to sound rude. But this is the longest I've been away from Mom and Phee in my life, and it's starting to panic me. "They're all here, aren't they? Will we be together soon?"

"Of course, my dear. Trust me, there's a method to my madness." Wren gives me a little wink. "I've always felt incredibly indebted to your father. I very much want you to love this community, like he did," he continues. "And I desperately hope this place will become your home."

His words spring a river of questions in my mind, but I keep them dammed inside. I find myself just nodding. I don't know what else to do.

"Please, take advantage of our food, our drink. Our company." Wren stands and rests his hand on my escort Quentin's shoulder. "Brother Quentin, I paired you with quite a lovely dinner partner tonight, didn't I?"

Despite the fact that I still feel somewhat out of sorts, I can't help but blush at Wren's compliment.

Quentin takes a quick peek at me, his face the same color as mine. "Yes, Master Wren."

Wren bends down and leans into Quentin, whispers what I'm sure I'm not supposed to catch: "And dare I say, in nights further, a union for the heavens."

My face is now hot, my throat closing. *A union for the heavens?* What's he talking about?

Could I have heard him right?

I'm so flustered that I miss Wren's next whisper, something that sounds like a code, a string of numbers, before he pulls away from Quentin's ear.

"Tonight, my lambs, we're having venison, chard, and mushrooms," he says to our small crew of eight.

On cue, the entire table chants, "Thank you for the Standard, the only Standard, the lofty Standard."

I nearly jump out of my chair.

Wren smiles. "Please enjoy."

"Robert—," I call out to him, but he's already halfway out the door with Wren, and a man in black is sidestepping his way into our room, with a huge tray of plates in his hands. I smell the food immediately, and for a moment, I forget about the disconcerting chanting, the weird chill Wren left in the room. I push aside the bizarre way our group has been separated in this hotel, and try to think only of the dish in front of me.

After the delicious, painfully slow three-course meal, through which I smile and nod at Quentin against a backdrop of total silence, I finally speak.

"Quentin," I whisper, quite aware that our companions can hear me. "I need to see my mom and sister now, okay? Can you take me to them?"

I give him a long minute to answer, and when he doesn't, I slowly push my chair behind me to stand.

But Quentin grabs my wrist. "Please, Sister Skyler." His voice is soft and shaky. "It's clear that Master Wren wants to share the Standard with you. And if he wants you to stay here, you must." He looks up at me, tentatively meeting my eyes, as if even explaining this to me is sacrilege on his part. "There are many ways of accepting Master Wren's will. I promise you, this way is . . . easiest."

His words cut right through my chest and swat at my heart. I have no idea what he means, but the warning behind his tone is crystal clear.

I sit and stay quiet as the waitstaff cleans up our table. Quentin eventually takes my arm, staying tight to me as he leads me back to my suite, then finally says good night.

Once I'm alone in my room, I count to a hundred, then five hundred for good measure, before I peek my head out and down the blue-carpeted hall. My body wants nothing more than to lie down, but my mind is reeling. I need to check in with the others. I need to know if anyone else's encounter with the Standard was as unsettling as mine. And it's worth a temporary truce with my sister.

So I trudge through my exhaustion and tap softly on each of their doors, starting with Mom's, and move quickly across the hall to Phee's. Then I knock on Ryder's, back to Phee's, then on Ryder's once more. I press my ear to his door, but hear nothing.

Frustrated, I build my knocks to raps and then to all-out pounds. I finally lose patience and grab the handle to Phee's door. The door catches on its wood frame, but it eventually snaps free, and I stumble into the dark.

"Phee," I huff, too loudly to count as a whisper. "Phee!"

"Whatever are you doing, Sister?" a voice I don't recognize answers.

A tall form rises from the bed. My eyes start to adjust in the dark. It's a woman—dark hair, thin frame, not too much older than I am.

But she's definitely not Phee. And I saw Phee settling in here earlier. I'm sure of it.

"Where's my sister?" I stammer.

"I am your Sister," the woman implores sleepily. "As you are mine."

My stomach plunges to the lobby below. Is Phee all right? Did they take her somewhere? Is she still in this hotel?

I run back into the hall, open Ryder's door. A boy I don't

know answers, looks at me questioningly. Asks with shy eyes whether Master Wren sent me.

And Mom's room is now empty.

I back up cautiously, an animal suddenly very aware of its cage.

So did they move everyone else? Are they on a different floor now? *Why?*

I think about running down the hall, knocking on every door—going floor to floor until I find my family, Ryder and Sam. But Quentin's cryptic, disconcerting warning echoes through my mind. *If Master Wren wants you to stay here, you must . . . this way is . . . easiest.*

I think about my lonely dinner, the bowed faces of my supper companions, and Quentin's hesitation to even speak.

My mind begins to free-fall.

This way is easiest?

What is this place?

Why would Mom's friend take us here?

Is this just happening to me, or are the others being cajoled and threatened too?

I slowly recede into my room. I shut the door tight against the frame, but there is no lock, no way to assure I'm safe from whatever lies on the other side.

I hug my book bag to my chest and don't get up to go to bed. The little sleep I get is captured on the steel-tiled floor of the bathroom.

I wake up to pounding on my room door. So I thrust off the comforter I don't remember wrapping around myself, and stumble into the small entryway. But when I go to answer, I realize I'm still locked in.

The latch on the other side slowly clicks open, and Robert tentatively sticks his hand around the door frame. "Phoenix? Can I come in?"

"Yeah." I sit back down on the bed, confused, as Robert lets himself into my room. I rack my brain for what happened last night. That spooky dinner in some random hotel room. That guy who was with Robert—Wren—who told me that he'd prayed for years about a way to repay my dad, and God listened and brought us here. All those silent creeps around my table, who started chanting and giving thanks to a freaking hotel. And my goon of an escort, Francis, this guy nearly my mom's age, who called everybody "Elder" and "Sister" and "Master" and then went mute after we sat down to dinner. And when I told Francis that I needed to find my family, then got up and left, he started threatening me—and we ended up in a rumble in the middle of the hall. He managed to drag me back to my room, and then locked me in.

"Are you all right?" Robert stands over my bed.

I look down at my arms—there're a couple of small

black-and-blue marks, but nothing I haven't dealt with from the whorelords before.

"I guess. Robert, where is everybody?" I try to remain calm. This guy's a buddy of my mom's, and dad's, from before I was born. I remind myself of that again, like I had to last night, when I realized how weird I was starting to feel here. "Why are we separated?"

Robert sits down on the bed next to me. "This wasn't always the way things were done. The Standard has . . . evolved." He tracks my gaze across the rows and rows of skyscrapers on the other side of the window. "As time goes on, Wren becomes more sure of his mission. And things are revealed to him that weren't revealed before. Now it's imperative that each Standard member finds their own path, without the distraction of friends and loved ones to cloud their journey."

I'm not understanding anything he's saying, and my frustration is just adding to my panic. "Robert, what the heck are you talking about? What . . . *mission*?"

"Wren's been saving this city slowly, Phoenix, one prisoner at a time, since the bombs dropped on Manhattan. He was lecturing in this very hotel when the city was hit, and he turned this place into a refuge." Robert reaches out and holds my hands. "We've given countless people a second chance here—through purpose, and devotion. Wren's Standard doesn't just save lives, Phoenix. It saves *souls*. And I really think if you give this place a chance, you'll understand. You'll come to love it just as much as I do. As your father did."

I find myself wanting to believe what he's saying, maybe even more so now than at the YMCA. Before I felt so alone.

Before I got into that wicked fight with Sky and basically told her she wasn't good enough for this city. I've been thinking about our fight, actually, all morning.

"But where's Sky, and my mom?" I ask. "I mean, I guess I get the whole 'my own path' thing in theory, but I don't go anywhere without them—"

"You'll see them soon," Robert interrupts. "But Phoenix, I need you to understand—it's very important that you exercise control here. That you're . . . *deferential*, in your path to joining our little community. No more fistfights, no more acting out."

I bristle. "But that Francis guy was totally bullying *me*. He was practically whispering death threats—"

"You're not in the Park anymore," Robert barrels over me again. "And Francis is an Elder, a missionary of the Standard. Which means you respect him, and listen to him, and don't fight back."

The idea of some Standard goon pushing me around for my own good just doesn't sit right with me. At least at the Park, they blamed it on the Red Allies. "Robert, I don't think I can do that."

He sighs and leans forward. "Phoenix, Wren is committed to saving you. We both are. Because of your father, because of everything . . ." His voice catches and he stops, collecting himself. "What Wren wants to happen *will* happen, Phoenix. There are many ways of accepting the Standard, and I want your transition to be as easy as possible." Then he looks me right in the eyes. "I'd hate for you to find yourself in a position that you just can't handle."

Again with these veiled threats, like Francis was doling out last night. But for some reason, they scare me more coming from Robert.

"So I need you to start cooperating, and then everything will turn out as it should," he adds. "I've even asked Wren for his blessing to work with you directly, to see what I can do. You remind me so much of your father, Phoenix. So impetuous, so outspoken." He pauses. "Too outspoken."

And even though I don't dig under people's words, like Sky, to figure out the story underneath them, it's impossible to ignore how deep the roots of his words run.

But I don't ask Robert what he means—I focus on what's important. "If I cooperate or whatever, can I see my mom and Sky?"

"Of course." He smiles. "In fact, Wren has arranged for a young missionaries dinner tonight, for you and your sister. It's been a while since we've welcomed born-agains, especially ones so young, and so important."

"But what about Mom?" I press. "And the guys we came with—Ryder and Sam and Trevor?"

"Ryder and Trevor are busy with their own lessons, finding their own path. And your mother and Sam are in the heavenly blue, like most adult members. You'll see them . . . after."

"Soon?"

Robert nods, but the smile's fallen off his face. "Soon. Now please, Phoenix, we have a lot of work to do. I suggest we get started."

Robert and I talk the rest of the day, all through our lunch, until the sky turns gray and the city's just shadows. He starts by asking me questions, like what I know about the world from Before, and about the war, and if I believe that someone's looking out for all of us. I give him a lot of one-word answers: first, 'cause most of what I know about the war and Before came from Mom's journal, and talking about it feels like spilling her secrets. Second, there're just some things I don't bother thinking about—things that don't seem relevant—like God and heaven and whatever else might sit above this city. But even though I don't say much, Robert still manages to take my words and twist them, wring them out like some wet towel.

Like when I say the war was obviously a tragedy, Robert says, "Well, depends on how you look at it."

When I say, "But so many people died," he says, "But sometimes things need to burn to light a fire."

Then he tells me that Wren knew it was coming, that the Red Allies were part of his grand prophecy. One that "ushered out the old world"—the world that lived in sin and filth and failed "God's test"—to make way for the new.

A world that adheres to a different standard.

The Standard.

And call me dense that it's taken me so long, but I finally figure out that this "Standard" thing isn't a hotel.

It's much, much more.

By the end of Robert's rant, my stomach's clenched like a fist, and all I want to do is see my family and bury my face in Mom's shoulder.

Finally Robert says, "I think that shall be all for today." He stands and moves to the door.

For *today*?

But I don't think about tomorrow, only tonight, and how I need to see my sister. "So you'll take me to Sky?" I scramble after him.

"Your escort will. He'll be here shortly." Before Robert closes the door, he fingers the lock on the other side, then waves the gold chain at me. "We want you to embrace the Standard with open arms, Sister Phoenix. We want you to *want* to be here. Today you've made great strides. Let's see how you handle yourself without restraints." He's about to leave, but then turns back towards me. "And please, Phoenix. Deferential," he reminds me.

Then he shuts the door.

My mind starts running as soon as he leaves.

Where has Robert taken us? What the heck is this place, where people get separated and worn down and talked in circles? Does Mom know how totally bizarre this is all getting?

And where the hell is she? Where's this heavenly blue?

But there's a knock a minute later, interrupting my thoughts, and the door slowly creaks open again. I peer around the corner to see Francis, my escort from last night, standing on the other side.

"You again."

He smiles. "Expect to see me for a while, Sister Phoenix."

Francis takes my hand and wraps his thick forearm around mine, squeezing my old bruises, revisiting last night's handiwork. He pulls me in tight to him as we pass door after closed door to another set of internal stairs. I keep my eyes peeled, but I don't see any of our crew on our way down.

We enter a windowless dining hall on the bottom floor, not as tight as last night's dinner but still cramped. There's one long table that spans the room. It's teeming with tiny candles, and china and glasses are set in front of each chair. Wren sits, smiling like a fat cat, in the center of a field of teens and kids, all cast-down eyes and pasted-on smiles. I scan the lot of them, my need to see Sky clawing at me like an itch. . . .

"Sky!"

I push off Francis, trying to unwind my limbs from his and sprint towards her. Her eyes get all wide and shimmery like they do when she's about to cry, and she reaches her arm out for me—

But before I can get to her, Francis grabs my neck and reels me into his chest. "I know Elder Robert thinks he can *talk* some sense into you, but Master Wren is doubtful. So if you can't behave like a good little girl, we'll take other measures." Francis eyes me up, then down, then up again. "In fact, I'm looking forward to it."

I'm not one for threats: Most times they feel desperate, and hollow. But Francis's message is thick and loaded, claws its way into my ears, down my throat, makes a home in the pit of my stomach.

I glance at Sky, who's slowly shaking her head in warning. I wonder what Robert and Wren have been saying to her. I wonder if she fully understands how off the rails this Standard really might be.

I let Francis shove me into my seat at the end of the table, catty-corner from Sky. He wraps his thick fingers around my thigh and squeezes with everything he's got till I yelp.

"That's the last noise you make tonight," Francis whispers. "Or your path to the Standard will take a detour."

I don't say another word through the first course, even though I'm dying to talk to Sky, especially now that she's so close. I'm antsy to start signing to her, to tell her that I didn't mean what I said at the YMCA. That I've missed her so much today, I felt like I was cut in half.

But all the times I look up, her eyes are on her plate.

"I know we usually have our meals in silence, but I have

some words to share, and God wants me to share them," Wren says as a team of men in black take away our first-course dishes. He beams at Sky, and then at me. "This is truly a special occasion, as it's been years since we've had the chance to welcome young born-agains into our community—but Sister Skyler and Sister Phoenix are more than that. They're the daughters of a man who gave everything he had to our mission, who laid down his life for the Standard. So I command each of you to make these children feel especially welcome."

Sky's eyes fly and lock on mine, and I know what she's thinking. Dad . . . *laid down his life?*

I think back to our conversation with Robert at the YMCA. When I asked if Dad was at the Standard, Robert *definitely* had said that Dad had died 'cause he was sick.

Is that what Wren means, or something different . . . something worse?

What happened to him?

"These young women are a gift from God," Wren continues. "They are part of his divine plan for all of us." He smiles. "So let us give thanks to the Standard."

On cue, the whole table chants, "Thank you for the Standard, the only Standard, the lofty Standard."

And everything I've seen and heard since we got here—Francis's threats, Robert's hours of talking things upside down, now Wren's babbling about us being part of his divine plan or whatever—it's all far too freaky. Whatever this place is, whether it's some miracle oasis or not, I'm pretty sure we don't want any part of it. And I need to get us out, before this gets even more out of hand.

"Wren, there's been some mistake," I find myself talking before I plan out what I'm going to say. "It's . . . nice that you think we're special and all, but I don't think this place is right for us. My sister, my mom—the guys we came with—we stick together. And it's really time we got going."

The entire table falls silent and stares at me. Twenty pairs of eyes.

Then something ripples across Wren's face. It weirdly reminds me of the times Sky and I snuck out to the Park Lake as kids, bent down in the grass, and peered into the murky water. We'd see waves on the surface, a flash of gray under the current—probably just a fish tail. But it always felt like more, a glimpse of a monster in the deep dark. And we'd scramble away from the edge, scared shitless.

"I mean thanks and everything, for dinner," I keep stuttering, and shove my chair to stand. "But we should really go. So if you can just get the rest of our crew—"

"Elder Francis," Wren finally says. "Take Sister Phoenix to the washroom to cool off."

Francis keeps my head under the water in the basin so long, I swear I'm going to pass out. I start thrashing my arms, my legs. Craning my neck up for air, as water starts to seep into my throat. "STOP!"

Finally he pulls me up out of the basin, and I choke and splay myself across the slate floor. My hair falls across me like a heavy curtain.

"You don't speak unless you're spoken to," Francis barks. "And you never, *ever* speak to Master Wren. I don't know why they're trying to ease you in. They should just show you the heavenly blue. Child or not."

I pant and roll onto my side, coughing up water. "Where

is this heavenly blue?" I barely manage to cough out. "I think that's where my mom is. I need to see her."

But Francis ignores me. "Dry yourself off and tie that hairy mess back." He points to a pile of towels resting on the bathroom shelves. "I'll be waiting outside."

I stay on the ground for a minute, heaving, fighting to collect my breath.

Cold.

Shivering.

Terrified.

I pull my knees in tight and try not to panic, but I can't seem to calm down.

So we're stuck here?

But Robert said we could leave whenever we wanted. Is he lying about seeing Mom and the guys too? Like he lied about trapping us here? Like he lied about Dad?

Why?

Tears threaten to rain down, a scream teases the back of my throat. But before I really lose it, I hear a soft musical voice from somewhere in the shadows of the bathroom.

"Yes, you're quite lovely," the voice says. It's rough and gravelly, but polite.

Ryder. Ryder is somehow in the belly of this bathroom.

"But my heart's for someone else," he says. "Now, I'm begging you, just a minute alone, okay?"

"But Master Wren said you're not to be alone," a soft, girly voice answers.

"Even to use the facilities?" Then there's a pause. I imagine Ryder flashing this girl one of his lopsided smiles, the ones I couldn't resist, even if I wanted to. "Thank you, Sister Ava. I'll be out in a sec."

I hear the softest of footsteps, and then an echoing tinkle of piss.

Ryder, alone. Ryder, steps away. And despite the fact that my own Standard goon's waiting for me outside, I've got to see him.

I throw a towel around my shoulders, tiptoe past the stalls of the women's bathroom, and follow the mirrored wall to a door, which opens into a dimly lit room of sinks. On the opposite side of the sinks, there's another door labeled MEN. I dash across the threshold and enter the men's stalls.

Ryder spots me before I can say anything. He runs to me, pulls me in gently, embraces me, like he's making sure I'm real.

"Where are you guys?" he whispers. "I looked for Sky last night and someone else was in her room."

I feel a twinge of jealousy but shake it off, just happy that he's here, and he's safe. "She's at my dinner, but they kept us separated all day," I start stuttering. "And I haven't seen my mom—Robert talked at me for hours about Wren's mission, which apparently we're part of—Ryder, this place is crazy."

"I know, they've separated us, too," Ryder says. "My escort's been telling me a little. Trevor got assigned to a 'junior ward' apparently, after he had this mini freak-out about being alone in a weird place last night. But I haven't seen Sam. My escort won't tell me much—just that he's an adult, so he's gone to the heavenly blue."

"Wait, yeah, that's where my mom is. Where the heck is it? Is it outside this hotel?"

Ryder shakes his head. "I don't know." He looks up at me, and his eyes widen, like he's shocked I'm crying.

"Phee," he whispers. "Oh, Phee, don't cry. You're tough.

Your whole family is tough as nails. Your mom's going to be okay. We're going to get out of here."

But I can't seem to stop crying. Christ, I can't even speak.

"Phee, you're the strongest girl I've ever met," Ryder whispers. "Listen to me. Start paying attention. The first step is finding each other. Note your floor, your hallway—your room number as you enter and leave."

He pulls me in closer, and I feel the soft, silky hair of his forearms on the back of my neck. Then his fingers in my hair, comforting me. And my fear and anxiety start to melt, replaced by a warm, teasing feeling in the center of my spine.

"They're keeping us isolated for a reason," he whispers into my ear. "It's up to us to find and save our families. Get Sky and find me, all right? Tonight. I'm in 825. I'll figure out where Trev is somehow. Then we'll find this heavenly blue and rescue Sam and your mom. I swear it."

"Room 825," I repeat, finally finding my voice.

And even though the world's starting to crack and break open, that teasing feeling crawls up my spine. It tickles the base of my neck, and then crackles like lightning across my shoulders. And the noise about everything wrong with this place becomes quiet, and all I can think about is the guy in front of me. His warmth, his arms, his scent of leaves and daytime.

As he holds me, I close my eyes and stop thinking. Stop breathing.

My hands reach up and wrap around his broad shoulders. Then I lean my lips into his and push.

He pulls away. "Phee—," he whispers, but he lets my name hang between us. I search his face for an answer. He looks . . . confused, but good confused or bad confused, I don't know.

But I want to, I need to . . . does he feel what I feel? God, does he share it?

"Brother Ryder, what are you doing?" a female voice cuts across the stalls. We both look to the door.

Ryder's escort has the door propped open, and she's tapping her foot and shaking her blond head like she owns him. "You're going to be sealed with me. Don't touch her."

It takes everything I've got not to run across the bathroom and clock her.

"Sister Phee," Francis rumbles for me from somewhere inside the women's bathroom.

"Find me later," Ryder whispers. "825."

Then he walks to link arms with his watchdog in the corner, apologizing like crazy to her before they're even out the door.

I stumble back into the girls' bathroom, my cheeks still on fire. Francis stands at the girls' room entrance. "Where'd you go?"

I keep to the shadows, not wanting him to see me flushed. "I took off my clothes to dry them a little. You soaked me."

That must satisfy him, 'cause he turns around without another glance in my direction. "Let's go. Master Wren has missed our presence for too long."

I follow my designated thug back to the table, my hair and clothes still thick and damp against my skin. A plate of delicious-looking apple stuff is at my seat, glistening in a china bowl under the candlelight. But I don't want it. Wren and his psycho Standard can't buy me off with dessert.

I push the bowl away and will Sky to look up at me.

She finally does, once Wren starts droning on about youth missionary duties. She sees me across the candlelit table—hair slick, clothes matted. Her eyes open wide, and she starts signing. *Are you okay?*

It's the first time we've spoken since our fight at the YMCA, and I want to say so many things. Things that signing just won't do justice.

What happened? she asks.

I slowly put my hand to the back of my neck and thrust it forward gently. *He tried to drown me—scare me is all. I'm fine.*

She nods, but I can tell she's freaked.

I quickly point one finger towards my eye, then circle my hands forward, like I'm riding a horse with invisible reins. *I saw Ryder.*

Her eyes fly open. *What?*

I nod towards the restroom, trying to remember our sister language signs for "shared" and "sinks." *Near the shared sinks, in the bathroom.*

She folds back into her seat for a minute. The relief on her face is obvious—but it's not just relief. It's longing, maybe even jealousy, that I saw him and she didn't get the chance. It annoys me, that he's between us now. That he's just making the wall that we somehow built higher, making it harder to see her on the other side.

I want to be a bigger person right now, but her face, that *wanting*—it triggers something ugly in me.

Sky lifts up her palms. *Where is he now?*

I think of Ryder's hands in my hair, his lips on my lips— then I picture Sky holding his hand back at the YMCA, and how seeing it felt like someone took a knife and cut me. My mind taunts me with an image of Ryder's hands in Sky's hair, his lips on Sky's—

Before I think better of it, I shake my head: *I didn't find out.*

Sky collapses back in her seat, defeated.

I know lies have caused us nothing but trouble—Rolladin's treachery, then Robert's.

Now mine.

But I owe myself a chance. Just a minute alone with Ryder, without Sky around to make things more complicated. And once we finish our conversation, figure out if there's more between us, then Ryder and I will grab Sky and find Mom and the rest of our family. It won't change anything—no harm done, just a little white lie.

I carefully point at her, using my own water glass as camouflage. *Where's your room?*

She sits up again and wraps her fingers around her wine and water glasses, folding the right number of digits around each one. Nine, then two, then four: 924. Then she points to me.

I'm about to start signing my own number when Wren pushes away from the table. "Time to retire." He nods to Francis and Quentin. "Take our esteemed new members to their quarters." He looks meaningfully at me and my sister. "I'll catch up with both of you in the morning."

Francis pulls me away from the table, but I manage to point at Sky before he grabs my hands. *I'm coming for you.*

I lean against the glass wall in my bedroom, counting the minutes until Phee finds me. I've already spent hours combing Wren's bedside bestseller, *The Standard Works: God's New Test for America*, trying to figure out what other evils might await us in this hotel, seeing if I can learn Wren's language of divinity and destiny and somehow talk our way to freedom. But the book is nothing but a condemnation of a dead world, a call to arms for the devoted—a pale shadow of the monster we're facing now.

I try to lie down to relax, but I can't seem to calm down, can't seem to get a handle on my feelings and steer myself into a place of control.

My sister and I are part of the divine plan of a psychopath. My mom has been whisked away to some secret place called the heavenly blue, while Ryder, Trevor, and Sam are tucked away in the dark, secret corners of this cursed hotel. I think of Phee speaking up about leaving, and Wren punishing her with some time upside-down in a water basin.

There's a chance, I'm realizing, that we may never leave this hotel again.

It's been hours since dinner ended, and there's still no knock on my door. Still no sign of Phee.

I torture myself, and imagine Phee and Ryder in the bathroom again. Even with all that's going on, all we have to lose, I still can't shake the jealousy. Still wish it was *me* that was being bullied in the bathroom, if it meant that I was the one who had gotten to see Ryder.

For a second, I wonder if she was lying, and is in Ryder's room right now, browbeating him into liking her. I've never doubted my sister before, and it feels awful. Like I don't trust her, which makes it feel even more like the entire world is unraveling, coming apart at the seams. I don't think I've ever realized how much I need Phee to keep it stitched together.

I throw myself back down on the floor and will the calm, more rational side of me—the side that's shrinking every day—to take over. *I'm sure Phee's trying to find me.*

Then a new panic grips my throat. What if Wren caught her sneaking out and she's in trouble?

I grab my knapsack. I have to distract myself.

I first pull out Ryder's gift, *Waverley*, and run my fingers over the cover, my cheeks warming at the memory of him giving it to me. *This* is what I should read to pass the time. But I glance again at the backpack, at that taunting, addictive spider and its web.

I pull out the disguised journal. I'm angry with it, want to tear it in two. As if this book of secrets represents everything that's wrong with this island—the lies, the·double crosses, the truth hidden in pages and stored in safes.

I thrust open the journal, cracking its spine in punishment, and try to take my mind off the present for a minute.

> *November 10—The temperatures have been quickly*
> *dropping outside. But we stay warm from one*
> *another's body heat in the zoo prisons, and as*
> *POWs, we all get two meals a day.*

And life promises to get better. Mary, or "Rolladin" as the Red Allies call her, has somehow made nice with the enemy. The general releases her from our cells sometimes and takes her to his barracks to consult with her. She's given him information on where she last saw other New Yorkers and has helped him understand the city better. They've been strategizing the best way to use the zoo animals for food and clothing, and collaborating on how to plant crops in the Park for extra rations.

I felt like a traitor by association, selling out New York for a polar bear pelt, but Mary didn't agree with me.

"All that matters now is right here," Mary said, running her finger like a circle around her, the girls, and me. "And then, right here." She pointed to the survivors in the zoo. "There is no New York left to protect."

I just nodded.

I hardly ever fight her anymore. I don't want to.

December 25—Christmas. After the year we've had, Mary's present moved most of us to tears. She delivered it from the other side of the bars.

"We're moving to the Carlyle Hotel."

Whispers from the crowd: What? How is that possible? How did you manage it?

Mary shook her head, tried to calm us down, but she was all smiles herself. She knew she had delivered a miracle. "There will be guards on every floor and in the lobby. But we'll have beds. And doors. And windows."

The 6 train survivors were joyous, chanting, "ROLL-A-DIN. ROLL-A-DIN."

"Mary," I said, waving her over as the crowd bubbled over. "How did you do this?"

"I never gave them a reason not to trust me."

She grabbed my waist and pulled me against her, the bars in between us. Phoenix on my back in a harness. Sky beside me, holding my hand. It was a rough kiss, but tender, promising things to come. And I thought, This is my family. This is us, in a dangerous, new, savage city.

"Someday," Mary whispered, her eyes on fire, "this will all be ours."

I shook my head and laughed, asked her what she meant.

She just jangled the zoo keys in her pocket and told me she had big plans for us.

She released us from our cages, tens, hundreds of us. We stumbled like mad, happy drunks into the freezing air and, guards flanking us, we crossed the Park and poured into the Carlyle Hotel.

I look up from the journal and think about Rolladin's annual Christmas lecture at Belvedere Castle. It's the first time I've thought about the Park in a while. I can close my eyes and practically hear Rolladin's self-important speech echo through the Great Hall. But reading this, it sounds like maybe she *was* that instrumental. Because as dingy as the Carlyle is, it was better than the zoo was for Mom back then. It wasn't freedom, but it wasn't exactly prison, either.

I anxiously watch the door, praying for a sign from Phee. But still, there's nothing.

February 14—Winter has passed by quickly, easily. Short, quiet days where I curl up with the girls and read books in the Carlyle's small library, or play checkers or chess with Lauren in the game room. Sometimes I even get a sliver of an afternoon with Mary—she's barely here anymore.

Last week Bronwyn came back after disappearing into the Red Allies barracks for months. It nearly broke my heart when I saw her. Her once startlingly perfect face looked . . . distorted, as if it had been broken and healed over. And there's now a small bump underneath her sweater. Three months pregnant? Four? I guess now that she carries extra baggage, her Red soldier is done with her, has tossed her like garbage back into the Carlyle slums. I wanted to roar at the skies, just tear down the walls of the Carlyle for this broken girl . . . but I've become an expert at swallowing screams.

There's a few of them wading around here now, girls careless enough to get pregnant, eyes cast down, with small bellies that might as well be scarlet letters.

Women with no pride, no tribe.

Women with nothing left.

Sky won't go to Bronwyn now—it's like she

knows she's a different person. And after days of
trying to break through to Bronwyn, trying to help
her forgive herself, this city, God—everyone and
everything I know she blames for what's befallen
her—I've let her be.

I pray for that baby.

March 1—The Carlyle was aflutter with news and
rumors.

"The Red Allies are combing the streets again
for prisoners," Mary told us. "There're still other
survivors out there. They're bringing them to the
Carlyle."

The others folded in on themselves with
speculations and excitement. But I no longer had
any hope. I've let it go, left it behind in the darkness,
like Mary told me to, before yearning swallowed
me whole. No, Tom and Robert were gone.

Mary pulled me aside as the others compared
notes in the lobby.

"Remember what I told you," she whispered.
"Don't trust anyone else who comes through here.
We don't know what their motives are. As far as
you're concerned, there's only the 6 train."

I nodded but didn't give her anything more.
She'd been talking to me like this recently, almost
as if I was her prisoner, as if now there was
something that separated us. And deep down, I
knew there was—Mary had almost become our
warden, both aligned with us and aligned with our
enemy. I knew the pressure on her, the singularity

she must have felt, weighed heavy. So I decided to cut her some slack and threw my arms around her. Sky mimicked me by throwing her arms around Mary's leg.

"Don't worry," I told her. "We're all yours."

April 2—Another small band of prisoners has been brought to the Carlyle. They're packing us in tight here, and the once spacious hotel now feels like a tenement.

Still, we'll manage. We'll adjust.

These past few weeks, Sky has become a little person. There aren't too many toddlers padding around the Carlyle, let alone ones as happy as Sky, so people love her, and clap their hands in applause every chance they get. Her words have multiplied, and now she's chatting up strangers, sticking her nose into other people's business, making friends.

"She's a cutie," a man, about sixty, said to me from a couple of chairs away in the library. He'd been brought in with the most recent group of survivors, though I'd forgotten if he was captured in the subway or on the streets.

"Thank you."

"What's her name?"

"Sky. Well, Skyler," I said. "She was born when the day was breaking open, and then my husband and I couldn't name her anything else." But the words felt odd as soon as they left my mouth, and I realized I hadn't referred to Tom out loud in

months. "Late husband," I added, again without thinking.

I looked up into the man's eyes. They were dark and serious, and I immediately felt uncomfortable.

"Sky, come here," I said quickly.

"What's your name, dear?" the man asked me.

I didn't have to answer him, because Sky blurted out, "Mommy SA-RAH."

"Skyler," I admonished, and gathered her onto my knee as Phee slept on my other side.

"Is your husband Tom Miller?" the man asked me.

And then I couldn't breathe. It had been so long since I'd heard his name. "I'm sorry. Did we know you? I don't recognize you."

The man moved forward onto the edge of his chair. "Apologies for the twenty questions. Forgive me. Tom was just a friend of mine. From the tunnels."

"The tunnels? Where? How long was he alive for?"

"Oh dear, I—I'm sorry. I haven't seen him in months. He and that artist friend of his . . . Robert . . . they left with those missionaries, who came down from that West Side hotel. He was upset after the summit. He was . . . looking for answers." The man gave me a forced smile. "Tom always said, 'My lovely wife will protect her only piece of Sky, even in darkness.' I loved that. Your husband was a poet in the truest sense."

"Wait," I said, my whole body shaking. "Wait, where were you? Where was he?"

"We were moving around a lot, before we split,"

the man said. "But we were trapped on the 1 line when the city was first attacked."

"But that's impossible," I said. "Back in the summer, we sent Mary—our representative—with a list, to the E-train summit to compare the names of survivors. And his name wasn't on any list." Now my mind and my heart are both racing out of control. "Why wasn't Tom on your list?"

"Of course I remember the E-train summit." The man knew he had upset me, and he threw his hands up in surrender and shifted uncomfortably. "But Mrs. Miller," he said, shaking his head. "Tom was our representative."

My hands start shaking too intensely to keep hold of the journal. I throw the book aside, livid for Mom, enraged myself. The E-train summit—which Rolladin promised my mom she'd attended. Where she'd said she was jumped, her escort beaten and murdered. But if Rolladin had really gone to the summit, she would have found my dad. If she'd gone, Mom would've had our father. We would've had our father. Things would have turned out wildly different.

So why did Rolladin lie and say she went? Just to quiet my mother? Just to keep her, and our family, to herself? I guess Rolladin built an entire island premised on lies. So why not lie to steal, to *hoard*, a family?

Now I understand the full extent of my mother's hatred.

I can't imagine what the years of picturing Dad still out there in Manhattan must have done to Mom, wondering what could have been if Rolladin had attended the summit.

I think back to Mom's face when Robert told her that Dad

had found peace, that he'd gotten a second chance at the Standard. Robert's words had released her, and Mom actually looked freer, *lighter*.

A sickening, clawing feeling crawls up my throat when I think back to Wren's speech at dinner, how he'd said Dad laid his life down for the Standard.

Was anything Robert told my mom true?

What happened to Dad inside these walls?

What's going to happen to us?

I scramble to my feet. I need to talk to someone about all this, *now*, and the only person who will really understand is Phee. Regardless of what's going on with us right now, and how mad she got at me when I tried to figure things out the first time. I need her. I don't work right without her. So I scramble to the door, journal in hand.

I creep out into the hallway, carefully look each way, *will* her to emerge from the shadows.

But still, nothing.

For a brief, paranoid moment, I wonder if I gave her the right room number, and I check the big handwritten laminated sign, hanging from a nail lodged in the door: 924.

Exactly where I told her I'd be.

I close my eyes and try to collect myself before I head back into my room. I look at the sign once more and pick it up to inspect it more closely. Something's odd about it—it's stiff, and much heavier than I thought it would be, almost as if it's made of rock instead of paper. It takes some finagling, but I finally manage to squeeze open the laminate and dislodge the handwritten sign from its grasp.

But there's not just one piece of paper—there are many stuffed in there. Maybe ten or more:

924, 1025, 842, 934 . . .

A deep, petrifying truth starts to sink in and settle.

They didn't just move a few of us last night.

They're swapping and switching all of us, renumbering the rooms, the floors, this whole hotel. A panic rips through my abdomen, reverberates through my whole frame.

How are we going to find one another in this hotel if there's a shifting blueprint?

I'm standing in front of room 825. But I don't enter for a long time, just pace under the dim lights of the hall, in front of Ryder's doorway. I'm more nervous now than I was before the street-fights, than I was when the whorelords caught us on the roof. Than I was when Sky and I were dragged to the castle and we lied right to Rolladin's face. It all seems a million years ago, bush-league stuff, nothing compared to the anxiousness I feel tonight.

Ryder and I alone.

Ryder and I in a hotel room.

Ryder with his hands in my hair, his lips on my lips . . .

I finally work up the courage and knock on the door softly, once, twice, then push the door open.

Ryder's got a few candles lit, making the whole room feel soft, romantic, like a scene right out of one of Sky's lame romance novels. I wonder how he could have gotten them. Jealousy pinches me when I think they could've been a gift from his escort who caught us in the bathroom.

Brainwashed psycho. Desperate Wren groupie.

I'm so focused on mentally bullying this girl that I don't notice Wren and Robert sitting on the bed, as if they've got nothing to do but wait for me to show.

"What are you doing here?" I say, after I recover from the shock of seeing them.

"My dear Sister Phoenix," Wren says. "We should ask you the very same question. Robert told me he made it quite clear that you weren't to leave your room tonight." He stands and hovers over me.

Technically, it's true. After Francis dragged me back to my room, Robert stopped by to tell me that he'd heard about my outburst at dinner. That Master Wren was going to be watching me very closely. That it was important that I exercised restraint, and control, or else they'd be forced to use other measures.

"I'm quite positive he mentioned that solitude is mandatory at the Standard," Wren bites, "as is obeying orders. The Standard is your home, Phoenix. You need to start abiding by its rules."

But I ignore Wren. "Robert, please," I say. "You were friends with my mom and dad. At one point, you were a normal person—"

Wren brings his hand down across my face and slaps me, hard, against the jaw. "Don't you dare speak to Elder Robert that way—"

I rub my cheek, but the words keep gushing. "Robert, we don't want to be here, okay? This place is freaky, and we're alone, and I don't think my dad would've wanted any of this. So even if you meant well or whatever, you've got to let us go." I take a step forward, hell-bent on convincing him. "You've got to let us go."

Robert just backs into the corner, while Wren grabs my shoulders to pull me back.

"Robert, my mom *trusted* you," I talk past Wren. "She doesn't trust anyone, and she trusted you. And you're going to leave her here? Leave all of us to rot in this psychotic hotel?"

Wren slaps me again, but I shrug it off. "Robert!"

"Sister Phoenix, this is all part of God's plan." But Robert's eyes won't meet mine—they're still cast down to the floor. The coward doesn't even have the guts to look at me as he's signing our death sentence. "Your family was meant to find the Standard."

Wren leans over me, shaking my shoulders. "That's right, Sister Phoenix, you're part of a divine plan." He thrusts his face into mine, forcing me to look at him. "A plan set in motion by your father. I am your savior, child, and you *will* obey me."

"You're no savior." I think about all those numb, mute kids at the Standard dinner tonight. "You're just a guy messing people up. Wearing them down till they eventually just . . . throw their hands up and listen to your bullshit."

Wren gives a sharp laugh. "Like you'd know. You've never sat in a dark, dank conference room for months, wrangling chaos, shepherding hundreds away from madness. You've never begged God for the world's second chance as its skies tumbled down and this city dwindled to nothing. You have no idea, the heaviness of the burden on my shoulders," he tells me. "I am responsible for this entire community. All these lives, all these souls, are in my hands."

I try to back away, my shoulders aching from the pressure of Wren's hands, but he keeps me close.

"So don't you dare question me. Don't you even speak to me." Wren grabs my wrist and tugs me towards the door, past Robert, down the hall into darkness. We go up and up, until the stairs run out and dead-end at the top floor. He whisks me down the hall, stops at a door at the end, unbolts a chain on our side, and throws me into the room.

I try to claw my way back out of the darkness, shout with all my might, but he shoves my hands, kicks at my stomach, and closes the door with a *BOOM*.

"LET ME OUT!"

"You will stay here, Sister Phoenix, until you learn your place. Until you accept the gift that I am offering you," Wren barks through the door. "Redemption." Then, more quietly, "For all of us."

I don't see Phee in the mess hall for community breakfast, and I can't spot her in any of the classrooms I pass on the way to my mandated "lessons" for the day. I didn't sleep at all last night, between being worried that Wren found Phee trying to find me, and driving myself crazy that she and Ryder met up in this maze of a hotel. Or worse, that Wren decided to "seal" them. I shudder, still not able to shake Wren's *union for the heavens* comment.

I study the Standard kids as I float down the hall—young men and women with their eyes cast to the floor, little children as silent as ghosts. So respectful, so quiet. So barely present. As I look closer, I realize how many of the young girls are pregnant. Some of them are my age, but most are even younger. And each one is escorted by a young man. It makes me think of my own designated escort, Quentin, who I can't seem to shake. Thankfully, he had Hunting Training with "Elder" Robert outside the hotel, so my arm is free for the moment.

A middle-aged woman who introduces herself as my "headmistress" finds me amid the crowd, then gently grabs my wrist and pulls me, along with a few others, into a small glass room with a few round tables. She motions for us to find seats and returns to the hall to pluck out the rest of her students.

I sit in a chair in the far corner, next to a girl about my age, her stomach so wide and big that she sits a good foot or two from the table's edge. She has a nice face with small features, and thin, translucent hands that reveal a patchwork of veins running underneath them. I'm so lonely I'm bursting to talk to her.

As the rest of the class settles around us, I lean in to whisper, "I'm Skyler." The sound of my own voice shocks me—it's the first time I've spoken all day.

"I know who you are," my seatmate whispers. But she doesn't elaborate.

"Oh." I think back to last night's dinner, and whether I saw this pregnant girl at Wren's welcome soiree for Phee and me. She wasn't there, I'm sure of it. "How?"

"Everyone knows who you are. You're one of Elder Tom's daughters. You're here to fulfill Master Wren's divine plan."

Her words prick the back of my neck, rush over me in a cold fever.

"He's been waiting a long time, for God to give him an answer." She looks at me with guarded eyes. "You're his answer."

"Wait, what—what are you saying? Why? What do you mean?"

But the teacher settles at the front of the room before I can push my seatmate any further. Then it's so quiet, you could hear monkeys howl from Wall Street.

The teacher launches into her lecture—a regurgitation of Wren's *The Standard Works*, a manic sell that God ended the world to give us a new Standard, a promise that one day we'll all see the heavenly blue.

But I barely hear her over the beating of my heart. My

seatmate has just confirmed my greatest fear, the thought that has kept me up at night, tossing and turning and reeling until morning:

We're never getting out of here.

The walls of the classroom start inching towards me, demented in their slow march, intent on closing me in.

Without thinking, I shove my chair back from the table and stand.

"Sister Skyler," the headmistress admonishes. All eyes in the room fall on me, surround me like a swarm. "Please sit down."

"I need"—I barely hear myself over the staccato of my heart—"I need to use the restroom."

"Your escort isn't here today, and I clearly can't send someone else's escort with you. You'll need to wait until I can bring you myself."

"It's all right, I can find my own way," I tell her. "I'll be right back."

As I walk towards the door, four young men near the exit stand like a wall to block me.

"Sister Skyler, *please*." The headmistress gently grabs my elbow. "We believed that you were open enough to accept group lessons. If that's not the case, we shall arrange for other measures. I can speak to Master Wren."

I look behind me for some reason, to my seatmate, who's clutching the table so fiercely I imagine her fingers pressing right through the wood. She gives me the smallest nod, her eyes saying what her lips can't: *Don't be foolish. Sit down and do what they say.*

"I'm so sorry," I mumble. "I didn't realize the rules."

"That's quite all right, Sister." The headmistress exhales

as the four door guards sit down in their seats. "Class, where were we?"

Our teacher jumps back into her lecture, but I catch only bits and pieces: divine unions sanctified by Master Wren, the importance of obedience, the need to repent and show God we are worthy in the wake of so much disaster. I fade in and out of focus, and the same is true for the next day, and the next.

I become a shadow, a ghost, trying to blend into backgrounds and fade into walls, listen with dull eyes to my lectures all day. I keep mute during meals, where I'm attached to Quentin like a duped fly to a spiderweb, wriggling carefully, trying to pick up some clue as to where they've put my mom and Phee, and where Ryder, Trev, and Sam are being stored in this madhouse.

But no one gives anything away—it's as if they never existed.

At night I'm left alone in my room, with nothing but the view of the city and my backpack. One night I burrow through my bag, desperate for Mom's words, even if her journal has done nothing but raise ghosts and cut us on its sharp and jagged secrets.

But the book isn't there.

"No," I say. "No, no, no, no, no."

I fly through the room, tearing off the bedcovers, fumbling through the drawers, combing the bureau, the bathroom. "Where is it?" I demand of the room. "WHERE IS IT?"

I run to the room door and thrust it open, not caring for a second what Standard devotee might see me. I tug at the laminated room sign, pulling out the thick wad of false room numbers, and quickly sift through them. I've been trying to note my room every time I enter and leave, trying to piece together the shifting blueprint and keep track of it all. But the changes are haphazard: Sometimes I'm shuffled once a day, sometimes every time I leave. Mom's journal might be in any room in any hall, forgotten under the bed or accidentally left in the washroom by one of Wren's shuffling minions.

I look down the empty hall.

I'm tempted to run.

I could make it to the stairs, maybe even across the lobby and out the door before anyone would be the wiser. I could hole up in this city, or find my way to Brooklyn, and sail far, far away from this wretched island and the monsters living in its shadows.

But it's a tease, an empty option—not a real choice. I could never, *ever* leave without Mom and Phee. And the truth keeps me chained to this damned city, to this dark and shifty hotel.

I shut the door.

Then I break down. I cry messy, fractured sobs until my head feels like it's been cracked open and my throat is scratched and sore. For my family, for the journal. For everything.

I sink into a deep, dark river, and each day I feel more disoriented. Like even if I wanted to swim to the surface, I might not know which way to come up for air.

It's not until days later that any hope appears.

The hope comes and goes so quickly, I'm almost unable to see it through my fog. It happens one morning as our headmistress funnels children into different rooms. Ryder passes by the door and spots me in my classroom.

He appears like a mirage, his edges fuzzy and smudged, as if I've literally painted him from memory, wished him real. My stomach climbs to my ribs, and I stand instinctively.

Ryder doesn't hesitate.

Before the headmistress can grab him, he darts across the room, his hazel eyes wild, his blacktop hair sticking out in all directions, arms propelling him forward.

"Brother Ryder!" the teacher snaps as he runs. "Brother Ryder, get back here! Brothers, help me, please!" Ryder slips around the conference room table and into my arms. "This is not the way of the Standard!"

Ryder's arms tighten around me, and even in my dark well of despair, I know he's no mirage. I take in his smell and thrust my face into his neck. "Ryder," is all I can manage, before Quentin and two other boys grab his forearms and pull him away. Ryder struggles against their grip, wriggling like a fish on a hook, then leans into me and whispers in his gravelly voice, "The lobby stairwell. Midnight. Five knocks."

That's all.

He's pulled out the door, all the while apologizing, laughing for his stupidity—walking the same thin line, I suppose, between survival and submission. "Sorry, blokes." He shakes his head as they paw and thrust him out the door. "My mistake. Thought she was my escort."

"Never again, Brother Ryder," our teacher scolds. "Go to your classroom down the hall. Brother William shall take you. Now."

"Yes," I can barely hear Ryder whisper. "Sorry, Headmistress."

She shuts the door behind Ryder and his temporary escort, sealing us in our prison. Then the headmistress collects herself before beginning to repeat what she said the day before.

But in these moments, something else besides Ryder has escaped. Out of the corner of my mind, a fast and brilliant form emerges—a butterfly fluttering from a gray abyss. No more illusions, switching rooms and tricks and lies. I will meet him. I will have him. I will hold Ryder tonight.

The lobby stairwell.

Midnight.

Five knocks.

I've never been more excited for anything in my life.

I've been in the same room for days.

Maybe weeks.

I can't be sure anymore. The only way to tell that time's passing is the rise and fall of the sun outside my glass prison, and the two meals that get thrown into my room each day before the lock outside clicks and I'm alone again. I wish I had a piece of paper or something to keep track. I wish I had a lot of things, actually.

The time's been driving me crazy. It's given me way too much room to think. I find my mind fixating on things, questioning things, like it's picking every memory up and inspecting it, trying to see what it looks like under the light, from the other side. This is what Sky does: analyzes. Reexamines. Tries to figure out what it all *means*, why things are the way they are. I hate doing this.

I've been thinking a lot about Sky. About what she said to me at the YMCA. How all her hunches told her something was wrong with this place. How she tried to warn me.

About how I wanted the Standard to be a real answer, so badly that I didn't listen. Wanted there to be a home on this island, for me, Mom, Sky, Ryder, Trevor. Even Sam. Believed a freaking miracle could happen on Manhattan. Now we're here, trapped with these psychopaths. With some guy who's hell-bent on saving us, on making us find our own "path to the Standard." And what choice do we have, if none of us can get off the path?

I'm torturing myself, obviously. But I can't seem to make my mind stop.

After who knows how many days, I hear a knock on my door, and then the latch unclicks and Robert walks in. Half of me is excited to see someone, anyone, besides my shimmery reflection in the windows. Half of me wants to take him down and run through the halls.

"Sister Phoenix," he says. "I trust the Elders are keeping you fed."

"I guess."

He sits down on my bed, uninvited, and rubs his hands through his dark hair. "Have you gained any perspective through solitary?" He looks at me hopefully. "In your time alone, and with God, have you come to see the error of your ways?"

This guy is unbelievable. "The error of *my* ways?" I say. "Robert, you're like, delusional. You guys separate me from my family, bully me into staying here, throw me in this room for days . . . weeks . . . and you want me to just tell you it's all fine, that I get it?"

Something changes in Robert's face as he grabs my hands again. "But you're *not* getting it. You're not getting any of it."

And I finally place the emotion crawling across Robert's face. It's fear.

"I've been here a long time, Phoenix. I've seen the Standard evolve—and change. A few small steps, a few more steps, and things are very far from where they started." Then he hesitates. "And I've seen Master Wren grow, and change. There is more to all this than you could ever know." He breathes deeply, and I take a breath too, 'cause if he's scared, I can't even imagine how freaked I should be. "Now, I loved your father. And I care about your mother deeply—I care about you. But I've sworn my life to the Standard, and I believe in Master Wren." He looks at me. "I'm going to bring him in now. And I need you to tell him that you're done fighting, that you're open and ready to be filled. You're at the end of the line here, Phoenix. Do you understand?"

I know I'm supposed to say yes—I feel it, the weight behind Robert's eyes, the way his hands are twitching in mine. But I can't speak.

So all I do is nod.

"Good."

It takes hours for him to come back. But that's okay. I need the time to try to come up with a plan, like I always do. I've got to be resourceful. I need to find a way to get to Mom and my sister and break us out of this nightmare.

So I keep on spinning Robert's warnings around in my head, then throw around the threats of my idiot escort, Francis. And then I think about what Ryder said, in our meeting in the bathroom, about how Sam was in the heavenly blue. . . . *Ryder, Mom, Sam . . . the Standard . . . other measures, the heavenly blue.*

And then it clicks.

People keep saying Wren's got all these other measures to make people love the Standard. And they keep mentioning this "heavenly blue" place, this totally secret spot where only adults are invited. I need to get there and find my mom and Sam so we can blow this hotel apart. But in order to do it, I'm pretty sure Wren needs to know that nothing else will work—that he's got no choice but to send me there.

When Whackjob Wren comes back with Robert, Wren's got a hopeful glimmer in his eye. I know they both expect me to smile and say, *Thank you for the Standard, the lofty Standard* or some crap, but I've got another plan. A good one. And I've got nothing left to lose.

Wren sits down on the bed and takes both of my hands in his. They're cold and spiny, like a pair of lizards. "Robert tells me that this time of solitude has done wonders for your soul. That you're ready to accept the Standard." He smiles. Then he leans in, far too close. "Is he right, Sister Phoenix? What do you have to say for yourself?"

I take a deep breath and remind myself to stay strong, for my family. To not bow down to this monster till I hear the words "heavenly blue."

I lean in and whisper, "Take your Standard and shove it up your ass."

Robert buries his face in his hands as Wren flies off the bed. "This is all a waste of the savior's time!" he screams at Robert.

Robert starts mumbling an apology. "I thought I had explained, I thought—"

"Do it."

"But Master Wren, she's far too young—"

"Don't you dare question me, after this circus." Wren pulls Robert out of my room.

"Wait, don't go!" Panic pulls me to my feet—did I have

LEE KELLY

things wrong? What did I miss?—and now I'm trailing them, shouting, "I thought I was going to the heavenly blue! Please . . . I need to see my mother—take me now!"

But they shut the door in my face.

Then I'm alone again.

And the loneliness wastes no time. It climbs up my back and saddles my shoulders. It's so heavy it almost crushes me.

My meal that afternoon comes late. At least it feels late, judging from the sun. And even though I don't feel like eating, I take the plate and finish it in three bites. It's a soupy mess of meat, root vegetables, and corn, a fat piece of bread, a thick glass of water.

Then I lie down and just try to relax, just keep picturing Mom and Sky, and Ryder and Trev and Sam, imagine us all walking out of this hotel as it burns in flames behind us.

But it's weird.

Every time I close my eyes, bright red lights start pulsing, like there literally is a fire underneath them. I sit up to shake it off, but sitting up makes my head pound. The room starts dancing, each corner of the room shaking, moving towards me inch by inch.

I thrust my covers off and run to the door.

But when I round the corner to the small entry, the door feels a mile away. And the hall keeps expanding, getting longer and longer. My heart starts beating way too fast for it to stay in my chest for long, and I stumble towards the bed to lie down again and get calm. Maybe this is all a nightmare.

Maybe I just need to wake up.

But each time I shut my eyes, the red lights multiply,

become blue, then green, and then take on faces, until there's a thousand rainbow faces in the insides of my eyelids. I give a little shriek. When I open my eyes, the faces don't go away.

Something's wrong.

Shit, something is *really*, really wrong.

Since I've arrived at the Standard, my dinner seat assignment has been inching towards Wren, and tonight I'm sandwiched between Quentin and the master of ceremonies himself. And even though I'm sure any Standard girl would feel beyond "blessed" for such a prime spot at the table, a few times I have to actually sit on my hands so I don't grab my dinner knife and lodge it into Wren's chest.

I just keep thinking about seeing Ryder tonight. I remind myself that I just need to get through dinner so I can meet him. I *will* myself to stay in control. And I manage to do it— until Mom arrives, that is.

She joins us in the same private dining room I was in with Phee all those nights ago, but doesn't arrive until after the first course. She's escorted by Robert and another middle-aged man on her other side. I almost burst out of my chair when I see her. But I know the rules, so I stay cemented to my seat, nearly giddy just to be near her, to see her after so much time.

The trio inchworms under the light of the chandelier. . . .

Something's wrong. My mom's face . . . it isn't bruised or beaten . . . but it's empty. Twitchy and long. Her two frightened eyes are weighed down by heavy gray bags. Her luxurious auburn hair is sweaty and matted to her brow.

"Mom!" escapes me.

My body aches to run to her, my mouth twitches to scream. But I can feel Wren's eyes on me, and so with every ounce of self-control I have, I stay tethered to his side.

Wren relaxes beside me. "Sister Skyler," he purrs. "You mustn't worry. It's just your mother returning from the heavenly blue." He puts his hand on mine. "The first few trips are always the toughest. She'll adjust."

A thought finally snaps into place, fits into the puzzle of this hotel like the lone missing piece:

The heavenly blue isn't a place.

It's *drugging* people, reshuffling their minds, all for the sake of Wren's "divine plan." Drugging people so they can't fight back. So they can't even think.

I can't look at Mom. This woman, who can barely stand, who's laughing and crying like some hollowed ghoul, she can't be my mother.

But I pick myself off the floor and give Wren the best smile I can muster.

Thing is, I have my sister to thank for surviving this haunted hotel, if you want to call what I'm doing surviving. Phee, who can accept without question. Who doesn't bother siphoning out right and wrong, only what is from what isn't. I've thought a lot about what she said that night at the Park, before the 65th Street fights. When I was so adamant to break the Park rules open and show her how little there was inside.

Who cares how things should work? Phee had said. *What matters is how they do.*

Now I'm studying every motion, every gesture of the Standard devotees, mimicking them. Making them believe I'm being *handled*. And I'm positive they're buying my facade.

So as much as my legs are itching to run to Mom, pull her into a fierce hug, and wrangle her out of her gray misery, I know I can't risk it, for all of us. There's a chance they have Phee locked away somewhere, showing her the heavenly blue, or worse.

I shake my head. I can't, *won't*, let myself think about that. If I do, the few stitches holding me together will finally come apart.

Mom's two escorts help her into her seat. She doesn't look at me, not once during the rest of dinner, and my panic that they might have erased and ruined her threatens to consume me alive.

"You've adjusted so well to the Standard," Wren whispers. He gently strokes my hand as his waitstaff cleans up our dessert. I shudder at his touch but don't pull away. "You and Brother Trevor are the epitome of what we hope to cultivate here."

Trev. My God, I hope he's all right. I'm dying to ask, but I know the Standard rules on devotees' silence during mealtimes. So I just look at Wren with pleading eyes.

He nods. "You may address me."

"Master Wren, is . . . Brother Trevor in the heavenly blue as well?"

"No, he's finding his way without it. The young members of our community are welcoming him with open arms." Wren's face turns solemn. "I try not to take children to the heavenly blue, if I can avoid it. It's not for the weak of heart, or weak of mind." He breaks away from my gaze and nods as his devotees leave the table and retreat back to their rooms. Robert ushers Mom out too, and while I'm dying to follow them, I manage to stay in my seat.

"Brother Quentin, you should also retire," Wren says.

Quentin pauses a moment on my other side. My escort's face is torn, but he doesn't protest—no one ever protests. He crawls back into the shadows of the Standard, and now Wren and I are alone at the table.

"If I may ask, Master Wren, what . . . what about Sister Phoenix?"

"That bull of a child. She never keeps that mouth of hers *shut*, does she? She never does what she's told." His laugh sounds like a sharp *pop*. "Forbidden osculating with Brother Ryder in the bathroom. Violence. A refusal to accept her lessons. There is no option but the heavenly blue for her." He sighs and strokes my hand again. "She's so different from you."

Sweat creeps under my hairline, my throat begins closing. Is Phee safe? Have they gotten to her already? I think of my mother, who mumbled to herself all through dinner, and I nearly scream. *Is that what lies ahead for Phee?*

What was Ryder doing in the bathroom with her, anyway? Did she get caught . . . kissing him, and that's why she's being punished? My envy steps aside and makes way for rage. Is this all Ryder's fault?

I can't think about him right now, how he might be playing both of us. How, because he can't keep his hands off my sister, she might be drugged up in some dark corner of this hell.

I think only about getting us out of here.

So I focus on Wren's hand, floating suggestively above mine.

"The headmistress told us about the heavenly blue, Master Wren, that God instructed you in its divine power," I start cautiously, forcing myself to say the words even though my body's cringing as I say them. "Being God's mouthpiece, taking care of this community . . . you have so much on your shoulders."

Wren's face softens. For a moment, he appears fragile . . . younger, even. He looks like that hopeful, zealous preacher on the cover of *The Standard Works* in every bedside table in every Standard room. "You're right. I do."

"I'd love to help. . . ." I inch forward, carefully, cautiously, very aware that the predator next to me could snap and lunge for me at any moment. "I'd love to take on some of the burden. Maybe if I knew about the heavenly blue—"

Wren grips my hand. "Ah, Sister Skyler, you have already helped me far more than you could ever know." He studies me, his eyes roaming over my face. "Though maybe you *should* know. This is your destiny, as well as mine." He smiles a sad, conspiratorial little smile, like we're about to share a secret. *Yes*, I practically scream, *show me this heavenly blue, teach me what it is, tell me how to destroy it.*

Wren takes me up a few flights of stairs, down a hall, and into a dark, cluttered room at the end of an unmarked corridor. He pulls matches from his trousers and lights a row of candles on a side ledge, and the entire room jumps alive. Glass bottles and flasks and beakers crowd a wide island in the center of the room and cast odd, frightening shadows across the ceiling. Piles of folders and handwritten notes lie at odd angles on the corners of the island. And in the center is a tray filled with paper, cut like a cake into tiny quarter-inch squares.

"My life's work," Wren says, gesturing towards the tray with a flourish. "God's work. The heavenly blue."

When I look at him, confused, he smiles. "We dissolve the doses into the food. It's easier that way. And it only took a couple of years . . . and failed attempts . . . to perfect the dosage."

I know I need to keep up my facade, should be oohing and aahing over the concoctions of this mad alchemist, but I can force only one word across my lips. "Why?"

I immediately wonder if I've pushed too far, been too forward. After all, I don't need to know why. I just need to know *how*, and if there's an antidote.

But Wren's looking at me with that—*guilty? penitent?*—face again, and I know he's going to answer.

"It was after the island became an occupation zone, and the Red Allies had already started scaling back their numbers." He has a far-off look in his eyes. "I was beginning to lose the people. They were hungry, and tired, and our missionary work was starting to wane. There was a restlessness in this hotel . . . talk of abandoning God's work and finally surrendering at the Park. I prayed for an answer." He readjusts the tray of hallucinogens lovingly, like he's stroking a pet. "And then one appeared. A missionary team found a young raider scavenging the Financial District, a drug dealer in a past life." He smiles at the memory. "I gave Elder Francis answers, and he gave me ideas."

I nod towards the tray. "Like the heavenly blue."

Wren nods. "Like the heavenly blue. We introduced it at community services, and . . . *everything* changed. People were humble. People were afraid. They were God's children— my children—again." He looks at me. "Elder Tom didn't approve."

The mention of my father's name jolts me like thunder.

But Wren just shakes his head. "He tried to talk me out of it. When I argued that this was what God wanted, Tom started making noise, planning a defection. He said there were rumors from some of the born-agains that a native was running the Park as some kind of de facto warden. He said we needed to surrender. That the Standard had served its purpose, kept us alive, but now it was done." Then he won't meet my eyes. "I needed him to see."

And even though I've been hunting for the past in the rubble of this city for as long as I can remember, I'm not sure I want to hear any more. "What . . . what do you mean, *see?*"

"I never meant to do so much damage," Wren starts stammering. "I just wanted Elder Tom to feel the awe and the terror of God again. I must have given him too much, I . . ." The Master of the Standard collects himself. "He was broken, Sister Skyler."

Broken.

"I tried to keep him alive, but he was a lunatic, untamable . . . too dangerous, in such a dangerous world. I had to put him down." Wren grabs my hands in his, knocking into the tray, and a tinny echo screams through the lab. "But now you're here. Don't you see? I've been praying to God for years for an answer, for him to assure me that I'm still the chosen, that your father's death was a sacrifice, not a tragedy. And he has." He leans in close, the candlelight distorting his features. "And everything I couldn't give to Elder Tom, I'll give to you. Your family is my redemption, Sister Skyler. You're my second chance."

I think of that young man on the book again, the picture of the hopeful preacher tucked into my nightstand drawer. Then I look at the monster in front of me. This city turned him inside out, like the monsters in the subways, like the warlords in the Park.

The more I hear about the history of this island, the more I feel like it's drowning me. Like it's just a dark current, rising slowly, steadily, pulling me under.

But I can't show Wren anything. He's studying me, waiting for me at a crossroads. Will I follow him down his dark and twisty path, will I say what he wants to hear? Or will I question him, like my father?

"Thank you"—I choke on the words, but I manage to get them out—"for the Standard, the lofty Standard. The only Standard."

Wren bursts into a smile and cups my face with his hand. "You will make such a wonderful wife for an Elder one day." He strokes my arm, and I swear, I nearly vomit. "Although wouldn't it be nice to keep you in my harem with your mother? We'll decide. But in due time." Wren takes my hand and pulls me out of his lab. "Like everything, Sister Skyler. In due time."

I'm a thick, fiery ball of madness. In fact, I'm burning alive. And it's the fault of the red, blue, and green faces. They're attacking me, inch by inch. They haven't left me alone.

Click, click, click and a door is opening. Then three visitors stand above me.

"All the faces," I plead with these visitors. "All the faces are trying to rip me apart."

One of the visitors comes towards me with a knife in his hand—wait, I know this guy. It's Francis. And Francis isn't holding a *knife*, I see, as he gets closer. It's some kind of small, thin piece of paper. A tab.

I lie down to block out the faces, but the little guys are now everywhere. They've somehow escaped out of my eyelids one by one and are now marching all over the bed, poking and scratching me.

Francis says, "You must be ripped apart. To be broken and rebuilt." He shoves the tab into my mouth.

"Just give her one extra dose," says another guy who's with him. I can't open my eyes to see who it is or I'm going to throw up, but I know the voice. Robert. "The first one must have taken effect already."

"Keep an eye on her while I find Master Wren?"

But soon I'm alone. Robert and Francis have left me with the faces. They're growing legs and advancing. They're becoming an army. They're getting stronger. They're not going to leave me alone. Maybe ever again.

I'm sick, nearly paralyzed, with anger. About everything. Not just about the fact that my mom's being hollowed, or that Phee might be next. That my father's life was stolen from him right inside these smothering walls.

I'm furious with Ryder. I picture him running across the classroom, embracing me like I'm his whole world. And meanwhile he's making out with my sister, getting her caught while he walks free? What, has he actually accepted the Standard? Plans on keeping both of us on his chain, helpless, lost girls—until he decides?

There's no clock in my room, so I spend the better part of the next few hours staring angrily out the window, willing the moon to hurry up and rise. I count the minutes to what feels like midnight. I fall in and out of a superficial sleep, thinking only of Ryder's face when I tell him off tonight.

I wait until the night is so black that the downtown buildings have faded into the midnight canvas. I carefully open the door and glance both ways down the narrow, abandoned hall. I turn right and tiptoe to the stairwell at the end of the corridor and head down, then duck under a landing and wait.

Ryder doesn't arrive for what seems like a long time—so

long that I've started to doze off again, and only wake to the rushed scuffling of feet on the steps. That warm, antsy feeling I often get when I think about Ryder crashes over me like a wave. It's even stronger, now that I sense he's so close. But I try to remind my body how angry I am with him.

To be safe, I don't speak, and instead raise my fist and knock on the steel staircase below me.

Bum-bum-bum-bum-bum. Five knocks.

"Skyler."

I hesitate. Finally, "Ryder."

His footsteps migrate to my voice.

"Did you happen to bring a light?" he whispers.

"No. You?"

"No."

His face starts to materialize in the darkness, not fully, just hooded features.

"Who cares?" he says. "It's enough to almost see you, and know you're really here." Ryder breathes deeply. He reaches for me, but I dodge his grasp. I watch him balk, then recover. "We could run out of here right now, you know," he says. "No one knows we're gone."

"Just the two of us?" I ask, but he doesn't catch my bitterness, or else ignores it.

"That's how they keep us here, isn't it?" he whispers. "Dividing and weakening us. Keeping us all tethered to this hotel with isolated chains." He stays silent for a while, and when he next speaks, his voice cracks. "I haven't seen Sam since we got here, Skyler. They just keep saying he's gone to the heavenly blue."

An image of my mom, hollowed, drugged up, defeated at dinner, flashes through my mind. And even though I'm angry with Ryder, I don't have the heart to tell him what the heavenly blue means for Sam.

"This place is a gateway to hell, I'm sure of it," Ryder growls. "So they just brainwash and bully everybody? Why is no one fighting back? How do all these people just . . . *accept* it?"

His question oddly brings me back to Phee's words, the ones that I've been using as a compass through this hotel of horrors. *Who cares how things should work?* she'd said about the rules of the Park. *What matters is how they do.* Maybe dissecting everything, dubbing things as right and wrong, is a luxury. Maybe it's only possible to judge when you're not in the trenches, fighting each day to survive. "They've been fed the Standard doctrine so long, maybe they don't think there's even a choice," I whisper, still lost in thought. "And when it got darker, and deeper, it was too late to climb out of it."

"Oh, please. The Standard is just evil, run by evil, terrible people. Plain and simple," Ryder says. "And I'm floored you think any different. You're the one with all the bright-line rules on right and wrong. You're seriously going to give this place—Wren and Robert and all these Standard monkeys—a free pass?" His voice has grown louder, a little more heated, and it reminds me that I have some bones to pick with him, too.

"Stop twisting my words," I snap at him. "I hate this place for what it's doing to my family. *And* to yours."

I collect myself, take a few big, shaky breaths, and try to level out my voice, drain all of the heat out of it, so I can serve the next sentence icily cold.

"I'm just surprised you take such a black-and-white stance on the Standard," I say. "Since your own moral choices are pretty damn questionable."

I feel him recoil from me in the darkness. "What are you talking about?"

"Oh, you know what I'm talking about."

"Sorry, I'm afraid I don't. Enlighten me, Saint Sister Skyler."

I'm trembling before I can even get the words out. "My sister," I say. "If you're hooking up with my sister, I don't know why you're meeting me in the dark."

"What?"

"You got her in trouble, you know that? You got her locked up and punished by Wren himself. So you can stop thinking you're playing both of us."

"Wait, no. Skyler, stop. Listen to me—"

"I thought you were different. But you just show up and turn everything upside down." I know this isn't fair, to blame Ryder for existing. For coming into Phee's and my world and altering it forever, just by being who he is. But it's far easier to blame someone in front of me than to retrace the small steps and missteps that got us here. "Just leave me alone, all right? Good luck to you and your million wives."

I stand up quickly and start climbing the stairs.

"Skyler!" he says, and in a quick tornado of a moment, grabs my wrist and pushes me against the stair rail. He looks like a shadowy, haunted monster, only his pupils shining in the darkness. "I want *you*. Not your sister. And she knows that. At least she should—and so should you."

I'm livid, still don't believe him. But I want to. "Wren said you kissed her, in the bathroom. Why?"

"*She* kissed *me*." Ryder pulls away from me a bit. "It all happened so quickly, and the psychotic Standard girl I'm paired up with saw the two-second peck and made a huge deal of it. I'd never lead Phee on, least I didn't mean to—she's a friend, plus she's your sister." He sighs. "I would have stopped her sooner if I had known what was coming, Sky. You have to know I'd never put any of your family in danger. They're too important."

I don't answer him, even though his words are the right ones.

"Sky, please. You've got to believe me. I swear it. I swear it on my mother's life."

Then his hands cross the threshold between us, his fingers carefully finding their way across my stomach in the dark. I both shudder and warm at his touch.

"I've been intrigued by you from the minute I saw you. In the Park. Through the woods." His fingers find their footing, dance carefully on my abdomen and wrap around my waist. And I know he's waiting for me to pull away, to tell him to stop. But I can't breathe, let alone speak.

"This hauntingly beautiful girl, wishing on a moon," he whispers. He moves his hands from my waist, then runs his fingers up and down my arm cautiously.

"You're a student of the old world. A crusader for a moral future," he continues, nothing but hot whispers against my shoulder. Then he dares to place his lips gently underneath my ear. Touching, taunting—the effect is ripples through my entire frame. "And I can't say good-bye to you again. I won't. We're getting out of here, Skyler—together."

And even though part of me wants to stay here, buried in his arms, and just forget the world and all its monsters for a minute, a raw, almost primal ache for my family pulls me away. "I'm scared we're never going to find them, Ryder."

"Stop, Skyler, don't say that. We'll figure out a way."

The angry little army of red, green, and blue faces hasn't let me go. If anything, they've advanced farther—taken up permanent tents in my ears and mouth and mind.

It's time to get out of here, they whisper. *We need to seek redemption on our own.*

The army pulls me up, towards the entry, takes over my arms and pushes against the door. I don't know what black magic they use, but for the first time since I was thrown in here, the door just lazily stretches wide to the hall.

I don't hesitate. I don't question them. I stumble into the hallway, my mind just as unsure and untrustworthy as my footing.

To the stairs, the army cries.

We crawl towards the stairs, each step shaky, hesitant, like we're combing through a minefield. I stumble into the stairwell, grip the handrail like it's the only thing keeping me upright.

Two forms float out of the darkness, on the stairs. I can't see who these people are, but they're tangled. It's intimate here, and I feel like I've stumbled onto something sacred. I shouldn't be here.

Reverse course, I tell the army.

The army answers, *But there is no going back.*

The forms mold themselves out of the dark, like clay, it's—

Sky and Ryder, on the stairwell.

But it can't be.

Are they free? Are they together?

Did they forget all about me?

Did they leave me locked in that room?

Betrayal spreads like fire, singes my arms and legs.

"Phee!" Sky rushes. She untangles herself from the knot of limbs. "Thank God, where've you been—"

"Don't pretend like you care!" *Get me out of here, I'm serious,* I tell the army.

"Phee, stop—," Ryder says.

"No, you stop! Just leave me alone!"

"Phee, come on!" They surround me, try to pin me down. But something's snapped in me, and I can't stop moving.

"Phee, are you on something?" Sky says, as she gets a good look at me. "Ryder, Wren said he was going to drug her. She's on something, I know it. Help me, please."

Ryder looks deep into my eyes, tries to figure out what secrets I'm keeping. But I'm empty. The two of them have just gutted me clean. "Leave me alone."

"Phee." Sky's crying now. "Oh my God, what have they done?"

She reaches for me again, but I'm broken, and I can't control myself anymore. I slap her hand away, then bat at the walls, the air, the windows. It's all closing in on me. I want to go home. No, I want to go *back*, to the way things were. When I knew who I was, and who she was. When there wasn't anything between us.

Now the whole world's between us.

"Ryder!" Sky cries. "Ryder, we need to do something!"

"Phee." Ryder's voice grabs and shakes me in the dark. "Phee, please, please, are you in there?"

But I hate him right now. I don't want him. Not if he doesn't want me.

I close my eyes and will myself back in time. And the army listens. They carry me there. I don't know how, but they do, and then I'm lying in the middle of a green open field.

I smell the stew cooking, the thick scent of meat in the air.

And Sky's beside me. Not this Sky, but the one who gets me. The one who would never abandon me for a guy.

And then I know where we are. "The Park," I whisper. "Sky, the Park."

The army has grown louder and more restless, is angry that I've spoken. *Let us handle this*, they say. They are screaming from the inside, telling me to give in.

So I do. It's just too much. I can't hold them back any longer.

I let the army finish me off, collapse me piece by piece until I'm nothing but a void.

A black hole once known as Phee.

Phee's eyes go blank, dead. She's still trembling under Ryder's grasp, but the light in her eyes has been extinguished, pinched out like a flame.

My sister. My young, strong, beautiful little sister is quivering like a hollowed ghoul. She looks like Mom. New Mom. Empty Mom.

I fall to the ground. I can't catch my breath. I can't— I can't stitch my heart.

Ryder gently shakes Phee's shoulders, tries to wake her carefully, then he whispers again in her ear. "Phee. Phee, come on, Phee. We know you're in there."

But she doesn't respond, she doesn't do anything. "Is she breathing?"

Ryder listens to her chest and gives a nod. "Yeah, yeah, she's breathing. She must've passed out. Sky, I don't"—he looks up at me, helpless—"I don't know what she's on."

"I do." I hesitate. "They've given her a hallucinogen . . . called the heavenly blue."

A slow wave of realization passes over Ryder's face. But before he can answer, we hear footsteps. A hurried, panicked scuffling on the stairwell above us, maybe three, four pairs of feet.

"We need to go," Ryder says. He tries to pull me down the stairs, hide me behind the next bend, but I can't leave Phee.

"Sky, we need to leave," he whispers. "If they find us, we'll both end up like this. We're not going to help anyone by getting caught. Come on."

He's right. But my guilt keeps me hammered to the ground, wiggling against his grip.

I hover over the blank, frozen face of my sister. "Pick her up." My voice is high and strangled. "We'll move her." I start to pull her arm, but she's deadweight. "Help me."

Ryder tightens his hold around me. Then he pulls me off my feet, twists me over his shoulder, and carries me down two flights. He muffles my cry of surprise as the footsteps stop shuffling, and voices above begin speaking.

"There she is!" a familiar voice bellows above us.

"You better thank the Standard there she is, Robert. How could you have left the door unlocked?" another, mostly definitely Wren, answers.

"I ran back to my quarters," Robert sputters. "It was a minute, maybe two, I swear. She was out cold when I left her."

"You're way too soft on this one. You have been since the moment they got here." Wren doesn't say anything for a minute. "Well, she's definitely out now. She won't be any more trouble for a while."

As the feet above us begin to shuffle again, we hear grunts of exertion. They must be taking her out of the stairwell and back to her room. But I can't lose Phee to this hotel again. I can't let her be sucked into the twists and turns of its haunted halls until she loses herself completely. "We need to follow them," I whisper.

Ryder puts a finger to his lips.

"Should I give her another dose?" another man asks.

"Another dose might kill her. We'll give her another tomorrow morning. And the morning after that, and so forth. Put her on the official rotation. Have one of the head-mistresses start spending some time with her during the peak of the trip. She'll cave. They all do." A pause. "Pity, I do so hate using this method with children."

The footsteps start retreating back the way they came.

"Ryder." I'm about to lose it completely. "My dad. You don't understand. We need to follow them, we need to—"

He shakes his head. "If they found you, if they caught you, I couldn't live with it."

"You heard them, they're going to keep doing this to her. Until she bends, or until she breaks. I can't—"

"Skyler, please, I've already lost far too many people I care about—I couldn't watch this happen to you." He grabs my hand. "Listen, Wren thinks your family's special . . . some of the Standard kids, even the headmistresses whisper it." And even though I don't want to admit it, I know he's right. Wren's made that clear. "So we need to use that, Skyler. We need to keep you the model Standard citizen till we figure our way out of here."

"Ryder, I can't just sit in my room and . . . and *hope* that everything works out."

"No, we'll meet tomorrow, same time, same place, and regroup," he says. "And if I don't show up for some reason, you run away from here as fast as you possibly can. You leave alone, you got it?"

"I'd never leave without my mom or Phee." I gulp. "And I'd never leave without you."

He flashes me one of his off-center grins. "I promise, you won't have to."

Ryder's treads are so soft that I barely hear him round the stairwell. I wait in the darkness a long time, paralyzed, my thoughts circling like vultures, preying on my sanity.

I wipe my tears away, barely able to see. I picture my mom, a walking zombie, screaming and mumbling under the Standard candlelight at dinner. And Phee, thrashing at the world, and then nothing but a hollow shell.

My mother, Phee, Sam—if they're all being brainwashed, if they're being drugged until all the life leaks out of them, who's going to stop Wren? How are Ryder, Trevor, and I going to bring down a master of manipulation, and an army of devotees?

I promised Ryder I would go upstairs, curl up in those warm, suffocating covers, and wake up ready to keep playing at this losing game.

But I know, as much as I know that the sun rises over the East River, that if I crawl back to my room, we'll never leave this place alive.

I rack my brain, trying to think of a way out, a way to bring Wren crashing to his knees, but it's useless. I'm slip-sliding through my own mind, flailing, grasping for ledges that just aren't there.

There are no sanctuaries, no mercy, no answers in this hotel.

Then Phee's haunted words prick me.

The Park. Sky, the Park.

I sit up with a start, the rays of an idea dawning.

The Park.

Rolladin.

LEE KELLY

But it's not a real answer.

Last time we were in the Park, we were running for our lives, a price on our heads and warlords on our heels. We're wanted for murder: To go to the Park would be suicide.

But then I think, hopefully, wildly, about the journal. Rolladin loved Mom. It was obvious in those pages, even if it wasn't obvious to Mom. Rolladin might love us, too.

Might, a small, more knowing part of me scoffs. It presents evidence as clear as pictures—the extra chances, the extra rations. The leeway when others were given prison, or worse.

She loved you, too.

Is the leader of the Park the same woman, in some way, as the Mary from Mom's book? Could she save us? Would she?

Am I willing to risk my life to find out?

I think of the alternative, staying here, and know, beyond a shadow of a doubt, this isn't a choice.

This is our only chance.

I fly down the stairwell, my feet barely hitting the ground, crack the door at the bottom, and peer into the lobby. There are no armed guards here overnight, like there are at the Carlyle. Just two young minions pretending to keep watch and heavily making out in the corner.

I watch patiently from the stairwell. Finally, the girl, acting coy, slips away and runs behind the check-in desk. When her young suitor rushes to chase her, I slip through the glass hotel door.

In my thin wisp of a nightgown, I sprint out into the night, into the cold corpse of a city, a city I've hated since I was old enough to know what hatred was. I run up the High

Line, keeping the Hudson River on my left, sprint until goose bumps cover my flesh, until my teeth start chattering so wildly I think they're going to fall out of my head. I run until I forget that raiders and feeders could be lurking in the shadows, until my bones feel so stiff and cold, I swear I'm going to break.

Run, Sky, I can practically hear Phee's voice pleading in my ear. *Run.*

When the High Line dead-ends, I fly down a rickety flight of stairs and keep running. Past 34th Street, past 42nd Street, up Broadway through a maze of littered taxis, a graveyard of faded signs. I run and run, half-afraid of where I'm going, half-confident that almost all roads lead to the Park.

I stop only to breathe. Only when my lungs are about to burst and the cement has pounded my flimsy slippers to the point where my legs are about to shatter.

Finally the twists and turns of the cement jungle run into a forest of green and autumn gold. And for just a moment, I feel like Dorothy when she first arrived in Oz, the sheer, breathtaking beauty of the Park overwhelming me.

Then I remember my suicide mission. That there's not a minute, a second, to spare.

I reach down into the part of me that I never knew existed, not until these past few weeks, anyway. To my layer of malnourished courage, to my soft undercurrent of determination. I close my eyes and picture Phee beside me.

I channel her.

The last time the two of us ran through these woods together, we were sprinting from the zoo, running for our lives. Now I'm racing against time to get back in.

I take a huge breath and start dashing towards the forest.

I start yelling before I hit the trees, a deep, bellowing wail of a yell, not my voice. The voice of someone better.

Someone fearless.

"Please show us the lords' mercy!" I call into the darkness, my nightgown flapping behind me like a white flag. "Please show us the lords' mercy!"

I'm not myself, but I see myself. At least I see who I was, who I think I was—Phoenix. Blond hair, closed eyes, limp arms and legs. Me, I'm floating somewhere else now, just a voyeur without a body. Forced to watch.

Phoenix is being taken up the stairs by a team of men. They drag her through the hall, propel her forward, and she offers no resistance. She just lies in their arms, aware but unaware, present but somewhere else.

Like a puppet. Not a real girl.

The group enters Phoenix's room.

"Put her on the bed," Wren orders the men trailing behind him. "She's not going anywhere anymore."

The men lay her down, and Wren leans over her. "Sister Phoenix, this too shall pass," he purrs, petting her hair. She tries to flinch and pull away, but she can't move. "Bring in the boy."

"But, Master Wren," one of the men—Francis—says, "I thought I was to be sealed with her."

Robert nods. "Master Wren, the boy's too young—"

"How dare you question me, after the mess you made tonight," Wren interrupts. "*I* ask the questions! *I* am the embodiment of the Standard!" He sighs and collects himself. "If we give her to the boy, we win the boy. If we win the boy, we win that self-appointed guardian of his. Stryder or Ryder or whatever. We get him, we have his brother," Wren continues. "Then we'll have the girl's mother and sister, too. People are nothing but dominoes. Knock the right one down and they all fall. Come," he says. "Let's get the boy."

They grab me on the Great Lawn. At least ten of them—they move out of the trees, drawn like moths to the escaped field-worker going down in flames.

"Please show us the lords' mercy!"

Five, ten, then fifteen warlords converge on me, picking me off the ground, until I'm just a caught animal, stretched and ready for roasting.

"You must be suicidal," Lory hisses into my ear as the troop of guards carries me towards the castle. "Rolladin's had a price on your head for weeks. You've signed your own death sentence, marching back into the Park." She gives a tight, confused laugh. "You Millers are masochists."

We burst into the dimly lit hall of Belvedere Castle, the warmth of the firecups burning my frozen limbs like fiery ice. My arms are nearly ripped from their sockets as I'm pulled forward, down the entryway. The ceiling oddly looks lower, the hall shorter, than I remember, especially compared with the awe-inducing tower of glass we're trapped in now.

Rolladin is in her chambers when I arrive. She's waiting, already expecting me, the news of my return getting here faster than I could.

"We found her shouting through the Park." Lory gives me a small shove forward. "She asked for the lords' mercy."

Rolladin doesn't look at me, not once, has eyes only for her guards. "The lords' mercy," she says. "Hmm."

She stalks to the bar behind her desk in the far corner, the same one where she'd pulled the whiskey bottle out for Phee and me, all those nights ago. When my greatest fear was my younger sister overshadowing me, becoming a warlord. That fear seems a luxury, compared with all that awaits us at the Standard now.

Rolladin pours herself a half glass of whiskey and downs it. The warlords and I hang on her every movement, awaiting her word.

She thrusts the glass onto the table. "You killed one of my guards. Injured another," she finally says. "The lords' mercy is hardly appropriate." She looks at Lory as she delivers my sentence: "Solitary confinement. Take her to the primate tower."

No.

"Yes, Rolladin," the guards say in unison, tightening their grip, and pull me back out the door.

"It was an accident!" I stammer. "Self-defense. Cass was about to kill Phee!" I struggle against my captors, appealing to Rolladin with wide, pleading eyes. "I need your help! They're drugging them! My mom, Phee, we need you! Please!"

"Quiet." Lory spins me around, dragging me down the hall, as I thrash with all the energy I have left.

"Please, Rolladin," I wail over my shoulder. "They're going to die!" The tears spring forward. "You have to help me, please!"

Rolladin walks slowly behind us as we push and pull down the hall. I crane my neck, trying to see her, trying to get her to see me, to show her the desperation in my eyes.

I try to probe through the Rolladin exterior to the Mary inside her, the woman I read about, the one I came to see.

"My dear, the one thing I've really learned from the war," Rolladin purrs as I'm taken down the hall and back out into the cold. Her form gets smaller, her voice softer, like I'm drifting away from a shore. "Is that there's really no such thing as second chances."

Before the cold air outside the castle slaps me, I call out once more, "Mary!"

Then the doors close.

They leave me, alone and shivering, in the primate tower.

Phoenix doesn't stir. And I'm still here, watching her. Removed, a visitor at a horror show played out behind glass.

Two of Wren's men return with a basin filled with water and a cool towel to wipe Phoenix down, to prepare her for something I'm sure I don't want to see. They do their job quickly and place the basin and the towel in the bathroom. They leave one of their torches hanging in a slot attached to the wall.

There's silence for a minute, a lifetime. Then different voices enter the room.

"Master Wren." Trevor, who I haven't seen in weeks, trails Wren into the belly of the bedroom.

I see Trevor, now, for what he is. He's a teenager, even though when I was Phoenix, he was never more than a kid. He's tall and thin, with a kind, even face, confused eyes. And he looks nervous. But also happy, expectant. Unlike me. Unlike the girl on the bed.

"Brother Trevor, we find you most willing to accept the Standard," Wren whispers into Trevor's ear. "And we reward those whose souls are empty and ready to be filled. As I promised, this Sister is our gift to you."

"Gift," Trevor repeats. His face looks puzzled, torn. Like he knows there's something wrong, but he'd rather not think about it.

"You are old enough to partake in the most sacred tenet of the Standard. Being sealed with another, creating new life to serve me and my Standard. Only then will you truly become part of us," Master Wren whispers. "Do you understand what I'm asking of you?"

Trevor's quiet for a long time. "I don't think I've ever been a part of anything."

"You will be tomorrow morning," Wren says. "Do not disappoint me."

Master Wren walks away from Trevor and out the door, leaving him with Phoenix. I want to wake her. I want to shake Trevor. But I have no hands. I have no voice. I have nothing left.

"How . . . how are you?" Trevor asks Phoenix.

Silence.

"I heard about you kissing Ryder from Sister Ava," he adds. "I don't care."

More silence.

"I love you," he blurts out. "I always have."

I watch him slide in beside Phoenix's body. He's tender with the girl on the bed. He . . . puts his fingers carefully in her hair, as if she might disappear if he moves too suddenly. He dares to put his lips against her shoulder, curling himself into a ball, imprinting his body next to hers.

"I know you think you're too good for me," he whispers. He carefully puts his hand on her stomach. He's testing the waters inch by inch. "You *are* too good for me," he says. "But maybe you'll feel differently. One day."

After a long time of lying next to her, he cautiously props himself on his forearms and leans over her. I watch his face turn gray. He knows something is wrong.

Something *is* wrong, Trevor. Something is really, truly wrong.

"The love potion will kick in soon, I promise," he says. "Then everything will be as it should be."

He inches closer to her, studying her drawn, pale face.

He lowers himself down to her lips. He grazes them softly, gently—

Then he stops.

His pause waters a tiny seed of hope in me. I try to make it grow. I push it out of my body like a new limb, will it to reach out and wake the girl on the bed. I try to breathe life into her, force her to speak with me. Beg her to tell Trevor what's ripping us apart.

"Please," we finally, barely, whisper. "Don't see me like this."

I'm jarred awake by a heavy blanket thrown at my feet. I don't remember falling asleep. All I remember is being bullied behind bars, screaming until my voice finally gave out, and curling into a ball of defeat in the corner. The stagnant air of the primate tower, thick with trapped humidity, must have finally knocked me out.

I jump at the scrape of a match. A burst of warm light illuminates the black hole of the prison.

I shield my eyes. "Who's there?"

"Who do you think?" a rough whisper answers me.

My eyes settle and there, in front of me, puffing on a long, thin white cylinder, sits the warden of the Park.

I'm speechless, but Rolladin doesn't say anything either. She just lifts the flaming roll of paper to her lips, offering me nothing but soft, hazy rings of smoke. But this feels like a chance.

"What . . . what is that?"

She eyes me carefully. "A cigarette."

"I've never seen one before," I whisper, very conscious that the fate of my family rests in this woman's hands. And in mine.

"I outlawed them in the Park." She shrugs, squashing the end of the stick into the cement floor with a flourish. Then, thinking twice, she promptly lights another. "Didn't need any temptation after I decided to quit."

I don't ask her why, if she gave them up, she's smoking one now. I don't know what to ask her, what to say. It feels like I've talked myself into a corner in about three seconds, until I remember a vague, borrowed memory from Mom's journal.

"You used to smoke, before the war," I say cautiously. "You had a lighter in the tunnels."

Rolladin doesn't answer.

"You used it to guide everyone up to Great Central."

"Grand Central."

"Right, of course. Grand Central."

It could just be shadows' illusions, but I swear the smallest of smiles plays at the corners of her mouth.

"We're . . ." Dare I say it? Do I actually dare to say it? *Stop it. There's nothing left to lose.* "Related," I finish.

She sucks in quickly on the cigarette, and a startled *"PUGH!"* escapes her lips.

She looks at me for a long time, until my stomach starts sinking, until my face becomes hot with anticipation over her impending rage. "Your mother finally told you that?" No feeling, no emotion. Just a question.

"In her own way," I hedge.

"Interesting."

"Why . . . ," I start, but there are too many ways to finish my question. Why did I have to read a journal to know that? Why did Rolladin lie about the E-train summit and tell my mother to give up hope on my father? Why does she act like she doesn't know us, not really?

And why is she here with me now?

"Your mother and I," she finally starts, but it seems that her words too, are betraying her. She fingers her crumpled pack of cigarettes, as if it might contain some answers. As I'm thinking the pack is probably older than I am, she pulls one of the sticks out and hands it to me through the bars.

"Thank you."

"Other way. Turn it around."

I reverse the cigarette and stick it into my mouth. It's got a wheaty taste, burnt cinnamon, and she snaps another match and lights it. A storm of smoke attacks me and burns through my nose and ears. "That's pretty brutal."

"If you can believe it," Rolladin says, smoke spiraling out of her mouth like silk, "each one gets better."

I try once more, peck the cigarette and let the smoke escape quickly, and manage to avoid choking.

"The thing about your mother is that she's stubborn." Rolladin takes a long pull from the bottle of whiskey I didn't realize was next to her. "And she blamed me for everything. Not just for that mess with the E-train summit, but all of it. Did she tell you *that*?"

It's obvious, I think. *She hates you, despises you.*

But I just shake my head.

"If you two were sick. If you weren't getting enough rations. If one of the soldiers looked at her funny. Anything. I was responsible for both of us. For all of us." I simultaneously cringe and soften at the word "us." "All the time. But I didn't mind."

I think again of the journal, about Rolladin on every page. How her smothering need to protect, her caging love for my mother, breathed life into Mom's words.

"No?" I whisper.

She closes her eyes, as if she's conjuring younger versions of all of us, long ago. "No." She takes another hard swig.

"That damn E-train summit, I swear"—and I get the sense she's no longer talking to me—"if I could go back and do it all again, I'd keep going. I'd find the damn meeting, despite the fact that we were attacked by those cannibals, Dave strung up and pulled apart like a roast. I'd die trying to do it, to say I did it. So there was no confusion. Though at that point, if I had found my brother"—she laughs—"I don't know what any of us would have done."

But I haven't heard the last part: I'm focused on the cannibals. I'm trying to remember exactly what Mom wrote about the E-train summit, trying to mentally conjure the pages. In the journal, Mary told Mom that she went to the E-train summit and had been attacked by the summit members themselves . . . then later, Mom found out she was lying.

There was never any mention of tunnel feeders.

"Did Mom know how you were really attacked?"

Rolladin stares at me with blank eyes, and I wonder if she really sees me, or if I've somehow become a window, a portal to the past. "Everyone knew we were attacked," she mutters. "But they didn't know by what. I said we were jumped. Wasn't about to tell a bunch of malnourished, terrified captives that Dave had been eaten alive. That I'd escaped within an inch of death. That living in the tunnels was turning people inside out, and there were nightmares down there, even worse than what was going on at the surface. So, no," she says. "I thought it best to keep that to myself."

But after the Standard, I'm not sure what sounds like truth anymore, and I get a sudden, feverish feeling that Rolladin might be lying. That she's put me behind bars to feed me this story and make some kind of bizarre peace with herself.

"Rolladin"—I try to remember my place—"if you had just told Mom about the tunnel feeders, don't you think she'd understand why you never went? Why you never found my dad?"

"Never got the chance to," she says. "When she found out I never went to the summit, Sarah stole one of my guns and escaped from the Park. Took the two of you with her. I didn't see her for months."

She lights two new cigarettes and hands one to me. Even though I feel my lungs shrinking away in my chest at the offer, I accept it through the bars.

"After she was brought back," she continues, "when they started the census, she was a different person. For years, I tortured myself with the idea that *I* had broken her." Rolladin shakes her head. "She pretended we were strangers, to the point where we *were* strangers." She takes a long drag, lets tendrils of smoke curl around her words. "Until she and her children hated and feared me, just like everyone else. It was devastating. I'd allowed myself . . . to hope for so much more."

I watch her, this woman wrapped around a bottle. Smoke clinging to her tight flame of red hair, her polar bear cloak hanging off her shoulder—our bloodthirsty, backbreaking Rolladin. And even though part of me wants to see *Mary*, more, perhaps, than I can even begin to understand, I can't see this woman as anything but my warden. Maybe that's what Rolladin mourns—having us see her in a different way, having someone know that there is, or was, more to her. But my mom killed that possibility. Or Rolladin did, when she drove Mom away.

It makes me think of Phee, of course, how we've drifted. Of the way we've been recently, missing and misunderstanding each other, growing apart. It makes me wonder how two people can ever go through something together and come out the same way on the other side.

As if sensing my thoughts, Rolladin asks, "What happened to you, when you left?"

I take a deep breath.

Then I tell her, about all of it—about the cannibals in the tunnels, about Robert. About the crushing void of the Standard, and what had happened to our Dad there. Mom, now comatose and disconnected. Phee, just an empty vessel. I tell the story brutally, honestly, quite aware that all our lives depend on its telling.

When I'm done, Rolladin slowly wraps her thick knuckles around the bars of the cage and squeezes. But she doesn't say anything for a long time.

"I'll help you," she finally says. "Like you asked. Tomorrow morning, I'll talk to my Council. You tell us where to go. We'll get them back."

"Rolladin, thank you. You can't imagine what they're doing down there. The Standard—they're monsters."

"This city, this world. It's full of monsters," she says. "The world's a terrible place. And despite what your mother thinks, it's still my job to keep you safe."

I get an odd prickly feeling at the back of my neck. *Keep us safe*. Keep us stored away in a park in the middle of a tiny island. Keep us dressed in lies. And for a minute I can't hold in my emotions any longer. I just need answers.

"Rolladin, the war," I say, before I can think twice. "Why'd you lie? Why didn't you tell us it was over?"

For a second, everything but pure anger drains from Rolladin's face. "Don't talk to me about things you don't know." She rages forward and grips the bars of the jail, rattling them, and I fall back in surprise.

I've blown it. With one bold, stupid question, I've blown my family's chance to be saved.

Rolladin slowly steps back from the cage. "You're young. I forget how young sometimes," she says. "So you can't understand. The people who survived this—our lives were *stolen*. Mine and your mother's and the hundreds of others who spent months crawling through the tunnels eating and praying and shitting alongside each other."

She begins to walk towards the stairs, then turns. "I rode into Jersey years ago, after the Red troops were pulled out of the boroughs and shipped to other fronts. After I didn't receive news from our captors for weeks, then months. Then years. Went as far as Pennsylvania on horseback. And there's nothing. Nothing but burned and riddled wasteland from a decade of attacks. The world that we were waiting for, gutted and gone. What was I going to do, let my survivors stumble out into a black hole? Let them know it was all for nothing?" she whispers. "Life is good here. Hard work and sacrifice give people a reason to live. They give people *meaning*. Our city—this Park—this is the seed from which the new world will grow. You'll see that eventually."

But that's not your call, I want to say. *That's not your call to make.*

"There are reasons for lies, Skyler."

She leaves me confused over whether I hate her, or pity her . . . or somehow understand what she's saying. And the idea of understanding her, this patchwork of a woman, this blur of misguided ideals and contradictions, angers me more than anything.

I wake up to Trev slobbering on the pillow next to me. And for a second, I get tricked into thinking we're back at the Park. That Trev's managed to fall asleep in our room, with Mom in our other bed, and Sky stuck with the floor. It's so comforting, this fake memory, that I nearly fall back asleep.

But it's not totally right.

The sun's too bright, for one thing. And the sheets are too white. Plus, my head's killing me. Then it comes back to me in a roar. We're not in the Carlyle.

We're in hell.

I sit up and nearly vomit from the head rush. My thoughts are tripping over one another, all mixed up and out of order. Things don't make any sense. Feelings have color, words have faces, memories are cut up and reordered, and some weird army of voices is barking them at me. When I try to box my ears to shut out the voices, they only become louder and more annoyed.

"Stop!" I finally scream at the voices, and Trev flies awake in shock.

Wait, Trevor's here. Trev's in my room at the Standard.

"What are you doing here?" I eye him. I rack my brain for the answer—for what happened last night—but everything's still running together and out of focus.

"Nothing," Trev says. But he looks guiltier than he did after stealing a second helping at the Christmas Reenactment last year.

I thrust off the covers and try to hop to my feet, but I nearly fall over.

"Are you okay?"

"Do I freaking look okay?"

"You look terrible," he says softly. Something about the way he says it rubs me a really weird way. Almost like he feels bad for me, like I'm someone to be pitied. I've never heard it in his voice before, and I want to shake it right out of him.

"I haven't seen you, or anyone besides Wren and Robert, in weeks. Tell me how you got here. I don't remember," I demand. I don't tell him how nervous I am that he's not real.

"You might not remember 'cause of the potion," he whispers. "Phee, keep your voice down, okay? They said they'd come back in the morning, to give you another—"

"'Cause of the *potion*? What are you talking about?"

Trev looks at me, flustered. "They give a lot of people potions, so they can fit in . . . so they can make a home here," he says. "Most adults get the heavenly blue, so they can see heaven. Most kids don't need any potions, 'cause our minds are already open. But I guess some do, like you. Master Wren said—"

"*Master* Wren?" I hate that he's said this.

"Wren said you're too angry with the world, too far gone to join the Standard without—" He stops talking and his face goes beet, I mean *beet*, red.

"Without what?" I start pacing, but my legs buckle and I sit down. I stare at him angrily. "Trev, without *what*?"

"Without a love potion."

"A *love* potion? You've got to be kidding me," I say. "Trev, my mind's all fucked up. I don't even remember last night. That wasn't a love potion, moron, that was poison."

He shakes his head. "No. Master—Wren would never do that. He said he'd never lie to me . . . that I always deserved the truth . . . that I was like a son." His blush turns almost purple. A *son*. Well, I'll give him one thing, that bastard Wren knows just how to work people. "He just wanted to calm you down, that's all," Trev adds. "He promised me he wouldn't hurt you."

"Wait." I'm still one step behind him, struggling to put the pieces together. "You mean you *knew* they were going to drug me up, before it happened? You were in on this?"

"No, I—"

"I could have freaking died last night, Trev. Do you understand that?" I ask. "So now you're just swallowing whatever crap Wren's shoveling? I mean, seriously, what's wrong with you?"

"Phee, come on, it's not like that." Trevor flies out of bed, rushing towards me in explanation. But I wave him off and crawl into the corner to think. I close my eyes and try to concentrate, try to piece together something, *anything*, real from last night.

And then, slowly, memories start to tiptoe out of the corners of my mind.

I remember eating dinner, all upset that Robert wasn't taking me to see Mom in the heavenly blue. I remember getting crazy paranoid.

I sort of remember running out of the room—then seeing Sky and Ryder on the stairs. A rush of anxiety floods me— they were *together* together—but I can't think about that now.

Then I was brought back here. To Trev. That memory I can see as clear as crystal: his face hovering above mine.

But then it cuts to black.

"What happened after you came in here last night?" I say softly.

"What?" He starts laughing, this high, panicked little laugh. "Nothing. I tried to take care of you."

I study his face. I'm not sure I know him. Right now, I'm not sure I know myself. "I bet you did."

"Phee, seriously, you've got to keep it down. Elder Francis said when you wake up, he's coming by with another potion. If he hears you, he's going to do whatever he did to you—"

"What *you* did to me."

"Phee, seriously, stop. I'd never hurt you. I didn't do anything. I wouldn't want to. Not like that." His voice catches, and now he's crying. "Come on, you've got to believe me."

I stay in the corner of my room and look out across our dead city. I can't remember anything past Trevor's face above mine. I don't know if he's telling the truth. But even if he is, for a minute I hate him, for being here. For seeing me like I was last night. I hate him for everything.

"Phee," he says through soft sobs. "I swear. I just thought—"

"What?"

"I just thought—"

"Seriously, Trevor," I snap at him. "You just thought *what*?"

"I just thought, if you could get love from a potion, then maybe you could love . . . me," he whispers.

Goddamn it, Trevor.

"I just wanted so badly to believe it." His breath catches and stutter-steps. "I wanted to believe all of it."

I pull my knees up to my chest and feel my own tears

coming. Not just because of my throbbing head, or the panic that still burns through me from the poison. And not just because of lonely, needy Trevor and his desperation to be loved.

But because of me, and the rest of this island, who just put their heads down, swallow lies, and wish them true: the fieldworkers who believe Rolladin's stories without questioning, Robert and the sad people of this hotel who cling to Wren's bullshit as a reason to go on. And me, who fell for Robert's act hook, line, and sinker, just so I'd never have to leave this city.

"I swear, Phee. I would never, ever hurt you," Trev's mumbling on the bed.

I walk over to him slowly. He's sobbing: *I'm sorry, I would never. Oh God, I'm sorry.*

I stand over him till he quiets down.

Then I slap him across the face. Once.

Again, on the other cheek with the back of my hand.

He lets me.

I slowly push him over, climb in next to him, spoon him like when we were kids and the world was less angry and complicated. I press my face into his back, bury my head under the covers, and let myself break down and cry.

I'm on the back of Rolladin's horse. I'm an afterthought, a sliver of a girl between the queen and the back of her saddle, as we ride from the stables through the changing leaves, across the cement labyrinth of Times Square, and over to the Hudson. We lead a team of a dozen warlords on horseback, a herd of armed guards galloping into dawn.

"You'll wait outside," Rolladin finally breaks our windy silence on the West Side Highway. "Me and my troops get your mother, Phee, and Trevor alone."

"Rolladin," I hesitate. I didn't bring this up last night, or this morning when I gave her every detail I could about the Standard and its security. But we're getting so close, I know this might be my last chance to beg her for another favor. "The men from Britain, the ones you found in the woods. They're good men."

"Skyler."

"They've saved our lives countless times," I plead. "They've become . . . like family."

Rolladin doesn't answer, not until I see the raised platform of the High Line, the Standard's twin towers of glass erupting out of the surrounding rooftops like crystal beacons. And as soon as I see them, my stomach wrenches. Dread, remorse, and anger, it all mixes and bubbles within me like a scalding stew.

"I can't have them in my Park." Rolladin shakes her head, and her broad back shifts me along with it. "It's too late. No, we're getting Sarah and the kids and going home."

The thought of leaving Ryder and Sam in that hotel, of never seeing my woodsman again, turns my insides out.

"But Rolladin—"

"Enough," she barks back at me.

I force myself to think beyond my own wants, to what's really most important. Getting Ryder and his brother out of that hotel. Regardless of whether I get to have Ryder forever, or if I ever even see him again.

"They don't have to come back with us. You could let them go to the boat they have, in Brooklyn. You could let them sail away. I told you what the Standard does. You can't leave them—"

"Stop blubbering," Rolladin mutters.

She snaps the reins of the horse and we break into a gallop. The cement gives way to cobblestones, the streets dividing and narrowing as we dance towards doom. *Clip-clop, clip-clop.*

"You're just a kid," she says. "There'll be other boys. Other lovers."

And the way she says this, so cold and removed, angers me more than her words themselves. "Right," I say bitterly.

I think of the Rolladin, or *Mary*, in Mom's journal. The one who'd do anything for my mother. The one who worked over the enemy from the inside out to give us a home in this city. The one who built a world of lies to keep us here. "So there were others for you?"

But Rolladin doesn't answer me, just grunts and kicks the horse in response.

"Stop here," she calls to the guards, once we've reached 13th Street. She pulls the reins taut, and we trot over to the black rusted stairs leading to the High Line, the shadows of the raised platform shielding us from the Standard's view. "Tie the horses. We'll scale the hotel from the fire escape, and each take a floor. We take no prisoners but the ones we came for."

The guards grunt in assertion.

Rolladin flips open the flap of her saddlebag and pulls out a folded red rifle, fills it with bullets, then snaps it back into one piece. Some lords dislodge red handguns from their boots and pockets, while others dust off old painted axes and knives and death tools I've never even read about before.

The spoils of war.

The last of Manhattan's weapons.

"Wait on the stairs." Rolladin pulls me into the shadows of the High Line. "You are not to move, you hear me?"

"I could come," I say carefully. "If you gave me a weapon, maybe I could help."

Rolladin looks at me, as if she's sizing me up. "All right, give me the extra handgun," she finally says, to no one in particular.

Lory steps forward and pulls a long, thin gun from the folds of her warlord cloak. She hands it to Rolladin, who, palms extended, hands it to me. "It took guts coming back to the Park," she says. It's the first, and likely last, compliment I'll ever get from Rolladin. "Stand guard outside the lobby. A ways down the High Line—be smart about it. You see one Standard freak try to escape, you shoot them in the arm, or the leg. Or the head, for all I care. Far as I see it, this is war."

Then Rolladin nods and motions for her guards and me

to follow her onto the High Line. We quickly and quietly file up the stairs.

As the warlords stealthily pour onto the hotel's fire escape, I fidget on the edges of the High Line's overgrown grass. Every worry and terror I can think of slithers out of the cement and coils around my legs, then up my stomach, to my throat.

I clutch the gun to my chest and pledge that Rolladin will do what needs to be done. That if it comes to it, I'll do what needs to be done.

God, if you exist, if you watch and guard this mess of a city, let my family all walk out of here.

I wake up to gunshots. Quick, hungry pops outside the door—*one! two! three!*—and then yelling and banging on the doors, up and down the hall. Trev's body jumps at the sound. We've been lying here awhile. All traces of dawn outside the glass walls are gone, and the pillows and covers are damp with sweat.

The gunshots make me think of my own little handgun. I haven't seen it since I got here, and after the shots in the hall, I feel naked without a weapon. *Who has it? Sam? Ryder? Wren?*

We hear grunts and groans as something heavy, like a piece of furniture, slides across the carpeted hall on the other side of our door. An army of fists pummels my door and shakes it from its hinges.

"Everyone out," I hear through the banging. It's a voice that sounds weirdly familiar. "Everyone up and out!"

"What's going on?" Trevor turns around and faces me.

"Put your shoes on," I tell him. "We're gonna find out."

We both walk down the short entryway and open the door.

The hallway's littered with people. I've never realized how many Standard drones were on my hall. Didn't any of them hear me screaming last night?

I look at the tired faces—a long row of empty eyes. Bodies that feel nothing. Eyes that witness nothing.

I don't know whether I hate them or pity them.

"Everyone should know better than to play games," the voice hollers again from around the corner of the hall. "We'll check each room to make sure you're not hiding them."

And then, pulling a turn around the corner, is Lory.

Lory, the guard from our Park.

Lory the freaking whorelord.

I'm positive I'm hallucinating again, that I'm picturing walking, talking memories. But before I can close my eyes and focus, Trev grabs my hand.

"Phee, they must have come for us," he whispers.

But I'm not afraid. Anything would be better than this hellhole—even the primate tower. So I step into the middle of the hall with one arm above my head, and I tug Trevor into the hallway alongside me. We're square in front of Lory, like we're about to begin a 65th Street fight. Only this time, there won't be any contest. We've already surrendered.

Lory drops her weapon when she sees us, and she starts running towards us.

I want to ask her so many questions. How'd she know we were here? Did she find Sky? Is my mom safe? How are we going to be punished when we get back to the Park?

But she's the one who starts barking questions as soon as she reaches us. "Where's your mother?"

I still can't believe she's here. It's only her rough grip around my forearm that tells me it's true, promises me she's real. "I don't know."

"We need to find her." Lory grabs my hand and Trevor's and pulls us down the hall.

She pushes open the door and ushers both of us into the dark stairwell. At each door we pass, Lory stops and yells into the hallway, "I have the kids. It's only Sarah left," and then again, "I have the kids!"

Some of the whorelords must be following her, 'cause I hear a growing stampede behind us as we round and round our way down. When I look back, I see some of the Standard drones are following us too. Are the whorelords bringing them back to the Park? To the lobby, for questioning? I can't figure out what's happening. There's too much commotion. Between all the stop-starts and Lory's hollers on each floor, I can't even sneak a word in.

"Lory, wait," I finally say, after we've rounded five or six corners. "My sister. We need to find my sister." Until I see her, I'm not going to feel whole.

"We have Skyler," she says. "She's outside. She brought us here. Now we need to find your mom and bring you home."

Wait—Skyler brought the lords here? How?

"Is Sky okay?"

"She's fine."

"Can I see her?"

"Not yet."

"Is Rolladin here too?" I ask as Lory pulls us down to the main floor.

"Yeah, we're here on her orders," she answers as we burst into the slick lobby.

I haven't seen the main floor since we walked in here all those cursed mornings ago. The stark light outside calls to me through the double doors, and I get the sudden itch to break through the glass and run into the fresh air. But Lory pulls me forward. The rest of the team of whorelords trails us into the lobby.

Then I see her.

She's got her stupid tiger cloak on, the pelt she wears for special occasions, all tied up around her neck. Some monstrous old gun's strapped across her shoulder. She looks crazy out of place against the sleek backdrop of the Standard. But I've never been so happy to see her, to see anyone maybe. My mom's sister, or lover, or my aunt, my warden. I don't know how to think of her anymore.

And I don't care.

I run to Rolladin and throw my arms around her. I do it before I can think better of it, before she sees me and can even react. And I hear the chorus of guns and knives and crossbows go up around me, a team of reflexes from the whorelords. But no one shoots. I can feel Rolladin stiffen in surprise at my touch, but then she relaxes into me. She puts her arm around me quickly, a flash of a hug in the middle of a circle of firearms, and then she pulls away.

"We need to find your mother," she says.

"Please get us out of here."

"I will. We're all going to go home. Together." She waves Trev outside. "Find Sky and stay with her."

Trev nods and hightails it out of the lobby.

"You should go too," Rolladin tells me. "You might not want to see this."

Unlike before, where I would have jumped at the chance to be on the front lines, in the center of the action, I feel no excitement. But still I say, "I'll stay with you," knowing I won't feel right until we have Mom. "Let's get her and go home."

Rolladin nods, then motions the whorelords to bring their Standard prisoners to her. Some of the prisoners resist, but most are deadweight. Rolladin pushes five or six of them to their knees, then paces back and forth in front of the Standard drones slowly, her massive gun now resting on her shoulder.

Finally she pauses in front of a young guy. I haven't seen him in weeks, but I remember his face from a dinner with Sky. Quentin, I think his name is. Rolladin shoves the nose of her gun right into Quentin's forehead, and his neck snaps back.

"Who runs this place?" Rolladin asks him.

But Quentin just keeps his eyes cast downward.

"Last time. Who runs this place?"

Quentin says nothing.

The boom from Rolladin's gun echoes through the hotel and rattles my eardrums, and Quentin's body collapses onto the floor. The rest of the prisoners start whimpering and trying to hold hands, but Rolladin's already moved down the line to an older woman, frail and shaking, long silver hair pulled back into a bun.

"Who runs this place?" Rolladin tries again, her gun now resting on the old woman's shoulder.

"The Master," the woman whispers. Her eyes dart back and forth to the other prisoners. She's so terrified, she's practically convulsing, and I almost can't watch. "Master Wren," she adds. "The senior Elders. The headmistresses."

"Where is Wren now?" Rolladin says, shifting her gun to the woman's other shoulder, like she's knighting her.

"I don't know."

"Last time. Where is Wren now?"

"I-I—," the woman stutters. "They shift us. We change rooms, constantly. I don't know . . ."

The next boom comes without warning, and the woman

falls into a heap on the ground, blood pooling around her like a red halo. I look away, and as I do, I catch some of the guards bringing a struggling Robert down for questioning.

"Rolladin," I say, pointing to Robert. "That guy knows where Mom is. I'm sure of it."

The guards holding Robert stop moving, and he looks up at Rolladin guiltily. And I realize they've got to know each other from a different life.

I follow Rolladin as she stalks over to him. "It's been a long time, Robert," she calls. "Glad you've been using your time wisely."

I expect Robert to kowtow, but instead he spits in her face. "Don't mock what you don't understand, Jezebel."

Rolladin brings the gun down, hard, against Robert's cheek, and he yelps. "Tell me where Sarah is and I'll spare your life." Then she shoves the butt of her gun into his features. "After all these years, you must know how to survive."

Robert hesitates. For a second. "She's in the Empire Suite," he whispers. "With Master Wren."

Rolladin pulls the gun out of his face. "Take us."

She nods to a few of the whorelords over the crowd. "Keep an eye on the rest of them. No one's freed until we get Sarah."

I follow Rolladin, slinking across the lobby and back to the internal stairs. I'm so focused on her that I almost walk right by Ryder. He's propping Sam up in the corner of the slate-tiled hall, the two of them huddled in the shadows, watching us, watching the whole thing. Keeping out of sight.

My stomach flips. It feels like a lifetime since I've seen them, though technically I guess I saw Ryder last night, nice and cozy with my sister in the stairwell. The memory bites at me, makes me want to ignore him, just pretend he isn't there. After all this mess is done, we'll go back to the Park, anyway—Rolladin will never let them come with us. It'll be like Ryder never was.

But I know, deep down, I can't be this selfish. I can't hate Ryder just 'cause he wants my sister, not me. If I care about her, I should at least care a little about him.

And I can't screw Sam. The crowd I'm swimming in keeps blocking my view, but I can still see he's totally strung out: all big breaths and bagged eyes and sharp angles. I think about what he's been through, weeks of the heavenly blue, and I know I've got to get him out of here.

But now I'm running out of time.

The sea of whorelords keeps bobbing me along, past the door and up the stairs. Right before I disappear from their view completely, I wave my hand above my head and catch Ryder's eye. I point, quickly and breathlessly, towards the door.

"Outside," I yell. "Go get her!"

"Sky!" I hear against the quiet of the morning, and my gun goes up in reflex. "Sky, it's Trevor! Where are you?"

Trev sprints out of the hotel towards me and hugs me as soon as he reaches me. He's crying.

"I don't know what happened in there," he says into my shoulder.

"It's all right, Trev." I squeeze him tight, so tight that I'm probably suffocating him. "It's over." I pull him back to look at him. "Did they find everyone?"

"Phee's with Rolladin," he says. "They're getting your mom."

Thank God. "What about—what about Ryder?"

"I don't know. I didn't see him or Sam in the halls."

I hear someone else call my name, and both Trev and I turn to find Ryder and Sam hobbling towards us. Sam looks terrible, weak and drawn—but he's alive. He and Ryder are alive.

I run to Ryder, throw my arm around his neck, and fold into his side, gun and all. Sam breaks away from us and slowly lowers himself down on a cracked wooden bench at the edge of the High Line.

"You okay?" Ryder lurches forward to help his brother.

Sam waves him away, then arches his neck over the back of the bench. He closes his eyes. His face is ashen even under the stark light of morning, and his clothes and hair are stiff with dried sweat. But still, he mumbles, "I'm fine. Just take care of your girl, Rye. I'm fine."

Your girl.

Ryder beams at me.

And then I can't stop myself. This could be my last chance. I paw at Ryder, run my fingers through his hair, pull him into me, kiss him fiercely. I drink him up, savoring this good-bye I was devastated I wouldn't have. He returns the favor. Trevor finally mumbles that he's going to check on Rolladin, then wanders a little ways down the High Line.

"It's over." Ryder laughs into my shoulder. "We're together now."

I don't answer, and just let him kiss me. I can't bring myself to tell him that this is probably the last time we're going to see each other. That we're going to have to beg Rolladin for their lives, and watch them walk away forever. That I want to stretch this moment on for eternity, until the details become a lifetime.

"Ryder." How am I going to do this? How does someone actually say good-bye? "Rolladin's going to send you and Sam away."

"Forget it," he interrupts. "We're not going anywhere."

"Please. Listen to me. I need to know that you're safe, that you and Sam are sailing into the horizon, to Bermuda or your wildest dreams."

"Skyler, stop it. Your family's coming with us. I'm not leaving without you."

"You don't understand," I say. "It's more complicated than I can explain right now, but Rolladin's never going to let us go. She's built an island of lies to keep us here. And if I can't leave, the only way I'll survive in this city is knowing that you're safe. And free."

Ryder stares at me a long time, so long that I think I've managed to trick fate. That my wish has been granted, and we've been given an ocean of time to float in forever.

But the spell is broken when Ryder leans in and kisses me.

He tastes both bitter and sweet.

The Empire Suite is on one of the middle floors, six or seven. I've lost count by the time we climb the stairs again and enter a stub of a hallway. This one's only a few feet wide and dead-ends at one door, unlike the tall, windy halls of the other floors. The ones with handmarked doors and never-ending corners.

"They're in there," Robert tells Rolladin. "Now stay true to your word. You said you'd let me go."

"You don't go anywhere until Sarah is safe." Rolladin pushes Robert towards the suite room door. "Knock."

Please, let Mom be in there. Please let her be all right. Not drugged up and crazy like I was. I need to see my real mother—the one who can shoot and skin a peacock in about thirty seconds flat. The one who always makes me feel beautiful and brave, even when I'm being a brat.

Robert raps on the door, with some weird system of short and long knocks, and it becomes obvious he's trying to use code or something to signal Wren. So Rolladin takes the butt of her gun, swiftly clocks Robert right in the temple, and pushes him aside.

"Backup, two rows of backup," Rolladin whispers, and the whorelords start pushing me out of the way, getting ready to move like a pack on the hunt. I try to elbow my way to the front, but I can't move. It's wall-to-wall whorelord, and as soon as Rolladin kicks the door down and enters the small apartment, I'm almost trampled.

We move to the kitchen. Nothing. The living room, nothing. Rolladin looks hungrily into the small glass box of a bedroom, nothing. Mom's not here, Wren's not here—

"Over here, hag," I hear from the other side of the breakfast bar.

Wren's leaning against the glass wall of the dining room, a small box off the main living space. His forearm's wrapped around Mom's shoulder, and his other hand holds a gun to her head. The gun's the size of Wren's palm. It's old and red, with a rubbed-away handle. And the floor of the suite nearly drops out from under me, sends me crashing to the lobby. 'Cause even from this far away, I know it's my gun.

The thing's only carrying one bullet.

But now it's cocked and ready to fire its last shot.

"No!" I run towards Mom, but Lory catches me.

"Let Rolladin handle it," she whispers.

Mom's eyes dart fearfully up to Wren, back to Rolladin, and settle on me. She looks horrible, strung out. Her usually solid body, thin and drawn. She looks older, much older, and it takes everything I've got not to run over to Wren and bash his face in. I hate him. I hate him more than I've ever hated anyone. He's worse than a liar.

He's a soul-sucking parasite.

"Let her go!" I yell at him.

"Phee," Mom answers. Thank God, she's kind of lucid. She knows it's me. But she just gives me a little shake of her head. *Don't move*, her looks says. *Don't do anything*.

"You have someone who belongs to me," Rolladin says evenly.

Wren laughs, long and deep. "*Belongs* to you? You're worse than the Red Allies were, Rolladin. So now you own the prisoners?"

"No." Rolladin's voice stays even and measured. "But they are mine to keep safe."

"You're delusional," Wren says. "This family *ran* from you. When they came to me, they were broken. Just like your broken brother. I've given them salvation. A chance for a new life. This is what's meant to be."

"It's over, you hear me?" Rolladin's voice is starting to crack. "Now let her go."

"Oh, it's far from over." Wren pulls my mom back into the far corner of the dining room, like there's some secret trapdoor or escape route we can't see. *Please, Mom.* I will her to hear me. *Elbow him and run.* But she looks like she can barely move. "See, when you sided with the Red Allies, you vicious bitch, you lost all perspective on what's going on. What it's like to live day and night in fear. This city needs me, just like this family needs me. We need each other."

Rolladin takes a step towards Wren. She doesn't raise her gun, but I watch her fingers twitch anxiously around it. Wren just grips my mother tighter, pulls her even closer to him. I jump forward instinctively to reach for her, but Lory holds me back.

"I don't negotiate with psychopaths," Rolladin says. "Last chance. Let her go."

Wren shakes his head violently. "No. This one's mine. I made a promise to God that I intend on keeping. Take the problem child, and the boys. But not this one."

Lory drops my hand and reaches carefully for her gun.

The movement's so small and contained that I barely catch it, but her gun keeps rising, slowly, inch by inch.

"This woman is my family, you understand?" Rolladin barks at Wren. "I will *not* walk out of here without her."

Wren starts waving his gun. "No, she's part of my family," he spits, then points his gun at Mom's belly. *What?* Wait—did he—has he been with Mom? Is he talking about a baby? I'll kill him.

I leap forward. I'll kill him.

"My future. Leave us. Leave all of us!" Wren screams.

And then I don't know what comes first, next, or last.

I hear a gunshot, Lory's gunshot, her bullet cutting Wren's face in two. But not before Mom doubles over, not before she collapses to the ground, and Wren's gun—my gun, now empty, clangs to the floor.

Mom. Oh God. Mom.

I run to her.

Rolladin's now beside us, wailing. "Sarah. Oh my darling, Sarah."

"Mom!"

But Mom's eyes are closed, and her stomach's nothing but a red, angry hollow.

No.

No. No. No.

No. No. No. No. No.

"We need to get this wound wrapped!" Rolladin's screaming at her guards, pushing them around, barking. "We need to get her downstairs, now!"

"Rolladin—," Lory begins, but Rolladin's already pushed her aside, has my mom propped up on her shoulder. "Help me," Rolladin pleads with me.

I rush to Mom's other side, finally given something to do, a way to help. I can't think about what's happened. This can't be real. If I do what I'm supposed to do—if I get Mom downstairs, one step at a time—this is all going to be okay.

This has to be okay.

We burst out of the hotel, into the white light. I can't feel my legs. I can't feel my heart. I think I threw up two times on the way down the stairs.

"Sarah, darling Sarah," Rolladin just says it, over and over, until it becomes a mantra. Until I start saying it. If we both say it, maybe it unleashes a miracle. A miracle that will put Mom together again. A miracle that will give us all a second chance.

Sky, Ryder, Trevor—they're now beside me, asking what's happened, but I don't have any words. I can't bring myself to speak. It's as if the gunshot carved me out, has made me nothing more than a red, angry hollow.

Rolladin lays my mom down on a small tuft of grass on the High Line, a few steps from the hotel. Mom's sputtering, coughing, but she's alive. I roll the mantra over and over in my head, thinking it's working. *Sarah, darling Sarah.*

I don't remember Sam sidling up to me. I don't remember collapsing into him, crying and wailing like I'm some infant. I just find myself there, with his shaky arms and shakier words wrapped around me—*Just breathe, it's not your fault, desperado. Just breathe—*

"Oh my God, Phee," Sky's whimpering next to me.

Finally Mom moves, just rolls over to cough, and I rush to her side. A sea of blood parts from her lips. "Mary," she says.

"Don't you dare die on me. You can't. I can't." Rolladin angles herself on the ground beside Mom, so that their faces

LEE KELLY

are inches apart. Mom looks up at me and Sky, and she reaches for us, pulls our hands close to her, right over her heart. "Give me this, Mary. Let them go."

Rolladin just reaches out and strokes Mom's bloodstained face. "I won't have it," she tells her. "You've got to fight. You've survived worse. Much worse. You've got to fight."

"Mary, it's time," my mother whispers. "Let us go. Girls." She pulls us closer. She's digging for something underneath her clothes, and Rolladin starts arguing with her not to pick at her wound, not to touch it. But she keeps digging. I want to tell her to just focus on fighting for every breath. But I can't remember how to speak.

Sarah, darling Sarah, Sarah, darling Sarah, Sarah . . .

"I only saw what I wanted to see with Robert. I'm so sorry," she tells us. She starts to cry, and I wish to God she would stop. "I just wanted so badly to give you more."

"Mom." I finally find my voice. "You've given us everything."

She looks up at me and Sky, and I think, I think she smiles.

Out of the wet magenta folds of her clothes, Mom pulls out a small pouch. "I found this in Wren's suite. This belongs with you two." Then she peels back the flap. Inside, there's a blue book. *The* book. The one that's always been the Property of Sarah Walker Miller. "It should have belonged to you a long time ago."

With that one last look, I see everything Mom's ever been to us—a friend, a guardian, a protector. A chance. But I can't watch her go.

I'm not ready. I'll never be ready.

"You two gave me meaning," Mom says as she passes us the journal. Her last words: "You make me proud."

April 5—Betrayal. It rumbled out of my core and flooded my throat, made me taste bile.

When I heard about the E-train summit, it was as if the sound was pulled from the room. I couldn't hear the man's voice as he mouthed, Are you okay?

I couldn't hear Sky's cries as she pulled on my sleeve, scared since I'd gone so still.

I got up quickly and gave the babies to Lauren. I ran down the torch-lit library stairs of the Carlyle, rounded the sharp, chair-railed corners of the halls. My limbs were still thin and weak from the months on bed rest, but I welcomed the pain. Tom, how could I have trusted her? What had I done?

Mary's room door was locked, unlike any other room in the hotel. I screamed at her to open up, and didn't waste any time. I railed at her, question after question, about the E-train summit.

She gave me some line, like, "The E-train summit? You mean back in the summer? What has you asking about it?"

I got up real close to her face, saw the small rings of wrinkles around her eyes that weren't there a year ago. "You never went, did you? Tell me.

Tell me now or I swear I'll run back down to the lobby and let everyone know you're a liar."

That got her motivated. She pushed me against the textured walls with her forearm, pinned me next to the window. "You don't know what you're talking about. You hear me? There's more going on in this city than you could ever imagine. And people were, are, counting on me to keep them safe."

"We were counting on you to find our loved ones!"

Then she admitted she needed to tell me something. Something important. Something, I'm sure, in typical Mary fashion, that would wipe away all her lies and bullshit and make the world right again.

But a knock interrupted us. As always, there was someone else with needs more immediate, and my panic attack was forgotten as Mary answered the door for one of her new groupies, Samantha. Mary has her own squadron of "warlords" now, since she's sold her soul to play Red Allies henchman, and the Red general lets her handle the smaller matters concerning us Carlyle prisoners.

The young guard immediately started stuttering, asking what to do about Bronwyn Trevor, the pregnant Red whore who tried to kill herself. She wondered if solitary confinement made sense until Bronwyn birthed, or if she should just be lumped in with the rest of the prisoners.

Bronwyn.

Poor, lonely, broken Bronwyn.

My heart seized for my beautiful charge, the

lost girl of the 6 train . . . but I knew I couldn't risk giving my concern a voice. My own family's future was on the line, my babies' father, their freedom. And this child of a guard Samantha had gifted me a sliver of time.

So I grabbed Mary's red-marked gun—a little toy from the Red Allies, like a spiked collar on some kept dog—and the box of ammo that rested on her nightstand. I slipped them into my pocket and excused myself. Just glided out the door without saying good-bye.

I knew Mary would visit me later and try to explain everything away. Somehow weave the truth with inventive lies. Lies I've even asked for, lies I've come to need, to survive. But they've cost me too much, a second chance at my life back, with Tom. And Mary can't fix that.

When she comes knocking, I won't be there.

I'm taking the girls, and we're leaving tonight. Uptown, downtown—anywhere but here. We'll take the subways. We'll find Tom on our own.

April 15—I know you want to know what happened, but I still can't talk about it. It will break me.

I'm already broken.

April 20—I'm sorry. The words still won't come. I thought they would but they won't. I'm just empty.

I wonder if from now on I'll always be empty. If they stole everything that used to be inside.

April 25— ~~After I left Rolladin's room, I packed up the girls and ran to Lauren's quarters. I told her about Bronwyn, and her poor cursed baby. I begged her to take care of them, just like I begged her to help me, to hide me and the girls until we could sneak out the fire escape. Until the newest night guards were on rotation, the ones who would believe me when I lied and said Mary was sending me on official business or some crap like that. I wasn't thinking. If I could go back, if I could do it all differently—~~

May 5—Some days I can't shake the memories. They haunt me and tell me that I'll never be right again. That it would be better for all of us, to end it.
~~I think about jumping. I think about dropping the three of us, like deadweights, down five stories below.~~

June 15—Summer's here. I feel it, in the hot midnight musk draping the city when I scavenge corner stores, and in the garden I've started to work in on our rooftop. I feel real gratitude these days, for my two little guardians padding around in the grass. Sometimes it hurts to watch them, like my heart's growing right along with them. Just expanding, pushing hard against my ribs, threatening that one day I won't be able to contain it.

My girls have made the world feel new again.

Maybe I can be new. Maybe there's a way to start over.

*July—That night, when I left the Park. I've wanted
to bury it. I've wanted to sink it so deep that it
would disappear. But it forces its way to the top,
bubbles to the surface in the middle of the night.
Comes out in nightmares. Through screams.*

*But I need to tell someone, and you're better
than anyone else. After all, you never tell. You just
take my words at face value, never judge. Never
share.*

*I snuck down to the 6 line on Madison. Without
a word, just packed up my bag, gun in pocket and
torch in hand, and ran with Sky and Phee, one
on each shoulder, underground. It's ironic to think
about it now, but I was hopeful. As if returning
to the dark we'd escaped from somehow wiped
everything clean. It gave me the feeling that I was
starting over, being reborn.*

*I crossed over at 42nd Street, eager to get to the
West Side. Inner voices taunted me that Tom was
dead somewhere, that I was too late to find him,
but I didn't listen. I kept plowing through the dark
with my torch, with my sleepy babies.*

*I saw the group coming towards me on the
tracks around Houston. It might have been because
of the children, the constant low wail Sky and Phee
started when we reached downtown, sonar that
bounced around the subways and coaxed all the
trash out of the shadows.*

*There were about ten of them, a mixed crowd.
Men, women, old and young. They reminded me
a bit of our ragtag family, Rolladin's crew at the*

beginning, when we were fending for ourselves, feeding on nothing but hope and canned goods scoured from the surface.

I should have picked up on the warning signs. The smell of old garbage and rotting meat. The fading torchlight painting the thinnest coat of dried blood around their mouths. I should have seen, I should have known, but I was electrified with hope.

"Hello." I took the offensive. "Thank God I've found you. I'm looking for someone. Someone who was on the 1 line when the city was first hit."

No one answered me. They started to circle us, a crowd of vultures, taking their time.

I told them about Tom. I described him. I told them the story of the E-train summit, how Tom and I were ships passing in the constant night of this damned city.

Finally one of the larger men, my age, told me that they didn't know any Tom.

"We'd heard about the summit," he said. "But we're not out for more politics and pleasantries. This is war, you know."

I asked if he might have any idea where I could find my husband. That it was important. That my kids' lives depended on it. I begged him.

"He could be with the crazies, the ones who think this is all part of some master plan," he said. "Sending missionaries into the tunnels like fucking end-of-the-world Jehovahs. Suppose they think God's going to put a bubble around them when the bombs start dropping again." Then the man smiled. "Or, of course, this Tom could be dead."

Then he walked even closer to me, so close that I couldn't see anything but his magenta lips, couldn't feel anything but his arms gripping around me. Then he whispered words to the others that have kept me up every night since, words I think I hear outside my door, on the roof, behind every corner: "Take the kids."

I begged. Moans and blubbers and desperate cries. Me for them.

I can still feel their hands on me. I can still see Sky and Phee's eyes as they watch me—

They grabbed me and start ripping my clothes off. The women were cheering:

~~Your babies will feed us for a week. After we~~ ~~fuck you senseless we'll eat these things for a week—~~

Phee and Sky could see everything.

The women were holding them, measuring them, as if they were weighing them.

I found the gun. Somehow I broke out of the cage of limbs and tongues and found that small pistol in my pocket.

The bullet shocked, and everything stopped for a second. I'd managed to hit the leader, and as he fell over, I rolled away, then aimed and fired at the women in the corner. Then I grabbed my children and ran.

They followed, I heard them, I still hear them on my tracks. I just kept firing. One, two, three bullets behind us, Sky weighing my arm down.

Me carrying both babies like two tons of bricks.
Adrenaline gave me the strength of an army.
Adrenaline saved our lives.

   I took the next set of stairs. I reloaded. I fired.
I ran until my back was breaking, until my feet
were scabbed and sore, until Sky and Phee stopped
crying. I holed up in an abandoned apartment
building, and I have truly never crawled out.

August—The rooftop garden is working. I'm
thinking we might be able to stay here until some
kind of peace is declared. The bombs have stopped,
and I don't hear gunfire ring against the night sky.
It's been awhile. Maybe even months.

September—I still only hunt at night, in case, but
the streets are clear. There're no more bodies. The
troops must be cleaning up after themselves. I
wonder if the war is ending, or if this is only the
beginning of a long, long battle. I've managed to
scavenge enough cans out of nearby Wall Street
apartments to last us a long time. At least through
the winter. I'm trying not to be so afraid. I think the
girls are old enough, now, to sense it.

   My prayer every night is that they don't
remember the subways.

October—On Phee's first birthday, a Red Allies
soldier found me and the girls picking through
a place on Fulton Street. He must have seen me
shaking, convulsing as soon as I saw him and

his gun, because he laid down his weapon and approached me slowly. He spoke English, and he told me he needed to take us back to the Park. I nodded, all the while carefully folding my own gun into Phee's Ergo carrier. A true child of the new world, Phee didn't protest, my little warrior hiding our deep, dark secret as if it's nothing but ordinary to travel with a gun.

As the soldier led us downstairs, he explained. The island surrendered, or rather, had been surrendered by the rest of the country. It's an official enemy occupation zone, a casualty of the war. The Red Allies are now conducting a census of survivors on the island, and everyone's being ordered to the Central Park internment camp.

He assured me that the conditions are adequate, luxurious for wartime, and that the Red Allies will treat their prisoners of war in line with the Geneva Convention. That one of the island's own, a woman—Mary, I'm sure—is helping as de facto warden, and he thinks it's better, for all of us. That eventually, census restraints will be lifted, and I can come back here, or go wherever I want, on this skeleton of a dead city.

I was beginning to think this kind, careful soldier was an angel, that I'd died and war had even disrupted the heavens, when he walked me and the girls to the seatless body of a helicopter filled with other survivors picked up from around the island.

And I knew I wasn't ready to go. I couldn't

face Mary without killing her. I couldn't leave my freedom. I couldn't look at anyone at the Carlyle anymore. Not after the subways. Never again.

The soldier, Xu was his name, was once again kind. He had a soft spot—his own family at home, miles and miles from here. He told the pilot to leave and brought me back to the Lower East Side by tank, to my apartment to say good-bye. "The need for closure," he said in his impeccable English, "is a great and weighty need."

As we drove along the water, I saw the scorched Brooklyn skyline. I absorbed the wide, gaping hole in the underbelly of Manhattan, a gash that ran from the Bowery to Chinatown. I finally accepted the truth, as the Red Allies soldier steered his tank through the wreckage of the Lower East Side:

The city has been conquered.

The island is dead.

It's now almost midnight in my old apartment. My girls are sleeping, and our escort, the Red Allies soldier, sits outside the unit's door. This enemy trooper trusts me to stay inside, to just enjoy my last hour in our old home. He took a real risk, of course, letting us come back here. I could have hidden grenades or firearms, could come out of the apartment with guns blazing and take him down before running with my daughters into the night.

But he knows, like I know, that there's nowhere left to run.

This is just a good-bye.

One last look at a life stolen, uncompleted. A

last stop before I go to Central Park as someone else. Tonight I return as a woman broken and rebuilt, recycled for just one mission:

My girls will survive this. They will live to see a better world.

My journal, my friend, my keeper of secrets. As I bury you in the depths of this safe, I promise us both that I'm burying part of me with you. So much hatred. So much hurt.

I know I need to let it all go. I need to let you go, along with my weapons. My gun, and my pride.

This isn't about me, or Tom, or even Mary anymore—sometimes the past should stay in the past.

Instead, this is about the future—my daughters, the two halves of my heart. I will give them a chance at a real life in this city that's been raped and left for dead.

From now on, nothing else matters.

Mom takes her last breath on the High Line.

We stayed with her, long after, into the afternoon, Phee and I asleep next to her, as if when we woke, someone would tell us that we've been dreaming.

Rolladin assured us that she'd make arrangements. That we were to go and never look back, but that Mom's resting place should be Manhattan. That she's a New Yorker, through and through. I guess it's true.

She'll never see Europe or Bermuda.

She'll never see old age.

We'll never again feel her strong arms wrap around us.

We'll never see her again.

Someone's cut me right down my center and stolen my heart, gutted me open.

It isn't real.

Sometimes the grief is so intense I swear *I'm* dying, inch by inch of me burning, and there's no water to put it out. I'm just going to keep crumbling, until one day all that's left is ash.

Rolladin gives each of us a weapon and torches. She stays silent as she and her warlords escort us across town to First Avenue to brave the tunnels into Brooklyn. She doesn't say a word after we thank her for saving our lives. It's only when we begin to walk towards the L line stop that she dismounts from her horse and waves Phee and me back towards her. "Girls."

We leave the guys for a minute and go to her.

Twilight is falling over the city, and the harsh cast of gray light does Rolladin's face no kindness. We can see all the track marks and battle wounds the city has inflicted, the heavy baggage of time and compromise weighing her down.

"It was brutal, all of it. It still is," she says to Phee and me. "But you didn't see it all fall to pieces. So I don't expect you to understand. I don't expect you to ever understand why I did what I did."

But still, she looks . . . hopeful.

And the words rumble out of me, before I'm sure of what I want to say, or at least, how to say it. "I think you're right," I try. "I don't think we'll ever be able to fully understand."

I think of the Park, and about the Standard, and the story in Mom's journal. I think about all the prisoners of this city, prisoners to the past, just wading through the rubble, just trying to find someone or something to fight for as we make our way through it all, inching forward day by day to survive.

So I force myself to look at Rolladin—not at her tiger cloak, not at her red rifle thrown over her shoulder like an afterthought—and find *Mary*. "But we know who you did it for," I say, as I grasp Phee's hand in mine. "We know."

Rolladin nods and presses her lips into a tight line, and then she only has eyes for the cracked cement of 13th Street. "All right, girls."

I feel a release and an absence all at once, even before she and her warlords gallop back through the East Village, towards their oasis in the middle of a dead city, taking Mom's remains with them.

There's no other way into Brooklyn but the tunnels, but still, all of us become paralyzed as we hover on the edge of the stairs to the L line. The monsters that roam the deep caverns of this city might be miles from the stretch of subway that runs from Manhattan to Brooklyn.

Or the feeders could be waiting for us.

But we can't let the terror consume us. After everything we've been through, we know the only way to fight through the fear is to keep going, to push through it together.

Our group moves quickly and silently down to the platform and through the tunnels, just a chorus of soft footsteps and tight breaths as we travel under the East River.

All of us grip our guns and crossbows and arrows, the weapons slick with sweat and fear.

The darkness is limitless, extends like a scroll—my sadness and longing so crushing, it's like I'm walking through a black hole, being pulled apart into nothing.

When I've nearly given up, when I hear nothing but guttural groans, whispers, taunts from the hungry darkness— *are they real are they in my mind am I actually going crazy—*

A small beacon of light shines hopeful onto the platform ahead of us.

We emerge in a place called Williamsburg and walk to the Brooklyn Yard from there. We stay camped out in its shambles for a couple of days as Ryder prepares the boat to go. But it's a blur—a lost period, someone taking over my body and propelling it through time and space, doing what I can't imagine doing: moving forward. Moving on.

I can't look at or talk to anyone. But I stay attached to Phee and Ryder, constantly next to one of them, as if our bodies are saying what words can't. *You have me. You'll always have me. You can lean on me, as I'll lean on you.*

But my mouth doesn't move. I don't speak.

A few times I find Phee huddled into a tense, tight ball behind a wide storage unit, her sobs more like the clipped howls of a wild animal, her hair a golden net, trapping her in despair.

But I can't go to her—I'm too broken.

Until the day I know I need to.

Until the day I can see her need like it's a third person, motioning for me to sit with them, and see what I can do.

I sit down beside Phee and pull her into my arms. My little sister. My wonderful, brave and brutalized, hero and child of a sister. She's lost her mom, like I have. But she's lost her home—for as much as I want to leave this city, she wanted to stay. And she needs me, like I need her, to get through this. To get through anything, we need each other.

We've found that out the hard way.

"I'm so sorry, Phee."

She claws at me, her tears coming down quickly, her sobs muffled by my shoulder, and I pull her in tighter.

"I love you," I tell her.

"I love you, too. Sky, I miss her. I don't—I don't know how to do this. I don't . . . I don't—"

"It's okay," I tell her. I taste my own tears, and my rage. My grief, my melting loneliness. I taste it all. "It's all going to be okay."

A few days later the boat is finally ready to leave the dock. Our food's been stored and budgeted, the route to Bermuda—Sam's choice, though no one argues—charted and settled. And we've also settled into some kind of balance, an odd cast of characters for a second chance.

Like Phee, Sam's on the road to recovery from the heavenly blue. He doesn't share much about what happened to him, just bits and pieces.

That every day he waded through nightmares: nightmares of things that had happened and things that hadn't.

That with nowhere to run, nowhere to hide, the past caught up to him.

That the only thing that kept his world right side up was thinking about Ryder, and getting a chance to make things right with him.

I guess we all have our compasses that lead us out of the darkness.

After the few days of rest, Sam says he feels strong enough to captain our journey. Naturally, Phee's declared herself his first mate. Sometimes I think the matchup is a terrible idea, that they're actually going to kill each other. But after the bickering, they settle as well, almost as if they speak a language of barks and jabs that the rest of us just don't understand. And Trevor, begrudgingly, has settled for the role of junior sailor. For now, at least.

Now Sam and Trevor are perched at the helm of the ship, and we're about to break from the Yard. I rest on the thin shelf of seats on the deck, pull the blanket Phee and I are sharing over my shoulders, and look out over the water.

"I think I can do it," Phee says, breaking the silence. It sounds like it's out of nowhere, but really, she's answering a question I posed to her days ago.

"We don't have to."

"I want to," she says. "After all, it's like Mom said. We're the reason she stuck through it. We're the reason she got up every day and faced the city. We're the second half of her story."

Ryder emerges from the small bedroom chambers below the boat with fresh water and extra blankets. But as soon as he sees the two of us talking, he veers off and joins the boys. He's giving us space, something he's learned Phee and I need. Something *I've* learned we need. I think Phee and I both took it for granted until recently.

"So who's going to write it?" I ask Phee, relieved that she's okay with this. I miss Mom desperately, and putting the rest of her story on paper, letting it breathe and see the light of day, feels like a way to keep her with us forever. "Me or you?"

She gives me a trademark huff. "Why's it have to be one or the other?"

I lean my head against the rail. "That's the way stories work, Phee. Somebody has to tell them."

Phee puts her head beside mine and gives a little cackle. It's been a long time since I've heard her laugh, and I've forgotten it's what home sounds like. "For being so smart, Sky, you're awfully one-way sometimes," she says. "Come on, you've got to know there's two sides to every story."

I think about what she's said, until her words settle around me. Until I feel like I'm floating on their calm, simple truth.

She's got a point, of course.

There are two sides to every story. And maybe there's not always a clear right and wrong, hero and villain.

Maybe there's just people.

I study my sister, think about how different we are, and I know that we're two sides of the same story. How easy it could have been to lose each other, like Mom and Dad, Dad and Wren. Or Mom and Rolladin. And how lucky we are to be here, together, side by side.

From the little I've seen of this world, it seems quite selective with second chances.

The boat starts bobbing off the dock and into the restless water, and Ryder finally joins us. He kisses me without thinking, and I instinctively look to Phee, judge how she's reacting. If this is too much, too soon. If she's okay.

But instead of balking, she smiles and looks up at me with big, genuine eyes. I let the air I've been holding fall right out of me.

"So how are we going to start our story?" I ask her.

She shrugs her shoulders, knocks hers into mine with a little nudge. "Well, the story starts with me, of course."

Ryder gives a little chuckle beside me as he perches his head on my left side, so we're three ducks in a row. "Typical," he says. But it's a loaded "typical." A grateful "typical," a "typical" that says things are on their way to getting better.

Phee cackles again and hits Ryder on the back playfully. Then she drapes her arm around me and whispers, "But it'll end with you."

Dawn is just breaking across the dark skyscrapers in the distance, a charcoal scrawl of a skyline flanking the river on each side. But for the first time in my life, the dark towers don't remind me of impartial watchmen, stoic in their guard, their border as closed and claustrophobic as a fence.

Instead I see a gateway, long forgotten, swinging open and whispering, welcoming us to the world. Our small ship bobs forward, closer and closer to the unknown, and I think of all we've seen, all we've lost, and dream of all we might gain.

And then I let my mind go to that deep, fragile place inside me, and I let myself see her with us. See Mom as I want to remember her. Her tan, taut arms hanging over the side of the boat, her long auburn hair streaming in the wind. Picture her laughing beside Phee, eyes blazing, finally at peace as her daughters sail forward into the future. A future she paid for dearly. A future she fought for, tooth and nail. I close my eyes and thank her, not with words, but with the beating of my heart, the rise and fall of my chest. The life that pulses inside me.

I take Ryder's hand with my left, and grab Phee's with my right—

And I wait for what's beyond our city.

ACKNOWLEDGMENTS

This book, at its heart, is a story about family, and so I would especially like to thank mine. A huge thank-you to my dad—my life coach and biggest fan—who taught me to chase my dreams and that the secret to success is persistence, and to my mom—my champion—who read this manuscript way too many times and declared from day one, *This will be a book*. Thank you to my sisters, Bridget and Jill, for not only inspiring this story but for making my life so much better by being in it, and to my son and sweet pea, Penn, for being totally lovable and the world's best distraction.

And a million thanks to Jeff, my partner, my rock, my best friend—thank you for telling everyone you know that your wife is a writer, for your limitless support, and for handling the household on weekends while your wife keeps plugging away at her dream. You are incredible.

Endless thanks to my talented, insightful, collaborative editor Navah Wolfe, for never making this feel like work, for her excitement and tireless commitment to this story, and for her partnership in making this novel the absolute best it could be. And thanks to the rest of the phenomenal team at Simon & Schuster's Saga Press, including cover designer Michael McCartney, production manager Elizabeth Blake-Linn, production editor Jenica Nasworthy, and copy editor Valerie Shea.

City of Savages would not exist without my wonderful agent, Adriann Ranta, who took a chance on me and who never wavered in her dedication or enthusiasm for this book. She is a superagent, and I'm beyond lucky to have her.

I'm also indebted to the Freshman Fifteens, the Class of 2K15, and the Fearless Fifteeners, my YA author debut groups, for their camaraderie and support, especially my amazing critique partner, Kelly Loy Gilbert, my fellow bloggers and confidantes Chandler Baker and Virginia Boecker, and the fabulous Kim Liggett, Jen Brooks, and Lori Goldstein. More thanks to my writing buddies Erika David and Lisa Koosis—for their friendship and their excellent notes on early drafts—as well as Loretta Torossian, whose infectious enthusiasm kept me committed to seeing this story through to the end.

And finally, thank you to the readers. I still can't fully believe my words are in your hands. And for that, I am wildly grateful.